IS FAT BOB DEAD YET?

Also by Stephen Dobyns

Blue Rider Press / New York

IS FAT BOB
DEAD YET?

A Novel

Stephen Dobyns

blue
rider
press

An imprint of Penguin Random House LLC
375 Hudson Street
New York, New York 10014

Copyright © 2015 by Stephen Dobyns

Grateful acknowledgment is made for permission to reprint lyrics from "(Ghost) Riders in the Sky
(A Cowboy Legend)," from *Riders in the Sky* by Stan Jones. Copyright © 1949 (Renewed)
Edwin H. Morris & Company, a Division of MPL Music Publishing, Inc.
All rights reserved. Reprinted by permission of Hal Leonard Corporation.

Library of Congress Cataloging-in-Publication Data

Dobyns, Stephen, date.
Is fat Bob dead yet? : a novel / Stephen Dobyns.
p.   cm.
ISBN 978-0-399-17145-1
I. Title.
PS3554.O2I8   2015   2015017213
813'.54—dc23

Printed in the United States of America
1   3   5   7   9   10   8   6   4   2

Book design by Gretchen Achilles

For Betsy

IS FAT BOB DEAD YET?

ONE

It's an early spring morning in late winter, a welcome oxymoron with balmy breezes that send Connecticut College students back to their dorm rooms for shorts and flip-flops. Bare legs proliferate. Businessmen loosen their ties. One mad rogue, the owner of a coffee shop, moves two small tables with chairs out to the sidewalk. Motorcycles emerge from winter hibernations. It would be wrong to say it's a good day on which to die, but surely one can imagine worse days.

This is Bank Street in New London, Connecticut, the name referring not to commercial activity but to the curving riverbank of the river Thames, which the street follows. We can see the river if we look across the cellar hole next to the Salvation Army thrift store, where a dozen rusty pilings rise from the ground. The lot contains a depressing collection of broken glass, plastic bags, plastic bottles, and decrepitating cardboard boxes, but we can ignore that. Down the slope and dividing the back entries of Bank Street enterprises from the train tracks is Water Street: more of a wide alley with pretensions than a street. Then comes the river with a few pleasure piers and the coast guard's three-masted, 290-foot cutter, the *Eagle*, which is a wonder to see under full sail. Across the river in Groton, those great gray square buildings flanked by yellow cranes are part of the General Dynamics shipyard where submarines are made, though few get made nowadays.

Bank Street is a hodgepodge of eighteenth-, nineteenth-, and twentieth-century buildings, ranging from the beautiful to the ugly, granite Gothic Revival to redbrick Victorian to the brick-and-tin Salvation Army thrift store, a small-box version of a big-box store next to the granite Custom

House. In an early version of urban renewal, Benedict Arnold and his Hessians put prior Bank Street buildings to the torch in 1781.

Back by Firehouse Square is where the historic district begins as modern streetlights change to retro streetlamps and Bank Street changes to one-way, heading downtown. The Greek Revival–style F. L. Allen Firehouse is now an art gallery, while a sign on the three-story granite house of Captain Benjamin Brown across the street advertises a Chinese-medicine practitioner. A bucket truck squats by the traffic island, and high in the air a service technician fixes the streetlight. Two traffic lights hang below an arm extending from the same pole; they sway slightly as the fellow in the bucket does his work.

If we could take his place for a minute, we'd have the chance to in-spect the nature of this Monday morning in early March: cloudless sky, men and women carrying their coats over their arms, kids already in shorts, one fellow parked in front of the Firehouse Art Gallery has put down the convertible top of his blue Mazda Miata, people pause to ad-dress friendly remarks to one another as they go about their business, sunlight reflects off the river where we see seagulls, and from an open window we hear one of those older rock tunes heard mostly in supermar-kets: the Eagles or Fleetwood Mac. It's a day that feels like unexpected forgiveness.

Beneath us a blue Mini-Cooper waits at the light. The driver's elbow, hidden in a brown leather sleeve, pokes from the open window. He makes his left turn from Tilley and drives slowly down Bank Street, looking for a parking space. There, he's found one. Gingerly, he pulls up behind a four-door Chevrolet Caprice sedan, which has to be twenty years old. The original dark cherry paint has faded, giving the big car a mottled as-pect. The trunk is held shut with a length of rope, and a busted-up tear-drop spotlight hangs down the side of the driver's door. The man climbs from his Mini and glances at the Caprice with mild interest, but before he can cross the street, he's startled by a blast from a train's air horn. About forty passenger trains come through New London each day, and two-thirds stop—Amtrak's Northeast Regional and the Acela Express, as well as a commuter line between New London and New Haven. And each blasts its horn. As if in response, the Mini goes *beep-beep* as the locks click shut, and the man continues across the street to a shoe-repair shop. The Greek shop owner has been there for more than thirty years and prefers to be called a cobbler.

The man is on his way to pick up a pair of shoes, new soles, heels, and a good polishing for his black Bruno Magli slip-ons, a rush job because he only took them in on Saturday. The shoes were a gift from his older brother, Vasco; actually they're hand-me-downs that Vasco found too tight. Vasco has rich tastes, and over the years his brother has benefited. Another item taken from Vasco is a purposeful stride, leaning forward and walking quickly, which, when a teenager, our friend liked enough to copy and which makes any destination seem the only one possible.

The man's name is Connor Raposo, though his Portuguese parents baptized him Juan Carlos and into his late teens everyone called him Zeco. But just before college, he decided he needed a new identity and changed his name to Connor. He's in his mid-twenties—thin, six feet tall, straight nose, chestnut eyes, moderately handsome, black hair that grazes the collar of his jacket, though if we were really looking down from a cherry picker, we might see an incipient bald spot, which in twenty years, if he lives that long, will overspread his dome. Besides his purposeful walk, he has a purposeful face. Connor will appear somber even when telling a joke. But his expression derives from the shyness he felt as a kid; it discouraged people from talking to him. You know that bromide "He's laughing on the outside but crying on the inside"? Connor's just the opposite.

Unlike the pasty winter faces of others on Bank Street, Connor's face is tanned, which is no surprise, since he left San Diego a week ago, and yesterday, dropping off his shoes, was his first visit to New London. What else? He wears jeans, running shoes, and a brown leather jacket he's had since college.

But to move along: Connor has given the elderly cobbler his claim ticket, and the cobbler has held up the black Bruno Maglis for Connor's inspection. He sets them on the counter, where they glisten like anthracite. The leather soles are a change for Connor. Usually he wears soft, rubber-soled shoes and he walks as softly as a wink, whether to sneak toward something or sneak away, he can't be sure. The cobbler counts out a fistful of one-dollar bills—Connor's change—while apologizing for having nothing bigger.

"You want a bag?" The cobbler has gray tufts of hair sprouting from his ears, woolly entanglements to snatch the oncoming words one by one.

"Never mind, my car's right across the street." He stuffs the bills into his jacket pocket.

A sound grows audible, a distant purr, which leads the cobbler to shake his head. "The first of the season, just like robins." Then, seeing Connor's blank expression, he adds, "Harleys—spring, summer, and fall they come roaring past."

The distant purr changes to a low rumble that increases in volume and reverberates off the stone buildings. It's an intrusion that loosens the mind from previous thoughts. Indignant seagulls flap away toward the water.

"We have noise restrictions in California." Connor had a noisy Harley in college and loved it. "Can't you make a complaint?"

Before the cobbler can answer, the Harley flashes by, twin headlights, a blur of candy orange, Stinger wheels, Tommy Gun pipes, lots of chrome, a growl like a brontosaurus. It's a snapshot shooting past the window. The plate glass shivers.

Then everything gets faster yet: the roar of a second motor rises above the roar of the Harley, a woman screams, a squeal of rubber to make Connor brace himself. Next comes a packed combination of noises: a collision of metal against metal, a wrenching shriek, glass breaking, the crunch and clatter of hundreds of little bits scattered across the pavement; a window shatters, and hidden within the variations of smash is the sound of a speeding biker striking an immovable object.

Connor hurries to the sidewalk. A large green dump truck has backed out of an alley and across Bank Street, ramming a parked BMW 300-something, shoving it over the curb into the now demolished display window of a music store. The guy on the Harley has hit the side of the dump truck.

But it's worse than that. The truck's dump box rides high on the axles, and the lower part of the Harley—wheels, V-twin engine, transmission, chrome pipes—has passed beneath, while the top part of the Harley—twin headlights, handlebars, gas tank, and half of the biker—has not. They've been separated. The rider has been ripped in two, so his bloody torso lies in the street, while under the truck at the end of a red smear are the legs, one with a boot, one not. The head has been detached from the neck and has vanished. Connor turns away so as not to lose his breakfast.

Blood and body fragments paint the nearby cars and windows of shops. The street is a mess of color. The truck has continued to roar; then the driver cuts the engine and climbs from his cab, his face creased with astonishment. A young man in a formerly white shirt stands across the street from Connor with blood streaming from his shoulder. It's a little after ten o'clock. Connor smells gasoline mixed with the smell of the river at low tide. For a nanosecond the scene is without movement or sound, except for someone retching.

Then, as if a lever were yanked, all becomes noise and action. People cry out. A young woman in shorts covers her face with her hands. If Connor were closer, he'd see spots of blood on her white legs. Some people hurry away; others run toward the wreckage with eye-popping avidity. There's a rush of randomness and instability that people try to reduce to order. Another young woman spits into a handkerchief and dabs at red spots on her blouse. A man in a blue business suit sits on the sidewalk with his legs outstretched, cleaning his glasses with his necktie. Cars honk as drivers are forced to stop farther back at Firehouse Square and have as yet to realize the reason for the delay. Soon comes the sound of sirens. Seagulls circle.

Connor stands twenty feet from the accident. He stares not at the truck or the biker's multiple bloody fragments but at a black leather Harley cap by the edge of the curb. He stoops to pick it up, half expecting to find the top part of a skull. But there's nothing, a few sweat marks, a few black hairs, and grease from whatever stuff the dead man put on his scalp. Oh, yes, the Harley cap has a red satin lining and on the lining is written a name in black ink: MARCO SANTUZZA.

A pair of broken aviator sunglasses lie in the gutter. Closer to the truck lies the torn black sleeve of a leather jacket in the midst of broken glass and pieces of metal. A hand extends from the cuff; silver rings embellish the fingers and thumb, one with a blue stone, another showing a skull. Connor again turns his head to avoid being sick and looks into the faces of twenty men and women gaping past him, their features magnified by disbelief.

Connor's sensory receptors are on serious overload as the street grabs his attention, but the strain creates a fog, and he has to half close his eyes in order to see. Now he shakes his head to free it of bloody images. He wants to get into his car and leave, but the street is jammed with cars and there'll be no freeing his Mini-Cooper until these are cleared. Just beyond the square is fire headquarters, a two-story brick building with two large bays. Out of one pokes the red nose of a hook and ladder truck. This is where the fire marshal has his office, but because of the traffic jam, the firemen won't go anyplace unless they walk.

People try to direct traffic, waving their hands to urge drivers to back up to Tilley Street, but some drivers have left their cars and have run forward to see the drama. People raise smartphones to take pictures. A police car half on the sidewalk makes earsplitting horn blasts as it pushes past the cars. For Connor the noise comes from inside his head: it's his brain's response to the awfulness. He tucks the Harley cap under his arm, meaning to keep it as visual proof of what he'd rather forget, and leans against the cobbler's window. The door is open, and the cobbler is down by the smashed Harley, staring at something unpleasant near his feet. Connor retrieves his Bruno Maglis from the cobbler's counter and makes his way between the jammed cars to lock the shoes in his Mini-Cooper.

This would be the moment to use our cherry picker again, but how much can be said? Once we've reached a point beyond belief, words are unreliable. "I can't believe this is happening!" At least a dozen people say this. Clichés soothe at such times; they link the horrific to the banal and make it tolerable. A few seagulls peck at bits of bloody tissue. Connor still hasn't seen the biker's head, which is just as well. It's been smashed to fragments, or on a rooftop, or is bobbing down the river.

N ow we come to a difficult introduction. Standing across the street by the crushed BMW is an elderly, homeless man who has a tail. No, no, he doesn't really have a tail, but he is certain he woke this morning with a tail, a long, gray, scabrous tail without fur. Perhaps the fur has fallen out; perhaps it never had fur in the first place. This is something he can't recall. Right now the tail is no more than a sinuous dark shadow, but the man's hands have begun to shake, and the more they shake, the sooner his tail will reappear, unless he gets a drink first.

The previous evening, in the bushes beneath the Interstate 95 bridge, he had blended a fifth of Everclear with five packets of grape jam snitched from a Greek diner. This reduced the alcohol proof from 190 to about 187, which he still saw as potent. He chose grape because he meant to make something winelike. Perhaps he had succeeded—he can't remember, because he blacked out almost immediately. This, to his mind, is a good thing. Erasure is what he's after, the more the better.

The man's name is Fidget, but it isn't his real name. It's just what he's called. As for last names, he's had a bunch of them. Nor is he sure of his age, though he knows he's over sixty, but that's been true for a while, so maybe he's seventy by now. He wears a Red Sox cap, a torn raincoat that once was beige, pants of an uncertain dark color, and muddy sneakers. In

place of laces, he uses twine. His gray hair is currently short, and if his
cap were removed, we'd see that it has a ragged look. A girl under the
bridge cut it in exchange for three cigarettes. And Fidget is thin enough
that his body seems to vanish beneath his raincoat, as if the coat were
draped over a parking meter. His long face is gray, unshaven, and somewhat disarranged from years of violent readjustments. The middle of his
nose, for instance, makes a distinct curve to the left, something like a
question mark. His eyes resemble those of a pug dog: dark brown and
protruding. It's not an ugly face, though it's seen a lot of use.

But the tail is a concern. There's no hiding a tail five feet long that
won't stay wrapped around his waist. It likes to flip about like the tail
of a disgruntled cat. Fidget wishes he could meet these downturnings of
fortune philosophically, but as his age increases so his patience decreases.
A few years ago, he had paws instead of hands, and once he had the
hooves of a palomino horse, which were noisy. So a rat's tail is a step up,
as long as people don't see it. Fidget believes if he just had an alcohol
drip, as he once had a morphine drip, he wouldn't be plagued by illusion-
ary appendages.

He'd been on the sidewalk by the music store when the accident took
place, and although he is shocked by the man's death—the tearing asunder and general horror—he also looks for opportunity, as he always looks
for opportunity. This morning he thinks he has found it. He feels sure he
has seen something he can turn into money, maybe a lot of money, if he's
patient.

Right now he focuses on how he'll spend his money, and these imaginings are a lively pleasure. He'll say good-bye to sleeping under the bridge.
He'll rent a single-room apartment with an electric fire and an armchair
where he can sit in the evenings and chew on a good cigar. It's a happy-
making image; it also strikes him as suitably modest, so modest that he
feels sure of its fulfillment. But as for patience, Fidget knows no patience,
unless it's the open-ended patience called forgetting.

Fidget has moved into the street closer to the scene of the accident to
a spot that he believes is free of the dead guy's fleshy remnants. He wears

no socks, and his sneakers have holes. No way does he want bits of the dead guy glued to the bottoms of his feet. A city detective talks to the driver of the truck as they stand by the open door of the cab. Fidget wants to know what they're talking about. The keys are in the ignition, and a steady *ding-ding-ding* comes from the cab. A TV truck has driven up Bank Street to the other side of the dump truck, and a cameraman films the dead guy's feet, one with a boot, one not. No way is that shot going to make the evening news.

Fidget takes a step closer, then turns his back to suggest a lack of interest. Coming toward him along the sidewalk are ten firemen pulling a very long hose. They grunt and stumble and press on, as if pulling a full-size elephant by its trunk. Shielded by firemen, Fidget takes another step toward the detective. He's had dealings with this man, whose name he can't recall, and he knows the more pissed the man becomes, the more quietly he speaks. At the moment the detective is not raising his voice above a whisper. As for the driver, he's saying something about the brakes or how his foot slipped. He holds his hands in front of him with his palms facing out; a drop of sweat hangs from the tip of his nose. He's a middle-aged guy with a big belly, and his face is as round as a poker chip.

Three uniformed cops make their way toward the truck, shooing gawkers from the scene. Fidget knows these cops from a multiplicity of threats and head slaps he's received in the past. None can he call friends, but he'd like to hear something useful before he's yelled at. He steps over the fire hose to the wall of a vacant furniture store across from the music store, and he stands quietly except for giving an occasional thump to his tail. It's again begun its serpentine gestures.

Fidget had seen the truck back out of the alley and shouted, "Hey!" or "Watch out!"—he can't recall which—but nothing could be heard over the noise of the truck and the approaching motorcycle. Then, in a second, it was too late. He barely had time to duck into the music store's alcove and crouch down with his hands over his head. The destruction of the Harley, the truck hitting the BMW at the curb and pushing it onto

the sidewalk, the smashing of the music store's display window have cre-
ated serious wreckage, and if it hadn't been for the BMW, the truck
would have broken through the window to crush the shiny trumpets and
trombones.

Now the nearest cop shouts at him, "Get the fuck outta here, prick-
head. You some kind of pervert?"

Fidget moves back up Bank Street. No way does he want to get hit
with a nightstick. His tail flaps back and forth. He smacks it to keep it
quiet, but this only excites it. Over the years he's had many humiliations.
The tail is just the most recent. But Fidget can't let it distract him from
future profit.

Detective Benny Vikström stares at the truck driver's belly, which
hangs over his leather belt like a slab of snow curving over the edge
of a winter roof, although this particular slab is covered by a blue work
shirt. Vikström tries to guess how many gallons of beer over how many
years produced a gut like that.

"I still don't see why you couldn't hit the brake."

The driver, Leon Pappalardo, shifts from one leg to the other. "I tried,
I slammed down my foot but only hit the gas. I already told you I never
drove this truck before. The pedals are different, I mean the space between them, like, it's narrower. Then the gas stuck, and before I could fix
it, I hit the Beemer."

"And the guy on the bike?"

"Like I said, he ran into me. I feel bad about it."

Vikström lifts his eyes from the man's belly to his face and decides he
doesn't look as if he feels bad. He looks scared. Vikström has seen this
look often: pretend calm and confidence with fear leaking from the guy's
face like water from cupped hands. And Pappalardo's dyed black hair
suggests a vanity that, to Vikström's mind, sits uneasily with the belly. It
might even suggest a kind of ambition.

Benny Vikström's name is Swedish, which should surprise nobody. He likes his name, though he's tired of people asking, "Whadja say it was again?" And when he spells it for someone, he adds, "With an umlaut," which leads to more questions. He was born and brought up in New London, but his parents came from Malmö fifty years ago. Soon after that his father, Acke Vikström, took a job at Electric Boat.

Vikström is forty-five, thin, a few inches over six feet, with one of those long, angular faces that appear cut from granite. His high cheekbones have an alpine look; his eyes are bright blue. His thinning blond hair is turning gray and is cut short with a fringe in front. He's been a New London cop for fifteen years and a detective for five. By his figuring he should be a detective sergeant by now, but women fucked up the competition. He doesn't complain, for the most part. It's this equal-opportunity stuff. Even the police chief's a woman, for crying out loud.

"I still don't see why you couldn't hit the brake."

Leon Pappalardo's head shakes like a bobblehead doll's, and he squints up at Vikström. "Aren't you fuckin' listening? I already—"

Vikström reaches out and taps on the beer belly with a knuckle, not a gentle tap. He's half a foot taller than the driver and looms. "What did I say? You be nice, I'll be nice. Didn't I say that before? But I don't have to be nice. Generally I'm not a nice person, or so the wife says. Generally I'm vicious."

Vikström wasn't scheduled to work this morning, but someone called in sick. Not that Vikström thinks the guy is sick. On a glorious day like this, he's most likely gone for a walk on the beach, like Vikström wanted to do instead of getting bent out of shape by the guy on the motorcycle. No, that isn't right, not by the guy himself—by the guy's many little parts. Their confetti-like aspect makes him queasy.

Vikström's gray suit coat brushes Pappalardo's belly. "You mean you got excited and just couldn't tell the difference between the brake and the gas? What kind of shit is that?"

Pappalardo again bobbles his head. His dyed black hair is held in a ponytail, which sways back and forth.

"I got big feet, just look at those feet." The men stare at the feet, encased in old work boots with the shiny edges of the steel toes breaking though the leather. "D'you see many like that? Size fuckin' fourteen. I'm lucky to get them in the cab."

"So you killed this guy because you got big feet?"

"No way. He was going like a rocket. It's, like, both our faults."

"Maybe you were talking on your phone and not paying attention."

"I lost my phone. I mean, it's in my house someplace. I'm always losing it."

Leon Pappalardo's sober, Vikström can tell that. He's Vikström's age, and he's nervous. But he's got a right to be nervous; maybe it's not guilty nervous, maybe it's *I fucked up* nervous. That's the main thing—for Vikström there's no clear reason to back up and hit the biker on purpose, which doesn't mean it didn't happen.

Firemen stand nearby holding a dry line, and by now the police have pushed the gawkers thirty feet up Bank Street. Vikström knows some, like Fidget and the cobbler and the black gay guy who runs an art gallery—what's his name?

Maurice, and who doesn't like it when Vikström calls him Mo—pause—*Reese*, which isn't a black thing like the guy thinks but goes back to the old cigarette ad: "Call for Phillip Mo—pause—*Reese*!"

Vikström sees his partner, Manny Streeter, talking to a man farther up the sidewalk, getting another version of the story. Vikström has already given the truck driver a ticket for reckless driving leading to an accident, which is a big ticket and could cost him his job, but Vikström would like to give him something bigger, if only because a guy got killed, though "rent asunder" was more accurate. As for the big-feet business, it's bullshit.

Vikström pats Pappalardo's stomach. "You a Budweiser man?"

Pappalardo looks up in surprise. "Sometimes. Mostly it's Nasty-gansett, the new Nasty-gansett."

"You're from Rhode Island?" Narragansett is a Rhode Island beer.

Again the driver looks surprised. "Brewster. It's on the coast, the first town up from Charlestown. I live in Brewster."

"I know Brewster," says Vikström. "I got friends there."

"Mostly it's a quiet place," says Pappalardo. "If you like quiet."

TWO

C onnor Raposo's Mini-Cooper remains trapped. There's no getting it out until a lot of other cars are moved. He holds the dead man's motorcycle cap and stands on the curb near the cobbler's shop, trying not to be pissed off. Who's he going to get pissed off at, the dead guy on the Harley, Marco Santuzza? Connor has work to do, money to liberate from other people's pockets, like it or not, and he won't make a dime by standing around Bank Street.

A few feet to his left, the street is blocked with yellow cop tape, while on the other side of the dump truck is a red pumper and a hook and ladder, as well as a white TV truck. The Harley's busted fuel tank has spread gas over a patch of street, and the pumper is supposed to spray the pavement, but there's an ethical problem, says the fire marshal. Since maybe twenty pounds of dead guy's bits and pieces are stuck to the street, washing it down means sending ten percent of him into the sewer. So the fire marshal looks to ask permission, but he's not sure who to ask: maybe the mayor, maybe a priest. Actually, he's not looking for permission so much as looking for somebody else to share the blame. But that someone had better show up soon, because all that accelerant is a disaster waiting to happen.

Connor has already spoken to two detectives about what he saw, which was nothing except the flash of the Harley going by. One of them was Benny Vikström, the other was his partner, Manny Streeter. About twenty people stand near Connor, and thirty more are in the street and on the opposite sidewalk. Half are drivers of blocked cars, others are gawkers. At the moment Connor stares at an old bum in a Red Sox cap swatting at something behind him, though Connor sees nothing behind him. The swatting is secretive and angry, and what seems especially odd is the old guy keeps looking in Connor's direction, though Connor is sure he's never seen him before.

Forensics specialists lift small, unidentifiable bits with tweezers and put them into plastic bags. Two TV film crews interview bystanders. Print journalists clutch notepads, and one young female reporter has a photographer in tow. When the TV people asked Connor what he'd seen, he said he hadn't seen anything and was only there to pick up some shoes.

Ambulance attendants stand on the other side of the tape, waiting to be told what to do, not that a stretcher will help. A mop and shovel would be better. Connor is struck at how he's gotten accustomed to the horror, but the Harley is hidden behind the cops and forensics guys, and he can almost imagine that the body is gone. The fact that the street is speckled with blood, tissue, and body parts is ghastly, but from this distance it's an intellectual understanding.

Many people's faces remain distorted by disgust, horror, and intense interest. Some have their eyes squinched half shut as if the scene's too bright; some are bug-eyed as if they can't get enough; some take videos with their smartphones. By afternoon they'll be on YouTube for the world to see.

Connor scratches a spot, a small lump, on the front of his leather jacket, that he suspects might be a dollop of gore. This seems unlikely, because he was inside the cobbler's shop when the crash occurred, though he got outside as fast as he could. Maybe the force of the accident threw bits of the motorcycle guy high in the air, where they hung for a moment before plummeting downward. With a little more picking, he realizes it's a dab of oatmeal from breakfast, and he laughs.

"I'm glad somebody thinks this is funny," says a man slightly behind him. "I just want to get the fuck out of here."

Connor turns to see shiny black hair swept back from a brow, a pompadour vaguely like Elvis's. The pompadour's owner is shorter than Connor, and the hair, adding a few inches to his height, is at eye level. Connor realizes he knows this man, but he keeps his face blank till he's sure the guy isn't part of a work-related problem, which is why he and his friends left San Diego in the first place.

Connor explains his confusion, that what he thought was a dollop of gore turns out to be a dollop of oatmeal. He laughs again, but mostly he wants to know where he's seen this guy. It wasn't on the West Coast, he's sure of it, and it wasn't recently. In fact, it's the hair he remembers, and then, gradually, he recalls the rest: black caterpillar eyebrows, flat shovel nose, thin lips, square chin, and a restless shifting of his shoulders as if he were preparing to slug someone.

The man wears a black shirt with the top button unbuttoned to display some gold chains. He has a tan jacket folded over his arm, and he holds it up, which shows off a gold Rolex. "The jacket's got maybe twenty spots on it, blood and other shit. I could get it cleaned, but I wouldn't like the memory."

Connor sees blood spots on the lapels and takes note of the Rolex. "You must have been standing close."

"Close enough."

"Is your car stuck here?"

"Fuckin' right." The man points. "It's the hunka junk in front of that toy car."

Connor pauses a beat, then says, "That happens to be my toy car."

"Yeah, well, I didn't mean to insult your wheels. No offense."

"None taken. Looks like your car's had a lot of use." The Chevy Caprice must have a broken suspension system: each of its four corners is at a different height.

"What my car's got is bigness. It's the cop package. Full of power."

"It must have its advantages."

"Yeah, no one's going to steal it, but right now the battery's dead. It drains quick if it's sitting. I didn't think I'd be here so long. Is that the guy's cap?"

Connor puts on the cap. "Just a souvenir. It fits pretty well."

"Dead man's cap. I saw him go by. It's bad luck." The man pats his hair in case any strands are out of place. Several gold-nugget rings twinkle.

Connor laughs. "I'll take the chance. Did you know the guy?" The man has no trace of a New England accent. If anything, it sounds like the Midwest, squeezing words together and giving "dead" two syllables.

"Nah, but I'd recognized the bike. Fat Bob."

"Is that his name?"

"It's what they call the bike—it's the model."

The fact the bike has a name makes it real again. It's like two people being killed. "You saw the accident?" asks Connor.

Another train approaches, and its horn blasts them into a few seconds of silence. Then the man says, "I was looking in the music store. My kid wants a trombone so he can march in the school band. You know how kids are. So my back was to the street. I turned when the truck came out of the alley and the biker hit his brakes."

"It must have been awful."

"Yeah, you could say that."

During this talk Connor keeps trying to place the man. It's an expanding question that he can't set aside. For the past year, Connor had a black mustache that he kept to please his girlfriend. When they broke up before he left San Diego, Connor shaved it off. However, he'd grown used to smoothing it back with his index finger and thumb, and though Connor has lost the mustache, he's kept the gesture. He's doing it now. It's a gesture that accompanies thought.

"You ever been in Detroit? There's a guy you remind me of."

"What's his name?"

"I never knew. He was a guy I'd see around the casino. Maybe he's a relative." But Connor knows that while a relative might have the man's height, eyebrows, and nose, he wouldn't have the pompadour.

"I don't know any family in Detroit. I'm from Saint Louis."

"Never been there. I'm from Minneapolis," says Connor, who was actually from Cleveland. He sticks out his hand. "Name's Connor Raposo."

The man's handshake is almost painful. "I'm Sal Nicoletti. You Italian?"

"Pork and cheese."

The caterpillar eyebrows go up half an inch. "Say what?"

"My dad was Portuguese. He liked to call it 'pork and cheese.'"

"Funny guy."

"Yeah, sometimes."

Connor is sure he hasn't heard the name Sal Nicoletti before, but he's also pretty sure he's seen this man in a Detroit casino, probably the MGM Grand, where Connor worked for a year. "I used to have a Harley, a small one. I had a few close calls and got uncomfortable on it. So I sold it."

Connor continues to talk, easygoing and disengaged, the way men talk when they are waiting for something else to happen: a car repair, a ball game. Sal's office overlooks the river, which is a good thing, but it's also about twenty yards from the train tracks, a bad thing. "Fuckin' train horn knocked me outta my chair the first coupla times." But Connor's mind keeps grinding away, seeking a clearer memory. Sal's in his mid-thirties, wears jeans, a black shirt, and genuine eelskin boots, which add several inches to his height. All Connor can recollect about the person he's trying to recall is something's not right about him, something destructive.

N o way it wasn't an accident. You kiddin' me? Course it's an accident." Detective Manny Streeter is talking to his partner, Benny Vikström, next to the dump truck. "Where's your evidence?" Manny's a stocky fellow and walks like a brick on legs. His chin, mouth, and nose, even his eyebrows and ears, seem oversize, and he shaves his head to conceal his hair loss, going bald by choice rather than be "fucked over by the fickle finger of fate," as he's said more than once. He wears a blue suit, and the jacket is open to expose a silver belt buckle the size of a fist with a replica of James Earle Fraser's *End of the Trail*, showing a dying, spear-carrying Indian on a skeletal, staggering pony. It's so distinctive that most people notice the belt buckle before noticing Manny.

"I don't have any evidence," says Vikström, "but we'll keep looking." He now carries his jacket over his shoulder because of the heat. They've been at the scene two hours, and it's past noon. Having talked to some people and picked up what information they could find, they're ready for lunch. But the information isn't much. A truck backed out of an alley, and a man on a motorcycle crashed into it. The dead man's name seems to be Robert Rossi, which is the name Vikström gets when he calls in the plate number. But the victim's wallet is missing, and this bothers the detectives. The wallet was attached by a chain to the biker's belt loop, and only a bit of chain remains. Presumably the chain snapped and the wallet was flung somewhere. Just like the head. They've directed a few policemen to look for it.

"So let's say it was premeditated," says Manny. "What's the motive? Why'd he come barreling down this street instead of another? And the driver—what's his name, Poppaloppa?—you think he's got the brains to plan this? No way, José."

"Lardo."

"Say again?"

"Pappalardo."

"Whatever."

Vikström, with his mind on lunch, leans back against the truck. Just as he's getting comfortable, his face changes; a memory has struck him. He turns quickly and says, "Do I got that dead guy all over me?"

Manny inspects the back of Vikström's white shirt. "Well, maybe here and there. Some red spots, a few sort of grayish. But they don't look bad. I mean, they don't look like parts of a dead guy." Manny keeps a straight face in such a way that Vikström can see that Manny is trying to keep a straight face.

"What the fuck does that mean?" Vikström twists his neck, attempting to see the back of his shirt. He thinks he sees a suspicious blotch that wasn't there before. "You could've said something when you saw me leaning back."

"I thought you knew."

"You thought I'd been leaning on top of the dead guy on purpose?"

"I figured you'd already checked out the truck, know what I mean?"

"No," Vikström says, "I don't."

We should step back and look at this exchange, because it's at the center of their relationship. Manny tries to drive Vikström crazy, Vikström tries to ignore it. They've had many such exchanges that conclude with Vikström feeling diminished in a small way. Vikström's sure Manny does it on purpose, but he's not *totally* sure, and of course Manny denies it. For Vikström such exchanges add needless tension and distrust; for Manny they add moments of joy.

Vikström and Streeter have worked together ten months, but they've never been close. Vikström thinks Manny's too competitive, meaning too ambitious, while Manny thinks Vikström is too loosey-goosey or goosey-loosey, he can't recall which, but it means Vikström follows his intuition while Manny likes everything down on paper. That's how it was at the start; then it got worse.

Vikström wants to strip off his shirt to look for splotches. Instead he bends his features into a semblance of indifference. He's pretty sure that Manny has done this business about not warning him on purpose, and he's sure that Manny knows that he knows, which is Manny's ambition.

"I'm not saying the accident was premeditated," says Vikström, as if nothing has happened, "but neither am I saying it *wasn't* premeditated. The driver wasn't telling the truth, or all of it, and I'd like to spend more time digging around."

"How'd he know the Fat Bob was coming? How'd he time it?"

Vikström shrugs. Manny hates it when Vikström says, *I just got a funny feeling about this one,* so he says, "I got a funny feeling about this one."

They walk back up Bank Street to where the trapped cars are being freed. Vikström furtively wipes the back of his shirt and then inspects his hand. Nothing. Two cops direct traffic. Cars honk. Soon the truck will be towed to a garage where its brakes, accelerator, and clutch will be checked. But right now the forensics guys are still picking up bits of Robert Rossi, and technically, as Vikström says, the truck should be sent to the morgue along with a good hunk of pavement. Manny doesn't laugh; outside the confines of his home, he limits his humor to irony, sarcasm, and mockery. Both men have considered transferring to another section, but each wants to remain in the Detective Bureau, so each waits for the other to make the first move.

Up ahead they see Fidget collecting spare change from people whose cars remain stuck. Fidget slaps at something behind him, level with his coccyx.

"I bet he's got fleas," says Manny, who doesn't want to get too close.

"Hey, Fidget," calls Vikström, "hold up. I want to talk to you."

Without turning his head, Fidget hurries forward, but his knees are iffy and keeping them stiff makes him look as if he's walking on stilts.

Vikström catches up with him and puts a hand on his shoulder. "Going deaf?"

"Jeez, Detective, this is prime picking time. If I don't get these people now, they'll be gone."

Vikström shakes Fidget's arm. "What'd you see when the bike hit the truck?"

"Bike?"

"The motorcycle," says Manny, "the motorcycle!"

"Yeah, I saw the Harley hit the truck. Is that what you're talking about? It was awful. I got blood on my coat."

Vikström and Manny look at the multilayers of gray that cover the once-beige raincoat with an impasto effect. No bloodstains are visible, which doesn't mean they aren't part of the porridge.

"I mean, did you see anything you should tell us about?" asks Vikström.

Fidget swats a hand behind him to quiet his tail that's flicking back and forth like a twenty-foot bullwhip. He knows what Vikström is saying, but he also knows if he has any chance to turn this event into cash, he has to keep quiet. "What's to tell? I saw a Harley smash into a dump truck and a biker turned to splop. What's more to say than that?"

THREE

The gravel access road to the Hannaquit Breachway is the victim of months of bad weather and resembles, to Connor's mind, a long ravioli mold with indentations on either side. Half are filled with water, and Connor steers his Mini-Cooper around them as he heads toward the beach. At times he's thrown against his seat belt; at other times he's bounced up to bang against the roof. As protection he wears the black motorcycle cap from the accident. It helps a little.

On a ridge above the water, a white, older model Winnebago Journey has been drawn into a campground parking slot reserved for self-contained RVs. The campground, of course, is closed for the season, but Connor was told that an assortment of deals had been made, the truth of various falsehoods had been asserted, and bogus regulations had been upheld, all of which had permitted them to park illegally. When he questioned this, he was informed that the coast of Rhode Island was full of fellow Portuguese and that close associates had settled matters. In any case, the details hardly signified, because now, with a salt pond behind it and the ocean in front, the thirty-nine-foot Winnebago with two open slides is the sole vehicle in residence, which is how Connor's friends like it.

It's four-thirty, and Connor hasn't eaten. Getting boxed in on Bank Street upset many plans. Still, he's rented a post office box in New London, picked up a rush order from a printer's, made various purchases, and acquired several telephone books.

It would be wrong to say that Connor's mind remains a blur from the accident that morning, but he suffers from a sort of double vision as the bloody display of the biker, disassembled and confettied against the side of the truck, is repeatedly projected upon the scene around him: blue sky, sand, and tall pines, a breeze rippling the surface of the salt pond, the ocean extending to the horizon. So Connor exists in a state of wince, with his hands clutching the steering wheel.

He parks behind the Winnebago next to a gray Ford Focus rental. The Winnebago is at the end of the breachway, while to the left are about twenty empty RV slots. Farther on stand a row of summer cottages on stilts. Connor pauses to admire a snowy egret pretending to be a bush at the edge of the pond; then he gathers his Bruno Magli slip-ons from the front seat and takes his parcels from the back. The phone books he'll get later. With arms full, he makes his way around the side of the Winnebago to the front door, which is open. It's low tide, and the sea does little more than slosh. Gulls seek snacks along the waterline. From somewhere comes a rhythmic *thump-thump-squeak*, over and over.

Sitting in a lawn chair by the door is a man or a boy in a bulky black sweatshirt with his back to Connor. He's small, and his straw-colored hair is mostly cowlick. Leaning forward, he focuses on a yellow pad of paper balanced on his lap.

The question of whether he is man or boy is a question asked by many. His cheeks are pink and show no sign of facial hair. If we touched them, we'd be struck by the smoothness of his skin, and if he stood up, we'd see he's five feet tall. But he doesn't seem short as much as unfinished, as if he were waiting for two or three more growth spurts to top him off. Nor does he seem short when he walks, because his step is purposeful and his back straight. He will look businesslike even in a casual dawdle along the beach. As we might suspect, he copies this from Connor, whom he admires, just as Connor has copied it from his brother Vasco, but the boy or young man exaggerates the walk to the point that, in motion, he appears robotic.

Observing him, we might think him anywhere between thirteen and thirty. His head is long and shaped like a loaf of bread, with a high forehead, a stub of a nose, and a round chin. Along with the sweatshirt, he wears jeans and pointed black boots. Oh, yes, his nails are clean and nicely trimmed. This wouldn't need to be said, but it's the result of obsessive behavior, so Connor thinks. The fellow spends hours keeping them perfect, filing and painting them with clear nail polish. Another thing: his left eye is blue and the other green, and at times he seems to glance at you with the blue one and at times with the other; and the blue eye shows his feelings as one way and the green shows they're another, but they never show the same together.

All in all, the man or boy is a mysterious fellow, and Connor, who has known him a month, hasn't figured him out, meaning he never knows what he's thinking, if he's thinking at all. The most Connor can say is he's pretty sure he has Asperger's, or something like it; on the other hand, he might be simply weird. As for his name, or real name, Connor doesn't know it, though he and the couple inside the Winnebago call him Vaughn, because his voice has the same rippling, velvety baritone as the late singer Vaughn Monroe; and whenever Vaughn speaks, Connor feels a faint thrill, the same as he felt years ago when he first heard Vaughn Monroe sing "Riders in the Sky," which was one of Connor's granddad's favorite songs. But Vaughn, or whatever his name is, has never heard of Vaughn Monroe. Or so he says.

Vaughn has another talent: numbers to him are what colors were to Van Gogh. He's a math whiz, which, for our purposes, means he's a whiz with computers and has developed formidable hacking skills. Perhaps he can't get into Pentagon computers or the computers of those pesky Russkies, but the computers of moderate-size businesses or organizations pose no problem. He's a twenty-first-century Peeping Tom. Not long ago he peeped for the sake of peeping, rather than for financial reward. But that's changed.

At the moment Vaughn is drawing squares on a yellow sheet of lined paper. These come in three shapes and are as exact as if measured with a ruler. The large squares form three across the top of the sheet and six down. Then three medium squares are in each of the large squares and three small squares are in each of the medium squares. But these are just today's squares. In his suitcase he has many other sheets of paper with squares of various sizes and configurations. When asked what they're for, Vaughn explains they represent his thoughts.

As Connor approaches, he asks, "Where's Didi?"

Vaughn turns and stares in Connor's direction, but he doesn't exactly look at Connor himself; instead his blue and green eyes stare at something past Connor's shoulder. Even after a month, Connor finds this unsettling, but he no longer turns to see who is behind him, though he may get a tingle in the back of his neck. Also, if an hour or more has passed since they were last together, Vaughn will act as though he's never seen Connor before. He does this now, as Connor smooths back the absent mustache that he shaved off when he split from his girlfriend. A moment goes by as Connor and Vaughn remain inert. Then Vaughn nods to the door of the Winnebago.

Again Connor hears *thump-thump-squeak, thump-thump-squeak.* "Eartha?"

But Vaughn is focused on the black motorcycle cap perched on the back of Connor's head. "What's that?"

Connor takes it off and turns it over in his hands. The red satin lining flickers in the sunlight. "A cap I picked up in New London."

"Can I have it?"

"Why should I give it to you?"

"It's my birthday."

"Is that so? How old are you?"

Vaughn continues to stare slightly over Connor's shoulder, and the stare seems as fixated as that of a snake hypnotizing a bird.

Connor can't think of a reason not to give Vaughn the cap, so he tosses it to him. "Happy birthday."

The noises from inside—*thump-thump-squeak*—continue.

Vaughn holds the cap up to the sun. "Who's . . . Mar-Co-San-Tuz-Za?"

"The previous owner. He doesn't need it anymore." In fact, thinks Connor, he has no head to put it on.

"It has blood spots."

Connor hadn't seen them earlier, but now, bending over, he sees a few dark spots on the brim. Vaughn licks a finger, rubs at a spot, and holds up the finger, which has a red blush on the tip.

"You want to give it back?" Connor asks him.

Vaughn puts on the cap. It's too big for him and wobbles a little before coming to rest on his freckled ears. "I like blood." He nods to Connor and claps a hand over his heart. "I'm internally grateful."

Connor opens his mouth to speak and then changes his mind to say, "I've got phone books in the back of the car. Get them, will you?" Then he climbs the steps into the Winnebago and shouts, "All right, cut the racket! I'm home!" He crosses the floor to the dinette and empties a bag of cell phones onto the Formica surface of the table next to three laptop computers and a printer. From other bags he takes boxes of envelopes, order forms, receipts, and letterheads. The RV is a dozen years old, and the interior is shabby. The maple veneer peels from the cabinets and trim. Covering the couch, the love seat, and the cushions of the dinette set is an off-white plasticized cloth with gray baroque designs that resemble, in Connor's mind, spiders and spiderwebs and are meant to camouflage stains, spills, smudges: the weekly overflow. The tan linoleum resembles tile, and it, too, has camouflage properties so it can go weeks without cleaning and the interior of the Winnebago might still seem presentable. A propane tank takes care of the stove and hot water.

Connor sleeps on the couch, which folds out into a double bed with a very thin mattress. Vaughn sleeps on the love seat. The others, whose names are Didi and Eartha, have a queen-size bed in the rear bedroom. The living area smells of grease with a stronger smell of mold. From the bathroom comes a disagreeable smell that Connor can't identify. Perhaps a squirrel was trapped in the metallic maze of the Winnebago's undercarriage and perished.

The bedroom door bangs open, and Didi appears. He's Connor's uncle, or that's what he says, because two months ago Connor didn't know he had an uncle by the name of Didi, which is short for Diogo. If anything, he might be his father's cousin, since his name is Lobato rather than Raposo. But Connor's father has six brothers, and no way can Connor keep track of them. Possibly Didi isn't related at all, but Connor doubts this, because their business is a family business of many years' standing and Didi claims to be Portuguese. "You're a tugo; I'm a tugo," he says.

Didi is about fifty and, as he says, "in tip-top shape"; he'll also say his thick, silver-gray hair "is completely natural." He parts it down the middle, creating swanlike silver wings at the sides of his head. His face is nearly a perfect oval; his nose is long and straight. The rims of his ears have small scoops at the back as if something had taken a bite from each. Didi tucks his T-shirt into his jeans and then zips his fly. He wears the self-satisfied expression of a man at peace with his libidinous wishes.

"Where the fuck you been?" he asks without animus.

"There was an accident in New London. My car got trapped." Connor describes what happened as Didi goes to the refrigerator for a Dos Equis.

"You're kidding," Didi keeps saying, "you're kidding!" He holds the beer out to Connor, who shakes his head. Didi flips off the bottle cap, throws back his head, and drinks.

Eartha emerges from the bedroom, interrupting Connor's story. She's a young black woman, and she's naked except for the bottom half of a red bikini; she twirls the top half in her hand. Under an arm is a rolled-up towel. "You think it's warm enough to lie on the beach?"

Connor turns away, though he knows it doesn't matter. Eartha often walks around naked, drying herself after a shower, braiding her hair, or even cooking up a couple of eggs at the stove. Vaughn never pays attention, nor does Didi for the most part, leaving Connor to think he's being oversensitive and stodgy. But Eartha is a "black knockout," which she repeats just as Didi repeats that he's in tip-top shape. In fact, her skin is a rich bronze. Maybe she's thirty. Her name isn't really Eartha; she's called that because she has a purr like Eartha Kitt. This is helpful in their work, which we'll get to shortly. Her real name is Shaw-nell, though sometimes she says it's Beatriz, a Brazilian name. And sometimes Didi says they're distant cousins.

Connor finds it difficult not to look at Eartha's breasts, which are melon-sized and nicely balanced. The nipples are pierced with silver nipple bars that have small rubies at the tips, which twinkle in the light. At times Connor thinks it's the nipple bars with their ruby dollops that attract him, but this is unlikely. His interest isn't aesthetic, which is why he turns away. He's afraid Eartha will think he's leering, and the occasion has not yet arisen when he can say it's the nipple bars that interest him and not their mounts. Since they've been together for only two weeks, Connor tells himself he'll soon get used to Eartha walking around naked, but so far it hasn't happened. Didi has said the breasts have been enhanced by implants and "have a nice bounce to them." But they look real enough to Connor.

Didi puts the empty beer bottle on the counter. "Connor saw a guy on a motorcycle smash into a garbage truck. He absolutely exploded."

Eartha puts a hand to her mouth; her large brown eyes grow larger.

"It was a dump truck," says Connor, "a green dump truck. The driver backed out of an alley and boom!"

Connor continues his story as Eartha puts on the top half of her bikini. Didi ties it for her. Vaughn has entered with the phone books from the car and has set them on the table. He seems not to be paying attention to the story, but Connor knows he always pays attention. Connor is annoyed that the banality of his words doesn't convey the horror of the scene. "Boom!"—what the heck does that mean? He wants to exaggerate, gesticulate, make faces, but he does none of that. A guy on a Harley piled into the side of a truck. It cut him in two. The pieces flew all over. *I should have taken a video with my iPhone,* thinks Connor.

"I have his cap," says Vaughn in his deep Vaughn Monroe voice. "Connor gave it to me for my birthday. It has blood on it."

Eartha inspects the cap but sees no blood. Didi says, "Is today really your birthday?"

Vaughn looks shrewd. "I got a special condensation."

There's a general silence as the others consider making a comment and then don't. After a moment Eartha says, "If you'd said something earlier, I'd have baked you a chocolate cake."

Thirty minutes later Connor sits at a spot above the water where the grass meets the sand. He has a ham sandwich, a Dos Equis, and is practicing not looking at Eartha, who lies on a yellow towel nearer the water to his right. He likes her all right, but he has no romantic feelings. At the moment she's stretched on her back; the ruby tips of the nipple bars sparkle, and her surgically enhanced breasts rise and fall with each breath, or maybe they're affected by the movement of the tides, maybe the moon governs their rise and fall. Connor ponders this and then turns away to free himself from their fleshy distraction, eat his ham sandwich, and study the ocean.

Directly across from him, he thinks, is Portugal, perhaps even Lisbon, where he's been twice to visit a great-aunt in Baixa, the old town. What he likes best about Lisbon is it allows him to forget the United States, to forget people and institutions who want something from him. Lisbon is a city full of strangers, which for Connor is its major appeal. His Portuguese is limited to "hello," "good-bye," and "thank you." Why know more than that? It solved a lot of problems and gave his brain a rest: a city of red roofs on the hillsides that glitter in the morning light.

But soon his thoughts drift from Lisbon to Sal Nicoletti in New London, or rather Nicoletti's mysterious familiarity. If Connor had in fact seen him in Detroit, then why did Sal lie about not having been there?

Earlier, when their cars were freed, Sal's battery had been dead just as he feared. It made only a clicking noise. Instead of calling a garage, Sal wanted to get a cab and go home, where he had another battery already charged in the garage.

"I'll give you a ride," Connor said, "if you don't mind riding in a toy car."

"As long as you got room for a dead battery."

So Sal opened the hood of the Caprice to display an engine that seemed to have been dipped in rust. He removed the battery and put it in the back of the Mini-Cooper. "I appreciate this. Like, you don't know me."

"No problem." Once they had turned around on Bank Street past Firehouse Square, Connor asked, "What's your office like? You said it faced the train tracks?"

"An office office."

Connor expected Sal to follow this up with a further remark about the view or the convenience or places to eat, but there was nothing. Sal had his eyes closed.

"You lived in New London for long?" asked Connor.

"No, not long. The wife's got family here."

"And you moved here from Saint Louis?"

"What're you gonna write, my life story?"

"Sorry. I'm just making conversation." He glanced at Sal, who had shut his eyes again. Earlier he and Sal had been involved in a certain amount of light chat: comments about the accident, questions about the missing head, and the general nuisance of the truck blocking the street. Now Sal's mood had changed.

Connor turned south on Ocean Avenue, which ran more or less parallel to the river: a mix of modest Victorian and early-twentieth-century houses; and then, past the railway tracks, larger Victorians with big lawns and big trees, still leafless in March, interspersed with brick ranch houses from the fifties. Sal lived on Glenwood Place, a loop of split-levels and ranch houses off Glenwood Avenue.

It was sunny, and the car's windows were down. Connor heard several chain saws tidying up from a February storm. On the sidewalk a woman in blue shorts pushed a jogging stroller in which a blond child snoozed. Connor's usual way of starting a conversation, especially with strangers, was to ask questions, so he pressed ahead despite Sal's apparent irritation.

"You got kids?"

"Yeah."

"How many?"

"Boy an' a girl, little ones."

"They must keep you busy."

Sal stared straight ahead. "The trouble with talk like this, it's like eating air. It's got no content, no protein. What's the point?"

"Aren't you curious about people?"

"Not unless they got something I want."

"That's pretty cynical."

"Yeah, yeah, yeah. Outside sports and cars, I don't see the purpose."

"Talk's good for the jaw muscles. It keeps the face trim."

Sal kept staring straight ahead. "You're a funny guy," he said disagreeably.

Connor laughed. "Yeah, yeah, yeah."

Sal's house was a brick ranch house with a large and treeless lawn. A light blue Chrysler Town & Country was parked in the driveway next to a small red tricycle with a white seat. Connor pulled up behind the Chrysler.

"I'd invite you in," Sal said with no trace of sincerity, "but the place's a mess. Kids, know what I mean?"

"You want a ride back downtown?"

"No thanks, the wife'll do it."

They got out of the Mini, and Sal retrieved his battery from the back. Connor kept thinking about Detroit and the various places where he might have seen Sal. Robins chittered fragments of song in nearby leafless maples; their bits and pieces sounded like the hurried excuses of the guilty.

"Let me open the garage door."

"No thanks, I'll get it."

The screen door banged open, and a woman came out onto the steps. The sight brought Connor to an abrupt stop. What was most evident, after her beauty, was her height. She was at least six feet, easily taller than Sal, and she looked athletic. Perhaps she was a runner or played tennis.

Her black hair hung past her shoulders. She wore white shorts and a white T-shirt. Her legs went on and on.

"Where's the Chevy?"

"Battery went dead downtown. I gotta change it." He turned to Connor. "Thanks for the ride."

The woman's skin tone was dark, and Connor guessed she might be southern Italian or Greek. Her eyes were black, and her nose was straight. She gave him a half smile, as if she knew his thoughts. She had a large mouth and full, sensuous lips that Connor thought would be ugly when she got angry, like an activated wood chipper. But the smile was beautiful.

"Hey, Connor, you hear me? I said you can go now. Like, thanks for the ride." Sal grinned, but his eyes were stony.

So Connor had gotten into the Mini again and reversed out of the driveway. His eyes, however, remained fixed on the woman talking to Sal. She glanced at him again, and he stared back. There was a sudden honking; Connor had nearly rammed into a mail truck.

FOUR

Connor, sitting above the ocean, decides that the way he'd looked at Sal's wife isn't the way he looks at Eartha. With the other woman, Connor had taken her in from her yellow flip-flops to her black hair. It wasn't a generalized look; it was absorption. With Eartha his look is more focused, though she also is beautiful.

As if his thoughts have called her, Connor sees Eartha standing next to him.

"Mind if I sit down?" She has draped the yellow towel over her shoulders, and it remains slightly open. Connor finds this more evocative than the bare breasts. He wonders if there's something wrong with him.

"Of course not."

"It's getting colder, don't you think?" She crosses her arms over the towel.

"It's supposed to snow tomorrow. A real storm."

"That's great. It never snows in San Diego. I've only seen it on mountains."

"You can get tired of it pretty quickly."

The purr of Eartha's voice generates a vibration in Connor's duodenum. He wonders if that's the effect she produces on the phone. But of course it is; that's why Didi brought her along. Just like Vaughn, she has a skill that Didi intends to use.

"I stuck my foot in the water and nearly froze it off."

Connor makes a sympathetic grunt and keeps his eyes on the ocean.

"It must have been terrible for you this morning, seeing that man killed."

"I expect it's the worst thing I've ever seen, and I didn't even see it. I heard the crash and ran outside."

"And it was an accident?"

"I guess so, but I heard two cops talking, two detectives, and they weren't sure—at least one of them wasn't."

"Like it was murder?" She says this in almost a whisper.

"I doubt it. The detectives weren't sure, that's all I can say." Through this exchange Connor looks at the water, then at a tree, and then at his feet. He and Eartha are silent a moment.

Eartha clears her throat, a theatrical noise, a soft-palate growl. "Does it bother you, I mean me sitting here? You don't look at me."

Connor laughs. "I'm sorry, I don't mean to be rude. I think I've got a fixation."

Eartha glances down at her towel-covered breasts. "You mean my boobs?"

Connor laughs again, but his laughter has a metallic quality, a palpable insincerity. "That's right."

"That's what they're for, the implants, to cause fixations. Before, they were nice enough but pretty usual, know what I mean? Not too big, not too small."

"There's nothing usual about them now."

Eartha nods with satisfaction. "That's what I wanted."

"You're not afraid it makes you a kind of stereotype?"

"Like a sexpot? Jesus, Connor, who the fuck cares? I like being looked at."

They go back to staring at the ocean. The tide has turned, and the sloshing is louder. Soon they'll have to move.

Connor says, "I saw an incredibly beautiful woman this afternoon, and I can't even remember her breasts. I don't know if that's a good thing or a bad thing."

"What made her beautiful?"

"Everything: her face, her body, her hair. And she had incredible legs."

"You're a romantic," says Eartha. "That can be a problem. I bet she leaves her dirty underwear on the floor just like I do. She burps, farts, and has messy periods. Really, Connor, you've got to imagine the whole package."

Benny Vikström and Manny stand inside the double overhead door of Hog Hurrah, a motorcycle shop specializing in Harleys on the other side of I-95. The six men working on bikes all have ponytails, even the bald guys. They wear black boots and jeans with silver chains connected to belt loops and fat wallets stuck in back pockets. Most wear black Harley T-shirts, some with flames, some without. They look like a family of bad brothers. Vikström is surprised he doesn't know any of them, meaning he's never arrested them or seen them in the station. He doesn't mind Harleys, but he hates the noise. No one has looked at him, though they've seen him. There's constant racket: a radio playing heavy metal, the hiss of an air hose, the clank of a tool hitting the concrete, the whine of a power wrench, the banging of metal on metal. The smudges of grease on their faces make an abstract painting.

After being ignored for ten seconds, Vikström takes a hammer from the floor and hits it against the side of a metal barrel. He keeps hitting it until the other noise stops, even the radio.

"I need information about Robert Rossi."

The men shake their heads. Their expressions indicate mental vacancy, dim thought, and negation. They start working again.

"Rossi was killed on a motorcycle this morning on Bank Street. He was cut in half. I need to notify his next of kin, and you're going to help me find them."

"Cut in half?" says a man standing by the door of a small office. The studied blankness of the men's faces changes to shock and focused attention, which again gives them a resemblance.

"Maybe he was broken into a hundred pieces, but the top half and the bottom half were the biggest chunks," says Manny. "And we can't find his head."

The men wince. This evidence of human feeling warms the detectives.

"I knew him best," says the man who'd spoken. "I'm Milo Lisowski. This is my place. Fat Bob worked here sometimes. Fuck, he's dead? He owes me money."

"Fat Bob? That's what you called him?"

"Everyone calls him that. He's got a bunch of Fat Bob bikes, the model. He collects them—or collected them. He had six or seven, all colors."

"Fat Bob on the Fat Bob?"

"That's right."

"You got an office?"

Vikström and Manny follow Lisowski into an office with a window looking onto the garage. He's about forty-five, of average size, and he wears gray overalls. He's got either a wandering eye or a glass eye, Vikström can't tell which. Benny is unsure which eye to look at, making it difficult to gauge the man's thoughts. Lisowski's hands are black with grease, and he picks at the larger bits with a fingernail.

"These guys work for you?"

"No, no, just one of them. The others use the space and tools at so much per hour. That guy by the lift is a dentist. He gives me a deal on my teeth." Lisowski opens his mouth to show his white teeth. "We got all sorts. It's a moneymaker."

"They got the biker face," says Manny, who hates motorcycles, "like the world could explode and it'd be a nuisance."

"They aren't bad guys. They got families, most of them. They go to church. This place is like a clubhouse without the obligations. They're only part-time tough. In school they were straight-A students, and they feel guilty about it. Here they can sound tough, swear, and talk dirty. They throw away their neckties—it's liberating. But if a couple of real biker-gang members showed up, these guys would shit their pants." He sits down on a beat-up swivel chair next to the beat-up desk. The chair squeaks. "Tell me about Fat Bob. Fuck, he said he'd give me my money this week."

Vikström stands. "Did he like being called that?"

"Sure. Fat Bob riding a Fat Bob. It was his special form of ID. He was nuts about that particular bike."

"And was he . . ." Vikström pauses a beat ". . . overweight? Did he have a belly?"

"He was husky, barrel-chested, and my age. The belly was a work in progress. It's the name that was important. He was part-time tough, like I said. Basically he's an accountant and works at a place downtown. He's really dead?"

"Well," says Manny, "I didn't check his pulse, but he was in two pieces."

Lisowski grimaces. "I've known him a bunch of years, but we weren't close. Not that I wanted him dead or anything. How'd it happen?"

So Vikström describes the accident. "A truck backed out of an alley. . . ." He keeps it short, not wanting it to inflate the event, but even the simplest description held its drama. "There wasn't much left to identify."

Lisowski keeps grimacing as if each word had a sharp point. "Bobby rented time here like the others. I got his wife's address someplace. They're split up." He searches through the papers on his desk. "He was just here this morning. You can die quick—I guess that's no surprise. I can't get my head around it. *Bam*, you're gone!"

"When was he here this morning?" asks Manny.

"He was waiting when I got here. Then he left around nine-thirty with another guy. Both were riding Fat Bobs. I think Bob was trying to sell him one."

"Fat Bob selling Fat Bobs. What's the other guy's name?"

"Marco Santuzza. He's also an accountant."

Vikström leans against a file cabinet. "They were friends?"

"They work on old bikes together. Or *worked* on bikes, make them look like new and sell them. So yeah, you could say they were friends with a business connection. Marco had a '54 Harley Model KHK they put back together and sold for a chunk of change. I don't know how much, at least fifty thousand. Beautiful bike. An art piece. But, you know, they all are if you spend the time."

"What's this Santuzza look like?"

"Mid-forties, heavy, and he's got a full beard he keeps trim. And earrings, he wears a coupla earrings. Gold ones."

"Give us his address as well if you have it," says Manny. "Okay?"

C louds moved in late that afternoon. Soon the bits of the dead biker would be washed from the surfaces of Bank Street. Detective Manny Streeter thought that was a good thing. He had come back again to seek out the clerks, store managers, office workers, even janitors employed in the buildings near the scene, which was still blocked off by yellow tape. Earlier he had talked to people out on the street; now he'd talk to the people in the buildings. This wasn't something that Streeter had decided to do on his own—Benny Vikström had decided it for him.

Manny still felt it had been an accident. No way had Pappalardo meant to run down the biker, identified as Fat Bob Rossi. To prove Vikström wrong, Manny intended to interview everyone he could find, and once he had his proof, he'd put it into his computer, print it out, and toss it on Vikström's desk. But Manny wouldn't shout, he'd only look disappointed. As for why he thought it was an accident, the main reason was that Vikström didn't. He liked it when Vikström was wrong.

Disappointment tending toward cynicism was a major emotion in Manny's life, at least out of the house, and one of his larger disappointments was Vikström. But it hadn't been always that way. When Manny had begun to work with Vikström ten months earlier, he'd been prepared to be friendly, or friendly for Manny—that is, less disappointed. He'd admired Vikström when watching him in the Detective Bureau and earlier as a patrolman. Vikström was stubborn and hardworking, and although he put too much value on hunches, at times the hunches paid off.

Then came the big disappointment. It wasn't that Manny stopped admiring Vikström, though the admiration had changed to grudging admiration, even bitter admiration. It wasn't that Vikström outranked him due to the length of time he'd spent as a detective. It wasn't that he went to a different church or ate sushi or voted Republican or was thin. No, it was more personal than that.

You see, Manny loves karaoke—not as much as his wife, Yvonne, does, but close; and the previous summer he'd gone so far as to build a karaoke box in the spare bedroom. After all, the kids had grown up and the bedroom was just wasted space. Some karaoke-loving friends helped him—they weren't cops—and in total it took a month to finish.

The karaoke box had a small stage with a karaoke system that included a lyric screen, a record option, and five thousand songs. It also had a stand-up mike, two handheld mikes, four Bose speakers, and Disco DJ stage lighting with strobes that made the rhinestones on the gold-stucco ceiling jump. Then, to create the right atmosphere, he'd added a fog maker and a bubble machine. There were four round tables and eight chairs as well as a bar and refrigerator. He even had a popcorn maker with flashing neon lights. The walls were padded, the windows covered. Yvonne was happy, as were Manny's friends, and mostly they liked the older singers: Perry Como, Rosemary Clooney, Patti Page, and occasionally a young guy like Tony Bennett.

Manny and Yvonne have a beagle named Schultzie, who's like a child to them, a replacement for the adult children who live out west. Whenever Manny gets up on the stage and sings Eddie Fisher's "Oh! My Pa-Pa," Schultzie howls his little heart out. This brings tears to Yvonne's eyes, which indicates the emotional intensity available in a karaoke box.

By the time the karaoke box was finished, Streeter and Vikström had been partners a few months. They worked okay together. If their wives had packed sandwiches, they'd often share them, each taking half a tuna fish and half a ham and cheese. They weren't friends, but Manny thought the karaoke box might bring them closer. So he invited Vikström to the opening.

He sprang it on Vikström one Monday night in fall in their unmarked car, a dark blue Impala 9C3, over by the high-rises. Vikström was driving.

"You busy next weekend? I got a treat."

"What's on your mind?" Vikström had an eye on the sidewalk, looking for drug deals.

"It's for you and the wife. You both gotta come."

Vikström glanced at Manny. "So? What is it?"

"You'll be impressed, I promise you. You'll love it."

"Okay, okay, so what is it?"

"A karaoke box."

"Say what?"

So Manny explained what it was: the lights, the music, the singing, the fog, the bubbles, the little refrigerator, and so on. Halfway through his description, Vikström drove the Impala over the curb, blowing out a front tire. A parking meter knocked off the driver's-side mirror.

Manny thought Vikström was suffering a sudden attack, which in a way was true, because Vikström was laughing deep, uncontrollable belly laughs, laughing so hard he had to wipe away his tears with his handkerchief as he hit the wheel with a fist. "Oh, that's good!" he kept saying. "Bubbles? That's really good!"

Manny rubbed his chin and looked out the window. "You don't like music?"

"No, no, I love music. You really get up on a little stage in your spare bedroom?" Again he laughed.

Manny wished he could put a bullet through Vikström's skull, and the fingers of his right hand toyed with the butt of his Glock. Instead he remained silent as they waited for the police tow truck to arrive and fix the front wheel. Vikström was silent as well, though every few minutes he'd chuckle. Then he'd say, "Sorry, sorry, I can't help it," then he'd chuckle some more.

The next day Manny asked the supervisor of the Detective Bureau, Detective Sergeant Masters, if he could be transferred. She said it was impossible, unless he wanted the Mountain Bike Patrol. Manny didn't think so.

"Whatever your problems with Vikström," Masters said, "get used to them."

But the laughter was like broken glass in his gut. No way could he get used to it. Anyway, he stopped complaining. "I've internalized the problem," he told Yvonne.

When disappointment becomes central to your life, it's like a religion. It takes up all your spiritual space. Are you Baptist? Are you Methodist? No, I'm Disappointed. That's how it happened with Manny.

So the disappointment provoked by Vikström left its mark, just as other disappointments had left their mark. It was a disappointment he'd lost his hair. It was a disappointment he was forty-five instead of twenty, a disappointment he was overweight, a disappointment he hadn't made detective sergeant, a disappointment that his kids had moved to California— the two sons to L.A., a daughter to Bakersfield—a disappointment that his cat, Flutie, had run away. It made a long list; and if Manny was sitting in the car—on a stakeout, for instance—he'd tot them up once again and find more. And looking in the mirror, he saw that each disappointment had carved a new wrinkle on his face until the wrinkles formed a portrait of his disappointment, which in itself was disappointing. So this was how it was with Manny: the sun-drenched, rolling hills of karaoke on one side, an alp of disappointments on the other.

"He walks like he's got a tombstone on his back," Vikström told another detective.

Late in the afternoon, Manny talks to twenty people in stores and offices near the alley that opens onto Bank Street, and as he makes his way from one to the next, he has a quiet talk with himself in the area of lexical semantics. Is it disappointment that obsesses him or is it grievance? Both identify loss, but grievance also suggests resentment, holding someone accountable. So perhaps his disappointments are in fact grievances. On the other hand, he might have disappointments and grievances at the same time. He's disappointed with Vikström, but he also has grievances against him. Manny's burdens seem to double. He staggers, and an elderly woman across the street shakes her head over evidence of intemperance in an otherwise respectable-looking gentleman.

When Manny thinks he's almost done talking to people, he calls Vikström to see what he wants next.

"Have you checked all the upper-floor offices?"

"I'm working on it," says Manny untruthfully.

"I think it's a good idea. Don't you?"

Over the next half hour, Manny talks to four people who occupied upper-floor offices. They'd all heard the crash and hurried to their windows, but by the time they looked, the accident was over, while its very drama made them incapable of examining the details of its display—that is, they were at a loss for words.

That changes when Manny talks to a middle-aged woman who works above the music store. She's a smoker in an office where smoking isn't allowed and where her boss, a data supervisor, has told her more than once that if she must smoke, she has to do it out on the street. But perhaps it's raining or she doesn't care to hunker in a doorway as if selling illegal substances. At those times she rolls her chair to the window, sticks out her head, and unless the wind blows directly in her face, lights up for a few puffs. Across the street is a three-story, flat-roofed building of gray granite blocks. To the right of the building is an alley, and within the alley that Monday morning she'd seen a large green truck with its motor idling.

The woman—her name doesn't matter—describes this to Manny at some length, but then she reaches the important part.

"All at once the truck backed up, and it didn't do it slowly. It rushed back, and I knew the driver wasn't looking both ways. It made a roar, and suddenly there was the motorcycle. I pushed my chair back from the window, but I heard the crash. It was terrible. I still hear it."

Manny takes her through her story several times, but the important part stays the same. The truck had "rushed" back into the street, and the driver hadn't looked to see if any traffic was approaching.

"You see any brake lights on the truck?"

"Not that I remember."

"What happened to your cigarette?"

"I dropped it, I was so frightened. I just hope it didn't hit anyone."

Looking from the window, Manny envisions the scene. The worst part is that it suggests Vikström was correct: the truck driver, Leon Pappalardo, had backed up in order to put the truck in the path of the motorcycle. Manny's sorry about this. It's ugly when Vikström turns out to be correct. But how did Pappalardo know when to back up?

Manny thanks the woman, leaves the building, crosses the street, and finds the stairs to the second floor. A minute later he's talking to J. Arthur Madison, LL.M.

"The exhaust was pouring into my office—pure carbon monoxide, as you can imagine. I'm still queasy from it. It went on for about five minutes, and when it became unbearable I went to close the window—such a pity on a beautiful day. Then I saw a man across the street in front of the window of the music store."

"And what'd he do?" Manny believes he already knows what the man did.

"That's just the thing, I didn't wonder about it at the time, because the truck made this roar and a frightful cloud of exhaust poured in through my window. Later I put one and one together, and now you're here as well. The man's hands were behind his back. Then he took one out, the right one, and made a small flipping gesture." J. Arthur Madison makes a flipping gesture with his right hand, like a shy child waving his daddy good-bye. "That's when the truck began to roar, so I didn't hear the motorcycle at first. The man stepped back into the alcove of the music store. Then I saw the motorcycle. The biker tried to stop, but . . . well, he couldn't. . . ."

"Can you say what the guy looked like?"

"He wasn't a tall guy, that's for sure, and he had thick, black hair, like Elvis."

And Detective Manny Streeter thinks, *Damn Vikström anyway.*

FIVE

So what's this business Connor Raposo has gotten into? Is it legal? "It's been a family business for four generations," says Didi with the self-deprecating laugh of someone hiding pride's shining light under humility's handkerchief. During a business lunch at the Asti Ristorante on Fifth Avenue in San Diego in November, Didi told his nephew that the name of the business was Bounty, Inc. This was over their shared antipasto: gamberi e capesante al limone. Then, over the fish, salmone marechiaro, Didi said the name was Step Up, Inc. And twice over grappa and espresso he called it A Shot in the Arm, Inc. Perhaps it was all three; perhaps it was all three and more; perhaps it was something else entirely.

Bounty, Inc., by any name, raised money for charities—Didi couldn't say how many. When it began in the early 1930s, it consisted of Didi's grandfather Vado, a great-uncle, and several other relatives going door-to-door to solicit funds for organizations such as the Holy Sisters of the Blessed Little Feet, the Dust Bowl Relief Fund and New Homes for Old Horses. Vado, short for Osvaldo, would pick a town—like Topeka—pick a neighborhood—say, around Southwest Twelfth and Southwest Fillmore—and then he and his associates would solicit door-to-door for two days and get the hell out. The next day they would show up in Omaha or Kansas City or Tulsa.

But it was easier then. First of all they only dealt in small amounts of cash. Next their charm and the apparent need of their cause to elicit sympathy for groups like One-Legged Veterans of the Great War was enough to establish their credibility. Vado would say that deception was to him what singing was to Caruso, and if he couldn't bring five people to tears on any day of the week, the day was wasted. No mail solicitations, no phones or computers: it was all face-to-face. And there weren't the legal constraints and licensing complications that exist today, so many mission statements, papers of incorporation, and boards of directors. A few snapshots of one-legged veterans or the decrepit motherhouse of the Holy Sisters of the Blessed Little Feet were enough. As for the groups for which they collected, or groups with vaguely similar names, they always received a money order for fifteen percent of the funds raised. So the Little Sisters and the rest were grateful, even if the amount was only ten dollars.

For a few years after Vado retired, Bounty, Inc. was inactive. Then his oldest son, Robert, called Betinho, came up with a new plan, and off they went again—half a dozen family members blowing into a midsize city to squeeze a bit of money from the softhearted. They might be villains, but they were public-spirited villains. One or two went to jail, one or two others had warrants served. They never grew rich; it was a modest living, a job like any other. As Betinho said, the game meant as much as the money. And the charities—Childhood Victims of Hoof-and-Mouth Disease, Organ Grinder Monkey Retirement Ranch—received their pittance.

We doubt if Didi hoped to make big money. The notion of putting Bounty, Inc. on the road began when he met the young man he called Vaughn Monroe, allegedly a distant cousin, in a halfway house in Imperial Beach, south of San Diego and across the fence from Tijuana. Didi never revealed his real name, and Vaughn claimed to have forgotten it. What made Vaughn valuable was that Didi's target group was the silver generation, folks between the ages of fifty and ninety; so Vaughn was Vaughn, and Didi was happy.

Still, it's unlikely that Didi would have revived Bounty, Inc. if imitating the voice of Vaughn Monroe were Vaughn's only skill. At most he might have managed a small career for Vaughn in karaoke bars. What energized Didi's ambitions was Vaughn's skill as a computer hacker. It meant getting two skills for the price of one. But when Connor met Vaughn, he had his doubts. Was he reliable? He seemed, as Connor said, *weird*. Didi gave a self-confident chuckle. "Everyone's got a little weirdness in them someplace," he said. And then, more seriously, "Remember, he doesn't have any parents. We're all he's got."

"Is he a minor?" Connor had asked.

"Not technically, nor legally either for that matter. He's just weird."

This was the start of Didi's master plan. After that he signed up the young woman he called Eartha Kitt, who had formerly been Shaw-nell or Beatriz. She, too, was a distant relative, a Brazilian, and her surname was Barbosa. Didi claimed it gave her a tugo connection, though she hadn't known it till then.

Lastly came Connor, who was working as a slot attendant at the Viejas Casino, thirty-five miles east of San Diego, and was sick of the drive, sick of the noise, sick of the gloomy faces. Before coming to San Diego, he'd been a slot attendant at the MGM Grand in Detroit, which was tolerable because his brother Vasco often passed through and seemed to work for MGM Grand. "Seemed" is an essential word when describing Vasco. This was after Connor had taught high school English for two years at Iron Mountain in the Upper Peninsula, until the school system downsized, meaning he was fired. Despite a master's degree and glowing recommendations, he hadn't found another job. Schools solved teacher shortages by increasing class sizes. Then, when Vasco called about a casino job in Detroit, Connor gave up on education. His ninth-graders brought in cake and ice cream for a going-away party. So long, kids.

A problem with Bounty, Inc. was that men who came after Vado and Betinho often grew impatient, even greedy. Then the line between legal and illegal wasn't so much crossed as crushed. Could this happen to Didi? Connor worried that Didi's ambitions might land them all in jail. But Connor's life was stagnating; he needed a change. Gradually his worries diminished, and then they stopped, or almost. So he told Didi he'd give it a try.

Didi's first task was to raise the cash for the Winnebago and "put the show on the road," which meant doing fund-raising in San Diego. Here Vaughn's computer skills were essential. He hacked the websites of San Diego veterinarians, and soon he had a list of older folks who owned beagles, as well as a list of the dogs' names. Although unlawful, it was for a good cause, Didi said, and sacrifices must be made. As for other legality issues, Didi said that the papers of incorporation were "pending." He waved a sheet of paper at Connor, declaring it was a mission statement. And the board of directors? Didi made Connor a member; Vaughn was one already. Armed with claims like "We'll get the legal shit settled in no time," Didi had his group make calls for Free Beagles from Nicotine Addiction, Inc., meaning beagles used in medical research rather than beagles hanging out on street corners.

"Is your puppy at risk of becoming a smoker?" Vaughn would melodiously rumble into the phone. "A crooked lab could snatch him right off the street."

"Cigarette addiction for your Suzy would be an awful thing," Eartha might whisper. "You can't protect the good beagles if you don't protect the bad."

This was Didi's strategy: scare them, then soothe them. If a man or woman contributed, Didi sent a certificate stating that so-and-so was a member in good standing of Free Beagles from Nicotine Addiction, Inc. "Just your small contribution," he'd say in a phone call, "has saved another pup." The donor would receive a form, and then cash (preferred) or a check made out to FBNA, Inc. would be sent to one of several post office boxes.

As for the voices, they gave Vaughn Monroe and Eartha Kitt the credibility of familiarity. Often a customer would ask, "Don't I know you from someplace?" Their hesitations and stutterings indicated awe. "I thought you died in 1973."

Vaughn might answer, "Only technically."

The fund-raising went well until complaints against FBNA, Inc. began to build up and the police department's Financial Crimes Unit took an interest. But by then the used Winnebago had been purchased and Didi said it was time to "fly away to the highway." Had fifteen percent of the earnings been sent to the Humane Society? Didi said that it had. "Would I cheat a pooch?"

But Connor worried. "Give me a better reason I should I go with you."

"The cops will see you as an accomplice. But as a first-time offender, you'll get a suspended sentence or probation, meaning no jail time."

"Are you serious?"

"It's best to expect the worst."

The danger, as Connor saw it, was that Didi's ego let him confuse the possible with the certain. If he thought a thing was true, it must be true. If he wanted a thing, he must deserve it. Take his hairstyle—silver and parted in the middle with a brushed-back wing on either side. Didn't they remind Connor of the wings on the helmet of the god Hermes, Didi had asked. "No," Connor told Didi. "They don't."

"Hermes," Didi said, "god of travelers, god of wit, god of deception, god of thieves and gamblers, god of poets. He's the trickster. You see how fitting it is?"

"I don't think a judge will buy it," Connor said.

But Didi held these beliefs lightly, as he held everything lightly. Why put your cards on the table if you didn't have to? He saw life as book-ended by the tragic and the ridiculous, which weren't necessarily independent: the tragic occurring on Monday and the ridiculous on Tuesday. If his philosophy had a flag, its symbol would be a banana peel on a sidewalk, and its focus was the man giving amusement to people on the street by stepping on the peel and flying into the air, only to spend the rest of his life in a wheelchair. The "tradiculous," Didi called it. "Think of the Supreme Being as the one who drops a flowerpot onto your head from a celestial window." The universe, he argued, is governed by whimsy.

Connor said that Didi wasn't "dependable" or "trustworthy," but they weren't the right words. They were only symptoms of a larger issue.

"You don't take life seriously."

"What's to take? People pretend to take it seriously because they're terrified. They say there's no such thing as a coincidence, or what goes around comes around. That's like chewing gristle. It's hard work. The flowerpot falls on your head because the maid bumped it, not because you deserve punishment. Get real."

But what's real? Didi was sure he traveled along a straight line, but we know how it is. The straight line develops a kink. Didi thinks he has the future figured out, but he knows nothing about Fat Bob, Marco Santuzza, and Leon Pappalardo, nothing about Sal Nicoletti and his sexy wife, nothing about Manny Streeter and Benny Vikström. Call them flowerpots waiting to happen.

As for Connor, despite his doubts, his mind was changed when Didi said they were heading to New England, because right now Connor's brother Vasco—the previous owner of the black Bruno Magli slip-ons—is in southeastern Connecticut for a few weeks doing some work at a casino, although Vasco hasn't said what.

At times Vasco appears to be a general consultant; at other times he's a security consultant or a slot adviser. The job remains vague. But spending time in New England will give Connor a chance to see him. In fact, this Monday evening Connor is supposed to have dinner with Vasco at Paragon, the most exclusive of the Foxwoods restaurants.

Detective Benny Vikström's wife, Maud, at times makes Vikström a casserole for dinner that he especially likes: salmon, sweet potatoes, shredded carrots, egg yolks, and yellow raisins. They have it tonight, and Vikström thinks of it as their "orange dinner" apart from the raisins, which are almost orange. With the dinner comes a nice green salad with orange sweet peppers and butterscotch pudding for dessert, maybe with whipped cream, possibly turned orange with food coloring.

So it is with a degree of irritation that, as Vikström is tucking his napkin into his shirt collar, there comes a familiar *tap, tap-tap, tap, tap,* which signifies that his partner, Manny Streeter, is waiting on the porch.

Vikström understands that Manny could have arrived a half hour earlier or a half hour later and it wouldn't have mattered, but Manny knows that his partner eats dinner at seven o'clock on the dot, and he has timed his arrival for its nuisance value. It's a way for Manny to share his existential disappointment.

"Not again," says Maud.

Vikström goes to the door. The weather is turning cold, and Manny wears a charcoal gray overcoat and a blue watch cap to protect his shaved head.

"I got news for you," he says.

Vikström lets Manny enter and waits. Manny hangs up his coat on a peg by the door but keeps on his blue watch cap. As he walks through the living room, he says, "They still haven't found the head. It's absolutely vanished. They brought in a dog, but even the dog can't find it." Reaching the dining room, he pauses and nods to Vikström's wife. "Good evening, Mrs. Vikström. Sorry to interrupt your dinner."

"May I get you a plate?" This is nice of Maud Vikström, because what she really wants to ask is, *What head?*

Manny stares at the "orange dinner" longer than is polite. "I don't think so, not tonight. Looks good, though." Manny glances around the dining room as if he has forgotten the reason for his visit.

"So what's going on?" asks Vikström. "Or is this a social visit?" He stands by his chair, uncertain whether to sit down. He hopes that whatever is "going on" won't mean leaving his dinner to be heated up later in the microwave. Maud Vikström stares at Manny's large, silver belt buckle showing the dying, spear-carrying Indian on the dying horse. She always stares at it. Maybe she doesn't know it represents a work of art; maybe she thinks it indicates a kind of fetish.

Manny assumes a *Would you ever believe it?* expression, lifting his eyebrows and pursing his lips. "It looks like it wasn't an accident after all—I mean the truck and Fat Bob business. It looks like it was done on purpose." Manny's been holding this back so that he can drop it on Vikström at dinnertime like a sharp object. He describes his talk with the woman over the music store who told him how the truck rushed backward to the street, and he describes his talk with J. Arthur Madison. "The guy said he saw a man signaling to the truck driver—what's his name, Poppaloppa."

"Pappalardo."

"Whatever. He was making hand movements and Poppaloppa hit the gas. They had it all arranged. The guy doing the signaling looked like a short Elvis, or at least that's what the witness told me."

"A short Elvis?"

"You know, the hair. That's what J. Arthur Madison said. He's a lawyer. Do you remember seeing anyone like that? I vaguely remember something."

"Maybe. He may have been talking to a young guy with a tan, like he was the only person on the street with a tan. They drove off in his car, a little blue thing."

"So they're in it together," says Manny.

"And maybe they've got nothing to do with it. Maybe you're rushing things. Can I get back to my dinner now?"

Manny shuffles his feet and gives Mrs. Vikström an apologetic look. "We need to talk to Fat Bob's widow, and we need a picture."

Vikström has sat down and was just lifting his fork, which is now suspended in midair. "You kiddin' me? That was supposed to have been done this afternoon."

He gets up again. He knows that Manny has put off this final bit of information for the moment when Vikström felt he could again sit down.

"Phelps and Joanie were supposed to do it, but they got called off to a drug bust. You'd better get your coat. Temperature's dropping."

Vikström makes a point of never swearing in front of his wife. As a result he's tongue-tied.

Manny looks sympathetic. If we have crocodile tears, we should also have "crocodile sympathy"—a wincing, squinched expression suggesting emotional pain. "Sorry to mess up your dinner," says Manny. "Maybe we can grab a burger. G'night, Mrs. Vikström."

Manny pushes open the storm door as Vikström grabs his coat; then Vikström has to catch the door as it swings back and nearly hits him. He hurries out to Manny's Subaru Forester parked at the curb. Manny prefers the Subaru to the Detective Bureau's dark blue, unmarked Impala, saying that the Forester's 2.0XT Touring model "has got big teeth," meaning it does a good job of gripping the road. This is pure vanity on

Manny's part, but at least he's had the Subaru equipped with a police radio at his own cost.

As Vikström gets in, the Subaru starts to move.

"Hey!" he calls.

"Sorry, sorry."

But Vikström knows he isn't sorry; it's just that tonight's steady flow of passive-aggressive behavior seems less passive than at other times. He also knows it goes back to that damn karaoke box. What can Vikström do at this late stage? There's no point in saying sorry, no point in asking to be invited to the next musical evening; he can't even shout, "Sing to me, sing to me!" It's too late for that.

Sometimes two weeks will go by when Manny's passive-aggressiveness slips back to dormant aggressiveness. Then it begins again. Vikström doesn't know why. *Was it something I said?* he wonders. So Vikström remains on alert, which is tiring. Two months back, around New Year's, Vikström had been hearty and chummy and willing to let bygones be bygones, but Manny had seen through it. There'd been a mocking grin, a sarcastic snippet. "Who says you get off so easy?" Manny had asked.

Now Vikström contents himself with brief displays of long-suffering patience. He sighs a lot.

SIX

I t's nearly eight, and Vasco had promised to meet him at seven, but Connor expected that—when had his brother ever been on time? Connor sits on a stool at the Scorpion Bar at Foxwoods, nursing a Corona and bypassing the many kinds of tequila and tequila drinks as he surveys the assortment of glitter with a south-of-the-border motif. The skulls on display at the entrance must belong to former customers. More skulls dot the walls around the room, as well as gaudy silver crosses. Behind the bar in a large glass box, a six-foot rattlesnake slithers back and forth. The music is loud, and Connor's been told the go-go girls get busy at ten o'clock. The bar is one of those places meant to be an event by itself: the people sit quietly, while the bar, with its decor, flashing lights, and constant music, enacts the party. It saves people from the need to talk. About ten other men and women also sit at the bar; three jokers at a table share a forty-ounce turquoise tequila drink.

When Connor called Vasco ten minutes earlier to see where he was, he got his voice mail. Connor asks himself how often this has happened in their life together. More than he can count. Slot machines chuckle in the distance; the casino has fifty-five hundred, over fifteen hundred more than Detroit's MGM Grand. For several years the sound excited him; now it's the sound of disappointment.

As Connor waits, he thinks about his morning: the accident's havoc and spectacle, but also Sal Nicoletti and his wife, especially the wife, with her long legs and then her black eyes, but they couldn't really be black, maybe a dark brown. He thinks about her mouth and full lips, the curve of her figure. Recalling her, it's as if Connor's memory rests in a soft place. Then Vasco arrives.

"Hey, Zeco, it's great to see you. You mind if we eat here instead of the Paragon? I got an appointment coming up."

Connor gives his brother a hug, feeling the love and exasperation he often feels with Vasco, who is the only person who calls him Zeco, the name he changed when he left high school. "You mean burritos instead of wild boar tenderloin?"

"You're a sneaky guy, you've been peeking at the menu. Anyway, they got more than burritos. Me, I like the salads. You wearing the shoes? Let's see." Vasco steps back to look down at the Bruno Maglis. "Shit, Zeco, they make you look like a million bucks. Let's grab a table in the back. I like to keep it private."

"You look pretty great yourself." Connor follows Vasco to a table.

Vasco wears a pin-striped suit with a vest, gray on gray, and black crocodile handmade Italian lace-up shoes that make the Bruno Maglis seem shabby. His black silk tie on his black silk shirt is no more than a shadowy flutter; his watch is a Rolex Day-Date with little diamonds instead of numbers. Vasco once told Connor that he had the left sleeves of his suit coats cut a little shorter than the right in order to show off his pricey watches. Connor had thought he was joking.

Otherwise Vasco is thirty-two, about six feet, thin, and dark with black hair—a display of Portuguese Moorish blood. His face is narrow and long like an El Greco saint. When he smiles, his perfect teeth seem too white and his eyes don't change. But he doesn't smile often. He saves his smiles for when they count.

Vasco shrugs. "You got to play the role. After all, it's theater. The Rolex is a rental. How's Bounty, Inc.? Still a bunch of clowns?"

A cute waitress arrives with menus. "You know what you want, Mr. Raposo?"

"Just a salad or something. I'm not that hungry." He glances at the menu.

Connor is impressed the waitress knows Vasco's name and that she calls him "Mr." But this is what Connor always does: he lets Vasco impress him. If Vasco works at the casino, there's no reason the waitress wouldn't know his name.

When she leaves, they talk about Bounty, Inc. Connor makes it sound more businesslike than it is. He doesn't mention the Eartha Kitt and Vaughn Monroe routines.

"You would've made more money if you'd stayed in Detroit or at Viejas," says Vasco. "You would've been promoted. I was seeing to that."

"Thanks, but I got tired of the casino life."

"Too much ring-a-ding and too many losers. That's what I like about it."

"Right at the end, there was a guy who sat at his slot for forty-eight hours. He never left. When he had to shit or piss, he did it in his pants. That's when I decided I'd had enough. They had to drag him away."

"Yeah, we've had those. The stink upsets the other players, but you get used to it."

"Seriously?"

"When am I ever not serious?"

As they talk, Vasco keeps glancing around the room, speaking to Connor but looking elsewhere. Connor knows he does this with everyone, but it makes him feel temporary, as if he were only occupying Vasco's time while he waits for someone more important. He also knows this is how Vasco wants him to feel.

"I saw an incredible accident this morning when I was picking up the shoes. A biker smashed into a dump truck in downtown New London. He was ripped in half, and his head's still missing."

Vasco glances back at his brother. He has slow, dark eyes that make him look as if he were always watching combinations of numbers drift across an interior screen. "I saw something about it on the six-o'clock news. These bikers don't get it. You go fast and don't have a helmet, you get killed. It's as simple as that."

"Pieces of this guy were thrown all over the place. I got stuck there. The street was closed for hours."

Connor continues his story, speaking rapidly to keep Vasco's attention, but in his hurry his words turn the story into a dull outline stripped of the elements that Connor can't forget. Vasco looks away again. For him the biker story is over.

"The guy's name was Marco Santuzza. I knew a kid named Santuzza in high school. You remember that name? And I saw a guy I knew from Detroit, maybe the MGM Grand. I was going to ask you about him. He said his name was Sal Nicoletti, though it meant nothing to me. He's got thick, black hair swept back over his head. A short guy, with a finger-busting handshake: does that sound familiar?"

As Connor talks, his brother's attention becomes more focused.

"This is in New London?"

"Yeah, right downtown. You remember Nicoletti? I'm almost certain that's not his real name." Connor feels uneasy. Maybe he shouldn't have mentioned Nicoletti. He decides not to mention Nicoletti's office on Bank Street or that he lives nearby. "He lives outside of New London someplace, not in town."

As Vasco stares at his brother, he again seems to be counting up numbers. Connor's afraid his face will show that he's lying. All the years they spent growing up, he could never lie successfully to Vasco. And what does he know about his brother's work? He'd only mentioned Nicoletti to get Vasco's attention. He wishes he'd kept his mouth shut.

"Don't know him," says Vasco. "But yeah, I remember the name Santuzza from high school, a girl. She must've been your friend's older sister. Cute."

Connor watches Vasco survey the room. He's afraid of getting Nicoletti in trouble, but he can't keep his mouth shut. "Maybe Nicoletti had problems in Detroit. Maybe that's why he's here."

"Like I say, it rings no bells. You probably saw him in San Diego."

They fiddle with their drinks: Connor nurses his beer, Vasco pokes at the lemon in his Coke with a swizzle stick. If Vasco knows anything about Nicoletti, he won't share it. They wait for their food.

"You think those skulls are real?" asks Connor, not knowing what else to say.

Vasco didn't so much look at him as give him a look, a long one. "Plastic, Connor, they're plastic. And the antlers are plastic, the long horns are plastic, the marble tabletops are plastic, the silver crosses are plastic, the drinks are watered, the serapes are made in China, and the big-titted go-go girls have implants. Fuck, Connor, smarten up. Nothing's real in here, not even the people."

"What about the rattlesnake?"

Vasco laughs one of his metallic laughs. "It's a drone."

"How so?" Connor tries to conceal his surprise.

"Its movements are controlled by an iPad behind the bar. They used to let it out on the floor on crowded nights, but it caused serious panic. So now it slithers back and forth in its box. It's plastic, too, as well as titanium and other shit."

"You joking?" Connor tries to see the snake from where they sit, but people are in the way.

"You're doubting me again? Why should I lie to my little brother?" Vasco glances toward the bar, adjusts his black tie, and then turns back. "You know how long you'll be here? Where're you staying?"

"Maybe two weeks or less. Didi says it depends on the 'pickings.'"

"He's a sleazebag. You know that? You can't trust him."

"I like him. He's odd and sarcastic. I thought you didn't know him. Anyway, he's your uncle or something like that. He's family."

The cute waitress shows up with their food. Vasco gets a Mexican Caesar salad with shrimp. Connor has the buffalo burger.

"When I knew him, his name wasn't Didi," says Vasco. "It was Leonor, and people called him Nonô. That's some years ago. Maybe he isn't any kind of relative—maybe he isn't even a tugo. But he's been around for a while. He's a con man. He's lucky not to be in jail. Fuck, I ought to report him."

"Don't do that, I need the money."

"You could work here."

"I'm done with casinos."

Vasco pushes away his barely touched salad and gets up. "I'm late. Call me if you want to have dinner again. We'll go to a real place next time."

Connor hesitates and then asks, "You going to say anything about Nicoletti?"

"Give me a break. Why should I talk about someone I don't know?"

As Vasco turns, a big man in a dark suit approaches. "Hey, Vasco, where you been? I thought you weren't going to show up."

Vasco again offers his metallic laugh. "Not me, Chucky, I was just leaving. I want you to meet my little brother, Zeco. He worked in Detroit for a while."

Connor gets to his feet. "It's Connor. Not Zeco, Connor."

Chucky grabs his hand with a hand the size of a catcher's mitt. The sausage fingers show off a few classy rings. Connor expects a strong handshake, but the hand is soft, sticky, and hot. It's like putting his hand inside a warm pudding.

"Shit, Vasco, I didn't know you had a kid brother." Chucky's over six feet and bloated rather than fat. His small teeth seem made for nibbling rather than biting. He wears several gold chains and looks like a former bouncer who saved his pennies and bought the bar where he once worked. His grin is a salesman's grin—half affable and half hungry, but his small, dark eyes give no sign of humor.

"He just showed up from San Diego."

"That's great. Give him some vouchers. You should've said you'd be late."

"Zeco saw that accident in downtown New London this morning. He says the dead guy's somebody called Santuzza, not Robert Rossi."

Chucky turns his small eyes toward Connor without turning his head. After a moment he says, "Nah, the bike belonged to Rossi. The cops say the dead guy's Rossi. Zeco's wrong, that's all."

Connor wants to describe finding the dead man's biker cap with the name Marco Santuzza written inside. Instead he asks, "Who's this Rossi?"

"A gambler," says Vasco. "A bad one."

Chucky again shakes Connor's hand, and again it disappears into the warm pudding. "We got people waiting. You know how it is. Come back tomorrow and we'll get acquainted, have a few drinks."

Vasco shakes his brother's hand. "Duty calls."

Vasco and Chucky head for the exit.

Connor strokes the hairless area of his upper lip. He decides that Chucky is his brother's boss. This shouldn't be strange, but Vasco hasn't mentioned working for anyone. And he was deferential to Chucky. More significantly, he was cautious. Connor realizes he's been left with the check.

A fireman sprinkles a smoking Fat Bob with a booster line from the pumper while two other firemen stand on the sidewalk playing rock-paper-scissors as they wait for the first fireman to finish. There's a smell of burned rubber. The time is seven-fifteen, and it's dark, but the scene is lit by the lights from the fire truck and from four New London police cars drawn up at different angles in front of a medium-size house with a bay window. A dozen onlookers stand outside a ring of police tape talking with one another. Not much has happened, despite earlier excitement, and they get ready to go home. A light rain is falling; soon it will snow.

"Looks like we're late for whatever's going on," says Manny as he pulls his Subaru Forester up to the curb by the red pumper.

"Maybe someone's told Mrs. Rossi her husband's dead," says Vikström, getting out of the car.

"Yeah, and she got so pissed she ran out here and blew up his motorcycle."

Vikström stops ten feet from the bike. "Are those bullet holes in the fender?"

Manny can't tell, so he only grunts.

The detectives pick up their pace and join the fireman holding the booster line, who has just shut off the water. Manny asks what's going on.

"Someone took some shots at the Harley," says the fireman, "put a few holes in the gas tank. It blew up. Detectives are inside."

"You've any idea who?" asks Vikström.

"You'll have to ask your buddies about that."

As they continue to the house, Manny says, "They're sure to have told Fat Bob's wife that her husband's dead."

"Let's hope so," says Vikström.

Three cops are on the walk, and there's a fourth at the door. Vikström nods to them. These are men he's known for years.

Inside, they hear a woman shouting, "They want to kill him, they can kill him! I'm sick to death of him!"

Manny and Vikström pause at the edge of the living room. Who's she talking about? The voice comes from the kitchen, and they make their way toward it.

Angelina Rossi sits at a kitchen table. Standing across from her are two New London detectives, Herta Spiegel and Moss Jackson. They give Vikström and Manny stoical looks. Herta is about forty and stocky. Moss is the squad's one African-American. He'd been a light-heavyweight boxer at UConn ten years earlier, but now he's mostly known for being gloomy.

Fat Bob's ex-wife eyes Herta and Moss Jackson as a Sunday school teacher might eye a group of snot-flicking ten-year-olds. She wears a blue blouse and jeans. Vikström thinks she is beautiful in a dark, southern Italian way, thin, with dark hair on her bare arms. She is perhaps forty-five and has very white teeth. Manny feels she has too many teeth. He finds them too aggressive, or what he likes to call proactive. And he can't get past her mustache. It scares him. Women like that throw things.

Vikström moves forward. "Excuse me, who're you talking about?"

Herta looks at Vikström as if he's slow in the head. "Her ex showed up to get something."

"Fat Bob's alive?" Vikström regrets the question as soon as he asks. The woman at the table and the two detectives give him *What a dummy* looks, while Manny moves back a few steps to separate himself from his partner. He stares at his fingernails to show that his thoughts are elsewhere.

"I thought he was killed downtown. He crashed his bike into a truck."

The *What a dummy* looks intensify. "It wasn't Robert Rossi on the bike," says Herta. "But the bike belonged to him all right."

"Rossi busted in here thirty minutes ago," says Moss Jackson. He speaks so slowly that he could turn a vivid description of the Crucifixion into a series of yawns. "He's not supposed to come within thirty feet of the house, so his ex called the cops. Before they got here, some guys in a green Ford shot up the Harley. Rossi ran out the back door. The Ford took off when they heard us coming. Neighbors heard more gunshots, but we haven't found any bodies."

Angelina Rossi gives Vikström a cool look. "Bob's got money hidden in the house. That's what he's after. Technically it's mine, for all the shit I been through. He owes me. If he's dead, I inherit. I'll go straight to Vegas."

Vikström finds Angelina's remarks too complicated for an intelligent answer. He turns to Moss Jackson. "So who was killed downtown?"

"Don't know," says Jackson.

"Do you have any idea?" Vikström asks Angelina.

She cocks her head at him. "Some asshole."

"Anyone go after the Ford?" asks Manny.

Herta and Moss look at each other and shrug. "Not really," says Herta. "It was gone when the patrol car got here, and it took the officers a few minutes to hear about it because of the fire. Then they called it in."

Manny laughs. "Now they'll pull over every green Ford in the county."

"Where do you think your husband's gone?" asks Vikström.

"To hell, I hope." The tendons in the woman's neck form a distinctive V, vanishing into the darkness of her blouse. Her hands are long and thin, and the nails are painted bright red with little white designs: maybe *A*'s for Angelina.

"That's not a constructive answer," says Manny.

Angelina stares at him until he looks away. Manny thinks that women like her put curses on perfectly respectable people, like police detectives. He thinks that underneath her blouse and jeans she's covered with black fur, or just thick black hair. The image scares him.

"Do you have a picture we can borrow?" asks Vikström politely.

"I burned every picture the day the divorce went through," says Angelina, pushing back her dark hair. "Burned his postcards and birthday cards. A whole lot of stuff: shirts, magazines. Did it in the backyard."

"What about a list of his friends?" asks Vikström.

"He has no friends."

"Oh, come on," says Manny, "everyone has friends."

Again she stares at him until he looks away.

"What about close acquaintances, business associates?" asks Vikström.

Angelina turns in her chair, giving them her back.

Herta takes her notepad, rips out a clean sheet of paper, and puts it on the table in front of Angelina along with a yellow No. 2 pencil, almost new. "You don't want to answer these questions downtown. Start writing some names."

Angelina picks up the pencil, snaps it in half, and tosses the pieces to the floor. Then she begins tearing the sheet of paper into thin strips. The detectives think it will take a straitjacket and a lot of rope to get her out of the room.

"Can't you see we're trying to help you?" There's a whine in Vikström's voice.

Angelina doesn't turn. The detectives wear their professional faces—serious, menacing, and impatient—but they're thinking about if the dog has been walked and if there's time to watch any TV tonight.

Manny's cell phone rings, a rising and descending trill. Putting it to his ear, he says, "Uh-hunh, Uh-hunh, Un-hunh, Oh-oh," and cuts the connection. He waves at Vikström. "We gotta tear ourselves away."

"We done here?" Vikström feels like a dog freed from the pound. He nods to Herta. "Take Angelina downtown. Use a straitjacket if you have to."

He and Manny hurry toward the front door, ignoring the shouts that come from the kitchen. Out on the porch, Vikström asks, "What's going on?"

Manny runs down the steps. "They found the head, but they're not sure who it belongs to. I mean, they know it belongs to the dead guy, but they're not sure of the dead guy's name."

It comes as no surprise that many men and women are filled with phobias. This one's sure he's about to be sucked up into the sky; that one must snap his fingers three times whenever he sees a white dog. Indeed, we're fortunate to have only two or three, since they can be a physical handicap like any other—like the man who has to hop fifteen times to get to the bus stop.

One of Benny Vikström's greatest embarrassments is his fear of heights. He's seen shrinks, he's taken antianxiety pills, he's been hypnotized. Nothing works. All he needs is to climb onto a three-step stepladder and his body becomes someone else's. His knees shake, his belly flips over, his hands tremble, black spots flutter before his eyes. He might even get teary.

It's remarkable that he's kept this phobia hidden during his years as a cop, but his deception has taken hundreds of little lies. For instance, if an assignment requires him to drive across the I-95 bridge over the Thames River between New London and Groton, he'll get someone else to drive while he sits hunched in the passenger seat with his eyes shut, whispering, in a musical way, "La-la-la-la-la."

"What're you singing?" Manny Streeter might ask.

"An old Beach Boys song from high school. I can't get it out of my head."

"Too modern. The old tunes are the best tunes, as far as I'm concerned. How come you hum it every time we drive over the bridge?"

"I guess the water sets me off. Do you know 'Surfin' Safari'?"

"No," Manny might say, "I really don't."

Manny is perhaps the only cop who knows Vikström is terrified of heights, but he keeps it to himself so not even Vikström knows he knows. This seeming ignorance offers Manny a wide range of subtle chastisements to increase the frustrations in Vikström's life, which in turn decreases Manny's level of general disappointment. Seeing Vikström terrified cheers him up.

The issue of Vikström's phobia once more declares itself when they reach Bank Street, where the head has been found. A hook and ladder from the fire marshal's headquarters up the street is parked in front of a three-story building. On the first floor is a used-clothing store called Never Say Die. A ladder extends from the fire apparatus to the top of the roof. Four cops and firemen stare thoughtfully upward, while three firemen on the roof stare thoughtfully down. Manny decides they are sharing a philosophical moment and that finding a severed head, which has been thrown one hundred feet onto a rooftop, is more than enough to make one thoughtful. It's raining slightly, and misty auras wreathe the streetlamps.

Manny and Vikström approach the truck. It's their job to look at the head before forensics removes it. They make their greetings and exchange handshakes. The fire department has been searching the roofs for the head for several hours, and now, a fire captain tells Manny, they've hit pay dirt.

Manny's disappointment, which has become one of our leitmotifs, is like a nagging sore throat: sometimes better, sometimes worse. As Manny realizes the pleasures that lie ahead, the sore throat fades entirely. He pauses to speak to a fire lieutenant and then hurries after Vikström.

"Guess we have to go to the top," he says. "Like, it's part of the crime scene."

"We take the stairs?"

"Nah-unh, it'd mean busting into the building, and the fire marshal doesn't want to do that. We'll take the ladder."

Vikström stares at the ladder, which to his subjective vision extends into the dark for half a mile. His belly begins to flip-flop. "Why don't you go up, and I'll stay down here and keep an eye on the car."

"That's no problem." Manny calls to a patrolman. "Hey, Wiggins, keep an eye on the car while Benny and I climb up to the roof."

"Sure thing, Detective."

"Okay, Benny, let's get a move on. I'd like to be home before midnight."

We'll skip over Vikström's excuses—for example, sore ankle, upset stomach, useless duplication of effort—because Manny shoots them down one by one like he was shooting hippos in a kiddie pool. Soon Vikström stands on the truck at the base of the ladder staring upward as if into a grinning human skull. The only good thing about the climb, or rather the least bad thing, is that the ladder has handrails, so Vikström can climb with his eyes shut while hanging on to the rails.

"I'll go behind in case you take a tumble—ha, ha, ha," says Manny.

The temperature has continued to drop, and the wind has increased. A few snowflakes make their appearance.

Vikström puts a foot on the bottom rung. Time passes. *I'm a fraud,* he tells himself. He considers turning to the men on the street and confessing his phobia. He'll shout it out, and then, when the laughter stops, he'll hand in his badge and move to Florida. These are the thoughts his fear triggers. He takes another step, and now both feet are on the ladder. The metal handrails are cold against his hands. Maybe thirty rungs rise above him before he gets to the top.

Manny thinks Vikström moves as slowly as a fast-growing plant. He bangs a hand against the ladder. "Get cracking, Benny. Life's going by. You need a push?"

"I'm moving, I'm moving, I've never been on one of these things before. There's no other way to get to the roof?"

"Only the fire escape."

The truck's engine idles and creates a vibration, which Vikström doesn't like. It should be said that Vikström is a brave man. He's had people shoot at him and he's shot back; he's fended off rabid dogs; he's run into burning buildings; he jumped into the Thames last November to save a toddler who fell in the water. That stuff meant nothing to him. It's heights he doesn't like. He also hates exposing himself to these other guys, to have them think he's cowardly. He loves their praise, hates their criticism. That's not unusual, is it? Lastly, he's ninety percent sure that Manny knows the truth about his phobia and is tormenting him on purpose.

"You don't start moving faster," shouts Manny, "I'll jab your ass with a pin!"

Vikström has climbed five rungs. He hears guys down below laughing. Of course he thinks they're laughing at him, but perhaps one has just told a joke about a parrot. Vikström shuts his left eye; the right's open only a crack. He doesn't go "La, la, la"—it seems too small, too picayune, for such a climb. Instead he picks a rousing marching song to distract him from imminent death. Very faintly he sings, "'Over hill, over dale, we will hit the dusty trail, / As the caissons go rolling along.'" Manny appears not to notice. This, however, doesn't last. By the time Vikström's climbed ten more rungs, he's singing loud enough for the others to hear. By the time he's climbed fifteen, he's gone operatic. But no, we exaggerate. At most Vikström's singing is an operatic mutter. Manny hears it, though, and several cops down below, rascals that they are, join in.

It's a pity that Uncle Didi Lobato isn't here to enjoy the fun, because it would be one more example of the tradiculous: singing cops below, severed head above, one miserable musical guy in between. Surely the god of capriciousness and whimsy looks down from a cloud and rubs its paws. Such gods feed on humiliation. But probably every cop has a phobia that could lead to a collapse. For one it's spiders, for another it's snakes, for a third it's going into the attic. Of course their exteriors look tough. There's nothing they can't handle. But deep in their guts is a small square of Jell-O.

It takes Vikström several minutes to get to the top. A fireman on the roof reaches over to help him up. Vikström staggers a few feet to catch his breath. Then, abruptly, he asks the fireman, "How'd you get up here?"

The fireman points to a little building that looks like an outhouse but is actually the top of the stairs. "I busted the lock," he says.

Vikström spins around, meaning to hurl Manny from the roof, but his partner has joined the group surrounding the head. He knows it's dangerous to dawdle. Vikström bends over with his hands on his knees until he breathes normally and his wish to murder his partner has temporarily passed.

Five lights illuminate the mess on the surface of the roof. The cops look like Boy Scouts around a bonfire. The head is squarish, with short black hair, a black mustache, and a trimmed beard, at least on one side of his face. The other side is mostly gone. One ear has been torn off, but the other sports two gold earrings. Teeth are broken. The neck is a savage slash. No one wants to look, and each keeps turning away, but then each turns back again, unable not to. "Didn't some witnesses say he was wearing a cap?" asks a cop. "I wonder what happened to it."

"Someone probably swiped it," says another.

"You can get in trouble for that," says a third. "Swiping shit from a crime scene, that's a felony."

Vikström turns to his partner. "It's Santuzza."

SEVEN

Connor Raposo has had a bad night, rolling around on the Winnebago's thin mattress. He thinks of how Vasco had grown alert when he'd described Sal Nicoletti, then how Vasco had gone blank and denied knowing Nicoletti in any way, shape, or form. Vasco is an operator, a fixer, a jive artist who knows a lot of people and hangs out with bad guys. He isn't a bad guy per se, or so Connor tells himself, but in the world of operators, information about someone like Nicoletti might be salable. Why had Connor mentioned him? Only to get his brother's attention, to impress him.

Vaughn sleeps nearby on the foldout love seat. He, too, on that night is a restless sleeper. Every so often he shouts out a word, like "connubial" or "walrus." When these nocturnal outcries occurred on their first night after leaving San Diego, Connor leaped from bed, thoroughly unnerved. "Despair!" "Heartbreak!" But the words had no clear applicability or context, and soon Connor grew if not used to them at least tolerant. But tonight Vaughn shouts more often and with greater force: "Bucket!" "Boyfriend!"

The wind has been building all night, and around three in the morning the snow begins to come down hard. Connor hears ice crystals clicking against the glass. Fleetingly, he feels the excitement he felt as a child from hearing the season's first snow against the window in his bedroom. Jumping from bed, he'd look out toward the streetlight to see the big flakes swirling down. School might be closed, and there were sledding possibilities.

He's woken at seven by Vaughn shouting, "Wow, wow, wow!" as he looks out the window at the snow. It comes down hard enough to obscure anything more than fifteen feet away, making the Winnebago an island in an ocean of white. Vaughn's a Southern California kid, and to him this is a big deal. Soon Eartha emerges from the bedroom tying the cord of a yellow silk robe. She joins Vaughn at the window. "Neat," she says. Then she begins cracking eggs for breakfast: twelve eggs in one big omelet with onions, mushrooms, and cheese.

Didi wanders out of the bedroom in a matching yellow silk robe. His silver-gray hair is disheveled, the silver wings droop, and he's out of sorts. "Fuckin' snow, I sure hope we don't get stuck here."

Connor hasn't seen Didi since he returned the previous evening from the casino. "Is it true you used to be called Nonô?"

Didi pauses in midstep. "I take it you've been talking to your brother. I've had a number of names, but now I'm definitely Didi."

"I like Nonô," says Eartha. "It's cute."

And Vaughn says, "No, no, no, no, no!"

Again Didi swears as he enters the tiny bathroom and then adds, "Didi, Didi, Didi!" Vaughn is pulling on his jeans and boots. Before Connor can even think of getting out of bed, Vaughn is out the door, which he leaves open. Eartha pushes it shut.

"Has your name always been Connor?" asks Eartha.

Connor begins to say no and then pauses. "My aunt in Lisbon calls me Zeco, which is short for Juan Carlos. My brother calls me Zeco as well. After high school I changed it to Connor."

"So we all have phony names?"

"I wouldn't go that far. It says 'Connor' on my driver's license and tax forms, so that's who I am. It's an Irish name, and my mother's part Irish."

"Zeco," says Eartha. "I like Zeco. It's different." She repeats it to herself as she moves to the stove.

After Connor gets dressed, he goes to the window. Onions are sizzling in a frying pan. Didi's on the phone, complaining to somebody.

Connor sees Vaughn running down the beach through the falling snow with his arms outstretched and his tongue poking out to catch the snowflakes. Then he runs back. Marco Santuzza's black leather motorcycle cap bounces on his head with sympathetic exuberance.

The day's business starts after breakfast. Didi hands out lists of names and phone numbers retrieved from local veterinarians for Free Beagles from Nicotine Addiction, Inc. He also has the phone numbers of Catholics who may be interested in the Holy Sisters of the Blessed Little Feet, which has been a steady moneymaker for seventy-five years. Some charities are less specific, like Mittens for Mothers; some are very specific, like Homeopathic Bras for Big-Breasted Homeless Women; some are surely impossible, like Orphans from Outer Space. But today they concentrate on the beagles.

We might think Didi would have more success with more familiar charities, like those helping flood victims and cancer patients, but that's not the point. He wants "to push the envelope," he wants to see what he can get away with. Some days he talks of it as an art piece, other days he describes the book he plans to write about gullibility. Although when he suggests Halfway Houses for Homosexual Horses and Toilets for the Indigent Left-Handed, Connor and Eartha vote him down. But Didi knows the name doesn't matter. What matters is the spiel, the patter, and he once raised a thousand dollars with his pitch for Victims of Roadkill Gastronomy. Even Orphans from Outer Space has brought in several hundred.

Absurd, we say? Yes, but that's the point: How absurd a story can someone swallow? Didi lives for that moment when the potential donor is balanced between yes and no as if on a knife blade. He or she leans first one way and then the other. Didi gives another nudge, and the potential donor topples toward the yes. When he received his first contribution for Orphans from Outer Space, he bought a jeroboam of champagne. Sure, it's far-fetched, but think: nearly half the population believes the earth is less than ten thousand years old, and right now we can probably find one hundred galoots praying to a potato that loosely resembles the Virgin Mary. Consequently, Orphans from Outer Space stands a chance.

When Connor calls his uncle cynical, Didi laughs it off. How is it cynical to identify folks ready to send checks to Orphans from Outer Space? They're grateful he's put his finger on a problem that's been troubling them. He's doing them a favor.

"Solemnity's a kind of fear," he tells Connor. "It's walking rigidity. Have you ever seen a laughing general? No? That's why we have wars. Flexibility demands the possibility of the comic. If we knew that nobody, absolutely nobody, would ever again slip on a banana peel, life wouldn't be worth living."

"So is Bounty, Inc. meant to raise money?" asks Connor. "Or is it meant to prove your peculiar philosophy?"

"A bit of both, actually. But I'm not cynical. You want cynical, go talk to your brother Vasco. Me, I'm full of hope."

So by eight o'clock the calls begin. Eartha has a list of older beagle owners, and she starts at the top. "Hi, Mandy? Mandy Adams? Do you want little Spikey to cough his lungs out in an awful death?" Eartha uses her best mix of purr and growl.

A pause follows as Mandy Adams thinks, *Don't I know that voice from someplace?* Then, nervously, "Who is this?"

"Coercive nicotine addiction kills thirty thousand beagles a year."

Hushed voice: "Have we met before?"

"Most were snatched off the street by nomadic bands of canine thieves. I hope you keep little Spikey under lock and key."

Another nervous pause, then, "He's here on my lap, safe and sound. I know your voice, I'm sure I do."

"Think of me as an old friend," Eartha purrs. "Think of me as loving little Spikey as much as you do. Beagles that smoke develop yellow lips."

Didi claims that if you can get a customer this far into the conversation, he or she is certain to contribute. "It's just plain science," he says. "They take a bite, then another bite, and then the sandwich grabs them."

So Vaughn and Eartha work their Walmart cell phones, and Didi prepares the envelopes and forms to be mailed to the good citizens who have pledged various sums of money.

But Connor, what's he doing? Standing at the window, he stares at the snow swirling onto the beach and thinks about his brother. He tries to explain to himself all the ways he might be mistaken about Vasco's ill intentions. It's a short list. He also tries to calculate the possibility that his brother is telling the truth and he's never heard of Sal Nicoletti. But the chances are low. And Connor knows that he *wants* his brother to be telling the truth, and that by itself is a reason to distrust him.

Connor goes to the bedroom to telephone in private a guy he'd worked with in Detroit, a blackjack dealer called Roy, although his real name is Franklin. The golden satin sheets are bunched into a ball, and the overheated room smells of sex and sweat. Connor tries not to let this bother him. Ripped condom packs dot the rug. Some are scarlet, some are cobalt blue. Connor turns to face the wall.

Roy's been asleep. "Yeah?"

Connor identifies himself and asks a few general questions like "How've you been? What's the weather like?" Roy interrupts him. "You fuckin' wake me up out of a sound sleep at nine o'clock in the morning to ask how I've been? I got home at five, and I'm tired, that's how I am. So screw you and—"

"Don't hang up! This is important. I need to find out about a guy who I think used to work at the casino. Right now he calls himself Sal Nicoletti."

Roy is silent a few seconds. "I don't recognize the name. Why's it matter?"

"I'm ninety percent sure he worked at the MGM Grand, but he denies it. He says he's never been in Detroit." Connor describes Nicoletti: his height, his pompadour, his swagger.

"And where are you calling from?"

"Rhode Island."

"That's where you've seen this Nicoletti?"

"More or less."

Roy appears to be thinking. Connor can hear him sucking his teeth. "Let me get some coffee." He puts down the phone, and Connor hears him walking away across a wooden floor. Five minutes later he hears him walking back.

"About eight months ago, the attorney general's office brought a case against a Detroit casino because of discrepancies between the revenue counted in the soft room and the numbers passed on by the revenue audit manager. He was charged, as were others. Originally, the revenue audit supervisor was also charged, but charges were dropped when he agreed to testify. The supervisor was the main witness, but the trial ended in a hung jury. Jurors may have been compromised—like, threatened. Now I hear the attorney general's office is in the process of beefing up their case while adding charges of jury tampering."

"What about the supervisor?"

"He disappeared."

"Dead?"

"The feds spirited him away. He'll testify in the next trial, if there is one. I don't recall his name, but it wasn't Nicoletti. I never laid eyes on him, as far as I know, except I heard some guys talking about his hair. The guy you're describing and this supervisor might be the same guy. On the other hand, he might not be the same guy."

"Can you get his name?"

"Why're you interested?"

"I heard Vasco talking about someone," lies Connor. "It sounded like someone I'd met here in town."

"Well, your brother's the type who'd know. You talking to him about it?"

"He won't talk, but he swears he's never heard of this Nicoletti. I think he's lying, and it worries me."

"That still doesn't say why you're interested."

"I guess I don't want Nicoletti to get hurt. He's got a wife and kids. Don't mention this to anybody, okay? It could be a nightmare."

"I'm just a little guy, and little guys stay safe by keeping their mouths shut. I don't squawk about good news, I don't squawk about bad news. So how'd your brother learn about this Nicoletti?"

"Because I was stupid, really stupid. One last question: Vasco seems associated with someone named Chucky. You know him?"

There's silence from the other end. Connor waits and begins to suspect a dropped call when Roy says, "Let me give you two answers. The first is, I know nothing about him. The second is, stay away from him." Roy cuts the connection.

Benny Vikström gets a phone call at seven Tuesday morning. It's his partner, Manny Streeter, who often tells Vikström that a mentally healthy person, like himself, needs only four hours of sleep per night. Vikström needs eight, and on his days off he likes to get ten.

"Rise and shine, Detective, ha, ha, ha!"

Vikström lies on his back in bed with his cell phone pressed to his ear. "What do you want?"

"There was a break-in last night at Burns Insurance, where Robert Rossi's a CPA. Fat Bob, remember?"

"And?" Vikström sits up and stares down at his toes. The nails need cutting.

"The only thing stolen was Fat Bob's computer. The thief busted through the back door to the alley. There was nothing subtle about it. There's an alarm, but the guy was gone by the time the cops arrived. He knew exactly what he wanted. Oh, yes, security cameras. The guy was wearing a big winter hat and a big coat. For that matter, we're not even sure it was a man. You want to check out the scene? I'll be at your house in five minutes. I got the four-wheel drive. But make sure you wear your boots. We got snow."

"That's great news," says Vikström as he gives his cell phone the finger. Looking toward the window, he sees the snow. His wife says, "Remember to button up." Vikström wonders why she thinks he would forget to button up.

Vikström is making a cup of instant coffee when Manny arrives. His watch cap, his boots, and the shoulders of his coat are snow-covered and drip onto the kitchen floor. "You don't have time for that," says Manny.

Vikström ignores him and pours the coffee into a travel cup. "Is there any news about Fat Bob?"

"Not a whisper. Either those guys last night caught up with him or he got away. Like everything—either it happens or it doesn't."

Vikström leaves this morsel of philosophy untouched. "Are we to think Fat Bob's the guy who was meant to be killed on the Fat Bob?"

"Maybe yes, maybe no. Like, it's logical, but it also might be logical that Fat Bob wanted to get rid of Santuzza."

Vikström gets his coat and puts on a pair of rubbers. The two detectives leave the house. "And why," asks Vikström, "make such a display? Why do it on a busy street instead of, say, in a dark alley?"

"It's the TV. Everyone's got to be an entertainer. Nothing's subtle anymore." Paused on the steps, Manny holds out his arms to the weather: the junipers shagged with ice, et cetera. "Isn't this beautiful?"

Vikström doesn't like snow; he's never liked snow. He didn't like it as a kid or as an adolescent, as a young adult or a cop. Snow is one of the *unnecessities* of life—that's Vikström's word—things that exist simply to annoy, like mosquitoes.

The detectives climb into Manny's Subaru Forester and put on their seat belts. It's snowing hard enough that the windshield is covered again with fat flakes. The defroster is on full blast. No plows have been down the street, and the tracks of previous passing cars are nearly invisible. Snow puts white hats on the telephone poles and accumulates on the wires. The birds are in hiding.

"This could be a fuckin' picture," says Manny. "It makes everything clean. We're supposed to get half a foot or more. Don't you want to roll around in it?"

Vikström doesn't answer. He's sure he once told Manny he hated snow. He also realizes his rubbers will be inadequate and that the only reason he didn't wear the boots was Manny had told him to.

Manny accelerates quickly, and the back of the Subaru fishtails a little. "Hang on to your hat!" he shouts. "Feel that four-wheel drive grab!" He steps on the brake to demonstrate. Vikström is thrown against his seat belt.

Burns Insurance is on Eugene O'Neill Drive, which runs parallel to Bank Street. There's not much to say about it. Office buildings, small apartment houses, and parking lots have taken the place of historic architecture, but the thick blanket of snow gives it some beauty. City trucks plow the downtown streets.

Mr. Burns meets them at the door. He's a plump fellow nearing middle age, and he wears a blue down jacket and a Greek fisherman's cap. His nose ends in a flat vertical, as if the original tip had once been snipped off. "Terrible weather. I don't know how anybody stands it. Mind you stamp your feet."

Mr. Burns's dislike of winter pleases Vikström; Manny Streeter, on the other hand, thinks he's a jerk. They stamp their feet and follow Mr. Burns into a large office with six desks. "I called everybody and told them not to come in today. No one answered at Bob Rossi's house. He lives alone since he and his wife separated. He has his own office over here." Mr. Burns leads them to a windowless office against the side wall. "He's got a number of his own accounts and he does some outside work, so technically he's only a part-timer, and he pays his own rent. Take a look at his desk. You see? No computer."

The detectives look thoughtfully at the space where the computer had stood. A computer-size square area is a little less dusty than the rest of the desk. Wires lead to a surge protector and a printer. Wires also lead to a pair of little speakers on either side of the cleaner area. All have been cut rather than disconnected.

"You got keys to the desk?" asks Vikström.

Mr. Burns holds them in his hand. "I knew you'd want them."

"Was his office busted into?" asks Manny.

"I expect it was open. We're pretty honest here. I hope this doesn't set a bad precedent. I always tell my employees that *distrust* is 'the unaffordable expense.'"

"Very clever of you," says Manny tonelessly.

Vikström opens the drawers, and he and Manny poke through their contents: files, stationery, envelopes, blank insurance forms, photographs of buildings. The belly drawer has chewing gum, pencil stubs, paper clips, a stapler, notepads, and a brown apple core. Neither Vikström nor Manny knows what's important or what's not, so they don't know what they're looking for. Manny's sorry there isn't a .45 automatic in the belly drawer to give the desk some flair.

"Show us the back door," says Vikström.

Mr. Burns seems uncertain. "Aren't you going to dust for fingerprints?"

"Not today," says Manny.

The back door opens onto a parking lot. It's been wrenched from the frame by someone using a forty-eight-inch gooseneck wrecking bar that has been hidden under the snow until Vikström accidentally kicks it.

Mr. Burns makes a *tsk-tsk* noise. "It will be impossible to find anyone to fix the door on a day like today. Darn the snow anyway."

Vikström can think of no appropriate response and remains silent. He picks up the wrecking bar. Manny starts to say, *Life sucks*, but decides against it.

"By the way," says Mr. Burns, "Bob also works part-time as an auditor in the casino? I hope this doesn't get him in trouble."

Vikström's and Manny's thoughts veer off in the new direction.

Vikström asks, "Why would it get him in trouble?"

"Many of my clients are religious."

"And they don't like gambling?" asks Vikström.

"They frown on it. Doesn't the Bible say, 'Neither a borrower nor a gambler be'? Even though Bob is a part-timer—freelance, basically—if customers knew he worked at the casino, they might worry."

Vikström tries to recall that part of the Bible and says nothing.

Manny thinks, *That's Shakespeare,* but he keeps it a secret.

"So Rossi works part-time for you and part-time over there?" asks Manny. "That must be a lot of hours. How come?"

Mr. Burns assumes a gloomy look to hide his pleasure in passing on news of another's ill fortune. "Messy divorce."

"How messy?" asks Vikström, recalling Angelina Rossi, her dark arms, and what he thinks of as her fiery nature.

"His wife caught him banging a secretary on his desk."

Manny looks astonished. "'Banging,' Mr. Burns? Did I hear you use the word 'banging'?"

Wiping drops from his brow, Mr. Burns seems surprised that particular word rolled off his tongue. "Well, you know what I mean, and that's what his wife called it. 'Banging.' I was quoting her. Her lawyer demanded a lot of money. She got the house, the cars, the children, and the beagle."

"You mean banging her on his desk right here in his office?" says Manny, still astonished.

"It was after hours, way after hours."

Vikström says, "You got Rossi's new home address?"

"I'll write it down for you." Mr. Burns retreats to his office.

"You could mess up your back banging someone on a desk," says Manny. "It wouldn't matter if you were the fucker or the fuckee. They got no give. You ever tried it?"

"Me?" says Vikström, shocked. "Me?"

Fat Bob now lives in a small Cape Cod on Montauk Avenue a few blocks from Lawrence + Memorial Hospital; it's a clear step down from the pretty gable-front house on the other side of town where his wife lives. The new house has all the majesty of an empty beer case. It's still snowing, but the temperature is rising. Chunks of snow plop down from trees. A few brave souls walk dogs. Montauk was plowed earlier in the morning, but more snow has accumulated. On the drive from downtown, Manny slams on the brakes four or five times as a way of testing the efficiency of his Subaru Forester's four-wheel drive. Will he go into a spin and hit a tree? No way! The Subaru stops as quickly as it would on dry pavement.

"See that, see that!" Manny shouts. "What a car!"

Manny pulls in to Fat Bob's driveway, plowing through eight inches of snow. It seems no one has been in or out since the snow began. So either Fat Bob's still inside or he spent the night someplace else.

"Look at that, no prints," says Manny.

"How can I fucking look at something that's not there!" Vikström puts all his pent-up frustration into his answer. Manny glances at his partner in faux surprise as he gets out of the Subaru.

The snow rises over Vikström's rubbers to his ankles. He can feel his socks begin to dampen; in another minute they'll be sodden.

"Don't say I didn't warn you," says Manny.

Vikström tries to walk in Manny's tracks. His mind fills with hostile thoughts. Manny's blue watch cap seems to bob up and down with each step. Vikström thinks the back of Manny's head could make a target for a snowball. Maturity robs a person of many reasonable actions.

Manny discovers the front door is locked. "Let's check the back. You go that way and I'll go this. You don't mind the snow, do you?"

Vikström calculates the annoyance factor of Manny's question on a scale of one to ten as he trudges around the small house. Maybe a six, maybe a seven. The ends of his pant legs drag though the snow. But Vikström gives no sign he's annoyed. His face is a mask of virtuous calm. Isn't this the case with people we see on the street? This man imagines a vicious assault on someone who has offended him, this woman plans to put roller skates on the cellar stairs before her husband gets home, while their blank exteriors show all the passion of a store mannequin. No wonder people become paranoid.

Manny stands at a window in the locked garage door. "You might want to take a look at this."

Vikström looks. Inside, five shiny Fat Bob motorcycles—blue, red, gray, a dark purple, and black—are parked side by side. "I wonder if he hid these from his wife when he was paying out the money. I guess he won't miss the one Santuzza used to smack into the dump truck."

"Or the one that got shot up in front of his former house."

"Maybe they're spares in case he gets a flat. You know Jay Leno has ninety-three motorcycles?"

"What kind of jackass owns a hundred bikes?"

"A rich jackass."

They walk to the back steps of the house. Before they've gone five feet, they see the door has been broken open with the same violence and efficiency used upon the back door of the insurance office.

"This is a bad sign," says Manny. "I bet it was opened with the same crowbar used on Burnsie's place."

The detectives stamp their feet and enter the kitchen. Drawers have been pulled out and cabinets have been emptied. Their contents litter the floor.

"This is a bad sign," Manny repeats. "You think someone was looking for something, or is it just trashing for the fun of trashing?"

Vikström doesn't offer an opinion. He leans against the sink, removing dollops of snow from his left shoe with a finger.

The living room and den have been similarly trashed. A computer has been taken, although the monitor remains on a small desk.

"This is a bad sign," says Manny. "It looks like—"

"Stop!" says Vikström. "Don't say it again."

"Say what again?"

"That this is a bad sign again."

"But it *is* a bad sign—"

"Don't fuck with me, Streeter!"

Manny widens his eyes to indicate astonished innocence.

Let's bring this little scene to a close. Suffice it to say they find nothing, which is what often happens when we don't know what we're looking for. The house is scantily furnished (Fat Bob only moved in a few months ago), and it's been searched from top to bottom by person or persons unknown, which suggests that the one who trashed it didn't find what he was looking for. Nor does anything suggest Fat Bob's location at the present moment.

"He's gotta be out there someplace," says Manny.

"He and everyone else," says Vikström.

EIGHT

I t takes Connor an hour to free the Mini-Cooper from the snow, even with Vaughn's assistance. Vaughn wears Santuzza's leather motorcycle cap. Connor is stoical; Vaughn is having fun. Fortunately, Connor has parked with the Mini's nose pointing down a slight hill, but he only drives ten feet before he gets stuck. He's got another hundred and fifty feet to go. But Vaughn is like a machine, shoveling-wise; he's a blur of white semicircles of flying white particles. Connor stares at him in fond amaze. He can't see how a person five feet tall can turn himself into a snow-shoveling robot. Vaughn lunges forward, takes a large scoop of snow, and shouts, "That's all for you!" Then he tosses it aside. Then another scoop, and he shouts, "That's all for you!" and then another scoop. Over and over. "That's all for you! That's all for you!" He wears black cowboy boots, jeans, and a black sweatshirt along with the leather cap, but gradually he turns white. Connor drives forward another ten feet and gets stuck. Then he starts shoveling again.

During a break, Vaughn says, "What would the extinguished gentleman be doing right now if he weren't the extinguished gentleman?"

"You mean the dead guy on the motorcycle?"

"The extinguished gentleman."

"He's just finished his breakfast and is drinking his second cup of coffee as he reads an article in the local paper about a guy smashing his motorcycle into a dump truck yesterday morning."

"Yes, that's what I thought he was doing." Vaughn goes back to shoveling.

Connor thinks the effect of talking to Vaughn and the effect of smoking weed are about the same. It's not that Vaughn is stupid or crazy; rather it's as if Connor were a regular cube and Vaughn an irregular octahedron, while the vision of one is no better or worse than the vision of the other, except that Connor is six-sided and Vaughn is eight-sided. This gives Vaughn an edge. But no way will they ever be on the same page. Earlier Connor asked Vaughn what he wants to be when he grows up. He guesses that Vaughn wants what others want: a modest middle-class life with medical benefits and retirement.

Vaughn said, "A soccer mom."

Connor digested that. "You going to have kids?"

"I'll get two or three rentals when there's a game."

"They going to have names?"

"Breakdown and Hellion."

"Sounds like fun," Connor said.

"And what about your parents, what are their names?"

"Gone and Goner."

Connor winced and regretted his question.

Of course, the chance exists to ask Vaughn what the hell he's talking about, but Connor has tried that in the past and was roughly dragged into Vaughn's irregular octahedron, where the world mystified him. No, it's best to keep quiet.

Connor also shovels, but he can't keep up. His jeans and jacket are wet, as is his baseball cap with the word TROUBLE printed across the front. He borrowed the hat from Vaughn, who in his energetic shoveling gets farther and farther away.

When they've finished and Connor has changed his clothes, he's able to drive out, though Vaughn has to push him free a few times. At last he sees Vaughn disappear in the rearview mirror, waving. The windshield wipers go *whap-whap*. There's only static on the radio.

This may seem a bad idea, but Connor is driving to New London to talk to Sal Nicoletti. One lane of I-95 is clear, pretty much. Traffic is light. A few cars have slid into ditches, but Connor stays on the road. Pure luck, he thinks. When he crosses the bridge over the Thames, he can't see the water because of the blowing snow. Gusts of wind elbow the Mini-Cooper sideways.

In New London the streets are nearly empty. Cars parked along the curbs are buried lumps. Yellow trucks spread sand and salt. Above the street, stoplights sway in the wind and light poles shiver. At least the snow would wash away the last of Marco Santuzza, Connor thinks. Bank Street will be clean again.

Connor turns left onto Ocean Avenue. Small late-nineteenth-century houses give way to bigger houses split into apartments. Though no two are alike, the snow lends them a family resemblance. Connor drives slowly. The closer he gets, the less he likes his plan. But if Sal's the man who testified against the casino employees in Detroit, then it's Connor's duty to warn him that his New London safe house has been blown. Connor, however, worries about his response.

A woman bundled up in a red parka shovels snow in front of Sal's house on Glenwood Place. No car is in the driveway, just indentations from snow-covered tracks. The woman's black hair is partly covered by her ski cap. She's tall. Connor knows exactly who she is.

He pulls up to the curb and puts down the window. "Excuse me," he says, "excuse me." He shuts off the motor.

The woman stops shoveling and looks at Connor, but she comes no closer.

"Is Sal around?"

"What do you want him for?" The woman has large brown eyes, a narrow face with a wide mouth and full lips. The tip of her nose and her cheeks are red with cold. Connor finds the face beautiful. It's hard for him to look away. He wants to keep staring at it; he wants it plastered across his eyeballs.

"I gave him a ride home yesterday after his Chevy didn't start. I wanted to see how it was, if he needed any more help with it."

"The car's fine. It's in the garage." The woman still hasn't moved.

"Is Sal home?"

"He's at his office."

"How 'bout the kids?"

"Watching TV. Why do you care?"

Connor worries that she thinks he wants to harm her or harm the kids. Even bundled up like an Eskimo, she's beautiful.

"I like kids."

The woman has nothing to say to that.

"We weren't introduced yesterday. I guess I left too quickly. I'm Connor."

The woman has nothing to say to this either.

"What's the address of Sal's office on Bank Street?"

She shrugs. "I've never been there."

"Haven't I seen you in the MGM Grand in Detroit? I'm sure I have."

The woman shakes her head. "I've never been to Detroit."

Connor thinks he has heard a slight hesitation. "I'm sure I saw you and Sal at the blackjack table, or maybe roulette."

"Like I said, I've never been to Detroit." She's turns her back and again begins to shovel. The scrape of the blade on the concrete is the only sound.

Connor wishes he could make her smile, but this is not the day. He decides if she and Sal are in a witness-protection program, then it makes sense for them to be suspicious. It's not personal.

"When's Sal getting home?"

The woman half turns. "Around six."

"So he'll be home this evening?"

"I don't know."

"Can I call him? What's the phone number?"

The woman doesn't answer. Connor is about to give up, but then she says, "Give me your phone number instead."

Maybe this is a step forward, maybe it's nothing. He recites his cell phone number. "Can you remember it, or should I write it down?"

"I'll remember it." She keeps shoveling.

"Don't forget to tell him Connor stopped by, okay?"

He doesn't hear her answer, but maybe there was no answer. He's irritated with himself because he wants the woman to like him, though he has no intentions as far as she's concerned, and hardly any hopes. It's all just fantasy stuff. He puts the car in gear and drives off. He doesn't wave good-bye.

Fidget leans against a wall on Bank Street. He's cold. The snow covers his Red Sox cap, raincoat, and jeans. His sneakers are buried in it. Around his neck is a thick, blue, and very expensive scarf, which is also snow-covered. What's a homeless guy doing with a pricey scarf? Fidget's long, reptilian tail makes mild moves of protest. It's half frozen, but Fidget doesn't care. "Fuck you, tail!" Let it suffer. Blanketed with snow and being so thin, Fidget looks like a permanent fixture, a snow-encased version of the parking meter to which he was compared earlier. His mind, too, is frozen, and his thoughts are slow. He's been standing here an hour waiting for the man whose office is on the second floor across the street to exit the building: his meal ticket, his bag of gold, his savior. Fidget has something to say to him.

Of course, Fidget can cross the street, climb the stairs to his office, and give a speech about helping the poor or else. But he worries the man won't be happy with this, that he'll become violent, even murderous. Hasn't he been murderous before? So Fidget decides it's best to talk in some public place, like the middle of the street.

Fidget has learned the guy on the Harley wasn't Fat Bob but Marco Santuzza. He has also learned, from overhearing two cops, that Santuzza's wallet is missing. It was attached to his belt by a chain, and the chain snapped in the accident. The cops thought the wallet had been thrown into the air, just like the head, and that it's now buried under snow someplace nearby. Fidget has looked a few places, along the curbs and behind trash cans, but the snow makes it difficult. So now he waits for the snow to melt. Fidget, being a street person, believes that all articles lost on the street belong to him. This makes the street, to his way of thinking, his personal backyard.

But first things first, thinks Fidget, which is why he concentrates on the man in the upstairs office. Why'd he want to kill Fat Bob? That's the question. Fidget has spent hours looking for Fat Bob, maybe to warn him, if Fat Bob gives something back in return. He had walked to his office at Burns Insurance, but the place was locked up. He walked to his ex-wife's place on Brainard, not knowing there was an ex-wife, and got yelled at by a cop sitting outside in a cruiser. He walked all the way to Fat Bob's new house, but he wasn't there either. Worse, the house had been broken into, and Fat Bob's stuff was scattered on the floor. Fidget took half a fried chicken from the refrigerator, two bottles of Bud Light, and an unopened box of crackers he'd found under a table. He would have taken more, but he got scared. Oh, yes, he also took from a closet this beautiful blue scarf that's keeping his neck as warm as toast. Then he walked back to Bank Street to wait for the guy with the black pompadour.

Vikström and Manny Streeter cross the I-95 bridge around nine that Tuesday morning on their way to Brewster, Rhode Island, at about the same time that Connor Raposo crosses the bridge, going in the other direction to New London. Manny might be thinking, *That's a cute little blue car over there,* but we have no information about that. Vikström has his eyes shut and is going, "La-la-la-la."

Manny swerves back and forth on the snow to see if he can get the Subaru to skid. Nope. The four-wheel drive keeps a tenacious grip.

Once off the bridge, Vikström bursts out, "Why do you treat me like this? We're supposed to be partners!"

"Treat you like what?" Manny's voice is as innocent as a politician's caught with his pants down.

"Like you're trying to drive me nuts!" Vikström wonders if he can get sick pay for a nervous breakdown. The thought of two weeks without Manny makes him sigh.

Manny thinks of the old joke: *Drive you nuts? It's only a short putt.* "I don't appreciate your attitude, Benny. Why should I drive you nuts?" Deep in his brain, Manny is laughing and clapping his hands.

"Screw you," says Vikström. He turns to stare out the side window.

Manny is silent for a minute. Then he begins to sing just loud enough for Vikström to hear: "'An old cowpoke went ridin' out one dark and windy day. / Upon a ridge he rested as he went along his way. / When all at once a mighty herd of red-eyed cows he saw / Come rushin' through the ragged skies and up a cloudy draw.'"

Yes, thinks Vikström, a nervous breakdown was possible, but would he get dizzy first or see black spots or pull out his hair? Would he bolt screaming down the street or strip naked in front of the police chief? Oh, madness has many symptoms he might soon discover.

But let's return to the bigger picture. Sometimes intimate details are just a distraction, mere tale-telling, and everyone has a right to his own secrets.

Vikström and Manny have decided to track down Leon Pappalardo. He, as we know, had been driving the green truck. If in fact he'd received a signal to stomp on the gas and rocket back across Bank Street, then the police would like a few words with him, as a prologue to arresting his ass.

But Pappalardo lives in Brewster, Rhode Island, which is off-limits to New London cops. It means they have no clout, which is offensive to those for whom clout is a raison d'être. Pappalardo in the safety of his living room can't be arrested; he can't even be bullied. He'd have to be extradited to Connecticut, which requires paperwork. Such a nuisance. But at least the Brewster chief might let them visit Pappalardo so they can extract the words to slap his ass in jail, even if that jail is in Rhode Island.

The Brewster police chief, Brendan Gazzola, is fairly new to his job, having replaced the realtor who preceded him: a *realtor*, for Pete's sake. Vikström and Manny haven't met Gazzola and know nothing about him, except that he is said to be an improvement. When Manny turns off of Route 1 toward Brewster, Vikström gives Gazzola a call. Common courtesy might suggest they should have called earlier; now Manny and Vikström are barely five minutes away. But the detectives justify the abruptness of their visit by saying that if Gazzola has a problem with their wish to question Pappalardo, they'll be right in his face in no time. It should come as no surprise that many city cops don't take small-town cops seriously, and if Chief Gazzola ever had a major crime, like a murder, he'd call the staties, as has happened in the past.

So Vikström calls, and it takes a minute for the chief's secretary to track down her boss. "He was outside smoking a cigarette. What else is new, right?"

Vikström can't comment about this.

Gazzola comes on the line. He has the raspy, gurgling voice of a broken sewer pipe. Introductions and explanations are made. As for Leon Pappalardo, Vikström says he only wants to talk to him, but perhaps someone from the Brewster police department should come along in case of difficulties.

Chief Gazzola keeps it short. "No problem. Glad to help. See you soon."

Vikström cuts the connection. "We're all set."

Chief Gazzola waits for the New London detectives on the front steps of the police station. He's smoking. Manny parks, and the detectives get out. A warm southern wind has begun to nibble the snow.

"Hey, I'm over here!" shouts Gazzola. In fact, he's the only other person in sight. He drops the cigarette and grinds it with his heel. Heaps of snow flank the steps, but the steps themselves have been nicely shoveled.

Greetings are exchanged. Gazzola is a tall, cadaverous man in his fifties. His fingers are stained dark yellow from tobacco, and his skin is as gray as cardboard. He begins to cough a series of phlegm-packed, liquid coughs that turn his face pink. Then he twists around to spit a yellow dollop into the snow.

"I do a lot of work out here," says Gazzola, looking around the steps. "I can smoke, and inside I have to chew Nicorettes. So I end up saving money."

"Very sensible," says Manny.

Gazzola gives him a look to gauge his tone but reaches no conclusions. "No reason to go inside. You know how it is: people always want something. We can drive to Pappalardo's right now. His wife works at a hospital in Providence, but I expect he's home."

The chief drives a spotless black Lincoln Town Car with super suspension. It has a soothing, aquatic motion. Closing his eyes in the backseat, Vikström imagines he's on a raft at sea. He conjures up sailboats and dolphins. Mermaids flit by.

"They let you smoke in this car?" asks Manny.

"The city council's putting it to a vote. So everything's up in the air till then, meaning no smoking. They were supposed to give me a driver, too, but no dice."

"It must be lonely at the top," says Manny in a way that makes Vikström snap open his eyes.

"It's not bad. They give me a lunch allowance."

Pappalardo and his wife live on Newport Street, a few blocks from Morgan Memorial Hospital. It's a gray Craftsman bungalow with two junipers in the front yard, which, in the snow, rouse Manny's memories of youth. No footprints mar the snow's smooth surface.

"I love the snow, don't you?" says Manny.

No one answers. Vikström thinks he's lying.

Chief Gazzola pulls in to the driveway. The men get out and wade through the snow to the front porch. Gazzola lights a cigarette.

"I hate to disturb the snow's pristine surface," says Manny.

Vikström thinks, *Give me a fuckin' break.* His shoes and socks are still wet from their visit to Fat Bob's. If he catches a cold, he'll instantly put in for sick leave.

Gazzola climbs the wooden steps and pushes the bell. They can hear it ringing inside the house. Nothing happens. Gazzola pushes it again and knocks on the door. Time passes.

"He must of left early," says Gazzola.

The covered front porch runs the width of the house, with a large window on either side of the door. Manny goes to the window on the left. Vikström goes to the right. They peer in.

"You goin' to head back to New London, or you want to get lunch? My treat," says Gazzola. "I can pick up Pappalardo once he gets home."

Vikström cups his hands around his eyes so he can see more clearly into the living room. At first he sees nothing; then that changes. "There's something over here you should look at, Chief."

Chief Gazzola isn't a reader and brags about it. "Books make you dumb," he's fond of saying. But if he read mysteries, he'd feel a chill when Vikström says, "There's something over here you should look at, Chief." It's a sentence we find in hundreds of crime novels. Manny recognizes it and joins Vikström. The three men peer through the window, bending forward and cupping their hands around their eyes. A brick fireplace faces the window, with an easy chair on either side. An archway on the right leads to a dining room. By the window is a dark library table.

"What's to see?" says Gazzola.

Manny draws a sudden breath. "Keep looking."

It takes Gazzola about three more seconds. "Are those feet? Bare feet?"

"This is a bad sign," says Manny.

"Don't start," says Vikström.

"You think he's napping?" asks Gazzola hopefully.

Manny goes to the front door. It's locked. Rearing back, he slams his boot against it just above the knob. With a cracking sound, the door springs open and hits a wall.

"Hey, you can't do that!" shouts Gazzola. "This is private property!"

But Manny is already inside, followed quickly by Vikström.

"You need a search warrant!" shouts Gazzola.

Leon Pappalardo lies on his back with his bare feet sticking into the living room and the rest of him in the dining room. The feet are huge and pink. They look like inflatables. He wears baby blue pajamas with gold stars. It would be wrong to say that he lies in a pool of blood. It's a lake.

Manny and Vikström feel surges of pleasure that the body is in Rhode

Island and not New London. Pappalardo has been shot in the chest, probably with a shotgun. A streak of blood and tissue is spread across the dining room table.

Gazzola stands back by the front door. "Is he dead?"

Neither detective answers. Vikström thinks that Pappalardo won't have to worry about his weight anymore, won't have to dye his hair. These are two of death's small consolations.

Gazzola joins them and fumbles for a cigarette. "Jesus, this is too big for me, way too big. I got to get the staties on the horn this very second!"

NINE

Yvonne Streeter is a woman of few doubts and many opinions, which she feels obliged to share with others. She lives in a twilight area between the assertive and pushy, and her opinions—or truths, as she calls them—exist for the benefit of her neighbors near and far. She likes being a policeman's wife—a detective, no less—and she feels that some of Manny's authority as a guardian of the people is borne on her shoulders as well. We might think its weight would become a burden, but Yvonne is a full-figured woman, size eighteen, and she looks upon women beneath size twelve with scorn.

Such qualities give Yvonne a high-minded heft, and she takes care never to act in ways she sees as undignified, by which she means silliness, girlishness, giggling, blushing, nervousness, and tears. She walks as a queen walks, with her full weight upon her heels, and imagines herself an offensive lineman on morality's football team. She does not brag, nor does she need to brag; she is amply defined by her measured words and movements.

In her own house, she relaxes a little, which doesn't mean she's relaxed; rather, she loosens her moral corset a notch or two. Her kids are in California, and she enjoys her vocation of helping her husband with his police work by giving him advice. And she loves karaoke. When she's up on the little stage of their karaoke box with the microphone gripped in her hands, she feels released from the day's troubles, released from the necessity of being right, released from her size-eighteen authority; she imagines herself a butterfly broken free of its restricting cocoon.

At times during the day, she takes a break from her housework or her volunteer hospital work, where she cheers up the terminally ill with recitations of life's hard truths, and slips into the dimly lit karaoke box, steps onto the stage, and, without recorded music or the lyrics unrolling before her on the computer monitor, she sings from a place deep in her gut, sings in the way she felt born to sing, and her little beagle, Schultzie, will jump up beside her and howl his heart out, howls that swirl around her forceful singing like a figure skater on ice. You'd have to be sitting at one of the small tables to feel the glory of the moment.

At times Yvonne loves Schultzie more than she loves karaoke, and at times she loves karaoke more than Schultzie, but mostly they run neck and neck through the allocation center of her desires. Schultzie is a two-year-old tricolor beagle with a jet-black saddle and light brown areas in the shapes of European countries. Although Schultzie cannot talk, he can howl meaningfully, while his mobile features form an exhaustive projection of idea and emotion.

At noon the day after Marco Santuzza's death, Yvonne's telephone rings. It's the landline, which is surprising because Yvonne and Manny rarely use the landline—they prefer their cells—and their number is unlisted. Yvonne stands in the hall in her tiger-striped bathrobe and eyes the phone suspiciously. After four rings she lifts the receiver. "Yes?"

"Madam, do you want little Schultzie to cough his heart out in the throes of nicotine addiction?"

The deep baritone voice carries within it the sound of galloping horses touched with distant thunder. It is a voice caressed by the melody of water swirling within an otherwise empty fifty-five-gallon metal drum. The faint vibrato creates for Yvonne images of dark shadows of rippling silk across a sunlit wall. And she fears that her heart might stop, so violently is it beating.

"Do you want little Schultzie snatched from the street by roving bands of beagle thieves and spirited away to midnight laboratories where he'll be forced to consume one coffin nail after another?"

Yvonne is so stunned that she sits down on the rug next to the telephone table, torn as she is between the medium and the message. She's caught within the rippling baritone, and the house around her vibrates as vigorously as a belly dancer's abdomen at the crescendo of her display.

"Vaughn?" she whispers. "Vaughn? Is it really you?"

"It's in your power to save Schultzie from a death as terrible as those faced by Christian martyrs. The needles and knives of medical research are a horrible fate for so sweet a hound."

Of course this isn't the real Vaughn Monroe, "Old Leather Lungs," but our own Vaughn who sits at the dinette table of the Winnebago parked in Brewster. He has made six calls, and Yvonne's is the seventh name on the list. He has instructions and a script written by Didi with promptings of what he might say. Squeezing the phone between his ear and shoulder, he carefully paints his nails with clear polish.

"Tell me," whispers Yvonne, "is this the real Vaughn Monroe? Will you sing me 'Racing with the Moon'? Please, please?"

Yvonne's response is like other responses Vaughn has received, though a bit stronger. The need, at this point, is not to let the woman get too excited. Otherwise she won't hear his pitch.

"Vaughn is my working name," says Vaughn, "but Vaughn's not usually my real name. My real name is . . ." Here we have to imagine Vaughn putting down the nail polish, taking off the black leather motorcycle cap, and looking inside. "My real name is Marco Santuzza."

Yvonne finds this disappointing, but she knows from a place deep within her that Vaughn Monroe's resurrection probably hasn't happened. Pity. She gets to her feet and shakes herself just as Schultzie shakes himself after a bath.

"Should I call you Vaughn or Marco?"

"Whichever works best for you."

"I'll call you Vaughn. You have his voice. It's wonderful. Tell me, Vaughn, can you sing?"

"Only for circles of intimate friends. Sorry."

Yvonne sighs. "Then how can I help you?" The disappointment in her voice could strip granite crumbs from a tombstone.

So Vaughn tells her about Free Beagles from Nicotine Addiction, Inc., or FBNA. He speaks of their dedication and hard work and of the many beagles they have saved because of the generosity of their benefactors. Thirty-five thousand beagles disappear into the nicotine labs each year, while twenty-five thousand others are used to test the effects on beagles of tear gas, car exhaust, and smog. Many of the beagles have been abandoned by their owners; others are bred on special beagle farms in Pennsylvania, where they are kept in cages and never see the light of day.

Yvonne is so moved by the magnificent baritone that she barely understands a word. She could easily listen to the voice all day. Vaughn is only a few minutes into his spiel when Yvonne withdraws a checkbook from her purse and promises to send him a check that morning.

"Where shall I mail it?"

It mostly happens that benefactors first receive a donation form, but at times the enthusiasm of a benefactor leads him or her to send a check directly to a post office box. Some even send cash.

Vaughn gives her the address.

"I'll go to the post office right away."

Yvonne puts down the receiver. The house feels suddenly smaller. But even though a melancholy sadness has settled over her shoulders et cetera, she feels cleansed, purified, and she gets busy making out a large check from her personal account.

I t should be said that Yvonne Streeter is not a generous person. When a neighbor comes to borrow a cup of sugar, Yvonne charges her a buck. Sometimes she's generous to her husband, Manny. Generally she's generous to her three kids in California as long as they don't make the trip to the well too often. And she might be generous to her brother, her sister, and a bunch of cousins. It depends on her mood. But when calls come from the United Way, Easter Seals, and various cop and firemen associations, the caller is unable to finish a sentence before the phone goes dead. A ten-year-old Cub Scout who knocked on her door to ask for a summer-camp contribution wept as he was berated for his arrogance and opportunism. These days cobwebs drape her doorbell.

So it may seem unlikely that she should give so generously to Free Beagles from Nicotine Addiction, Inc., but generosity is not the issue; rather, she is asserting her devotion to her dog, Schultzie. She is *celebrating* that devotion! And her gift is a result of Didi's two-pronged attack using research and pinpoint selection. With Vaughn's highly honed computer skills, Didi pries loose the names of beagle owners from the computers of vets in a fifty-mile radius. But not just any beagle owners. No. He chooses those who rush their dogs to the vet for the smallest excuse ("Smoochie's off his feed!") and who do it every few weeks.

The second part of the attack is Vaughn's imitation of Vaughn Monroe, but again Didi is selective. He mostly calls no one under fifty and prefers to call women, who statistically have more adrenalized relationships with beagles than men do. These are also women whose parents' musical preferences were fixed before the advent of rock and roll. It's nice that Yvonne likes Vaughn Monroe today, but what's crucial is that she grew up listening to Vaughn Monroe. She listened to him in her crib!

Yvonne, in fact, was *waiting* for Vaughn's phone call. This expectation was like a mild tickling in her cerebellum that had persisted for years. As a result, she topples faster than a sapling gnawed by a beaver. It was fated to happen. Our single surprise is that her large check wasn't larger, but no matter.

Benny Vikström and Manny Streeter spend most of the morning in Brewster, much of it in Pappalardo's Craftsman bungalow. Generally they are bystanders, even tourists, as the forensics team comes and goes and local cops trudge door-to-door to ask neighbors if they've seen or heard anything suspicious. Then around noon a state police detective, Woody Potter, shows up.

This guy, Manny thinks, looks nothing like a detective. He wears jeans and a barn coat, a Red Sox cap and boots. He drives a Chevy pickup, and a goofy-looking dog, maybe a golden retriever, is salivating out the open window. He's maybe forty: a tall, muscular man with short brown hair, dark brown eyes, and a chin that juts forward like a challenge.

Manny tries being a bit patronizing, but Potter buys none of it. He doesn't say anything, but his chin juts out a little farther and his eyes get a little darker. Manny decides that Potter is one of those difficult people who lack a sense of humor.

Woody Potter listens to Vikström's explanation of why two New London detectives are in Brewster; then he asks Vikström, with a straight face, "Are you one of those famous Swedish detectives?"

Vikström opens his mouth, but nothing comes out.

Once Potter realizes that no answer will be forthcoming, he points through the living room window to Gazzola, who's just crossing the street. "I need to talk to Chief Gazzola. We can talk after."

"What's this Swedish-cop shit?" asks Manny when he and Vikström are alone.

Vikström shakes his head. He has no idea, and it worries him. He dislikes distractions and wants to get back to New London and chase down Fat Bob. There's also the unknown person—Manny calls him "the phantom"—who either did or did not signal to Pappalardo to tromp on the gas. Manny says they also need to talk to Marco Santuzza's widow, because the person who shot Pappalardo might be a friend of Santuzza's, or possibly a friend of Fat Bob's, seeking revenge. "It might even be the widow herself," Manny offers.

Five minutes later Woody Potter hurries back inside. "Let's get out of here before Pappalardo's wife shows up. She's driving down from Providence. She works up there at a hospital. I can talk to her later."

"You don't like the wife?" asks Manny.

"I've never met her, but I'm told she's upset. I'd like to avoid the emotion. Let Chief Gazzola deal with it—he's the one in charge. Unless of course you want to talk to her."

"Not right away," says Vikström. "You think that's cowardly?"

"Only sensible," says Potter. "You're out of your jurisdiction."

"Can we get something to eat?" asks Manny. "It's lunchtime."

They go to the Brewster Brew, a coffee and ice-cream shop on Main Street in a former shoe store that now has round, marble-topped tables with sweetheart chairs. It doesn't serve lunch, but there are bagels and cream cheese, six kinds of Danish, and a variety of ice-cream sundaes. Potter orders black coffee. Manny gets coffee and two Danish—glazed apple and cheese and pecan—which he decides are lunchlike. Vikström gets a banana split with three scoops of ice cream, chocolate syrup, pineapple and strawberry toppings, crushed nuts, whipped cream, and a maraschino cherry on top. This is another example of the battle raging between Vikström and his partner. He orders the sundae not because he wants it but to annoy Manny, who loves ice cream yet can't eat a spoonful without gaining weight. Vikström is thin and never gains weight no matter how much ice cream he eats. He sees it as a special gift and believes that if a person has a special gift, it's his job to flaunt it.

Jean Sawyer, owner of the Brewster Brew, brings the banana split by itself on a shiny, chrome-plated tray as if she were presenting diamonds to a king. "I want you to know you can have as many maraschino cherries as you want." Jean pauses, thinks, and adds, "Up to ten." She returns for the rest of the order.

Woody Potter watches how Manny stares at Vikström's banana split and guesses that an enmity of some duration exists between the detectives. Vikström wonders what Manny will do to get even.

On a shelf behind the counter along the far wall is a row of antique coffeepots and grinders, while over the shelf is a watercolor of an old guy in an old-timey white wig who looks like a sickly George Washington. Beneath the picture are the words WRESTLING BREWSTER, OUR FOUNDER.

"Who's the old man in the picture?" says Vikström.

"Don't ask," says Potter. He turns to check the location of Jean Saw-yer, who's behind the counter putting their cups of coffee and Danish on a tray. Potter leans forward and lowers his voice. "If you ask, Jean will spend four hours answering your question. You don't want that. It's sup-posed to be a picture of the guy that founded the town, but it's not. Jean held a contest and picked the picture of someone who *might* look like Brewster. But don't mention it. We're here on business only."

Manny and Vikström nod their heads, mildly intimidated.

Manny leans forward and whispers, "Why was he called 'Wrestling'?"

Potter looks around again; Jean is approaching with a tray. "Because he wrestled with the devil," whispers Woody Potter.

"Ah," says Manny, as if this described everything. "Been there, done that."

Jean puts the tray on the table and distributes the coffee and Danish. The tray is scratched brown plastic rather than the shiny chrome tray that supported Vikström's sundae. The three men notice this but choose not to comment. Jean hangs over the table waiting for a word to be spo-ken so she can enter the discussion. No one speaks, and soon she retires, looking disappointed.

Vikström has told Potter little about why they are in Brewster, only that it concerns the accident yesterday in New London when Pappa-lardo backed up the dump truck and how Bank Street had been closed for hours. Now he explains that a witness saw someone signal to Pappa-lardo as the Harley approached, which was when Pappalardo tromped on the gas.

The Harley, a Fat Bob, belongs to another man: Robert "Fat Bob" Rossi. And the guy riding it, Marco Santuzza, had borrowed it, maybe meaning to buy it. So it's unlikely, but still possible, that Santuzza was the intended victim. In the meantime Fat Bob has disappeared, probably because yesterday evening a green Ford drove up to his ex-wife's house and a man, identity unknown, shot up his motorcycle. Fat Bob had run out the back door and hadn't returned.

Contrariwise, Fat Bob might have set up the whole business to kill Santuzza himself, and maybe he's being pursued by Santuzza's associates. As for Pappalardo, he may have been killed by Fat Bob or by whoever signaled Pappalardo to tromp on the gas. Manny uses the word "tromp" four times and gives it special emphasis each time, making it sound drumlike.

"But it might be something else entirely," says Potter. "Santuzza might have been killed by an enemy of his own—the same with Pappalardo. Someone might have killed him who has no connection to the business in New London. Even his wife might have killed him. I mean, it's possible."

"But not likely," says Manny.

"No, not likely, but you can't rule it out. Anyway, I'm glad it's your mess and not mine."

Manny chews on his Danish as Potter sips his coffee. Vikström works on his banana split. He eats it slowly, scooping up a spoonful, staring at it briefly with a fond smile, inserting it carefully in his mouth so no drops fall on his necktie, and looking up at the ceiling with a blissful expression. This is no more than show business. As for the motorcycle business, he's already guessed that Santuzza might have been the real target. So maybe Pappalardo was killed by a friend of Santuzza's seeking revenge, or maybe by a friend of Fat Bob's seeking revenge. Did Santuzza and Pappalardo know one another? Or did Fat Bob know Pappalardo? And who was the guy who signaled Pappalardo to *tromp* on the gas?

Woody Potter has finished his coffee and pushes away his cup. "I'll get Chief Gazzola to talk to Pappalardo's connections here in Rhode Island to see if anyone has a motive and if Pappalardo knew Santuzza or Robert Rossi. And there's the guy who signaled to Pappalardo. D'you know what he looks like?"

"We're working on it," says Manny, who chooses to keep the information about the black pompadour to himself.

"How was your ice cream?" Woody asks Vikström.

The banana split, the hugeness of it, made Vikström a little ill, and he knew he'd have to skip dinner. But he gives no sign of it. "I could eat another," he says.

"And what are you going to do?" Manny asks.

"Right now," says Potter, "my wife's making spaghetti carbonara, and I have to pick up some fresh bread and stuff for a big salad. This is supposed to be my day off." Potter heads for the door. "We'll be in touch."

TEN

A round noon Connor stops in Brewster to pick up groceries on his way back from New London and then continues to the beach and the Winnebago. The sky is turning blue, the temperature is rising, and the snow will be mostly gone by morning. Reaching the gravel road to the water where he and Vaughn shoveled snow, he guns the motor and fishtails forward to the Winnebago.

Connor parks next to the gray Ford Focus, carries in the groceries, and sets them down on the counter by the sink. Eartha and Vaughn are on their phones; Didi writes addresses on envelopes and inserts creative invoices detailing the amount pledged. What makes them creative is they have borders with photographs of beagles hooked up to smoking machines. Didi also inserts a fulsome letter of thanks and a return envelope with a stamp attached to make the return easier. The return address does not say Free Beagles from Nicotine Addiction, Inc. but FBNA, Inc., which stands for one of Didi's bank accounts: Frank Bishop Negotiating Accountant, Inc. The return envelope goes to a post office box at the U.S. Post Office on Masonic Street in New London, a massive three-story stone-and-brick building. It's an example of Classic Revival architecture and already on the National Register of Historic Places. Didi doesn't like his mail going to ticky-tacky P.O.s.

Near the FBNA post office box is another post office box. So if the first post office is watched, Didi can avoid suspicion by going to the second, which contains a few picture postcards. Didi imagines that if the "watcher" sees him fussing with a mailbox, he'll think he's opening the FBNA mailbox and try to nab him. At which point Didi will show the postcards and act out what Vaughn calls "righteous inflammation." This is a subtle stratagem, but not once has Didi needed to use it. Still, it indicates how Didi plans for all contingencies. After a week both mailboxes are closed for good, and the postcards perhaps go to the dead-letter office, now called a mail-recovery center.

Didi enjoys writing these postcards: *John, Call home, Jimmy hit by tree* and *Maggie, The baby wasn't Henry's after all* and *Louis, I don't know what they are, but they're quick and they're filling the cellar.* These are a few of many messages Didi has used, and he likes to imagine the nervous narratives that his messages inspire in agonizing clerks.

It should be no surprise that Didi likes to arouse those unsettled feelings that make people peer back over their shoulders. Letting sleeping dogs lie is not him. People shouldn't get too comfy. He wants them to stop being complacent and start feeling anxious, which makes them careless in their choices. This is one of the axioms behind Bounty, Inc.: Anxiety produces better donors.

Detectives Manny Streeter and Benny Vikström also inspire disquiet. It's part of their job description, though they're hardly aware of it. It's become second nature. They work to inspire insecurity in others. It softens them up and makes them eager to tell the truth. Dread, for them, is a tool.

Connor's brother Vasco arouses disquiet as well. His skill is to make others feel lesser. When he tells a person, "You're looking better," he or she will think, *Was I looking so bad before?* After that it's all downhill.

In each case the actor (Didi, Manny, Vikström, and Vasco) puts on a persona to get what he wants, an ersatz self whose role is to make others feel reduced. The actor may also value its comic element, but the victim is just a victim.

Connor sees this behavior in Didi and Vasco; and he may have seen it in Manny and Vikström, though he met them very briefly. After all, it's part of a cop's tool kit. For the cop it's a power issue: I'm stronger than you. For Vasco, it's an ego issue: I'm better than you. But Didi feels that people will have richer lives if they worry more. It gives them something to fight against. It teaches them to take nothing for granted. It undercuts complacency.

As for Connor, he takes life at face value. He's no patsy, but he leans toward the gullible. Nor is he skilled in convincing strangers to donate money to Free Beagles from Nicotine Addiction or the Holy Sisters of the Blessed Little Feet. He throws out the pitch, and people hear the lie. So they hang up. This is why Connor was chosen to run errands. He's at the bottom of the scammer's ladder, and it shames him. So he practices little lies to get the hang of it. Remember? "I'm from Minneapolis," says Connor, who is actually from Cleveland.

"Sixty-five thousand beagles are used in biomedical research each year," whispers Eartha. "By doing nothing you put a gun to their heads."

"Have you ever heard a hooked beagle hawk and spit?" murmurs Vaughn. "Have you listened to the smoker's gurgle in their lungs?"

"If you've noticed a white, unmarked panel truck cruising the streets of your neighborhood," says Eartha, "then your Snoopsie will be next."

After putting away the groceries, Connor takes a Dos Equis from the refrigerator.

"You got a call a while ago," Eartha tells him. She wears a tight turquoise turtleneck, and again her breasts, for Connor, become armaments of the amatory.

"Who from?"

"I've forgotten. Hey, Vaughn, what was the number?"

Vaughn spits out a number: Michigan area code, Detroit-area exchange. This is another of Vaughn's skills. He's their address book.

Connor recognizes it as the number he'd called that morning: Roy's number. He calls right away. When Roy answers, Connor asks, "You learn anything?"

"You're eager, aren't you?" says Roy.

Yes, thinks Connor, *I'm eager.* "Did you get Nicoletti's real name?"

"The fellow who gave evidence is Dante or Danny Barbarella. . . ."

"And his wife?"

"There's a woman involved. Her name seems to be Céline. Maybe she's the wife. Why the interest?"

"Just curious." *Céline,* Connor thinks, *what a wonderful name.*

"She's supposed to be beautiful."

"That's true, she is."

"This Danny Barbarella is no hero. People will soon be rearrested for the second trial. Some folks want him dead. Did the feds really hide him in Rhode Island?"

Connor wonders if he's making another mistake, but at least he hasn't mentioned New London. "Just keep quiet about it, will you?"

"I could make a chunk of change with this," says Roy thoughtfully.

"What can I say? I can't afford to give you money. You really want to be responsible for his death?"

"That's okay. These aren't guys I want as friends. If you give them something, they always come back for more. So don't sweat it." Roy hangs up.

Connor sits on the couch with his beer and engages in deep thoughts, though many would call it fretting. Despite the presence of Didi and the others, he feels alone in the room. He cares deeply for Didi, Eartha, and Vaughn, but they feel distant to him. It's like caring deeply for a vaudeville act. And can he believe Roy? What choice does he have? And what about Vasco? And who's Chucky with the soft hands who showed up at Vasco's table? What is this everyday persona that people adopt in order to meet the world? They appear serious and diligent, but underneath they're probably squealing as they dash like lemmings toward the ultimate pratfall. Whoops! And what do we have in the meantime? Maybe a few kisses in the dark.

Digging his cell phone out of the breast pocket of his jacket, Connor calls Vasco. The phone rings for a bit and then goes to voice mail. As sometimes happens, Connor feels a whisper of rejection. "I need to talk to you," he says.

Again he thinks about Nicoletti. He wishes he'd never spoken to him, and now he's carrying him on his back, or at least he feels that he's hauling a heavy weight, a weight he can't put down. Connor has no particular feelings for Nicoletti, but he's concerned about his future, or rather its duration. He's concerned about being responsible for his death. And there's the wife, Céline. Now he has a name for her. Connor gets up and grabs his coat.

"Where're you going?" asks Didi.

"I've got to go back to New London."

Marco Santuzza lives, or lived, across the river in Groton, the "Submarine Capital of the World." The Naval Submarine School is there, and it's where the first nuclear submarine, USS *Nautilus*, was launched in 1954. Santuzza's house is on Godfrey, just north of Electric Boat, an older two-story house that Vikström can tell needs several coats of paint. Three cars are in the shoveled driveway. A shiny black Buick sedan has a church sticker in the rear window: ST. MARY STAR OF THE SEA.

"Looks like she's got the God boys already chatting her up," says Manny as he gets out of the car.

Vikström makes a grunting noise. His upset stomach from the banana split eaten in Brewster has been worsened by Manny's sudden swerves and abrupt stops.

The detectives stand by the Subaru and reflect on what might happen next. Because Santuzza's head was found the previous night, they assume his widow has been notified of her husband's death, though by rights they're the ones who should have first brought the news, while accompanied by Groton police. That, however, is a labor they're glad to have missed. Now they want to talk to her about Fat Bob and to get the names of Santuzza's friends. It seems like a simple enough task.

But as they proceed toward the front porch, they hear a cry: half weeping, half screaming. It builds to a crescendo and descends. The policemen have come into scenes like this often—hysterical grieving people—and they hate it, though neither has confessed this to the other. Manny Streeter hates the noise, the raw emotion. Benny Vikström hates his inability to give comfort. The door is open. They walk in.

A woman shouts, "I'll tell you one fuckin' thing, I'm not going to bury him without his fuckin' head! No fuckin' way! It's not fair!"

"Maybe we should come back later," says Vikström, "or let the Groton cops handle this."

Manny pretends not to hear him and enters the living room.

A large woman in a baby blue Mother Hubbard sits in the middle of a cat-tattered couch. This is Caroline Santuzza, and her eyes are red and damp. A young priest sits to her left with a hand on her arm. He slowly shakes his head as if once again astonished by the world's ravages. Two other women, about the same age and shape as the woman on the couch, sit in cat-tattered armchairs. Five cats are in the room, three sleeping, two prowling.

Manny introduces himself and shows his ID; then he introduces Vikström. By rights Vikström should be doing the introductions, but Manny has entered the room first. Vikström wonders if this is meant to be another rudeness.

"You found his fuckin' head yet?" shouts Caroline Santuzza.

Manny takes a step back. "We found it last night. We thought you'd been notified. The Groton cops were supposed to tell you. We're New London."

"They only told me this morning Marco'd been killed! What kind of fuckin' cops are you that it takes so long to find a fuckin' head? It's got a beard, for shit's sake!" Mrs. Santuzza begins to weep again.

The young priest gets to his feet and introduces himself as Father William. He shakes their hands. Then he winks at Vikström. "Are you one of those famous Swedish detectives I keep hearing about?"

Vikström opens his mouth but says nothing. He thinks he's being baited in a puzzling way. He ignores the priest, walks to the couch, and sits down next to Mrs. Santuzza. "D'you mind if we ask a few questions? I know this is an awful intrusion."

Vikström waits as the woman continues to weep. She has dyed reddish hair with a straight valley of gray roots down the center of her skull. It makes Vikström think of Moses separating the Red Sea. Mrs. Santuzza's cheeks are round and pink, each like half a tennis ball; when she weeps, the tears pop straight out of her eyes and drop to her lap. "Like what?" she says after a few seconds.

Vikström glances at Manny, who is poking around in his ear with his little finger. The two other women stare at Vikström as if he were a film star. "Like why was he riding Robert Rossi's motorcycle?"

This brings on another attack of weeping. "He wanted to buy it. Bob called yesterday morning and said he'd let him use it. Just to try it out, the son of a bitch."

"Fat Bob made him take it," came a voice.

Manny and Vikström turn to see a man seated in a straight chair by the wall. He sits next to a large green plant with red berries, and the detectives think that the plant must have hidden him when they first came in. The man is thin and red himself: red hair, red-freckled face, red ears, red shirt, red hands. The face is narrow and long, with high cheekbones and a long nose that looks sharp enough to cut bread. Some people resemble dogs, some people resemble monkeys, this man resembles a flame.

"Who're you?" asks Manny.

"That's Jack Sprat," says one of the women. "He's Caroline's brother."

"Sprat?" says Manny.

"It's from the poem," says the other woman. "Jack Sprat eats no fat and Caroline eats no lean. He's always been Jack Sprat. It's like a nickname."

Jack Sprat's eyes are like shooting sparks. He's gotten to his feet, and in his narrowness and angularity he resembles a bolt of lightning.

"Why d'you say that Fat Bob made Marco take the bike?" asks Vikström.

The man shows his teeth. Maybe it's a smile. "'Cause I knows what I knows."

"That's not very helpful," says Vikström.

"Why the fuck should I be helpful?" says Jack Sprat.

"What's your real name?" says Manny. "Show us your ID."

There follows a brief verbal tussle as Jack Sprat says he won't show them any ID and Manny says that he will. This ends when Manny holds up his handcuffs and says he's taking Jack Sprat down to the Groton police station.

So Jack Sprat takes out his driver's license that indicates his real name is Giovanni Lambertenghi.

Vikström and Manny trade a glance in which they inform each other that if their name were Giovanni Lambertenghi, they'd prefer to be called Jack Sprat as well. But they worry that to say such a thing might be considered an ethnic slur, and so they decide that Jack Sprat is a piece of work and they'd best ignore him.

"When did Marco pick up the motorcycle?" Manny asks Mrs. Santuzza.

"I dunno. He left here about eight. Fat Bob said he could keep it for the day, that Marco could drive it wherever. He fuckin' took it to the cemetery."

"You call him Fat Bob?"

"Everyone does: Fat Bob on the Fat Bob."

"He and your husband were friends?"

The past tense of the verb "to be" leads to another spasm of tears. Then she notices Manny's silver belt buckle with the dying Indian, and the tears come to a stop. She wipes her eyes with a dish towel decorated with prancing kittens.

"I wouldn't call them friends," says Mrs. Santuzza, still staring at Manny's belt buckle. "It's a bike thing. I guess they're friendly enough."

"And what about you—you don't like him?"

"He owes Marco money. Fat Bob gambles." She says this as she might say Fat Bob beats his wife.

"He's a fuck!" says Jack Sprat, flickering and spitting flame. "He murdered Marco! He gave Marco the bike just to get him killed!"

"You have proof of that?" asks Manny.

"I don't fuckin' need proof!" says Jack Sprat, quivering. "I just know!"

Manny meant to ask more about the gambling, but Jack Sprat has distracted him. Instead he asks, "What'd your husband do in his office in New London?"

Marco Santuzza and Fat Bob were accountants, but Fat Bob works in an office at Burns Insurance and Santuzza worked by himself, doing people's taxes and keeping track of their money. He had a small office on Bank Street. When Manny and Vikström hear this, they make quiet "Aha" noises.

"No way am I going to ID Marco for you bastards. Father William says he's in a bunch of pieces, like a puzzle. Use the DNA. Cops on the TV are always yakking about the DNA."

The Groton cops had already sent a state forensics team to Santuzza's house for fingerprints and to take Marco's hairbrush and electric razor for DNA profiling. This means less work for Manny and Vikström. By now the remnants of the body and its head have been sent to the state police forensics lab in Meriden, about an hour away. Manny imagines the happy cries of eager medical examiners as they await the brainteaser of putting Marco Santuzza back together again. Creeps.

Vikström asks Mrs. Santuzza for the names of men that her husband knew. One that comes up often is Milo Lisowski, owner of the Hog Hurrah. Vikström writes down the names of five other men.

Manny, standing to Vikström's left, says "Poppaloppa" in a stage whisper.

"That's right," says Vikström, who has forgotten. "Does your husband know Leon Pappalardo?"

Mrs. Santuzza nods, dabs her nose, and again glances at the dying Indian. "They went to high school together in Brewster. They see each other now and then, mostly for fishing. And they've been here a coupla times for dinner. I didn't like it."

"Why not?" asks Vikström.

"He's got bad breath. Smells like ripe roadkill."

Not anymore, thinks Manny.

Vikström wonders what Pappalardo's response would have been when he heard he'd mistakenly killed a friend. Surely he was angry at whoever had paid him.

The next item to ask for is a key to Santuzza's office so the police can search it, but Mrs. Santuzza doesn't have one. She does, however, have a photo, which shows Marco sitting on an antique motorcycle and grinning. She'll lend it to Vikström if he promises to return it.

Several times Mrs. Santuzza has interrupted Vikström to ask about Marco's funeral and if anything can be done about the disconnected head. Each question increases the degree of Manny's irritation. The perverted woman keeps looking at his crotch, he's sure of it. He's slyly checked his zipper, but it's shut. And he doesn't like Jack Sprat either. He doesn't like how he seems to flicker. Guys like that can go haywire in a nanosecond.

"They can stick the head back on so you'd never know," says Manny. "Put him in a nice turtleneck. As for the rest, they'll put it in a plastic bag, put the bag inside the turtleneck, and put the turtleneck inside a black suit coat. Only the top half of the casket will be open, so nobody'll see he doesn't have feet."

Mrs. Santuzza begins to wail. Jack Sprat takes a step forward. Father William sits down beside Mrs. Santuzza and takes her hand. His face has turned red, and Manny thinks he looks like an angry beet.

"You boys should leave," he says. "You're just making things worse."

As they descend the front steps, Vikström asks, "Why the hell d'you say that stuff about a plastic bag? I thought Jack Sprat was going to jump you."

"That Santuzza woman kept looking at my crotch," says Manny angrily. "Anyway, it's Groton, what's it matter?"

Belt buckle, thinks Vikström.

———

Connor is parked outside Sal Nicoletti's house. It's early in the afternoon. There's no car in the drive; the garage door is shut. Spots of melted snow make dalmatian-like patches across the yard. He thinks about walking up to the house and ringing the bell, but what would he do if someone answered?

Well, if it were Sal, he'd ask if he was really the Danny Barbarella who testified against his ex-pals in Detroit. Then he'd see how Sal responded. Next he'd tell Sal that he's probably blown his cover by telling Vasco. The very thought sends small, icy feet prancing up and down the back of Connor's neck. Sal might possibly shoot him. Connor takes his cell phone from his pocket, looks at it for a moment, and then puts it away. Minutes pass. Nothing changes, neither Sal's house nor the weather nor Connor's problem. His options are to sit here until someone shows up or to do something. He again takes his cell phone and holds it tightly. Connor can almost hear the seconds click by. He calls his brother.

Unexpectedly, Vasco answers on the second ring. "Hey, Zeco, what's happening?"

Caller ID, thinks Connor. There are no surprises anymore. "Who's Danny Barbarella?"

There's a slight hesitation. "Who's it again?" asks Vasco. People are laughing in the background, and there is some kind of music.

"Danny Barbarella."

"Jesus, Connor, you keep asking me about these wops. I don't know any of them. We're tugos aren't we? Ask me about a tugo."

"Barbarella was revenue audit supervisor at the MGM Grand until he testified against some of his fellow employees in an embezzling case. You had to have heard of it." Connor hopes if he questions his brother aggressively enough, he'll break through Vasco's mild teasing—or is it goading?

"When was this?"

"Last fall sometime."

Vasco laughs a metallic laugh. "Look, I wasn't even in Detroit last fall. I spent two months working at some Biloxi casinos."

"What kind of work?"

"Work work."

"You got pepped up when I mentioned Sal Nicoletti. You saw it as something you could sell."

Vasco laughs again. "I never get pepped up."

"Okay, so you blinked several times. Here's this Sal Nicoletti, previously Danny Barbarella, in the feds' secret witness program, and I made the mistake of talking about him to you without knowing the case. And these guys who took the money haven't even been convicted yet. They're out on bail waiting for a second trial. If you sell the information, you'll get Sal killed and it'll be my fault."

"This is a pretty complicated story, little brother. How can I sell information about Nicoletti if I don't know him?" Vasco appears to be getting bored.

Connor starts to accuse his brother of lying, but why should he expect Vasco to tell the truth? For Connor the reason exists in their being brothers, that his relationship with Vasco needs the seemingly secure foundation that truth could provide. How foolish. Vasco has always kept him at arm's length, just as he keeps everyone at arm's length. What Connor wants is a lessening of that length, that despite appearances to the contrary his brother loves him. Yet none of this, Connor thinks, has anything to do with Sal Nicoletti. It just muddies the water.

"Does Chucky know him? You might have told Chucky."

"How can I tell Chucky anything I don't know myself? You seem confused."

"Because you work for Chucky. You realized from me that Sal was really Danny Barbarella, and you sold the information to Chucky."

"Fuck you, little brother, I know nothing. Call me the next time you're in town." Vasco cuts the connection.

Connor is squeezing the cell phone hard enough to make his hand ache. He releases it and looks toward the house. Still no movement. He's angry at Vasco's apparent lie, and his feelings are hurt that his brother lied to him. Again he asks, is Sal really Danny Barbarella? But he's ninety percent sure of it. In any case, all he has to do is ask Sal the question and see how he responds. Connor's angry that he let himself get into this mess. He knows he's being indecisive, but he has no wish to walk across the yard to the door. Is he afraid of Nicoletti? Well, yes, he is. When Nicoletti learns what Connor has done, he could explode. This scares Connor, but he's still positive he should tell Sal that he's talked to Vasco. No, not *should* but *must*. The wisest thing, Connor decides, is to wait in the car till someone shows up, whether it's Sal or Céline, but he'd prefer Céline. Then he wonders if he is emotionally capable of identifying the wisest thing.

We shouldn't hold Connor's discomfort against him. He's not a cop, he's not a soldier or a private detective. He's a former schoolteacher and small-time casino employee. His one fistfight was in ninth grade, and it was broken up by the assistant principal, which was fortunate because Connor was losing. It's wrong to think he's a coward; rather, he's never been tested.

M anny Streeter gets home around nine, having spent the past five hours with Vikström seeking out men who were acquainted with Fat Bob, these being men who worked on their bikes at Hog Hurrah. The first was the owner Milo Lisowski, whom Vikström had talked to the previous day. "It's not exactly that I *dislike* Fat Bob," Lisowski said. "He owes me money. He owes everybody money. He gambles. People look for him all the time."

"Why didn't you tell me this yesterday?" Vikström had asked.

"Because it had nothing to do with what we were talking about."

The fact is, Manny had thought, Fat Bob is a loser. He used his accounting skills, whatever they might be, to try to beat the system, to win at cards, roulette, even the slots, but as he kept telling Milo Lisowski, "It needs some tinkering." *It* being his scheme.

"He says it's surefire," Lisowski told Vikström, "one that'll make him rich." His wandering eye had drifted across the detectives like a curtain in a gentle breeze.

"So it's cheating," Manny said, making a statement.

"That's an exaggeration. He calls it a technique."

Lisowski had given them the names of half a dozen men, and they talked to three of them. All said what Lisowski had said: "He owes me money." But none actually *disliked* Fat Bob. They might be angry or peeved or disappointed, but they didn't dislike him. Nor, however, did they like him.

"The problem," said one of the men, "is that I see the money as a loan and Fat Bob sees it as an investment."

It seemed to Manny that none of these guys had a motive for murder. Why kill Fat Bob when he owed them money? They might want to kill him after they got their money, but not before.

Vikström disagreed. "Someone just got sick of him, so sick that the money didn't matter."

As it turned out, neither detective was correct.

Manny and Vikström also went back to Fat Bob's little house. The police had put a seal on the broken back door, and it was still in place. But when the detectives shone their flashlights through a window in the door of the garage, they saw that one of the motorcycles was missing. There were only four.

"Is it the gray one?" Manny had asked.

"I don't remember a gray one," Vikström answered.

So that's how matters stood. And for Manny, getting home and taking off his boots in the entry, it's been a day with lots of movement but little progress. Now he's cold, wet, hungry, and depressed. What he wants most is to grab something to eat, hurry to his karaoke box, and belt out a few songs. Some people are coming later for a song session, and Manny wants to limber up his throat. His little beagle, Schultzie, is doing a welcoming dance around Manny's feet as he makes his way across the living room. "I'm home," he calls, bending over to scratch Schultzie's ears.

Yvonne is in the kitchen, and there's the sound of dishes being taken out of the cabinet. She calls out to him. "You won't believe what happened today. I gave a thousand dollars to Marco Santuzza to save beagles like Schultzie that are hooked on cigarettes. Aren't you proud?"

Manny stops so quickly that he almost steps on the dog. He's aware of five of what he might call assertions, concerning *belief, money, Marco, hooked Beagles,* and *pride.* All, to Manny's mind, are false, and he means to beat them back one by one, by showing Yvonne her mistake. His immediate problem, however (his statuelike half crouch signifies confused thought), is with which one of the five should he begin?

ELEVEN

For Fidget it was the best of days and the worst of days, the luckiest of days and the least fortunate of days. For everyone else it was simply Wednesday, which doesn't mean they liked it. At daybreak Fidget hurried out of his hutch under the I-95 bridge to make his way to Bank Street, full of expectations. Yesterday afternoon had been warmish, and it rained in the night; today was supposed to be warm without rain, so the snow would continue to melt. Few cars were out at this hour. Delivery trucks crisscrossed the downtown. Fidget's tail was for the most part somnolent, apart from sudden flips, like those of a man experiencing bad dreams as he slept.

The previous day he had spent several hours on Bank Street looking for the "wallet," a word that blinked golden in his mind, as he willed the snow to disappear. The wallet had been attached to the dead man's belt with a chain that snapped at the time of the accident. That was simple fact. The question for Fidget was, what happened next? Clearly the wallet had flown into the air, but in which direction? This was a subject that required careful thought. The problem was that the wallet had been attached to the very region of the dead man that had been ripped in half. If the wallet had gone with the lower half, it would have slid under the truck; if it had gone with the upper half, it would have bounced *off* the truck. Unfortunately, the side wall of the truck didn't present a smooth surface. Eight vertical reinforcing ribs, each about six inches wide, separated seven panels. How and where the wallet struck a rib or panel would affect the trajectory of the ricochet. And perhaps, too, the wind could have influenced the distance the wallet was thrown. Fidget pauses to think. Had there been a wind? His conclusion, at last, is that the wallet could have bounced off in any direction.

A further complication was that the sidewalks had been cleared of snow and the snow pushed to the curbs; possibly the wallet was buried within one of those mounds near where the truck had been. Fidget knew he couldn't attack these mounds with his bare hands. People would notice. The work needed subtlety. So he had borrowed a cane from the Salvation Army store by hiding it under his coat and had spent a part of the afternoon and evening digging and poking into slushy snow piles. And he had to do it cunningly so no one would ask, "Whatcha looking for?" Well, the process took longer than expected, and a few times he was indeed asked, "Whatcha looking for?" Luckily, his answer was offensive enough to send people on their way. "I'm looking for the dead guy's fingers. The accident ripped off four of them. And his balls—his balls were cut right off. If I find them, the family will give me a reward." Years of lying had made Fidget the Babe Ruth of falsehood.

In any case, no wallet was found. As for the dead man, during the morning Fidget had called him Fat Bob, but then around noon he'd learned the dead man was Marco Santuzza. Since Fidget knew neither man, it hardly mattered what name he was called, except that increasingly Fidget would shout, "Where's the fuckin' wallet, Fat Bob?" This was later changed to "Where's the fuckin' wallet, Santuzza?"

But that was yesterday. Then, during the night, the sky cleared, and when Fidget emerged from his hutch at daybreak, it was with well-rested hopes. It shouldn't be thought, however, that with all this digging and shouting Fidget had forgotten the man with the black pompadour. If the wallet was a potential gift from heaven Number One, the man was a potential gift from heaven Number Two. But on Tuesday the man had appeared only once and hurried up the stairs to his office. Then he'd hurried back down the stairs and vanished up the street before Fidget had screwed his courage to the sticking place, meaning about five minutes.

This morning the mounds along the curbs were smaller, but Fidget ignored them to explore a new idea. He'd assumed that the wallet had been thrown either forward or back, but what if it had been thrown to the side, meaning into the alley itself? It was this prospect that sent Fidget to Bank Street at the crack of dawn.

A dozen yards down the alley were two dumpsters, and it surprised Fidget that he hadn't paid more attention to them earlier, because dumpsters were like mothers to him: they fed him, clothed him, they sheltered him from the cold. So he trotted down the alley to explore their environs.

There's no point in dragging this out. He looked under them and over them, in front of them and behind them, to the right and to the left of them. Of course he found the wallet, and it was in a space exactly in the middle between the two dumpsters. Some folks argue that the nonreligious can't have spiritual experiences, but for Fidget his discovery of the wallet was definitely a spiritual experience. And if he hadn't worried about attracting annoying attention, he'd have sung a hymn.

Fidget stepped back to the wall to inspect his discovery. It would be nice to say he was abruptly changed into a rich man, one of the glorious one percent, but this was not the case. The wallet contained seventy-seven dollars. But for Fidget this was a fortune. He could stay drunk for quite a while on seventy-seven dollars and might get something to eat as well, though Fidget hated to waste his money on food. He rifled through the rest of the wallet—credit cards, driver's license, all made out to Marco Santuzza, and Fidget wanted none of them. They'd only lead to trouble. So he dropped the wallet on the floor of the alley and headed back to Bank Street. But leaving the wallet where it could be found was a mistake.

At a coffee shop two blocks farther up Bank Street toward the train station, Manny Streeter and Vikström are sitting at a table by the window, but each has turned his chair so they don't directly face one another. Manny has also turned away from Vikström to conceal his black eye. Fat chance. We don't know if this has been your experience, but black eyes are harder to conceal than bright red pimples on the tip of your nose. Black eyes also lead to questions, amused looks, bad jokes, and bogus remedies designed *not* to test your patience—you've already lost your patience—but to test your ability to keep from becoming homicidal. Whatever.

Manny is drinking tea, Vikström is trying the Postum. At eight o'clock they will meet Marco Santuzza's landlord, who will unlock the door to Marco's second-floor office and let them look around. Right now it's seven-thirty, and Manny and Vikström are just passing the time, though delicately.

"I don't quite understand," says Vikström slowly after he has kept silent for ten seconds. "What does it mean, 'hogging the mike'?" He tries to keep every trace of emotion out of his voice—that is, he sounds like a benign robot. And he also tries not to laugh, that's very important. He thinks he may have a chance to mend fences, but only if he keeps himself under total control.

Manny still sits turned away from Vikström. "What the fuck you think it means? Hogging the mike means hogging the mike. He wouldn't give it up!"

"And he punched you?"

"He punched me with the mike. It hit me right in the eye. Fuckin' broke it—the mike, I mean. We were wrestling. He said it was an accident. Cheese!"

"Cheese?"

"Jesus Christ! What's wrong with you?"

Vikström sips his Postum. It doesn't taste as good as he'd hoped, or as good as when his mom made it for him forty years ago. "Are the mikes expensive?"

"I don't give a fuck about the mike! Each person has so much time to do their number, that's never more than five minutes. Those are the rules. So after fifteen minutes I decided to take charge, and he hit me with the mike. Maybe it was an accident, maybe not."

Vikström feels he can only nod sympathetically. If he says the smallest thing, like *That's a shame* or *People can be disappointing* or *No accounting for taste,* Manny will accuse him of sarcasm.

"'Jezebel.' You know the song? Frankie Laine? Normally I like it, but for fifteen minutes? 'If ever the devil was born, / Without a bunch of horns, / It was you, / Jezebel, it was you. . . .' D'you know it?"

A guffaw sneaks its way up Vikström's throat, but at the last moment he turns it to a cough and gulps more Postum. "Can't say I do."

"I told him never to come back. You think that's too strict?"

"Well, fifteen minutes is fifteen minutes."

"Exactly what I told Yvonne."

The difficulty, thinks Vikström, is that the whole conversation could be a test. Manny might be faking it in order to lure Vikström into making a compromising statement. Then Manny would shout, *Aha! I knew you were lying the whole time!* After all, it's happened before.

Vikström doesn't care if Manny likes him, though most people like him. What is important is to have someone he can trust, someone who will watch his back and whose back he'll watch in return. He's sick of this passive-aggressive bullshit that gets less passive every day. At times Vikström thinks the Mountain Bike Patrol might be an improvement, though he hasn't ridden a bike in twenty years. Even now Manny is staring at his mouth as if expecting wickedness to leap from it. And if Vikström makes the mistake of looking at his watch, Manny will accuse him of being bored.

Yesterday Vikström spent the whole day with Manny, and after visiting Mrs. Santuzza they talked to a dozen of Fat Bob Rossi's and Marco's friends and business associates. But Vikström's request for additional police assistance had been nixed by their supervisor, who said there wasn't enough evidence to show that Marco was murdered. Until Vikström and Manny found evidence that someone had signaled to Pappalardo, the death officially remained an accident.

"You kiddin' me?" Manny had shouted. "What about the guys that shot up Fat Bob's Fat Bob?" It had been past six-thirty, and Manny wanted to get home, though if he'd known that Yvonne had given a thousand smackers to Free Beagles from Nicotine Addiction, Inc., he might have sought out a motel.

The supervisor, Detective Sergeant Maggie Masters, stared at Manny until he looked away. "We don't have evidence to show the events are related. You've already said people were chasing after Robert Rossi because he owed them money. For all we know, Rossi gave his motorcycle to Santuzza to pay off a debt."

"But some guy signaled Pappalardo to back up his truck, a short guy with a black pompadour. How many times do I need to say it?"

Again Detective Sergeant Masters unleashed her icy stare. "Yes, somebody in a second-story office claims to have seen it, but we need more proof. Really, the man could have been scratching his ass."

Manny had shivered slightly as he labored to tighten the leashes of his self-control. "What about Fat Bob's house? Can't you send forensics over there? I bet the same person broke into his insurance office."

But that, too, might be tied to Rossi's gambling debts, said Masters. If people thought Fat Bob had just been killed, they might plunder his office and house to get what money they could. After all, one of his motorcycles was missing. The detective sergeant admitted it might be useful to talk to Rossi, but he'd never contacted the police about his house, nor was he charged with anything. "All he's done is lend a bike to Santuzza. That may have been a mistake, but it wasn't a crime. As for Mr. Pappalardo, if Rhode Island wants our help, they have to ask. So far they haven't."

Manny had wanted to keep arguing, but Vikström pulled him away. He felt it fortunate that Maggie Masters hadn't told them to forget about Marco and Fat Bob.

The afternoon interviews had led to little. Yes, Fat Bob owed people money because of his gambling debts, but the largest amount seemed to be five hundred dollars, which didn't seem enough to lead anyone to murder. The description of the man with the pompadour was passed around, as was the description of the tall young man with the tan. One person thought the man with the pompadour also had an office on Bank Street, but he couldn't swear to it. And there was the chance that Fat Bob's ex-wife might have some involvement with the death, since she still held a life insurance policy on her ex-husband, though that seemed unlikely.

But the interviews went too smoothly for Vikström's taste. Some people were too affable and forgiving. He suspected they were hiding something—that is, lying about the amount of money involved. But he and Manny wouldn't be given time to check their stories. Other work was piling up on their desks. The city liked it that the Detective Bureau was understaffed. It made everyone look busy.

In the coffee shop, Manny continues to talk about his black eye and how operating a karaoke box fucks up his stress levels. Maintaining a buoyant exterior as emcee takes an emotional toll, and some ingrates and scumbags say the job of master of ceremonies should be a rotating position. Vikström gives sympathetic nods, purses his lip, opens his mouth in disbelief, and shakes his head positively or negatively, until every muscle above his Adam's apple throbs.

However, as they're almost ready to leave, Vikström spots someone staring through the big front window over Manny's shoulder. He points. "Who's that!?"

If the seat of Manny's chair had been a bear trap ready to snap shut on his butt, he wouldn't have jumped any faster. He spills his cup, his chair falls back and lands on the floor. But he doesn't turn to look. "I know your tricks," he says coldly.

"Really, really!" shouts Vikström. "It's the little red guy we saw yesterday! What's he doing peering at us? I swear he's got more to say!"

"If you think I'm going to turn around, you're nuts," says Manny. Now indignation combines with the frigidity of his reply.

Vikström is on his feet and still pointing. Then he dodges around Manny to the door. When Manny is sure that Vikström's back is turned, he takes a quick look and sees the edge of a red coat disappearing.

"Hey!" shouts Vikström, now out on the sidewalk.

Manny's impressed by how far Vikström can go with his little joke. He exits to the sidewalk. The waitress follows, waving their bill.

Looking down the street, Manny sees that Vikström has shoved someone up against a wall. The man is half a foot shorter than Vikström and wears a red-and-black mackinaw cap and a red coat. "Jack Sprat," Manny says to himself as he hurries to join his partner. The waitress hurries after him.

It should be said, however, that Manny remains confident that when Vikström pointed to the window and shouted, "Who's that?" the sidewalk was in fact empty and that Jack Sprat appeared only after Vikström jumped to his feet. Threaten Manny with splinters of bamboo shoved under his fingernails and he'll still swear the whole business is a trick. This is a problem with Manny: in the struggle between belief and reason, belief often wins, no matter what the evidence may be.

Vikström holds Jack Sprat by the collar of his red coat. "Why'd you run?" he asks with the growl he uses only for police business.

"You were fuckin' chasing me!" Jack Sprat struggles to break free, but Vikström holds fast.

"I didn't chase you till you started to run."

"The fuck you say!"

"Why should I run after you if you weren't running yourself?"

"Beats me, but I bet you got some phony cop excuse!"

We may see in this exchange Jack Sprat's own liking for belief over reason, and though Vikström can't see it, Manny's nodding in agreement. The detectives had looked for Jack Sprat late the previous day and twice dropped by Caroline Santuzza's house, but no way would she squeal on her brother. Vikström recalls that Jack Sprat's real name is Giovanni Lambertenghi, but Manny has forgotten.

Manny pushes forward, elbowing his partner out of the way. "Cut the jokes, Benny!" He turns to Jack Sprat. "Where's Fat Bob?"

The small man stares at Manny's black eye, which glistens in the sunlight. "On his way to hell for all I know. And don't expect me to bring fuckin' flowers to his funeral."

"You gonna send him there?" asks Manny quickly.

"I should be so lucky. I told you, I don't know where he is."

Vikström now nudges his partner aside and again takes hold of Jack Sprat's coat. "Why do you think Fat Bob killed Marco?"

Jack Sprat spits on the sidewalk, a silver gob that moves at the speed of a slow bullet. "Bob owed Marco a lot of money. Marco wanted Bob to give him one of his Fat Bobs, but Bob said he didn't have the title, so Marco could use it for free."

"Who's got the title?" asks Vikström.

"Angelina's got it, and for other bikes as well. And she's got the title for his house. Marco told me Fat Bob was afraid the bank would seize his shit, so he put it all in Angelina's name."

"And you still plan to kill him?" asks Vikström.

"Nah, I got over it." Jack Sprat looks down at the sidewalk.

"You sure?"

"Sure I'm sure," says Jack Sprat, grinning.

This goes back and forth till Manny asks Jack Sprat what he's doing on Bank Street. Sprat says he plans to get breakfast at a diner down the street. Why there rather than elsewhere? It's cheaper; the waitress is a personal friend; they got real maple syrup.

This keeps up until Vikström puts a hand on Manny's shoulder. "We're late for meeting Marco's landlord. Let's go."

Manny checks his watch and then says to Jack Sprat, "You're going to see us again soon."

The detectives turn and nearly bump into the waitress, who still has their check. Vikström digs out a ten-dollar bill. "Keep the change!" He'd like to make a few critical remarks about her being a nuisance, but he wants no further delays.

As they walk back, Manny elbows Vikström in the ribs. "You see how Jack Sprat stared at my black eye? It's fucking insulting. Even the waitress stared at it."

"I don't think that's right," says Vikström. "It's hardly noticeable."

"You're a sly son of a bitch," says Manny. "You're glad I got a black eye. I wouldn't be surprised if you even sent that guy to my house to hog the mike. 'If ever the devil's plan, / Was made to torment me, / It was you, / Vikström, it was you.' I know exactly what you're doing!"

Vikström's wish to protest defeats his wish to remain silent. "How can you say such a foolish thing?"

In the sunlight a multitude of delicate colors flicker across the burst capillaries of Manny's shiner. "You're good, Vikström," he says. "You're really good."

They continue to Santuzza's office. Although the day is nearly as warm as Monday, it lacks Monday's air of celebration. Few people are about. Vikström turns to see if Jack Sprat is still on the street, but instead he sees Fidget entering a diner up the block on the right. Fidget seems to scurry.

"Have you ever known Fidget to spend money on food, like in a restaurant?" asks Vikström.

"What the fuck's that got to do with anything?" says Manny.

"I was just wondering."

Santuzza's landlord, James Polanski, waits for them on the sidewalk. He's a stout middle-aged man in a blue suit, whose apparent respectability is tempered by a gray ponytail.

Biker, thinks Vikström.

Polanski steps forward to greet them, though he's mostly focused on Manny's black eye. "That's terrible about Marco, fuckin' terrible. I just saw him last week at the Hog Hurrah, and he looked great."

Manny is tired of having his black eye confused with prime-time TV. He shakes his head. "*Sic transit gloria mundi.* Now he's in a thousand pieces."

Polanski stiffens. Vikström pushes past Manny and shakes Polanski's hand. "What my partner means is, you never know what'll happen next."

Polanski remains focused on Manny's black eye as if it were the symptom of a disease he might catch. "That's true enough." He holds up a set of keys and jingles them. "I'll let you into Marco's office."

The detectives follow Polanski up the stairs. Vikström whispers to his partner, "What're you, nuts?"

"He was leering at me."

"He was only looking at your eye."

At the top of the stairs is a short hallway with a number of doors. Polanski unlocks the first on the right.

"You've other offices up here?" asks Vikström.

"Four altogether—two facing Bank Street and two the river. Marco wanted one facing the street because the trains make a lot of noise. He's paid up till the end of April, so I guess it's still his. Or his wife's. I'm not going to get used to his not being here. We rode together."

"Cowboys till the end," says Manny.

"So who rents the other offices?" asks Vikström. He kicks at Manny's ankle but misses. They enter Marco's office. On the walls are five color- ful posters of Harley-Davidsons showing scantily dressed, big-breasted women with provocative smiles and hard eyes, lolling across their black leather seats.

Polanski gestures with his thumb over his shoulder. "The guy across the hall's oldest. He moved in when my father was running things. He buys and sells stamps, does pretty well at it. Maybe I bump into him twice a year. Then there's a woman in back who's some kind of psycho- logical counselor. She's not an M.D., I know that much. She's been here five or six years and has soundproofed the whole office. The fourth guy's been here a couple of months. I'm not sure what he does—something with numbers. I'm no good with them. My wife does the books."

"Is he an accountant?" asks Vikström patiently.

"Yeah, I guess so. I mean, he counts things. But he doesn't do taxes like Marco. You'll need to ask him what he does."

Manny stares at Polanski with serious disapproval, but whether he feels actual disapproval or is just trying to intimidate him isn't clear. He seems about to speak when Polanski's cell phone rings.

"Excuse me." Polanski steps into the hall.

Vikström turns impatiently to his partner. "What's wrong with you?"

"What d'you mean?" Manny looks bewildered.

"Why're you acting this way?"

"What way?"

"Like you're a nutcase."

"A nutcase? Are you calling me a nutcase?" Manny sounds hurt.

Polanski reenters the office. "Sorry about that. Is there anything in particular you're looking for?"

A desk by the window has a computer and models of ten motorcycles—Harley-Davidson Die-Cast Collectibles—parked side by side. File cabinet, bookcase, green leatherette visitors' chairs—more motorcycle figurines are parked on the two windowsills and on top of the file cabinet. They come in all styles and colors. Manny picks up one of them. "These must be a bitch to dust. Crazy." He begins poking through the desk drawers.

"Marco's customers were mostly bikers," says Polanski.

Manny looks up. He holds an address book. "Yeah, well, I didn't think they'd be old-maid schoolteachers."

"You ever see Robert Rossi here?" asks Vikström hurriedly.

Polanski sticks out his lower lip as he remembers. "Fat Bob came up here a lot. A lot of bikers did. It was a kind of social place."

"What about Leon Pappalardo, you see him here?" Vikström asks.

"Yeah, now and then. He used to be a biker, then he got too fat. I mean, too fat even for a biker."

Vikström and Manny leave with Santuzza's address book a few minutes later. Manny wants to take the computer, but Vikström doesn't see the point—or rather, there's no evidence it would be useful. Mostly Vikström is angry with his partner about his odd remarks.

"What's going on with you?" he says. "What's this business about old maids? That guy thought you were nuts."

"Just livening up the morning," says Manny with a shrug. "Just putting some pep into the day."

"Does your eye hurt?"

"Everything hurts. The black eye is just the tip of the iceberg."

Vikström thinks, *This is more of the same. He's trying to drive me nuts.*

"As least he didn't ask if you were a famous Swedish detective," says Manny.

TWELVE

The phone calls from Bounty, Inc. begin at eight o'clock Wednesday morning. Weekends, holidays, Christmas, Easter—any day's the right day to call, says Didi. He's in a good mood and expects Yvonne Streeter's thousand dollars today.

"You should take us out to a nice place for dinner," says Eartha.

Didi gives a laugh that means there's not a snowball's chance in hell.

Vaughn, sitting in the dinette, raises a finger. "That's a conspicuous assumption," he says.

Connor opens his mouth to speak and then closes it again.

One particular call is of interest to us here, and Eartha makes it at nine forty-five. She wears a headset so she can talk and do her nails at the same time. At the moment she's applying a gray lacquer called Concrete Catwalk. She dials and listens to a phone ring, or at least what passes for a ring in the twenty-first century.

After a moment comes a suspicious voice: "Hullo?"

"Hi, Bob, I want to warn you that beagle trucks are now cruising the New London streets and your chance to save little Magsie from agonizing nicotine addiction is decreasing by the minute." Eartha's purr is a fur-lined gargle.

There's a pause; then a man says, "How'd you get this number?"

"Only the speedy intervention of Free Beagles from Nicotine Addiction, Inc. can save Magsie now. Over sixty-five thousand pups vanish into biomedical labs each year. Bob, you want little Magsie turned into a statistic with yellow lips? Just think of your duty as a beagle owner, for Pete's sake!"

The man grows angry. "How the fuck you get this number? Who is this? I know I know your voice from somewhere."

Eartha changes her tone to long-suffering patience. "Bob, what's important are Magsie's two little lungs, his happiness as a pup. The rest is beside the point. . . ."

"Fuck Magsie, that's Angelina's dog!" the man shouts. "She's got him in the divorce, and I hope I never see the little shit again. How'd you get this number?"

Eartha quickly checks her list. "Isn't this Bob Rossi? You paid good money for Magsie. You had him fixed, you had his toenails clipped and teeth cleaned, and you had his ear sewed back on when that bad pit bull next door half ripped it off. Now you want to toss him to the midnight labs?"

Connor hears the name of Eartha's prospect. He writes a note and puts it in front of her: *His name's Fat Bob.* This was mentioned in Tuesday's New London *Day* when the victim in the crash was correctly identified as Marco Santuzza and not Robert Rossi.

"I told you, that's Angelina's dog. How'd you—"

Eartha interrupts him. "D'you mind if I call you Fat Bob? It'd be a treat for Angelina if you saved her pup."

There's a pause. "I know your voice. You been on TV?"

"David Letterman's a big contributor to Free Beagles from Nicotine Addiction. In the great wall honoring our donors, your name could be next to his. Just a small donation would help. Dogs are dying as we speak. Sometimes, late at night, I hear them coughing!"

Fat Bob breathes heavily into the phone. "You're a friend of Lisowski's, aren't you? You're on *their* side. Angelina's selling all my stuff, and I don't have a cent. So go fuck yourself!"

The phone goes dead. Eartha calls back. A mechanical voice answers, gives a number, and asks if she would like to leave a message.

"That didn't work very well," says Eartha, blowing onto her Concrete Catwalk nails. "Who's Fat Bob?"

"He's the guy who was supposedly killed on the motorcycle when he hit the dump truck," says Connor. "Then the dead guy turned out to be someone else."

"He sounded both angry and frightened," says Eartha. "He thought I was a friend of someone named Lisowski. I hope he doesn't find out where we are."

"There's not much chance of anyone finding us here," says Didi with a laugh.

We need to confess that we don't really know Sal Nicoletti. That is, we can see him from the outside, see his actions, but we don't know what he's thinking. His innermost thoughts are closed to us. This can happen to the best of scribblers: some folks are impenetrable. But it doesn't mean Sal himself is a mystery. We learn much about a person from periods of attentive watching, and we've done that. And we know his real name is Dante, or Danny, Barbarella, and that he was the revenue audit supervisor at a Detroit casino who faced being charged with embezzlement until he agreed to testify against his associates, some of whom were his buddies. We could hide this information. We could watch him from the outside and ask, *Just who is this fellow?* This, after all, is what Connor Raposo has done. But why bother? Sal Nicoletti is Danny Barbarella. It's as simple as that. Many people reading mystery novels pride themselves on correctly guessing who did what before their spouses, reading the same book, can make the same discovery. We want to save them the effort. Perhaps they guessed from the start that Sal Nicoletti is Danny Barbarella. If so, well done! But it's not important. It's like raising your hand in third grade and shouting out, "I know where flies go in winter!"

But we can't see what goes on in Sal's head.

One difficulty is his expression, which is sarcastic, disapproving, and superior. We could say more about it: the curved lip, the shrug, the bored nodding of the head, the hooded eyes, and the eyebrows—one can do a lot with thick black eyebrows. They're like hand gestures; they can be used as alternative speech. We can see this, but we don't know how deep it goes. Does it rest only on the surface, or does it go all the way to the bottom? Perhaps it's only camouflage, and a nano-inch beneath the surface Sal's trembling like a puppy in a hailstorm. Perhaps, in fact, he suffers from irritable bowel syndrome and all these arrogant facial expressions are an attempt to hide the problem when what he really wants is to go to bed and weep.

Then we have his black pompadour that increases his height by three inches, while his boots or elevator shoes take him up another two. Is it arrogance or compensation? When he works on his hair before the mirror, adding the gel, a touch of extra color, and wielding his hairbrush like a boxer wields his fists, does he think, *I look fantastic!*? Or does he think, *At least I look taller?*

We may have our suspicions, but we don't know. How useful is a plastic exterior that can be cast into a thousand insinuations while the unfortunate store mannequin has to make do with what it gets at the start? We have mentioned this before with Vasco, Didi, and even our two detectives, Manny Streeter and Benny Vikström. Their exteriors conceal conflicted interiors. It resembles apophatic theology: the one truth we can express about God is that we know nothing about God. We are ignorant. But at least we know they are male. That shouldn't be doubted.

So Wednesday morning Sal emerges from the bathroom with a white towel around his waist, redolent of a Chanel cologne for men that uses synthesized human pheromones for greater sex appeal. His hair shines like a smear of tar with hints of rainbow. His teeth sparkle. Looking at him like this, we see he's somewhat fleshy. But this disappears with his compression body shirt and his high-waist control boxer briefs, which themselves are hidden by tight black spandex jeans and a white silk skintight top with body art arm stockings displaying lunging orange-and-black tigers. Stick a pin in Sal and he'd pop like a birthday balloon, but as he inspects himself in the mirror, he experiences a sense of comfort, which we may see by his smile, even though he's forced to breathe in short, quick gasps.

His black eelskin cowboy boot—a style called Los Altos—are a natural 8-B, because Sal has small, delicate feet. However, the raised platform within the shoe and the raised heel increase his height by 2.75 inches. It's a pity his black silk socks can't lift him a trifle more, but they are as thin as a vampire's sigh.

Sal turns from the mirror, pauses, and listens. The house is silent. Céline is downstairs. And the children, where are the children? At this moment the house should be reverberating with Wednesday-morning cartoon shows. But, alas, there are no children. The two we've heard discussed are in fact rentals, just as Vasco's gold Rolex is a rental. It's so much easier in the long run. They belong to a cousin of Céline's who lives twenty miles away in Norwich, a single working mother who endures their absence during the week because their caretakers are paying big bucks to create the semblance of your average American family and she needs the money as well as the free time.

Sal turns from the mirror and pauses. Is he ready yet? Not quite. Opening a burgundy leather box on the dresser, he withdraws a yellow-gold curb-link bracelet; two yellow-gold hollow-wheat-chain necklaces, a yellow-gold solid Franco necklace, and, his favorite, a white-gold chain with a hundred one-carat diamonds. Then he adds a gold crucifix pendant with a gold rope-chain necklace, because Sal likes to go to Mass on Christmas and Easter. Is he done? Nope. Sal chooses from the box two yellow-gold nugget rings and a third nugget ring with a round diamond cluster. He is especially fond of nugget rings, because they remind him of brass knuckles. They are his trademark. Next he takes a gold pinkie ring with a large ruby, and then, last of the last, he removes his watch from a green leather box: a Rolex Oyster Perpetual GMT-Master II with an eighteen-karat yellow-gold case and an eighteen-karat yellow-gold bracelet and a sprinkling of diamonds, sapphires, and rubies. It jingles slightly and slips onto his wrist like a caress.

Again Sal considers himself in the mirror. His jewelry glitters like artificial intelligence. He has rich tastes, which is why he got into trouble in Detroit. Though his position as a revenue audit supervisor came with a decent salary, Sal believed he deserved more, or at least that's how it appears to us. This is a story we've heard a million times. We ask, "What would you like, young man? What would make you happy?" And the answer? "More, much more!"

Coming down the stairs, Sal meets Céline in the living room. She wears a full-length red silk robe. Her feet are bare. Her black hair is piled up on her head.

"How do I look?" asks Sal.

Céline walks slowly around him. "No cuff links?"

"I don't feel like cuff links today. Nobody in New London wears cuff links."

"Why the ruby pinkie instead of the diamond?"

"The diamond's a little flashy. It's more of a nighttime ring."

Céline put a finger to her lips; she's deep in thought. "I know!" she cries. "You forgot your pen! Where's your pen?"

Sal snaps his fingers: a small, petulant gesture. He runs back upstairs. Moments later he returns. In one uplifted hand, he holds a Montegrappa St. Moritz Limited Edition Woods eighteen-karat-gold rollerball pen with which he likes to doodle on his monogrammed stationery in his almost-empty office. The body of the pen depicts skiers, winter trees, and deep snow.

"Perfect," says Céline.

Sal heads for the door, pausing only to grab his black lambskin jacket from the closet. He's ready to face the world: tallish, thinnish, and be-decked with gold. And where is he going, this paragon of sartorial elegance? Why, he is going to die.

Around eleven o'clock Connor sits at the stone bar of the Exchange, a bar on Bank Street. He waits for his hamburger with blue cheese, mushrooms, and tomatoes, along with sweet-potato fries. He drinks a Coke. The bar itself is made of gray stone and forms a large rectangle, about twenty feet on the longer sides, with rounded corners. The bartenders serve from within it. Connor sits on a high-backed stool on the right. To his left are large windows looking out onto Bank Street; in the back extends the broad patio facing the train tracks and the Thames.

For the occasion Connor is dressed in a gray checked suit with a vest, and he wears his Bruno Maglis, because today he represents Bounty, Inc. and he's making what Didi refers to as "pickup calls," meaning that Connor drops by the dwellings of folks who are hesitant to trust their donations to Free Beagles from Nicotine Addiction, Inc. to the U.S. Mail. So he collects the money himself. For this he must be spruced up and somewhat elegant; he must be the clinching sentence to an enticing argument. And he must be charming. Of course, his elegance is nothing like Sal Nicoletti's elegance, but it's enough. The well-presented appearance of Connor and Sal brings to mind Ben Franklin's remark: "Don't judge men's wealth by their Sunday duds." But for some elegant illusionists, every day is Sunday.

Connor pokes at the ice cubes in his Coke with a blue straw and puts a few wrinkles in his brow, connoting disquiet. Through his relatively short life, he could not be described as a worrier, but he worries today. His first worry concerns these pickup calls, about which Didi is maddeningly casual. The reason? They may end with a cop answering the door. That's because the pickup represents the moment when the generous benefactor is balanced between "Is this a scam or is this not a scam?" As Didi has explained, "It hasn't happened often, but it's happened. That's why you must look your best." And since Connor at times doubts the veracity of Didi's remarks, he tries to deconstruct the words "It hasn't happened often" as he waits for his early lunch. This is one worry.

Next he worries about Sal Nicoletti. Has Vasco sold the news that Sal is the wanted Dante Barbarella for what Vasco might call "a chunk of change"? We know that Vasco has denied knowing anything about Nicoletti, but just what does it mean when Vasco says, "I know nothing"? What's his tone of voice? How is he drawing out his vowels and enunciating his consonants? As we've said, Connor isn't a liar, but that's because he's a bad liar. Yes, he's trying to get better. Recently he's pulled off a few minor lies without blushing or having his eyes get all strange. But he's a rookie. So his attempts to deconstruct the lies of others tend toward failure.

His third worry, which may be a subsection of his first, concerns what will happen when the police throw open the door of the incorrectly assumed generous benefactor and Connor must explain that he is the lawfully employed representative of Free Beagles from Nicotine Addiction, Inc. Can he do it without falling to his knees and crying, *I'm lying, I'm lying!* Connor thinks not.

This third worry leads to further worries. He worries about his nonrelation with Céline. He worries about how he looks at Eartha's breasts. He worries about Vaughn's strange remarks. He worries about paying his taxes or not paying his taxes, which would lead to additional exercises in falsehood. And he worries about his future.

This is the trouble with worrying. It evolves from a verb to a noun. It morphs into the State of Worry, a location competitive in size with New Jersey, a place where thinking is synonymous with fretting. Worse, the worrier in the State of Worry soon transmogrifies into Worry itself. Just as Manny is Walking Disappointment, so Connor would become Walking Worry. Worry would become the center of his being, obliterating other personality traits and requiring a constant diet of small worries to stay alive, since the alternative to the State of Worry is death or expensive psychoanalysis. And this from Connor, who is generally not a worrier but worries that he will become one: a condition generated by his inability to lie. Compared to this, the weight of the world's sins on the pope's shoulders is nothing.

Mercifully, Connor at this moment receives a slight bump from a man taking a seat on the stool to his right.

"My fault, my fault!" says the man, eager to confess the obvious. He's a bulky, dark-haired fellow with a red motorcycle tattooed on his left forearm.

"No problem." Connor didn't see the man come in and realizes he must have entered through the back.

"Glad to see that snow disappearing," says the man. "How 'bout you?"

"Sure am," says Connor. "It's nice today."

"Sure is."

Such introductory exchanges are like dogs sniffing one another on meeting for the first time. Significant content is negligible.

"Fuckin' snow makes it hard to ride. Slide all over the place."

Connor emits a knowing grunt, while seizing the chance to practice deceit. "I biked over the Rockies a few weeks ago. The easiest part was when the snow came up to the handlebars, because it gave me a cushion when I skidded out."

The other man grunts, a sound signifying impressed comprehension. "You bike a lot?"

"That's the sad part. Me and a buddy were out shooting pheasant. He hit one, and it bonked me in the head. Now I've got double vision. I need a straw to drink or I miss the glass. I tried to jump on my bike and fell to the sidewalk."

A waitress in a tight black tank top takes his order. At last the man says, "I've always liked pheasant."

"That's another thing: the pheasant was full of buckshot. It broke four of my teeth. Now I can only eat soft foods like rare burgers."

"I'm a well-done guy myself," says the man. "I hate blood."

The two men work on their cheeseburgers. Connor uses ketchup; the other man doesn't. Thinking about Céline, Connor reasons that having sex with her is no more impossible than spontaneous human combustion, which means it's possible.

"What kind of bikes you ride?" asks the man.

Knowing little about motorcycles, Connor is somewhat at a loss. "My brother's a DEA agent. They seized a bunch of Harleys in boxes. He gave me a touring bike, and I put it together in my living room. I've got a third-floor walk-up, and I had a bitch of a time getting it downstairs to the street. What do you ride?"

"I like Dynas myself: the FXDF with the twin-cam engine. Got a lot of them."

Often when a person lies, he or she feels scorn for the one who believes: the sucker, the dummy, the goof. But Connor feels an almost ten-
der appreciation. After all, his lies have been accepted. The man has
offered his trust.

"By the way," says Connor, sticking out his hand, "my name's
Connor."

The man offers a fist bump, requiring hurried revision on Connor's
part. Each man's hand shows off shiny grease spots from their burgers,
and a few are passed between them when they touch.

"The name's Bob." He tosses a twenty on the bar. "See you around."
Heading toward the back, he stops to speak to the waitress, who laughs
and looks at Connor.

The biker has a bowlegged walk: vaguely tough-guy, vaguely ape.
Moments later comes the sound of a motorcycle being started. The energetic reverberation of its 103-cubic-inch twin-cam ruffles the smooth
surface of Connor's Coke.

Connor gives the waitress a twenty and asks for change. "I liked that
guy. Was he saying something about me?"

She laughs as she counts out a ten, a five, and five ones. "Fat Bob?
Yeah, he said you're the worst liar he ever met. He said your eyes sort of
rotated like. Poor guy wiped out the other day outside on the street, piled
his bike into a dump truck. Got cut into lots of pieces. But it was his
buddy instead. Right now cops are looking for him. Other guys also. It
was nice of him to drop by, all things considered. . . ."

THIRTEEN

Now we again come to one of those troublesome sections, by which we mean requiring special care. Sal Nicoletti, formerly known as Dante Barbarella, has gone downtown after his Wednesday-morning toilette. He runs several errands, but eventually he reaches his small office on Bank Street. He drives the mottled dark cherry Chevrolet Caprice, which has seen better days. At each bump his muffler scrapes the pavement, and there's a wobble to the right front wheel. Sal hates the car, but it has its advantages. For instance, he sees it as modest, which is a virtue he's been asked to demonstrate these days: modesty and humility. This is hard work for anyone whose cologne is called Égoïste Platinum.

Sal's former car back home was a custom '51 Mercury—chopped, decked, nosed, frenched, magged, with a Cadillac grille and painted a glossy scarlet with black pin-striping. Regrettably, it was blown up by his former friends, and all he could salvage was the chrome die-cast skull suicide knob with ruby-red eye sockets, which he keeps in his sock drawer in Detroit.

He parks behind a black Yukon Denali with smoked windows, which, if the world were fair, would be Sal's car and not belong to an undeserving stranger. He gets out but doesn't bother to lock the door. If you stole his Caprice, you'd be doing him a favor. He pauses to admire the Denali and then walks quickly to the street door of a two-story brick building, enters, and hurries up the stairs to his office.

If you guessed that Sal has reached the same building that contains Marco Santuzza's office, you'd be correct, except that Sal's office is in the

back and he can look out over the river. But views for Sal are just distractions. Put him in a room with drawn shades and he wouldn't mind a bit.
The office's main disadvantages are the train tracks and, more specifically, the forty trains that go back and forth each day and blast their
horns. This is an important detail.

Sal intends to make some calls and send some e-mails. He's sick of
living in New London and wants to be moved someplace else. He's sick
of Céline, and he's sick of his rented kids. So every day he calls his han-
dlers to complain. Why can't they send him to Miami, a civilized place
where it's also warm?

Now we go back outside. It's too bad that Sal couldn't take a closer
look at the Denali, but the smoked windows constitute a problem. He
assumed that the Denali was empty, but, as with many other of his judg-
ments big and small, he's wrong.

All at once the back door opens and a figure gets out. We might
know him, or we might not. His face is hidden by his hooded sweatshirt,
which is pulled down to his eyebrows. But he is big and tall and quick.
He crosses diagonally to the corner of Golden Street, steps into the alcove
of an empty store, and waits.

A minute passes, and then the front passenger door of the Denali
opens and a second man gets out. We don't know him, but along with
the rest of his clothing—khakis and a dark jacket—he wears a gray fedora and Ray-Ban sunglasses with thick black frames. Possibly we might
recognize the driver, but the front door is open just a second and we see
only shadows. In a better world, we might knock on the door and inquire, but we lack the nerve.

The man in the fedora goes to the door of the two-story building that
Sal entered and climbs the stairs. He wears black Adidas Samoa sneakers,
and we can't hear a thing. He makes as much noise as a faint sniffle. He
passes Marco Santuzza's empty office, proceeds down the hall, pauses at
Sal's door, and listens. He hears some traffic from the street, maybe a
Harley, but no more. Now the man looks at his watch. Seconds pass. He

tilts his head to listen. Ahh, a train is coming. It's the Acela Express to Boston. The man waits a few more seconds; then he quickly opens Sal's door and steps inside.

Sal looks up with an expression of irritation. He means to say, *Who the fuck are you? Get the fuck out of here!* But between the thought and the articulation of the thought, the man raises a small black pistol—it looks like a Walther PPK—and puts a .32 caliber bullet in the center of Sal's forehead. It is the same model pistol that Hitler used to commit suicide, though this particular model was made in Maine. We don't hear the gunshot; the Acela is making a racket as it prepares to stop in New London. For a fellow like our friend in the fedora, planning is everything.

Sal, or in death maybe he'd like to be called Dante, leans back in his swivel chair, and we see a modest S-curve of blood curl down his forehead. Briefly it gets lost in his thick black eyebrows, then emerges to trickle down his nose, pauses at the tip, and drops onto Sal's white silk shirt. Most of the damage exists at the back of Sal's head, but we don't want to look at that. The red mess splattered on the wall tells us enough.

As the man in the fedora approaches the desk, he takes a red plastic rose with a short green stem from his jacket pocket, and with a little fiddling he inserts it into the bullet hole in Sal's forehead. He steps back, tilts his head, and appraises his work. Not quite satisfied, he leans forward and adjusts the flower to create a symmetry of petals on the left and right sides. There, he's got it. He tucks the small black pistol back into his waistband and walks to the door. Did we say he wears gloves? He wears gloves.

N ow the troublesome section begins. Directly across Bank Street in a second-floor office is a psychotherapist who at the moment leans back in his chair, makes a tent with his fingers, and rests the tent gently in the area above his heart. He's bored. His patient, or client as they're sometimes called, sits in a comfortable armchair turned slightly away from the desk and describes an aspect of his peculiar predilection in a monotonous drone. This has taken the first half hour of a two-hour session, and the psychotherapist is not only bored, he's sleepy. But at least he has a window looking out on the street. Without it his claustrophobia would send him loping from the office. So he has seen Sal Nicoletti park his Chevrolet Caprice behind the Yukon Denali and head for the door to the stairway. The sun is bright, and what is noticeable about Sal is how the light sparkles upon his gold chains and bracelet, also the nugget rings and gold Rolex watch. But the eelskin boots are also of interest, as well as the shiny black hair and his small stature. If one is truly bored, even an ant climbing a wall can become fascinating.

The psychotherapist has seen this man with the shiny black hair a few times before, and each time the man's glittering chains and rings have drawn his attention. In fact, the gold is so noticeable it's as if the gold were carrying the man and not the man carrying the gold. But the boots and hair are competitive, as far as getting noticed is concerned. In fact, the polished heels of the boots are the last the psychotherapist sees of Sal as he disappears through the door.

The psychotherapist's name is of no significance. He'll be with us only a short time. But we know some readers like to write down characters' names as they hurry along, and so, with them in mind, we reveal that his name is Dr. Hubert Goodenough. He's forty-five, and over the years when he introduces himself to a stranger, the person will often respond by saying, "And are you?" Meaning, of course, "good enough." This has happened a hundred times and is followed by laughter, the wiseacre assuming that he or she is the first person to spot the joke. Dr. Goodenough will politely say, "Ha, ha, ha." And his laughter is laughter in the same way that toothpaste forced through a dirty sock is toothpaste. In fact, he'd like to take the wiseacre by the throat and shout that the name Goodenough was originally Godinot, a Saxon name meaning "first settler," and that it can be traced back to tenth-century England, which is to say the name's *important* and not just a joke for the unimaginative. But Dr. Goodenough's tormentors could give a flying fuck, as the late Sal Nicoletti might say, while the self-discipline to remain silent despite unpleasant stimuli has taken the doctor years of hard work, for statistics show that many psychotherapists end their careers as mental patients.

But now a man in a hooded sweatshirt opens a back door of the Denali, crosses the street, and vanishes somewhere beneath the doctor, who can only bend his head so much before drawing the notice of his patient, who continues with his monotonous drone.

Then, a few minutes later, a man in a gray fedora climbs from the Yukon Denali, looks both ways, and slowly approaches Sal's building. Later, when asked to describe the man, Dr. Goodenough can recall only the fedora; as for the rest, it was "pretty usual," though the doctor also vaguely recalls dark clothing and sunglasses. In any case, the man's walk was relaxed and purposeful, as if he were on his way to a relatively unexciting appointment, for instance to a dentist for his annual checkup. One might ask if the man with the gold and the man in the fedora are business associates, or at least Dr. Goodenough asks this. Perhaps they are even friends. He thinks about it, while half listening to his patient. Same old, same old, he tells himself bitterly, as the man in the fedora disappears up the stairs.

The patient's name is equally unimportant. We shouldn't have to bother with it. But for those whose pens are raised, his name is George Ledbetter, though he's no relation to the blues singer Leadbelly, has never heard of the blues singer, and isn't African-American. Mr. Ledbetter has been seeing Dr. Goodenough three days a week for three years, and each appointment is a double appointment lasting one hundred minutes. The doctor has only six other patients, and so Mr. Ledbetter is a major source of income at five hundred dollars a pop.

At the start Dr. Goodenough was so fascinated with Mr. Ledbetter's complaint that he was happy to spend three hundred minutes a week with him, month after month, year after year. But now it's torture, and he has come to consider himself a prostitute forced to accept the dark confusion of Mr. Ledbetter's affliction just to pay the bills. And he wouldn't be one of those glamorous and high-priced prostitutes. Oh, no. He's the one who taps on your car window when you pause at a stoplight.

Hardly five minutes pass when the man in the fedora emerges from the building and hurries to the Denali. He no longer appears calm and quickly turns this way and that, even spinning around to see if anyone is behind him before jumping into the SUV and slamming the door. Then tires squeal, and the SUV drives off faster than Dr. Goodenough thinks safe. He sighs and turns back to his patient. "But you again avoided arrest," he says, stifling a yawn.

Mr. Ledbetter is a squeezer. His compulsion is to visit the bakery aisles of supermarkets to squeeze the loaves of white bread. And sometimes he pleasures himself, sometimes he moans, and sometimes he attracts the attention of customers who may complain. Indeed, Mr. Ledbetter makes no secret of his complaint as he pleasures himself with one white loaf after another, leaving behind a mutilated trail of loaves no longer in neat rectangular blocks but as various as the shapes in a geometry textbook, because Mr. Ledbetter likes to squeeze the loaves until their plastic pops, and then he pulls up his shirt and rubs the remnants against his white belly.

But now Dr. Goodenough has turned again to the window to focus on a thin, ragged fellow in a baseball cap and a filthy raincoat hurrying along the sidewalk. Hardly a minute has passed since the man in the fedora was driven away. The doctor has seen this ragged man often, and observing him has provided hours of relief from Mr. Ledbetter as the man solicits spare change from pedestrians and slaps at an invisible appendage extending from his backside. The man, of course, is Fidget, though the doctor doesn't know his name, and Fidget zigzags up the sidewalk because it's been years since Fidget has walked in a straight line. His destination is the street door leading to the upstairs offices. Fidget grabs the handle, looks slyly in both directions, passes through the doorway, and disappears.

Dr. Goodenough finds this of potential interest, because he knows that the only person in residence upstairs this Wednesday is the man with the gold and the eelskin cowboy boots, but he doubts that Fidget and the man are friends.

Of course, Dr. Goodenough often tells Mr. Ledbetter he can squeeze his loaves of white bread in the privacy of his home, but Mr. Ledbetter likes the variety found in supermarkets. He likes to choose and exercise his free will. He likes to be seen by others and enjoys their startled looks. But Mr. Ledbetter has grown unpopular in his first-choice markets, so his selections have grown farther afield as he seeks out a market that is virginal.

If we could eavesdrop at a convention of supermarket employees, we would find that someone like Mr. Ledbetter is a hot topic. Speaker after speaker would take the stage to describe how Mr. Ledbetter first clutches the middle of the loaf until his fingers touch, then he grasps both ends and twists, and as his excitement grows and his eyes roll to the ceiling in a manner suggestive of rapture, he gently pushes each end of the loaf inward, then pulls outward, then pushes inward again, as if the loaf were an edible concertina. It is here the moaning begins as the plastic pops and Mr. Ledbetter buffs his belly with the bread bits bursting from the bag.

Dr. Goodenough has heard this often, and he no longer offers advice or asks how it makes Mr. Ledbetter feel or if he had an unhappy childhood. Mr. Ledbetter, it's clear, has no interest in getting over his obsession; he wants only to share it with an intelligent person who won't talk. So the doctor's role is simply to endure.

But luckily the doctor has his window, and soon he sees Fidget burst from the street door and fall to the sidewalk. A passerby attempts to help him to his feet, and Fidget shoves him away. His face, as we often read in novels, is a mask of terror. He drops something. It might be a yellow necklace. He grabs it and then performs a zigzag sprint down the street until he disappears from view.

Dr. Goodenough doesn't recall that specific necklace, but he knows where Fidget got it. He's also sure it wasn't a gift, because why should

Fidget run and show such terror? No, he must have swiped it, and Dr. Goodenough waits for the man in the eelskin boots to rush through the door in pursuit. But no way will that happen.

As for Mr. Ledbetter, one shouldn't think he never offers up some variation of topic. No, every session has its wrinkle, and today Mr. Ledbetter expresses a concern about his age and weight, both of which are advanced. The trouble with white bread, he tells the doctor, is that the bran and wheat germ have been removed from the flour, thus increasing the carbohydrates and lessening the number of vitamins and nutrients. In addition, to make the bread whiter, various flour-bleaching agents are added, like chlorine dioxide gas and potassium bromate. Mr. Ledbetter wonders if this is healthy. It might even hurt him. Should he stop? Otherwise he might collapse or fall down dead on the street.

The chance of Mr. Ledbetter's falling down dead fills the doctor with such pleasure that he utters a sigh. Then he sees another man at the street door to the upstairs offices, and it's the man who helped Fidget to his feet. This is someone the doctor doesn't recognize, but he's young, tanned, and dark-haired. He wears a gray suit, and the doctor even identifies his Bruno Magli shoes, because he has often yearned for a pair. This, of course, is Connor Raposo, who has learned the location of Sal Nicoletti's office and intends to confess to Sal that he has inadvertently blown his cover. It has taken Connor great courage to reach this point. It's a pity he's too late.

"Multigrain and sprouted wheat!" shouts Mr. Ledbetter, because he's noticed Dr. Goodenough looking out the window. "I need twelve-grain loaves: sourdough and pumpernickel and German dinkelbrot. But I don't like them." He says the multigrain loaves are tougher than white bread, and the crumbs get into his undershorts and itch. "They've no give, no surrender." Squeezing a multigrain loaf would be like squeezing a skinny old lady. "They lack the youthful zest. They're born stale!"

Dr. Goodenough's indifference is as weighty as a dead gorilla. Even if Mr. Ledbetter said he'd eaten toads, the doctor would only yawn. It's as if Mr. Ledbetter were no longer human, hardly mammal, and although the doctor is mildly shocked by his own lack of concern, he also feels a sense of release. Mr. Ledbetter could burst into flames and the doctor would only feel sympathy for the chair. Mr. Ledbetter stares at him, eagerly waiting for a response. Dr. Goodenough turns to the window.

He's in time to see Connor slam open the downstairs door, stumble, and nearly fall. Though his face doesn't express terror, it definitely expresses shock. He catches himself on a handicapped-parking sign, pushes his hands though his hair in unstudied frenzy, and runs down the street toward the train station.

"You're not paying attention to me, Doctor," says Mr. Ledbetter sharply.

Dr. Goodenough looks back and raises one cautioning finger. "Please shut up." He reaches for the phone. "I believe I must call 911."

It's too bad that Dr. Goodenough has turned from the window, because he misses seeing the man with the hooded sweatshirt run across the street and enter Sal's building. However, it's unlikely the man does more than take a quick look, because a minute later he emerges from the building and disappears.

Manny Streeter and Benny Vikström stand in front of Sal Nicoletti's desk and stare down at his corpse with the red plastic rose protruding from the middle of his forehead. *How disgusting,* thinks Manny. *How odd,* thinks Vikström.

"Is that supposed to be funny?" says Manny. "I don't find it funny."

"Maybe it's a kind of signature," says Vikström.

"Yeah, well, I still don't find it funny."

"Maybe it's not meant to be funny," says Vikström.

If Didi were here, he'd say the rose protruding from the bullet hole in the forehead is comic. And, if pushed, he'd add that comic is to funny what beautiful is to cute. One is not obliged to laugh at the comic. Living, Mickey Mouse is funny; dead, he's comic. In fact, Didi would say the rose in the bullet hole is tradiculous while still belonging to the middle range of event. No, no, we might argue: the manner of Sal's murder lies outside any middle range, as does murder plain and simple. But Didi says we reduce the width of the middle range to make life tolerable. We shrink it to exclude criminal behavior, perversion, cruelty, even poverty. We say those things belong to the extremes and so don't belong to us. Didi, however, is a militant generalist. He says that Orphans from Outer Space, Inc. and Toilets for the Indigent Left-Handed, Inc. are also part of the middle range and deserve our attention. After all, that expanded middle keeps him in business, just as it keeps Manny and Vikström in business.

Perhaps Vikström is correct and the rose is a signature. No doubt that it is the focal point of the entire room. It even seems to take precedence over Sal Nicoletti's dead body, and it is difficult for the detectives not to stare at it. Manny and Vikström don't know Sal, nor have they heard of Dante Barbarella. But they recognize Sal from the day of the accident, and he was someone they wanted to talk to. After all, he was suspected of giving the all-systems-go sign to Pappalardo to tromp on the gas and send his truck into the path of the onrushing Fat Bob motorcycle, ridden by Marco Santuzza. So he was more than a person of interest. But they have yet to instigate a serious search. They hadn't gotten around to it. Busy days can be like that.

Manny remembers something else about Sal from when he'd noticed him at the accident. He'd been wearing a number of gold chains.

"Where's the bling?" he asks.

Vikström wears rubber gloves, actually cheap plastic. He moves forward and steadies the corpse with a hand on his shoulder. Then he checks Sal's pockets.

After another moment he straightens up. "Where's the wallet?"

Dr. Goodenough has given the detectives a full description of what he'd seen: first it was Sal Nicoletti, then a man wearing a hooded sweatshirt had gotten out of the SUV and walked away, then came the man with the fedora, next came Fidget, and lastly came Connor Raposo. Sal Nicoletti had never emerged. The others had run from the building "like their tails were on fire," the doctor said. He also said that when Fidget fell, he'd seen a flash of color in one of his hands like a yellow chain.

"Fuck me," Manny says, "Fidget's got the bling."

We said earlier that this Wednesday was for Fidget "the best of days and the worst of days, the luckiest of days and the least fortunate of days." The moment before Manny said, "Fuck me, Fidget's got the bling" was the highest point of Fidget's good fortune. Now it descends.

"And the other guy," says Vikström, "the one with the tan and wearing the gray suit. The one with expensive shoes. He's the guy who was talking to Nicoletti after the accident."

The detectives are pleased to make such quick progress. As for the fellow with the fedora, for the time being they don't wish to think about him. The trouble with wearing a fedora and heavy black Ray-Bans is that they will be all a witness remembers, which was probably the point of wearing them.

Lost in this excitement is the man who got out of the Denali and walked away. Dr. Goodenough said the man had crossed the street and disappeared somewhere beneath him. But perhaps he didn't walk away.

The detectives remain in Sal's office or out on the street until the body is removed. One of the forensics guys takes the rose from Sal's forehead, and he is criticized for this, but of course there are pictures. Much time is spent seeking out fingerprints. This, basically, is a waste of time, because none will belong to the man in the fedora. The wall behind Sal's chair is a wide splatter of blood and tissue, which leads Manny to say that the killer used a hollow-point bullet. He then digs it out of the wall with a penknife and shows Vikström how it has mushroomed. The bullet is a metal dollop. The shell isn't found.

In the file cabinet are phone books, empty manila folders, and receipts that may show how Sal was spending his time. The computer is taken to police headquarters. In the belly drawer of the desk is a small pile of porn magazines, a box of tissues, a deck of cards, a pack of peppermint-flavored sugarless gum, and a few bills from Sal's landlord and the phone company (Verizon). Manny calls the landlord, telling him to come to the office. The other drawers contain only dust.

Manny and Vikström, with other police officers, talk to clerks and store owners up and down the street. A number of people saw the Yukon Denali, but they didn't pay attention to the license plate. One said it was from Massachusetts, another said from New York, another from Rhode Island, others from Connecticut, New Jersey, and Kansas. People also saw the man with the fedora and dark glasses—or rather, they recalled the fedora and nothing else except that the man was "average-sized" and perhaps wore dark glasses. One claimed it was a woman.

Many recalled Sal, who'd eaten in the restaurants and cafés or just walked around as if he had nothing to do, which, given the contents of his office, was probably the case. But no one talked to him—or at least did more than exchange brief remarks. Sal made it clear he didn't want to chat. In fact, he was unpleasant. But some also recalled the gold chains and the bracelet and rings. "Showing off on Bank Street," says a man. "What a jerk." No one saw him signal to Leon Pappalardo to drive backward, other than the lawyer who told Manny about it on Monday.

Many also knew Fidget, and five or six say they'd seen him on the street that day. One disagreeable man says it would be good for everybody if Fidget were put in jail. The panhandling lowered the tone of the street. "And what tone is that?" Manny asked. But the man had no answer. Police are on the lookout for Fidget and patrol cars are actively searching.

No one recalled the young man with the tan, but that changes when Vikström reaches the shoe-repair shop, where the cobbler recollects the Bruno Maglis. As for their owner, he was young, moderately handsome, and had a tan. He was also driving a small blue car, which had been blocked from leaving after the accident. Oh, yes, he had a claim ticket for the shoes: Connor Raposo, but no address or phone number. The cobbler also recollects that it was a rush job and the shoes were only brought in the previous Saturday. The man was from out of town and would be leaving again soon. "How far out of town?" asks Vikström. Maybe from California, says the cobbler. Maybe San Diego.

Reporters and TV people start arriving, and the crowd near the ambulance increases. Manny sees a red-and-black mackinaw, but not the face of the person wearing it. Does he guess that it's Jack Sprat? Maybe. The detectives stay quiet about the red plastic rose planted in Sal's skull. The information would create too much excitement, which makes for an atmosphere the detectives dislike.

FOURTEEN

In the afternoon Manny and Vikström drive over to Sal Nicoletti's house. They have gotten the address from Sal's landlord for the office. They need to tell Céline that her husband is dead. The passing on of such information is a job they never look forward to, and recently with Mrs. Santuzza's hysteria and Fat Bob's ex-wife's venom they've had enough of that business to last a while.

They arrive at the brick ranch house on Glenwood Place around four o'clock and trudge up to the door. Each waits for the other to knock, then they reach out together, then Manny pulls back and Vikström knocks. They wait. Then Manny knocks. The street is quiet except for a barking dog.

When the door opens, Manny grins at Vikström as if the knocking had been a competition and Manny has won. But then they focus on Céline, who stands before them in short shorts and a black T-shirt. Her jet-black hair hangs loosely over her shoulders. She doesn't speak or make any expression. She just waits.

Manny and Vikström show her their ID. "I'm afraid we need to talk to you," says Vikström.

Still without speaking, Céline turns, and the two detectives follow her into the living room. It's not as if Manny and Vikström need to stare at her ass and legs; rather, there seems to be no other place to look, and looking feels both energizing and restful. *Tarty*, thinks Manny. *Stunning*, thinks Vikström. In both there arises a sense of melancholy, as if Céline's backside gave witness to what they have missed in life.

Céline turns to face them. "So how can I help you?" She's taller than

Manny but not as tall as Vikström. She doesn't sit down, nor does she invite the detectives to sit down. The living room is attractive but uninspiring: beige carpet, beige couch, beige armchair, and an ocean scene with sailboats over the mantel. Soon the detectives will learn that every bit of furniture is rented, but at the moment they believe it represents Céline's aesthetic choices, and they find them disappointing.

"I'm afraid we've bad news for you," says Vikström. "Your husband was killed earlier today. He was shot. We're terribly sorry."

Céline's impassive expression doesn't change. Maybe her dark eyes open a little wider. She walks to a red leather purse on a coffee table. "At least I can now smoke in the house," she says over her shoulder.

The remark strikes Vikström like a blow. He glances at Manny, who shrugs. Céline lights her cigarette with a silver lighter, inhales deeply, and then blows the smoke toward the ceiling. She wears bright red lipstick, which makes her wide mouth seem even wider.

"You'll have to identify your husband's body," says Manny. To himself he calls her one tough cookie. The description opens a door in Manny's head. Behind it waits his disappointment. Beautiful women disappoint him, insipid rooms disappoint him, and Céline's answer disappoints him. He glances around for other things that disappoint and finds no shortage.

"He wasn't my husband," says Céline.

Manny and Vikström raise their eyebrows in unison. "Your partner, then," says Vikström.

"He wasn't my partner. He wasn't anything. The whole business is a sham. Anyway, it doesn't matter now. But I'll identify the body. My pleasure."

Vikström ignores the possible pleasurable aspect of identifying Sal's body. "What do you mean, 'a sham'?"

"The house is rented, the furniture is rented, the dishes and silverware are rented. Sheets, blankets, rugs, lamps, TV, Internet, cars—it's all rented. Even *I'm* rented, and also the kids and little dog. It's a sham, like I said."

"But you were living with him," says Vikström.

"But he didn't fuck me. He even offered me money, and I didn't let him fuck me. He was disagreeable, and he slapped me once. I don't allow that."

"What'd he slap you for?" asks Manny.

"He caught me trying on his gold bracelet. He accused me of planning to steal it. It was too big for me anyway. I found him repellent."

"Didn't he have any good qualities?" Vikström feels mildly sorry for Nicoletti.

Céline smiled. It was her first change of expression. But it wasn't a friendly smile. "He could make a good omelet." She stubs out her cigarette in a green glass ashtray on a table by the couch. The filter is bright red from her lipstick.

"Jeez!" says Manny. He sits down on the couch. Fuck the invitation! He didn't need an invitation to sit down.

Vikström sits down to the left of Manny, whose arm rests on the back of the couch. For the first time that day, Vikström sees that Manny is wearing a Swiss Army watch with a white face, red bezel, and a black rubber strap. Without needing to look closer, Vikström knows that the model name is Maverick II. He knows this because he wears exactly the same watch. He's positive that Manny has purchased the watch to annoy him.

"So what's this all about?" asks Manny gruffly.

Céline runs a hand through her black hair. Then she shrugs. "The FBI put us here because Danny has to appear in federal court in Detroit in about a month. They thought he was in danger, so they invented this whole charade: the happy American family. I guess they didn't watch him closely enough."

Manny and Vikström feel a sense of liberation. It will be the FBI's job to find whoever shot Sal Nicoletti. Manny and Vikström will be no more than domestic help. If they weren't policemen, they might giggle with pleasure.

"Why d'you call him Danny?" asks Vikström.

Céline remains standing. "Because that's his name: Danny or Dante

Barbarella. He had a job in a Detroit casino. The FBI changed it temporarily to Sal Nicoletti. Danny liked it. He thought it was classy."

They ask if Danny had any friends or acquaintances in the New London area. No. Do they know their neighbors? No. Did he invite anyone
over to the house? No. Then Céline raises a hand.

"A man drove him home from downtown on the day of the accident,
but he didn't come into the house. And he came back yesterday looking
for Danny, but Danny wasn't here. He said his name was Connor. He
drove a blue Mini-Cooper."

"What'd he look like?" asked Manny.

So Céline described Connor Raposo: handsome, mid-twenties, dark
hair, dark eyes, straight nose, narrow face, tall and thin. "And he had a
tan," Céline adds.

Who is this fucking guy with the tan? thinks Manny. "Anything else?"

"Danny said he asked too many questions. And he kept looking at
me. He liked what he saw." She says this without expression.

Céline stands above the two detectives with her hands on her hips.
Her black T-shirt seems too small for her. Maybe it shrank in the wash.
With her black shorts and T-shirt, Manny thinks she looks like a sexy
ninja.

"I bet," said Vikström. "Was he rude or anything?"

"He was fine—just a polite guy working up an infatuation."

Manny and Vikström are quiet as they think about that. *Strumpet,*
thinks Manny. *Still gorgeous,* thinks Vikström.

"He ever get any phone calls?" asks Manny.

"Not really. Well, he got one Monday night. I answered Sal's cell
phone. I thought he was going to slap me for that as well. He didn't like
anyone calling him. The man said his name was Leon. When Sal took the
phone, I could hear this guy yelling at him, but I didn't hear any specific
words."

"Did Sal say anything?" asks Vikström.

"He kept saying it was an accident, that it wasn't supposed to happen.
I didn't know what he was talking about."

But Manny and Vikström knew what Leon was talking about, and the next day Leon was dead.

"What about his office?" asks Manny. "He say anything about people in the offices next to his?"

Céline thinks for a moment. "He mentioned the man in the front office. He called him Marco."

"What did he say about him?"

"Same thing he said about everybody. He called him a jerk."

"He's the guy who was killed on Monday. Did he mention that?" asks Vikström.

Again Céline's eyes widen slightly. "He didn't say anything about it. I heard it on television."

"Sal wear much jewelry?" asks Manny. "Someone saw a homeless guy come tearing out of the building and drop a gold chain on the sidewalk."

"Was Sal wearing any when you found him?" asks Céline.

"Nothing at all. Even his wallet was missing," says Vikström. "That's why we thought the homeless guy might have taken more than a single chain."

Céline lights another cigarette. "Sal wore some, but nothing too flashy. A couple of chains, a couple of rings, perhaps the gold bracelet I mentioned."

"Someone said he wore a Rolex," says Vikström.

Céline laughs her humorless laugh. "Yes, he got it cheap. He liked to brag about how cheap. It was made in China."

"Is there other stuff still in the house?" asked Manny.

"Not much. Maybe some cuff links. He usually wore what he had. Maybe there's another chain, I don't know."

Vikström isn't sure she's telling the truth. "And that was it?"

"As I say, he didn't want to call attention to himself."

Manny decides to change the subject. "Why'd you agree to come out from Detroit?"

"The money was good. I needed the money."

"What's that make you?" asks Manny. "Living out here with a guy for money."

"Practical," says Céline with a straight face.

Manny and Vikström consider this. Both have conflicting ideas about the word "practical." Manny thinks, *Gold digger.* Vikström thinks, *Provident.*

"Anything else before we go downtown for the ID?" asks Vikström.

"There's something I'd like you to take with you. I don't want it in the house." Céline leaves the room.

"For Pete's sake," says Vikström. "You practically called her a whore."

"So what? She didn't blink. I bet she's turned tricks for cash in her time."

"Watchit!" shouts Vikström.

Manny and Vikström leap upward from the couch with their hands on their weapons. They move surprisingly quickly for middle-aged men.

"Fuck me!" says Manny. "She's going to kill us!"

Céline has reentered the living room carrying a pump-action shotgun loosely in her left hand.

Vikström shouts, "Drop that immediately!"

Manny has drawn his Glock 22 and hopes he won't shoot himself in the leg.

Céline slowly puts the shotgun down on the rug and steps away. "Danny had that. I don't want it in the house."

"Where'd it come from?" asks Manny. He can see it's a Winchester 1200 with a twenty-inch barrel. He used to have one at home but sold it when he was building his karaoke box.

"Danny brought it from Detroit in case someone came looking for him."

The detectives have a sudden image of the rose sticking out of Sal's forehead. Vikström takes a handkerchief from the breast pocket of his jacket and picks up the shotgun. He sniffs the barrel. "It's been fired not long ago."

"Poppaloppa," says Manny. "That Rhode Island statie is going to be as happy as a pig in shit. What was his name? Rocky, Rocky something."

"Woody Potter."

"You sure it wasn't Rocky?"

"Positive."

"Rocky, Woody, what's the difference? We solved his case for him."

Vikström doesn't want to agree, but he sees no reason not to. He turns to Céline. "I guess we don't know your last name."

"Gaurige."

"Is it Greek?" asks Manny.

"Greek enough."

Neither finds this a satisfactory answer.

"Okay," says Manny. "Grab your coat. We're outta here."

It may be easily understood that when Connor Raposo fled Sal's office after seeing his corpse with a red plastic rose emerging from its forehead, he was not at his best. Shock, panic, and fear wrestled for emotional domination, while guilt, regret, and shame—the smaller fellows—jumped up and down to be noticed. If Connor were a Navy SEAL, he could laugh it off, but the closest he has ever come to a military connection was fifteen years ago when he was a Cub Scout. Once on the sidewalk, he knows that if he runs, he'll attract attention, but his hurried walk is on the cusp of a gallop.

The Mini-Cooper is parked twenty yards up Bank Street just across from the Exchange, where Connor had lunch and talked to Fat Bob, not knowing he was Fat Bob. On his way to his car, he passes several mildly startled people to whom he gives a rictus grin and gasps, "I'm late, I'm late."

Connor drives quickly to the granite-and-brick post office four blocks away, pulls in to a parking slot, cuts the engine, and rests his forehead on the steering wheel. Having a dozen thoughts clamoring for your attention is like having a dozen big people trying to crowd into an already crowded elevator—that's how it seems to Connor. He wonders if he can think himself into oblivion, but his temporary parking space is only good for fifteen minutes. Still, he attempts to regulate his breathing.

We've already said that Connor has had no experience with the rough side of life: guns, gangsters, and brutal behavior. This, for him, is TV stuff. It's beyond the pale, meaning on the other side of the fence. But what is this fence? Most likely it means beyond the middle range of event that Didi often talks about. In Didi's expansion of the middle range, Sal's murder fits as nicely as a pebble in a pig's snout.

But Connor isn't interested in nihilistic philosophies. In the past few days, many appalling images have shouldered their way into his brain. And how can he make sense of them when their sensational aspects disrupt what he calls his rational thinking?

Yet when a brief gap occurs in his confusion, like a bit of blue sky among a mass of clouds, all he can think is, *I've caused this!* He's sure Sal is dead because of what he told Vasco. And Vasco then sold the information. How simple. Connor had been unable to keep his mouth shut because he wanted to impress his fucking brother! As he thinks this, he slowly bumps his head against the steering wheel, but not hard enough to be painful. It's not pain he wants; it's new thoughts. This is Connor's education into the dark side, and future lessons will inform him that Sal's apparent two children are rentals and his wife Céline is not his wife but a high-priced escort. That's the trouble with education: it keeps bullying us with further unwanted information. No wonder political conservatives want to close the schools. Their wish is for a pre-Snake world, to return to those happy days of scratching one's balls. Good fucking luck, as the late Sal might say.

But Connor can't just sit in the Mini-Cooper bumping his head on the steering wheel. He has to retrieve the envelopes stuffed with checks from the FBNA, Inc. mailbox and get back to the Winnebago. It's a pity those times when we're called upon to think most clearly are also the

times most rife with commotion. Because Connor is afraid to go into the
post office and get the mail: he's afraid it's being watched. Other people, too, are entering and leaving the post office, and Connor could slip
among them as inconspicuously as a single crow among a murder of
crows, but he's sure that the moment he opens the door, a heavy hand will
land on his shoulder. So now he'll spend further minutes with his head on
the steering wheel as he tries to separate his tangle of thoughts and emotions, which is like peeling soft tar from a sidewalk with your fingernails.

No telling how long he might sit like this, but after another minute
comes a gentle tap on his window, which shoots boiling adrenaline
straight out of Connor's ears, metaphorically speaking. Turning his head,
he sees a pretty young woman standing in the street wearing a concerned
expression. Connor, in his present paranoia, thinks she must be an un-
dercover cop, but then clarity of mind reasserts itself and he lowers his
window, although slowly.

"Are you all right?" The young woman has a gentle voice, and her
blue eyes brim with sympathy through wire-framed glasses.

We should say that we don't believe in angels, nor are we acquainted
with this woman. We can only say that she performs an angel-like task.

Connor raises his head. "Just a little tired," he says.

But the woman doesn't believe him. After all, he's a dreadful liar. "Do
you need a doctor? Or perhaps a drink of water?" The sun is behind her,
and her short, spiky blond hair radiates color. She takes a bottle of water
from her backpack—these days all young women carry bottles of water—
and offers it to Connor.

He is still dazed, but he sufficiently knits himself together to reach
for it. Taking the bottle, he brushes her fingers with his own. He un-
screws the top and drinks. We wish we could say it's a magic elixir, but
it's only water. Connor takes another drink and tries to hand the bottle
back to her.

"Keep it," she says. "I have more."

"You're wonderful," says Connor.

Maybe she blushes. With the light behind her, it's difficult to tell.

"Are you okay? Did you have an attack? Why were you banging your head against the steering wheel?"

Connor wants to say he'd been struck a near-fatal blow by the world's ugly complexity, but instead he says, "I guess I've no good reason for that. But I'm fine now. Thank you for the water."

She smiles. "Then I'll be on my way."

Connor's knot of contorted emotions doesn't disentangle itself on his drive back to the Winnebago, but the strands loosen to the extent that they can join together without squabbling. The Latin term *morsus conscientiae* doesn't begin to describe his feelings, but he can only beat himself on the head for so long. What can he do to make it up to Sal? Nothing. Perhaps he could take care of Sal's wife and kids for the rest of his days, but he sees under this good idea a bad idea struggling to get out. The only one Connor wants to take care of is Sal's wife, Céline. And with this understanding, Connor's guilty feelings return, while beyond these feelings he sees Céline, a beautiful woman standing on a farther shore. If Connor were a drinker, he'd drink himself into oblivion. If he were a flagellant, he'd beat himself silly. But he's a relatively normal man with an average number of strengths and weaknesses. We, of course, like him, but we're prejudiced.

He parks behind the Winnebago, gathers the many envelopes taken from the mailbox, and gets out. The gray Ford Focus rental is gone. The sky is partly cloudy, and a stiff breeze blows clouds to the east. The ocean is choppy with whitecaps. A few gulls ride the thermals. Connor wants to wrap himself in a blanket and lie on the beach until the tide drags him away, but he knows that's impossible.

Walking to the door of the Winnebago, he finds Vaughn sprawled on the ground, fussing with the shells of eight horseshoe crabs arranged in a circle on the dead grass. "What's up?" says Connor.

Vaughn doesn't look at him. "I'm arranging crushed Asians."

Connor doesn't stop to talk, but he's glad to be back in the world of ordinary madness. Inside, Eartha plays solitaire on the dinette table. She's topless and wears only a pair of shorts. When she looks at him, her breasts swing in a gentle arc. Connor is positive he hears a faint whoosh as they pass through the air.

"Want to play gin rummy?" she asks.

"You'll have to put on a bathrobe." Connor stacks the envelopes on the kitchen counter. "Vaughn's outside crushing Asians."

Eartha grins. "At least he's happy." She wiggles her shoulders in a mild shimmy. "I thought you liked my tits."

"It's not a matter of not liking them. I told you, they're distracting."

"And I said that's their purpose. I sure didn't get them built up for reasons of health. Here in this damn Winnebago, they just get wasted—visually, I mean."

Connor looks at them quickly and looks away. "A guy I know was killed today. He was shot in the head. I found him sitting at his desk. Somebody had shoved a red plastic rose in the bullet hole. I think the whole thing's my fault."

Eartha puts a hand over her mouth. "Is that true?"

"I can't stop thinking about it. He was in some kind of witness-protection program. I didn't know that, and I told my fucking brother about him. I feel sick about it. It's like I shot him myself."

Connor hadn't meant to tell Eartha; now he tells her almost out of malice to take the attention away from her breasts. Bad news reduces their drama. He also wants another person to share the weight of his knowledge.

"His name's Sal Nicoletti. I mentioned giving him a ride from the accident the other day. He's got a beautiful wife and two little kids. I feel like something inside me's about to pop. It just presses against my gut."

Connor goes to the couch that folds out into his bed. He imagines being in the bed all folded up like the ham in a ham sandwich. He envies inanimate objects.

Eartha puts on a bathrobe and comes to sit by his side. "Did you see the person who shot him?"

"No. I went to Sal's office to talk to him, and he was dead. Nobody else was around except a homeless guy. I can't get that fucking flower out of my mind. I can't get any of it out of my mind. It just goes round and round."

Eartha puts a hand on Connor's brow. It feels cool to him.

"Do you want a drink? Didi's got some whiskey."

"No, thanks. A girl downtown gave me a bottle of water. It was nice of her."

"You want to go in our room and try to sleep? You can shut the door, and I'll be quiet."

"Maybe I'll try it." Connor gets to his feet and looks down at her. "You're a good person. I appreciate it."

Eartha gives another little shimmy with her shoulders. "I'm only a good person some of the time. Other times I can be a monster." She stands up and gets a glass from the cupboard. "Just a small glass of whiskey. It'll help."

Five minutes later Connor is lying on the big bed in the bedroom. He's taken off his shoes and finished his whiskey. The room reeks of sex. It's like a colorless, ectoplasmic blob suspended in the air, something the size of a hippo. Connor is positive he'll never go to sleep. Then he goes to sleep.

It's dark when Eartha wakes him. He has no idea of the time.

"You've got a phone call. It's a woman."

Connor scrambles out of bed. "Is Didi here?"

"He's not back yet."

Connor is sure it's the young woman who gave him the water. But he's wrong. It's Céline.

"Are you busy? Can you come over here? Can you come right away?"

FIFTEEN

Fidget sits cross-legged on a cheap blue poly tarp, which is the floor of his hutch. Another poly tarp forms the roof. The sides are cardboard reinforced by two shopping carts. A concrete bridge abutment forms the back. "Temporary lodgings" is what he calls it, because soon the police will demolish it or another, stronger, meaner bum will take the pieces for himself. Lots of unpleasant things can happen under the bridge, so he'd never think of it as home. That's just tempting bad luck.

Next to Fidget sits his Terror, and his Terror explains in its hoarse voice that Fidget has overreached. His Terror sits beside him because it's so big that there's not enough room for it in Fidget's interior. His Terror tells Fidget that he's endangered himself by being greedy. First there was the seventy-seven dollars in Santuzza's wallet. That was okay. Like, who'd ever know? Then there was the hundred twenty-six dollars in Sal Nicoletti's wallet. That was less than okay, but it wasn't terrible. It wasn't overreaching so much as stretching, the kind of stretch that can give a little cramp. But he should have been satisfied with the two hundred three dollars and quit while he was ahead. Who tells him this? His Terror tells him this. In fact, his Terror has been telling him lots of stuff and all of it negative—that is, it's terrifying.

On the surface of the blue poly tarp within the small well formed by Fidget's crossed legs lie five gold chains, three gold rings (one with diamonds), a gold pinkie ring with a large ruby, a gold bracelet, a Rolex Oyster Perpetual GMT-Master II watch with an eighteen-karat yellow-gold case and eighteen-karat yellow-gold bracelet, plus a sprinkling of diamonds, sapphires, and rubies. Anything else? Oh, yes, a Montegrappa St. Moritz Limited Edition Woods eighteen-karat-gold rollerball pen. Why couldn't Fidget have stopped himself? his Terror asks. What was he thinking? His Terror can easily count off the names of twenty men and several women who'd murder Fidget for only one of the gold chains. Fidget calculates that he has twenty thousand dollars' worth of jewelry. In point of fact, it's closer to five times that. Sal Nicoletti or Dante Barbarella carried his value on his exterior. His interior was worth about two cents.

A few minutes earlier, Fidget had put on the watch, the bracelet, the rings, and chains. Then, on a rumpled paper bag, he drew a smiley face with the Montegrappa pen. Momentarily he felt like a million bucks. Then his Terror took over. Two of the big nugget rings were on his right hand, and the one with diamonds was on the left along with the pinkie ring. Otherwise Fidget's hands were smeared with dirt and grease; black crescents of filth topped his fingernails. It formed a nice contrast. He was moronic, and his hands were oxymoronic. Fidget had hurriedly removed the jewelry and put it in the well formed by his crossed legs. Then he shivered a little.

What can Fidget do with the bling? Can he sell it? No. Can he pawn it? No. Can he trade it for a Cadillac car? No, no, no! The very first proof of its existence will get him killed. Or perhaps the cops will guess who it belonged to and beat the shit out of him. That would be the softer, gentler way. But Fidget is fragile. Even a mild beating would finish him off. And if he *did* manage to survive it, he'd land in prison, where he'd have to lick the toes of the tough guys. What was he thinking? But the very chance of having the gold had driven him crazy. Gold is like that: it drives you nuts. So it isn't his fault; it's the gold's fault. It made Fidget overreach himself. Gold has had a long and brutal history as the causative factor in that area of human experience.

As Fidget stares at the gold, his Terror explains that he must hide it and hide himself. The best idea would be to return it, but that idea is too painful even for his Terror. Anyway, who can he return it to? Sal's dead.

And Fidget can't stand the thought of the nugget rings leaving his hands and finding a home on another's. So he has to hide the gold and he can't hide it in his hutch.

It seems to Fidget that he now has a plan. In fact, he has only the shadow of a plan. He scoops up the gold, puts it in his pockets, and crawls out of his hutch. As for his tail, he doesn't have time to think of his tail, but it droops along behind him.

Manny Streeter and Vikström are back in the Detective Bureau's office at police headquarters: a bunch of scratched desks and wobbly chairs, light green walls, dusty fluorescent lights that hum. The sun has gone down, and the building is quiet. They've learned that Rhode Island has called the Detective Bureau to say the shotgun that killed Pappalardo was likely the same gun that Céline gave the detectives, though further tests need to be done. Manny and Vikström have expected this, but when confirmation came from the Rhode Island cop, Woody Potter, the New London detectives feel all the satisfaction found in finishing a good meal. And what's for dessert? Mrs. Pappalardo also told Potter that her husband and Marco Santuzza were friendly and sometimes hung out together, which corroborates what Mrs. Santuzza said. This, to Manny, feels like progress.

Manny and Vikström have also learned that forensics has found matches for the fingerprints in Sal's office. One set belongs to Céline, which is worrisome since she said she'd never visited his office. On the other hand, falsehood is familiar to the detectives. It comes with the job. So even though they hadn't expected a lie, it was almost as if they *had* expected one. In their world everyone lies.

But it seems unlikely that Céline had shot Sal. It had been too good a shot, and the red plastic rose didn't feel like Céline. It was tacky; she's not tacky. But neither did it feel like anyone else in New London. Most likely a guy is mowing his lawn in a Cincinnati suburb and he gets a call on his cell phone that sends him on a plane to Providence or Boston or New York. He's then driven to New London, given a pistol, taken over to Bank Street, and does what he's paid to do. Now he's back in Cincinnati trimming a hedge. As for the rose, who knows what it means? Hit men can be sentimental like anyone else. As for the Yukon Denali, Manny and Vikström assume it had false plates. They'll look for it, but it won't be an optimistic sort of looking.

Other fingerprints in the office belonged to Marco Santuzza and Fat Bob Rossi. Marco's aren't surprising. After all, he was Sal's neighbor down the hall. But Fat Bob's aren't so easily understood. What was the connection there?

It's clear, however, that Sal was the one who signaled Pappalardo to tromp on the gas and send the truck hurtling back across Bank Street. It's also clear that Sal expected Fat Bob to come roaring along on the Fat Bob and was surprised when the rider turned out to be Marco Santuzza. Whoops.

"So let's say," Manny Streeter opines, "that Poppaloppa doesn't mind obliterating Fat Bob for a fat chunk of change, but he wouldn't want to whack Marco, who's his buddy. What's he going to do?"

"Maybe it's more important to ask what Sal *thinks* Pappalardo will do."

"Maybe both," says Manny, "but I'll bet Sal no longer trusts him."

"Maybe Pappalardo tries to blackmail him," says Vikström. "Or threatens him or yells at him."

"In any case, he doesn't trust Poppaloppa to keep his mouth shut."

"So Sal whacks him with the shotgun, okay. But maybe Sal is whacked by a friend of Pappalardo's."

"And the plastic rose?" asks Manny.

"If it's not meant as a signature, maybe it's meant as a distraction. Like the fedora was a distraction. All people can remember is the fuckin' fedora. Anyway, the Rhode Island state cop is checking on Pappalardo's Rhode Island friends."

"What about Fat Bob? If Sal tried to whack Fat Bob with a dump truck, then Fat Bob must have a reason to have Sal whacked."

"Maybe the hit wasn't done by a guy in Cincinnati," says Vikström, "but by someone in Providence or Boston, someone in the East who Fat Bob could contact. These bikers have networks. They're like a cult."

"So who shot up Fat Bob's Fat Bob and caused it to blow up?"

"It had to be someone that Fat Bob owes money to," says Vikström. "Until that person saw the bike in front of Angelina's house, he probably thought Fat Bob was dead. When he sees he's alive, he figures he still has a chance to get his money."

"So he threatens him or scares him."

Vikström nods. "Maybe we should find out if Lisowski has a pistol permit."

Manny and Vikström have their feet up on their desks and lean back in their swivel chairs with their hands behind their heads. They would hate to hear this, but at the moment they share a family resemblance. The main difference is Manny's black eye, which has turned dark purple. So when he's not cradling his head, he sits with his elbow on the arm of the chair and his hand over the eye. In this way Manny looks as if he's engaged in serious thought tinged with sadness.

"You get many fights at your karaoke whatchamacallit?" Vikström asked earlier.

"It's happened." Manny's tone was suspicious, as if any mention of the karaoke box by Vikström was sure to lead to trouble.

"Police ever been called?"

"Why the fuck would the police be called? I'm the police!"

"I thought maybe a neighbor would call the police to complain about the noise. You know, the shouting and chairs breaking."

"It's soundproofed. Anyway, no chairs have ever been broken."

"Tipped over, then. I mean loudly."

Manny knew that Vikström had no interest in the karaoke box. Instead he was purposefully being irritating to balance out those occasions when Manny himself had been purposefully irritating. "I don't think the guy ever meant to hit me. He just happened to be swinging his arms."

"Like to the music."

"Yeah, to the music."

Now, as he sits with his feet on his desk, Vikström asks, "You ever have dancing in your karaoke whatchamacallit? You know, Charleston dancing?"

Manny doesn't like this, but he keeps quiet.

"I should think the Charleston dancing could make a lot of noise. And people could trip and fall."

"We got to find Fat Bob."

Vikström regrets that his chance to needle his partner has to come to an end. "Maybe he's dead."

"We still got to find him. That fucking red rose irritates the shit outta me."

"We got cars looking for Fat Bob."

"Okay, let's go find Fidget and see if he took the gold."

"We got people looking for Fidget as well. Maybe the gold was taken by the young guy with the tan."

"I doubt it," says Manny. "That shrink guy across the street saw Fidget drop some gold, or what looked like gold. Anyway, it's easier to start with Fidget. We know where he hangs out."

It's nice to have a plan, and the detectives mentally prepare themselves to rise from their chairs to make a businesslike exit: their muscles tense, and their thoughts focus on the I-95 bridge, where they expect Fidget to be found.

But there's an interruption. Detective Sergeant Masters enters with two men whom Manny and Vikström haven't seen before: about forty, very fit, neatly dressed, shoes polished, nice haircuts, shiny pink faces. Although the men are complete strangers, Manny and Vikström know who they are.

And the two men recognize Manny and Vikström, or at least they think they do, because they see two rumpled city cops leaning back in their chairs with their feet on their desks and their mouths slightly open to gape at the intruders.

Detective Sergeant Masters displays all the agitation of a society hostess introducing the hired help to local billionaires. Names are exchanged.

"I bet he's one of those famous Swedish detectives," says one man to the other. They chortle.

"You should have notified us before the forensics guys tramped all over the crime scene," says the other man. "Dante Barbarella's our baby."

Manny stands up. He sticks out his lower lip and appears clumsy, confused. "And who did you guys say you were? Maybe TV journalists, right?"

"Stop it, Manny," says Detective Sergeant Masters. "These gentlemen are taking over the case. Any assistance you can give them will be greatly appreciated."

The FBI agents' names are Orville Percival and Henry Lascombe, and they're here because Sal Nicoletti, also known as Danny Barbarella, is supposed to appear in federal court in Detroit as the main witness in an embezzlement case that we have heard about before. The agents only know that Danny is dead and that he was the victim of an apparent contract hit. They know nothing about Fat Bob Rossi or Marco Santuzza or Leon Pappalardo, nor are they interested. And if Vikström told them Fat Bob was a prime suspect, Percival and Lascombe—known to one another as Percy and Hank—would snort. Nor would they care that some folks have taken potshots at Fat Bob and blown up a motorcycle. It only muddies the water. And if Fat Bob were shot, they'd shed no tears, because for them Fat Bob's not part of the equation.

But Fat Bob's not dead yet. We don't know where he is; most likely he's out riding around. He's like a fly that refuses to settle. Fat Bob believes that people want to kill him—not just Sal, who he thinks is still alive, but lots of people. He's been afraid this might happen. He's wheedled too much money from too many folks and hasn't paid them back. It's like making a tower with playing cards. It's short-lasting. There's always a wind building up.

And people are blaming Fat Bob for Marco's death, but he still tells himself it was an accident. He'd lent Marco a motorcycle as collateral for the money he owed him. Fat Bob had no idea that he was setting Marco up to be killed. Does Fat Bob believe this? He's working hard to believe it.

Fat Bob knows he should never have tried to get money out of Sal. We see no reason to keep this secret. He had gone down the hall with Marco Santuzza to meet this new guy, this new accountant, and Fat Bob had recognized the guy from a Detroit casino. But he should never have called him Danny. He should never have let him know that he knew where he came from—meaning Detroit, meaning the court case—and that he'd been testifying against his former pals. Wiping out Fat Bob on a Fat Bob—that was Sal's or Danny's kind of humor, even if Fat Bob had mistakenly killed Santuzza. So no way is Fat Bob going to settle down someplace, except for nights of fitful sleep, when he imagines trouble on his trail.

The Winnebago this Wednesday evening doesn't offer much of a domestic scene. Connor is gone, and the others are having dinner: spaghetti and meatballs with a green salad. Didi, when he first contacted Eartha, didn't expect her to have cooking skills, though she's not a serious chef. She just cooks, and she often cooks topless, unless she's cooking pork chops or burgers and the oil splatters.

Eartha has told Didi that Connor arrived in the afternoon with a dreadful story. He'd described Sal Nicoletti sitting in his office chair with a hole in the middle of his forehead and a red plastic rose stuck in the hole. And he said that Nicoletti's real name was Danny Barbarella and he was from Detroit. Maybe Eartha forgets some stuff and maybe she gets some of it mixed up, but she remembers that Connor accused his brother Vasco. "He said Vasco sold the information to some other guys from Detroit and those guys got Nicoletti shot."

As he listens, Didi's fork is paused halfway to his mouth, while around its several tines are two neatly wrapped strands of spaghetti. He could be a model in a pasta ad. Vaughn, on the other hand, eats his spaghetti strand by strand. He takes one by the tip, holds it over his head and shouts, "Snakes in the kitchen!" Then he lowers it into his mouth. After that the process repeats.

"A fucking plastic rose," says Didi.

Vaughn says, "It's beyond my apprehension."

Eartha and Didi give Vaughn a quick look and decide not to comment. This often happens when Vaughn speaks. They're unsure whether his confusions of language are intentional or accidental, but they know if they ask, Vaughn will give an explanation that will drag them into his alternative universe. This is a scary place to visit. Eartha and Didi have been there before and beaten a hasty retreat, but like a pervasive smell, their confusion lingers for the rest of the day. So they ignore him.

"You know Connor's brother Vasco?" asks Eartha.

"I've met him a few times, but I can't say I know him."

Eartha is eating her salad. "Would he sell information like that?"

It should be clear that Didi and Vasco have features in common, though Didi is more than fifteen years older. Both are handsome, vain, well dressed, and have distinctive heads of hair. Both are sure of themselves. Both have more answers than questions, meaning they are self-confidently opinionated. And they're quick to share their opinions with others, meaning they're pushy.

But while Didi is a nihilistic optimist, Vasco is a nihilistic cynic. Didi's belief that someone might eagerly embrace the concept of Orphans from Outer Space derives from his love—perhaps only an affection—for his fellow man. Vasco's belief that someone might embrace the concept of extraterrestrial orphans only arouses his scorn. The fact that casino patrons are gullible fantasists leads Didi to sympathy and even tenderness. Vasco dismisses them as chumps. Didi looks on Vasco with mild pity;

Vasco looks at Didi with energetic disdain. Didi has a sense of humor, though it's eccentric, while the closest Vasco gets to a sense of humor is sarcasm.

"You're not answering my question," says Eartha. "Would he sell information like that?"

"Yes," says Didi. "He would."

"Could this mess up our . . ." She pauses and goes on. ". . . fund-raising efforts?"

"I'm certain it will, especially if it attracts attention to Connor." Didi turns to Vaughn. "What d'you call a plastic rose stuck in a hole in a guy's forehead?"

Vaughn doesn't hesitate. "An optical conclusion."

SIXTEEN

Let's get back to those folks who say there are no accidents and every-thing happens for a reason. Vasco calls them suckers; Didi calls them his constituency. In these folks' analysis of the world, Fate and the extended power digit, or middle-finger salute, of various faith-supported superfigures do a lot of heavy lifting. So they might think the prospect of an overlap between Free Beagles from Nicotine Addiction, Inc. and Prom Queens Anonymous, Inc. isn't a coincidence but "means something." It was destined to happen.

But Didi will say what it means is statistics: that given two hundred prom queens and one thousand beagles within a population of a hundred thousand women, there's an *X* percent possibility that *Y* number of prom queens will own a beagle. In fact, a few former prom queens will find spiritual sustenance *only* in the embrace of a beagle. Beagles don't care if you're no longer beautiful. They don't care if the great expectations you had as an eighteen-year-old knockout have become spilled jam pots on the dusty roads of life. That's why we like beagles and other canines: love and loyalty are more important to them than truth. You tell your dog you can walk on water and it will lick your hand. Its only fear is of being left behind, locked up, shut in the doghouse when you go to a fancy-dress ball or simply go shopping. Otherwise you're gravy.

Didi's target prom queens are women between forty-five and sixty-five—women dismayed by the creeping decrepitations to be found on necks, cheeks, foreheads, etc. Didi is the enemy of face-lifts. He doesn't want these ladies to be beautiful again.

He wants shattered glass to remain shattered glass. As girls they had great hopes. They were told that golden futures lay ahead. They saw themselves as celebrities in training, as proto–trophy wives. Maybe many also wanted to become doctors, lawyers, and airline pilots, and maybe some were successful. In fact, among family members, friends, and fellow workers, they might be superstars. But they're no longer beautiful. That's not to say they are ugly—they are faded.

Didi, of course, understands that some have made profitable transitions to middle age. For them their brief fame as prom queens is no more than a mildly diverting anecdote about the days when they posed in shining crowns and held bouquets of flowers. And some perhaps never liked their beauty. It was the child they constantly had to care for. They hated being ogled. They celebrated each new wrinkle.

But others may live in states of perpetual grief. Nothing has worked out as promised. Despite fortunes spent on makeup, their faces are little more than prettified accusations. Of course this isn't true, but it's how they feel. Instead of casting aside the delusion of ugliness, they embrace it. And perhaps they see it as the cause of all their failures: they lost their looks.

These are the customers of Prom Queens Anonymous: groups of older women sitting in church basements over sour cups of coffee and a few stale Oreo cookies discussing how the truths of youth became the falsehoods of age: unawakened Sleeping Beauties, Cinderellas for whom the pumpkin carriages never arrived, graying Rapunzels. As members of Prom Queens Anonymous, they push aside their mirrors' fabrications and get on with the business of living. They learn to forgive themselves for growing older. The lines and wrinkles of experience become more consequential than the pink and unspoiled surfaces of youth.

Didi doesn't know if groups like Prom Queens Anonymous exist, but he's confident there's a need. And where there's a need, he knows he will find women eager to contribute money, especially if they themselves are former prom queens. He has only to seek them out.

In the past this meant combing through old newspapers and school yearbooks, a laborious task where the game's hardly worth the candle.

But with Vaughn at his side, Didi can sneak into the computers of every high school in a fifty-mile radius. Then, with a few key taps, the girls' names burst forth on the screen. In fact, Didi's greatest success has been with high school prom queens, rather than college homecoming queens. Their fantasies are richer and age's encroachments grimmer, while the intensity of their response suggests they've been waiting for his call.

We haven't yet said that Angelina Rossi was a prom queen, but we say it here. And we may remember that Vikström found her beautiful "in a dark, southern Italian way." On the other hand, her black mustache repelled Manny Streeter. Let's say without further fuss that Angelina has no mustache. We see only a slight, dark shadow on her upper lip, perhaps a little more than a shadow. Manny also imagined thick locks of black pubic hair from her navel to midthigh. Even if this is true, she remains beautiful.

Angelina sits at her kitchen table smoking a cigarette at about eight o'clock Wednesday evening with her beagle, little Magsie, at her feet, when her cell phone abruptly starts buzzing. Her response is immediate: the world has arrived to pester her again. She clicks on the phone as Magsie begins to growl.

"Yes?"

A woman's low, breathy voice says, "Is it you, is it really you? Is this Angelina Carlotti, the Pumpkin Queen of 1985? Angie?"

Angelina's normal response to telephone calls is to cut the connection within two seconds. But tonight she hesitates.

"Yes?" she repeats. "Who are you? Your voice sounds familiar."

"I remember you walking to the center of the stage and everyone applauding and calling your name: *Angie! Angie!* You looked so beautiful in your pink gown."

Angelina, in point of fact, was crowned queen during the halftime ceremonies of a Friday-evening football game in November. And it wasn't on a stage. She sat atop a prickly hay bale on a wagon drawn by two undistinguished horses. Also, her gown had been blue. But she doesn't let these details bother her, because all at once she hears those voices calling, *Angie! Angie!*

"What of it?" she says unpleasantly, unwilling to surrender anything as yet.

"How hard these last years must have been for you. Believe me, I feel the same way. I've been betrayed by my body—I gain weight, my face sags. Angie, where did it go? What happened to the beautiful girl with a bright future? I've become a stranger to myself!"

Eartha sits at the dinette table in the Winnebago reading words from a script begun many years ago by other members of Bounty, Inc. and which has been added to and tinkered with ever since. The most recent words were written by Didi, though Eartha at times takes the opportunity to add a few, change a few, cut a few. "Organic stagecraft," Didi calls it.

Angelina doesn't answer. Even though she wants to hurl the phone through the window, she curbs the impulse. She feels a lump in her throat, or maybe she's getting a cold. It is, for her, an unfamiliar sensation.

"Isn't that the night you danced again and again with your husband-to-be, Robert Rossi? When later you both lay naked in the backseat of his car?"

"Fat Bob, the fat fuck, my ex."

Eartha hears her venom and backtracks. This is no time for venom.

"But he wasn't like that then. He was handsome and kind and generous—"

"He said he wanted to fuck me till the cows came home. I should have known then he was greedy."

"But there was passion—"

"He ripped my nice dress!"

"But you liked it."

"I was stupid. I liked anyone who was nice to me."

"What were your dreams that night, your dreams for the future?"

"I was going to be an airline stewardess."

"So men could stare at you but couldn't bother you?"

"Something like that. Who the fuck are you anyway?"

"Right now," said Eartha with a deeper purr, "I'm your best friend. Your sorrows have been my sorrows. Your tears have cut their furrows in my own furrowed cheeks. And what happened to those dreams?"

"Fat Bob knocked me up. And he kept knocking me up—knocked me up four times, but one of the kids didn't make it, a girl."

"I'm sure they're beautiful children."

"They got fat. They look just like Fat Bob."

Eartha keeps thinking she's heard that name and then realizes she heard it from Connor. "Didn't Fat Bob transition on a motorcycle the other day?"

"Transition?"

"Cross the great divide, go the way of all flesh, cash in his chips . . ." Eartha struggles to find an inoffensive euphemism.

Angelina snorts a laugh within which Eartha hears a growl of disenchantment. "No such luck. It was Marco got killed, Bob's buddy. Bob let him use his bike. That's why people said the dead guy was Fat Bob."

"How awful."

"Yeah, if Fat Bob got killed, I'd get the insurance money. I was counting on it. I need it for a face-lift, so I've been selling his Fat Bobs to make up for the loss. I sell them cheap, and it drives him crazy. Anyway, what the fuck do you want?"

Although Eartha hears Angelina's anger, she knows that Angelina isn't angry enough to hang up. "I'm like you were: a girl with lots of dates and lots of friends who was elected homecoming queen. They put a crown on my head and shook my hand and kissed my cheek, and hundreds of people clapped and clapped and shouted my name, and I thought my entire life would change and be wonderful. The shadowy future reached toward me with its promised embrace. But it never happened. I was left standing on the darkened stage of life. And it may surprise you to know that there're lots of us."

The lump in Angelina's throat gets bigger. "What d'you mean 'lots of us'? Are you a club?"

"We are Prom Queens Anonymous. We meet and talk about how things used to be and what they became. We work to defeat our disappointment and make our lives joyful again. We try to change ourselves, become part of society, to be useful. We rediscover our beauty as older women, and we set up groups all over the country. It takes time, but mostly it takes money."

We haven't counted the words Eartha has spoken, but they all lead to one larger word: "money." And Eartha hopes she has set that word in Angelina's brain as one might set a baby on a feather bed.

"I like the sound of that," says Angelina.

Eartha pumps her fist. *Yes,* she says to herself. *Yes, Yes!* "We've no wish to rehash the old stories. We move beyond the bad times. We realize our beauty is still within us, and we try to live productive lives. We move forward."

This is a fragment, just a taste of Eartha's script as she speaks faster and becomes more impassioned. She takes Angelina's bitterness and disappointment and works to soften the sharp edges. She takes her inflexibility and rubs and pummels until it is lenient and forgiving. She speaks until Angelina interrupts her.

"Wow! What can I do?"

So Eartha talks about how the group needs books, coffeemakers, and rent money for the meeting places. How the staff needs money for airfare as they fly around the country to start new meetings and to give encouragement to newly formed groups. They need money for babysitters and meeting lists, raffle prizes, posters, and bumper stickers. The list goes on.

"Of course, once the groups get started, they can pay for themselves with members' contributions, but we still help with the rent and some other stuff."

"You have a group near here? I want to go." Angelina speaks in a hushed voice, just as one might speak in church or at a funeral home.

"I'm afraid not. Right now all our groups are on the West Coast. That's why we're calling women in your area. We'd like to get busy in New England."

There's a pause. "So you're after money."

"Yes . . . well, a contribution, just to help us get going."

"Fat Bob's got some extra Harleys. Why not take one of those?"

"We prefer cash, or a check if necessary."

"I hold the titles so the IRS can't snatch them. Technically they're my bikes, just like his house. I'll give you one cheap, and you can triple your money."

"No can do."

"Maybe I can squeeze a few more bucks from Bob."

"Don't you have money of your own?"

"He's the one who fucked me, so he should pay. He stood between me and my destiny. I need every penny I can scrape together. Face-lift, boob job, tummy tuck, liposuction, butt implant, a chemical peel—you name it, I need it."

Eartha scans her script for a suitable response. She could say, *You can't let him rent space in your head,* or *It's time to live and let live,* or *You need to turn your life around.*

Instead she says, "Most women who join think that. They blame their ex. They won't take charge of their own lives. What's the point of dragging Fat Bob all the way to your grave?"

Well, the talk goes on. It's as if Angelina has been dipped in concrete that has hardened to give her a toughened epidermis and a stony heart. Eartha chips away at it, helped by the script prepared by Bounty, Inc.

After another five minutes, Angelina says, "What about ten bucks?"

Eartha has an answer for this. "Is this what your disappointment is worth? What your wrecked future is worth?"

"Okay, twenty. But you'd do better with one of Fat Bob's Fat Bobs. It would drive him fucking ballistic!"

Let's move away from their negotiations. Angelina is stubborn, but Eartha is determined, and if we stay, we'll be here all night. It should be evident that both Manny Streeter and Angelina are victims of disappointment. But it can also be said that both have allowed themselves to feel disappointed. Manny is more fortunate, because he has his karaoke box. It may be foolish, but it's the one place he can go and leave his disappointment at the door. Angelina has nothing like this except her beagle, little Magsie. Her disappointment is a twenty-four-hour job. Most likely the meetings of Prom Queens Anonymous could become her karaoke box. But of course Prom Queens Anonymous doesn't exist.

U nder the I-95 or Gold Star Memorial Bridge, we find about a mile between the riverbank of the Thames and the abutment where the bridge rejoins the surface of the highway. Five roads pass under the bridge within this mile, but closer to the river, along State Pier Road, are wooded areas, which are fenced off, but a fence is no more than a nuisance to those who are resolute, like Fidget. It's here he has made his hutch. In fact, he's made it many times, because it keeps being torn down. But to Fidget it's home, while nearby is the Homeless Hospitality Center where Fidget sometimes showers and gets a bite to eat.

The number of people who live under the bridge depends on the season and how often the police roust them out, which in turn depends on the complaints of people living nearby and the conduct of the homeless residents, meaning no fights, no fires, and no drunken parties. And sometimes the chief of police sends cops over to do a little rousting just because she feels the cops need exercise.

Manny Streeter and Vikström often had this task in their early years before they became detectives, and since then they've paid visits if they're looking for someone in particular, or searching for stolen property, or if a crime has been committed. The drug squad also pops in fairly regularly, as do other city and state agencies. Really, it's surprising anyone can get a full night's sleep. Before a good summer rousting, twenty people might be under the bridge: some local bums, some passing through, and others who find the hospitality center claustrophobic or have been kicked out for various infractions. But typically there are fewer than a dozen people under the bridge. On a winter night, we might find only two or three, and every year or so one poor fellow freezes to death down among the bushes.

Fidget, we believe, is the most permanent resident. Nobody can say how long he's been there, and neither can Fidget, for whom the past is only heavy fog. But it feels like forever. And though he's been rousted many times, he always returns. Even the most modest dwelling can elicit homesickness, and Fidget has a sentimental streak. So in looking for Fidget, Manny and Vikström, on this chilly Wednesday night in March, believe they know where to start.

We should recall that this was their plan before the arrival of Percy and Hank, the FBI agents, and now they go ahead with their plan simply to get Percy and Hank out of their minds. Manny and Vikström aren't dummies; they know the arrival of the FBI will save them work, but it's a blessing they'd prefer to do without. Both detectives admit to strengths and weaknesses, though they differ as to how they're allocated, each thinking the other has the more flaws, but they don't want their flaws discussed and their strengths denied by Percy and Hank. Better to have those fellows hit the road than to admit that their assistance is worth a roll of used flypaper.

But of course they won't hit the road. We may not see much of Percy and Hank, but they'll be in the background doing whatever they do. And most of the time, they'll be around the casinos. As for Manny and Vikström, they drive along State Pier Road to the area by the I-95 bridge as if Percy and Hank never existed. They work to cogitate the FBI agents into nonexistence.

Manny pulls onto Mill Street under the bridge, parks, and climbs from the car. He finds the place disgusting. "It smells like a fuckin' latrine," he says.

Vikström smells nothing; maybe he has a faulty sense of smell. He doesn't particularly like the local homeless, or trust them to behave, but he's got a bit of sympathy. "They've all had mothers," he says in a way guaranteed to make Manny grit his teeth.

"Yeah, and they all have scabies and fleas. They're alkies or addicts or nut jobs, or maybe all three."

They duck through a hole in the fence and bushwhack through the brush until they see a small fire at the edge of an open space. The ground is littered with bottles and broken glass, rusted bits of metal, wrecked bikes and busted shopping carts, but nothing that can be used, burned, or sold.

Manny and Vikström walk toward six men gathered near the fire.

"They're not supposed to have fires," says Manny.

Vikström shrugs. "Forget it."

"They make me itch," says Manny.

As the detectives approach, the men seem to withdraw into themselves and get smaller. None of them look at Manny and Vikström except out of the corners of their eyes. Maybe they've been chatting; now they're not.

Vikström asks if they've seen Fidget and where he might be found. The men shrug, raise their eyebrows, and make *Fidget? Who's Fidget?* gestures.

"Cut the shit," says Manny. "Where's Fidget?"

One of the men points to a bridge abutment about twenty yards away. He explains that Fidget lives over in that direction. "He's got a little cardboard shelter."

"Or did," says another man.

"You guys keeping your noses clean?" asks Manny, to be irritating.

The men mutter in the affirmative or nod. They want the cops to vanish. If they have bottles or drugs, they're hidden.

When we last visited Fidget's hutch, it was a relatively neat arrangement of two blue poly tarps and two broken shopping carts up against the bridge abutment. Now the carts have been tossed aside and the tarps are among the weeds. Vikström looks at a few large rags that started life as blankets. The contents of several boxes have been scattered: a dented saucepan, a frying pan, some magazines, old newspapers, a torn sweater, and some indefinables. The ground where the floor of the hutch once was has been dug up with a sharp stick or a piece of metal.

Vikström kicks through the stuff and throws the cardboard around.

"What're you looking for?" asks Manny. "You expect to find gold chains?"

"There's no spoon. There's almost always a spoon."

"He's probably got it on him. Who threw this stuff around?" Manny shouts to the men by the fire.

"Bad guys," says someone.

"Are you the bad guys?" asks Vikström as he and Manny walk back toward them.

"Nope, we're the good guys."

"Don't get wise with me," says Manny. "Who took his spoon?"

The men shake their heads. They'd like to say that they are honest citizens down on their luck, who'd never steal another man's spoon, but they keep still.

"When did you last see Fidget?" asks Vikström.

"He was here a coupla hours ago and left," says one.

"He doesn't keep us informed," says another lightly.

"Watchit!" barks Manny.

"You know any other place he hangs out?" asks Vikström.

But the men say they've no idea. They don't really know Fidget. He comes and goes. He stays by himself. He's not a big talker. And he smells.

"Maybe he's over at the hospitality center," says a man.

Manny tugs Vikström's sleeve. "Why don't you tell them he had a mother?" He laughs.

Vikström ignores him; the detectives walk back to the car. They check the hospitality center, but Fidget hasn't been seen all day. For half an hour, Manny drives up and down the nearby streets looking for Fidget. "What the fuck does that silly noodle think he can do with that gold?" he asks.

"Maybe he just likes wearing it. It's exciting for him."

"All dressed up and nowhere to go," says Manny.

Other police cars are also looking for Fidget, but no one has seen him.

"You ever notice," says Manny, "that when you're *not* looking for Fidget, you see him all over the place and when you *are* looking for Fidget, he's vanished."

"Let's drive over to Fat Bob's house and see if there's any change."

"Like what?"

"Like how many Harleys are there."

Fat Bob's house is dark, but when Manny pulls in to the driveway, the detectives can see that more windows have been smashed.

"This is a bad sign," says Manny.

Vikström digs his fingernail into his palm. The pain has a cleansing effect. He keeps silent.

They get out their flashlights and walk around to the back of the house. The back door to the kitchen is open again.

"I don't like the look of this," says Manny, changing his modus operandi.

Vikström keeps quiet. He considers hitting Manny with his flashlight. Of course he's not going to hit his partner, but he likes imagining it.

The refrigerator door hangs open and there's the smell of spoiled food. It's not bad yet, but it will be worse tomorrow when spoil turns to rot. Glasses, cups, saucers, and plates lie broken on the floor. The window over the sink is smashed.

"The city has to secure this," says Vikström. "They got to do it right away."

"They don't like coming out at night."

"That's not my problem," says Vikström. He goes back outside and walks to the garage. The garage door is open about a foot.

"I don't like the look of any of this," says Manny.

Vikström again digs his fingernails into his palms. He decides he needs longer fingernails. But he forgets his nails when Manny opens the door. Now there are two Harleys: a dark purple one and a black one.

Vikström grabs Manny by the arm. "*Tell* me you don't like the look of this! I dare you!"

Manny pulls away. "You ever been told you got a serious behavior problem? You're lucky I don't write you up."

————

Connor arrives at Sal Nicoletti's house around seven—or, since Sal's dead, maybe it should be called Céline's house. Connor has called his brother Vasco a dozen times since he ran out of Sal's office this morning, but Vasco hasn't picked up. In fact, the phone goes directly to voice mail. At first Connor's messages are simple: "Call me," he says, or "We need to talk." But then they grow angrier until he's shouting, "You fuck, you sold that information about Sal! You told them he was Danny Barbarella!"

Connor isn't sure who he means by "them," just gangsters, mobsters, bad guys. All he knows is that Sal won't be testifying in Detroit.

He's also terrified that Céline will learn he's the one who blew her husband's cover and got him killed. It doesn't matter if it was an accident. It was stupid, and if she learns about it, she'll never forgive him, or such is his thought. We may say that Connor wants to know Céline better, but he hasn't told himself what "better" means, nor does he define all the meanings of "know." She'd been a wife with two kids, and now she's a grieving widow with two kids, or so he thinks. To Connor any chance of "better" is over. He murdered her husband, and even though he didn't pull the trigger, it's still murder.

Now he stands on her front steps and rings the bell. The porch light is on. He straightens his jacket, fusses with his tie. If she greets him with a shotgun, he won't be surprised. Connor, of course, doesn't know she actually *had* a shotgun that the police took away earlier. There's lots he doesn't know. But Connor's a romantic. Céline's virtue seems clear to him. Only Vaughn, out of Connor's acquaintances, wouldn't find this absurd. She's a wolf in cheap clothing, he'd say.

The hall light goes on, and the door opens. Céline stands looking at Connor, and the light makes her black hair shine. Her face gives no indication of thought. The tops of fenceposts are more expressive. But Connor likes what he sees, and his stomach jumps up and down. She pushes open the storm door to let him in and returns to the living room. Connor follows her.

Glancing around, he sees that everything is beige, plain and uninteresting. He doesn't know that the house's furnishings have been rented. Instead he has assumed that since he finds Céline amazing, her house would also be amazing: Oriental rugs and antique furniture, wonderful paintings on the walls. But it's not.

Céline wears a purple velour robe buttoned to her neck with gold stitching at collar, cuffs, and hem. She's Connor's height, and her full lips are very red. Connor thinks the lipstick is her only makeup, but he's wrong. Her eyes, cheeks, cheekbones, chin—all have felt the subtle touch of her brush. Her "natural" look has taken an hour of preparation.

"I'm sorry about Sal," says Connor. "You must feel terrible."

"Yeah, now I'm a grieving widow." Céline motions to him to sit down; he sits on the couch. She stands with her eyes focused on him. He's struck by the hardness of her tone, and he sees no sign of the kids but forgets about them when she speaks.

"One thing about Sal, he always wore gold. He saw it as his trademark. But he didn't have any when the cops got to his office this morning. They said you'd been there. They described you, and I recognized the description."

She says nothing further. After a moment Connor becomes uncomfortable.

"He wasn't wearing any when I found him, but I got out as fast as I could."

"The cops said a bum had been there before you. They called him 'Fidget.' They said he'd taken the gold, but they didn't know how much."

Connor has a quick memory of Fidget, though he didn't know that was the man's name till now. Connor bumped into him as he ran out of the building and something fell to the sidewalk. He had no chance to see what it was before Fidget grabbed it and hurriedly zigzagged up the street. Could it have been a gold chain? Maybe.

"A guy who was maybe a bum came running out of Sal's building."
No, thinks Connor, *of course he was a bum.* And he recalls Fidget pan-handling the crowd after the accident. Connor had given him a dollar. "How much gold are we talking about?"

"Not much," lies Céline. "A couple of chains, a couple of rings. They're maybe worth about five thousand tops. It's the sentimental value that's important."

"You must have loved him," says Connor.

"Actually, I hated the fuck. Maybe there's more than a couple of chains and rings. There's a phony Rolex and a fairly expensive pen. But I want it all. I don't care about the money. I want something to remind me how much I hated him."

Connor feels as if someone has hit him, but there's no indication of Céline's hatred in her expressionless face or in the tone of her voice. "Why'd you hate him?"

Céline thinks. She doesn't want to say too much or too little, and whatever she says must be something to appeal to Connor's particular sensibility. "He wasn't a gentleman," she says at last. "Will you find those things for me?"

"I wouldn't know where to start."

Céline gets up from the armchair and walks slowly to Connor until the purple velour brushes his face left and right in a delicate slap. Then she moves back a step. "You'll find a way," she says.

SEVENTEEN

It is midnight, and we're in the small white house on Montauk Avenue where Fat Bob moved after Angelina kicked him out. Two rooms and a kitchen are on the first floor; two bedrooms and a bath are on the second. One bedroom contains six U-Haul boxes and a three-legged straight-backed chair that Fat Bob had hoped to fix; the other has a narrow floor-to-ceiling mirror by the window, two bureaus with drawers pulled out and clothes strewn all over, and a queen-size bed covered by a white comforter. The bed has the sort of mattress that adjusts to one's bumps and bulges while exuding soothing perfumes when one button is pushed and soothing sounds—breaking waves, wind through trees, birdsong, et cetera—when a second is pushed. Fidget knows that if he lies on the mattress, his fears will vanish. They'll be lulled away, chuckled away. Unhappily, he is lying not on the bed but beneath it as a serious ruckus consisting of shouting and banging rises up from downstairs.

Fidget is sure the noise is caused by bad guys in pursuit of his bling—gold chains, gold rings, bracelet, gold Rolex watch, and a limited-edition Montegrappa pen. He's fearful, and he'd check his racing pulse if he could, but the eight inches of space between bed and floor don't permit such activity. Indeed, if someone jumped on the bed, he'd be crushed faster than a jackboot can crush a cockroach.

When Fidget was hunting out a fine and private place in which to hide, he'd thought of Fat Bob's empty house as an entire house and not a thin sliver of space beneath a bed. With him are two half gallons of vodka he bought at a package store on Montauk, but there's not enough room to lift one to his lips. The pockets of his raincoat are crowded with nips, and in two paper bags he has a supply of liquor store food: beer nuts, peanut butter crackers, beef jerky, and Slim Jims. But in the space at his disposal, these treats are as distant as Mars.

He'd squeezed beneath the bed when he heard what sounded like a dozen boots tromp into the kitchen, open the refrigerator door, bang the cupboards, tromp into the living room, and then tromp up the stairs to inspect the bedrooms. "Nothing in here!" shouted one pair of boots. "Nothing here either!" shouted another. Then they tromped back down.

Fidget fears that without food or drink he'll die beneath the bed like a sailor marooned on a coffin-size atoll. But he needn't worry. The noise downstairs comes from disgruntled employees of the department of public works as they clean out the refrigerator, gather up the trash, and screw panels of half-inch plywood over the windows and doors. The midnight job, set in motion by Detectives Benny Vikström and Manny Streeter, is to make certain no more ne'er-do-wells take liberties with private property. Now it will require a tank to break into the house, and, as Fidget discovers, it will require a tank to get out.

Perhaps Fidget slept—he's not sure. But when he next turns an ear to the ruckus downstairs, it's gone. Silence reigns, and all is dark. Fidget spends a moment thinking the big boots are hiding in the closet and if he leaves his place of safety, they'll jump out with shouts and whistles, but then his growing need to pee defeats his fear of the boots and he begins to extricate himself. This is a detail mostly absent from adventure stories. Was there ever a moment when the Lone Ranger, galloping along after desperadoes, turned to his companion and shouted, "Hold up, Tonto, I've gotta take a whiz?" Very unlikely.

Once free and with his antique bladder accommodated, Fidget celebrates his release with several mouthfuls of vodka and a Slim Jim. He again listens and again hears nothing. He decides to stay put till morning, since the house is dark and if he begins to prowl around, he'll break a leg. So, after having a mouth-cleansing gargle with more vodka, he crawls into bed and pulls the comforter up to his nose. The bed tweedles birdsong noises. This was what civilization, Fidget thinks, is all about.

Some might imagine that Fidget will be lonely, marooned as he is in an empty house. But Fidget doesn't know the meaning of loneliness. Maybe he knew it once, but he's forgotten. His interactions with people are mostly negative, so he can't envision seeking out anyone for a chat. Maybe in the distant past it was different, yet when he tries to recall what it was like for him as a kid, he sees only shadows. As far as he can tell, he's always been as he is tonight: solitary. Does he have a wife? A dog and cat? Children? He won't deny the possibility, but with shadows in his past and shadows in his future, Fidget thinks the present moment is where he's meant to be.

Now, however, life has changed; he's turned the tables on the world. His rings twinkle in the faint light from the window. He has gold, and his joy is not yet diminished by the worry of its heavy responsibility. Life is good. He settles his head on a pillow and soon falls asleep. Does he dream? Only of rosy clouds at sunset and squawking geese flying south.

Around two a.m. he's awakened by the busy *putt-putt* of a motor scooter, but it takes a minute to determine the source of the sound as it gets louder and softer, louder and softer. Then, when the word "scooter" drifts across his cerebral cortex, the sound is already diminishing down Montauk. Fidget feels a touch of disquiet that someone would ride a motor scooter four times around Fat Bob's house at two a.m., but as he turns over, he thinks his disquiet can wait until morning.

We should state, however, that the scooter's rider is Jack Sprat and that he's still looking for Fat Bob.

Fidget sleeps late, and it's not until nine o'clock that sunlight creeps across the comforter and into his eyes. The room is warm, and he stares up at the ceiling that follows the slope of the roof. The walls are off-white and freshly painted. Fidget wiggles his toes. Although he doesn't believe in heaven, he feels that a room with sun streaming through the window has a heavenlike splendor. He takes a remote control from the bedside table, turns a dial, and the mattress begins to vibrate. The more he turns, the more it vibrates. The gold chains around his neck jingle, and when his remaining teeth begin to rattle, he lowers the dial to a more restful level.

Fidget goes into the bathroom to fill the tub. As the water rises, he uses the nail clippers found in the medicine cabinet to cut his toenails, which resemble the thick, dark scales on a nine-banded armadillo. Once his nails are done and the tub full, he lies on his back and admires how his gold sparkles in the darkening water. Half an hour later, clean-shaven and cloud-white, he leaves the tub, dribbling water behind him as he returns to the bedroom, rubbing himself with a towel.

When Fidget catches sight of himself in the mirror, he receives a little scare. Who's this naked, beardless man with the trimmed white hair caressing the nape of his neck? Never in all his vague memory has he appeared so virginal. He may still resemble a parking meter, but he's a very handsome parking meter. He raises his towel in front of his genitals and bows to his reflection. The reflection bows back. Then he skips two steps to the right, pauses, skips two steps to the left, and bows again. He jumps up and down three times, small jumps, nothing too strenuous, just enough to make the gold chains bounce on his narrow chest so they go *ching, ka-ching, ching.* He pirouettes and then skips again to the left and right. Again he bows, and with this last bow he has reached the pinnacle of self-appreciation.

Fidget stops when he hears a *putt-putt-putt,* the same *putt-putt* he'd heard in the night. He crouches by the window as the sound circles the house. Then it diminishes. Something red is disappearing down Montauk Avenue.

It's past nine o'clock Thursday morning, and Connor has walked several miles in search of Fidget. Now he's taking a breather by a large blue mailbox next to the round archway of Union Station, a two-and-a-half-story redbrick structure where Amtrak and commuter trains discharge and pick up passengers. It's springish and about fifty degrees. A March wind blows small billows of sand from where it had been scattered by city trucks during Tuesday's snow. At times Connor wipes sand from his eyes, and to someone across the street it might look like he's weeping.

But Connor is moderately happy. There's solace to be found in stroking the area of a missing hirsute accessory with finger and thumb even if the accessory is only a large black mustache, and as Connor massages his upper lip, he realizes it is nicer with the mustache gone than with the mustache in place. The memory is better than the actuality, which in truth was often a bother, as the mustache imitated the job of a steam locomotive's cowcatcher, snapping up bread crumbs, raspberry jam, and unfelt kisses. This also is one of Didi's firm beliefs: Life recalled is better than life lived. The imagination, after all, can edit, revise, and improve. Those ancients who pass to their reward in old folks' homes with smiles on their lips and songs in their hearts—who knows what illusory achievements and bogus epics warm their last moments? "Isn't it something to look forward to?" Didi likes to ask.

But to continue: Yesterday evening and into the night, Connor walked about fifteen miles, all in New London, as he searched for Fidget. He means to appropriate Fidget's jewelry, though Connor's verb of choice is "liberate." He isn't sure how this will happen, and in his imaginings he skips the theft part to the gratitude part, when Céline shows her appreciation with fleshy thank-yous between soft sheets. Made-up futures and made-up pasts: "Reality," says Didi, "is no more than a fleeting nanosecond that we straightaway begin to modify."

But earlier that morning, Didi had shown irritation as his reality came into conflict with Connor's over the issue of what Didi called Connor's irresponsible absences. "You're supposed to be working for us, not prowling around New London after some woman."

Connor rejected this. Céline wasn't just "some woman" but "an archetype of female sexuality."

Eartha disliked this talk. She'd taken out a sizable loan to have her own sexuality heightened, and now it was going to waste on a deserted beach in Rhode Island. To her mind, sexuality must be seen—otherwise her breasts were just a double splop of silicone gel. She scorns Céline, whom she's never met, as no more than "pussy with bells and whistles," which conjures up strange images in Connor's mind.

As Didi and Eartha made their complaints, Vaughn sat cross-legged on the floor bobbing his head and drawing squares on a yellow pad. When Eartha paused in her gripes to take a breath, Vaughn approached Connor, who sat in the dinette staring into a cold cup of coffee. Vaughn leaned over to whisper in his ear. "You're in a risqué location. For water's worth Didi'll burn you as a steak."

"Say again?"

"Stick your eye on a wheel and your shoulder to a boulder."

What was it about Vaughn's declarations that disturbed Connor? Or was it confusion as to Vaughn's meaning that gave him a chill, as if his words were hazy broadcasts from the Hermetic Order of Vanished Chances? He felt if he could understand Vaughn, then Vaughn would no longer trouble him. But Connor was unable to articulate the nature of his anxiety—or if a potential threat even existed.

"You confuse me," said Connor.

Vaughn looked kindly at Connor, as if he were a dumb animal in need of comfort. "You're in a dangerous salutation suffering from impassable dreams."

"How so?"

"Don't burn your bridges before you come to them. Remember, there's no time like the pleasant. Don't take the bad with the worse."

Standing in front of the train station later that morning, Connor decides he suffers from a dislocated agenda. He's not lazy. He wants to help Didi in any way possible, or so he tells himself. But the statue of his self-identity has been knocked askew on its pedestal by a few powerful thrusts, leaving Connor to stare off in new and worrisome directions. The first had been the motorcycle accident. The second was meeting Sal Nicoletti. Third was the moment that Céline had emerged from her house in her white shorts. Fourth had been telling Vasco he'd seen Sal. Fifth was Sal's murder and the red plastic flower planted in his forehead.

And there'd been smaller nudges, such as the confusion between Fat Bob and Marco Santuzza. And snow, how could he forget the snow? Then, in Wednesday's paper, he'd read about Pappalardo's murder. Drifting back and forth over these events was Céline, like a hawk in cheap clothing, as Vaughn might say. Lastly came Fidget and the theft of Sal Nicoletti's gold.

Only three years ago, Connor had been teaching in Iron Mountain, way up in Michigan's Upper Peninsula. Two years ago he'd taken a job as a slot attendant at the MGM Grand in Detroit. A year ago he'd taken a job as a slot supervisor in San Diego. In terms of the world, he'd been a baby. Excitement for him was an egg dropped on the kitchen floor. Then he'd been seduced by Didi's promise to widen his horizons, which included the Winnebago, Eartha's bare breasts, and Vaughn's hermetic mouthings. Now, in New England, his horizons seemed as misshapen as a kiddies' earthquake-struck jungle gym. Even gravity was problematic. As for Connor's small duties—errands to run, checks to pick up, et cetera—they seemed absurdly immaterial given his present frame of mind. Thus his dislocated agenda.

Connor is distracted from his disagreeable musings by the growing roar of a motorcycle as its sound reverberates deep in his belly. Up and down Water Street, people turn to look. A bright yellow Harley Fat Bob pokes along past the light at Bank Street and past the Soldiers' and Sailors' Monument, where a dozen men and women sit on the steps giving the bike the eye—some positive, some negative—while the female figure of Peace atop the monument's fifty-foot column keeps her back to the station as if to say, *Enough's enough.* The motorcycle slowly passes in front of the train station. The rider wears a black leather jacket and jeans. No helmet, of course. His dark hair with streaks of gray is caught up in a ponytail. He isn't fat; rather, his body seems swollen into a football shape. His face resembles the mug of a good-looking English bulldog having a thought.

Connor sees it's the biker he sat next to in the Exchange. Bob, the waitress called him: Fat Bob. This is who the police were looking for,

thinks Connor, because of the accident, because the crashed Fat Bob belonged to Fat Bob, and because Marco Santuzza had ridden the Fat Bob's
Fat Bob into oblivion.

Fat Bob glances toward Connor and gives him a slow salute. Connor
salutes back. Briefly, their eyes lock in a sympathetic exchange, and then
Fat Bob continues to poke along down Water Street past the bus station
and toward I-95.

Five seconds later, as Connor wonders if the salute had any special
import, he hears a high whine. A red scooter zips down Bank Street onto
Water Street. The rider wears a dark red coat and a red-and-black mackinaw cap. He is small, red-faced, and his narrow head reminds Connor of
a dull ax. The man leans over the handlebars to decrease wind resistance,
because the scooter is only fifty cc's and its top speed is maybe thirty-five
miles per hour. He looks neither right nor left but focuses straight ahead
to where Fat Bob is approaching I-95.

Connor takes two steps into the street. Perhaps he means to pursue
the scooter or pursue Fat Bob. But although Connor is a good runner, his
action is only symbolic. Not even the fastest runner could catch the
scooter, much less Fat Bob. Ahead of Connor, however, are the Grey-
hound bus station and the police department. Maybe one of these forms
his destination, but we'll never know, because at this moment his cell
phone makes its summoning tweedle and Connor comes to a stop. He
slaps at his various pockets, discovers the phone, and presses it to his ear
as he moves to the sidewalk.

It's Didi. "Have you picked up the stuff from the post office?"

"I'm almost there."

"What's the delay?"

"Traffic." Connor wonders if Didi can hear the lie.

"No more fooling around. Remember, we have an obligation to history. I've brought you to New England to train you in the business, and
someday you'll take my place. Eighty years of Bounty, Inc. stretch behind us. Where're your priorities?"

This is surprising and unsurprising to Connor. He hadn't realized he was being groomed, but nor had he understood why Didi should be so insistent that he come on this long trip. Didi's words clarified his intentions.

"What if I don't want to take your place? What if I don't want to work for Bounty, Inc.?"

"It's your destiny. You're a tugo, I'm a tugo. Now, pick up those checks and get back here." Then Didi chuckled and his voice changed. "Oh, yes, I wanted to tell you. D'you know what that crazy Vaughn did? He found some black paint and wrote 'Here lives an orphan from outer space' on the side of the Winnebago. What d'you think of that?" Didi laughs again.

"How're you going to get it off?" Connor began to say it was an irresponsible act, but the term seems inapplicable to Vaughn.

"Why take it off? I like it." Didi cuts the connection.

As he thinks of what it means to be included in Vaughn's inclusive "we," Connor has a glimmer of insight as to why he changed his name from Zeco. He hadn't wanted to get enmeshed in Bounty, Inc., and he still didn't. Being Portuguese was no reason to become a con man. Bounty, Inc. was a family business. It was the *family* he wanted to escape, not his family's nationality.

Standing by the train station, Connor shifts from one foot to the other. He can go up State Street to the post office or up Bank Street in search of Fidget. He takes a step toward State Street and then pivots toward Bank. Surely the post office can wait half an hour. He crosses to the head of Bank Street with the East Bank Gift Shop on the corner; its display windows are crowded with mannequins in multicolored, floor-length, faux-swank Indian gowns designed perhaps for faux romance.

Two shops farther along, Connor pauses at the display window of a small travel agency, his eye caught by a poster of the Pena Palace, a gigantic pink-stone confection perched on a mountaintop in Sintra outside Lisbon. He'd once spent a day with his great-aunt exploring its dozens of rooms, as his tongue occupied itself with repeating the word "splendiferous," the only word that seemed an apt description of what he was seeing. Staring at the poster, he imagines slipping into a small gold-spattered and leather-bound room, maybe a modest library, in one of the palace's high towers, falling back into an armchair, and taking a deep breath.

Connor can't know that his imagined escape duplicates Fidget's retreat to Fat Bob's boarded-up house on Montauk Avenue, but we know it and we share it here. Connor feels packed to his ear tips with opposing obligations, distractions, and anxieties. So for a few seconds, no more than that, he sees himself in a quiet, book-lined room looking out through a narrow leaded window over small white towns with red roofs and rolling summer fields to where a line of white selvage indicates the distant surf of the Atlantic. Oh, blesséd escape.

Then Connor realizes he's not just looking at a travel poster but also into the face of a young woman staring back. If he were chewing a baseball-player wad of bubble gum, he'd swallow it. Such is his surprise. The woman has short, unevenly chopped blond hair with blond highlights and wears wire-rimmed glasses. It's a familiar face.

She comes to the door. "Have you recovered from banging your head on the steering wheel? I don't see any bruises."

Connor likes to think he isn't someone who blushes, but he feels his face turn red. "No, I'm fine. You saved me from myself."

"Well, I'm glad beating your head isn't a hobby. Collecting stamps would be better. You must work near here. I've seen you go by." She stands in the doorway observing him with birdlike attention. She's thin, like a runner, and her blue blouse matches her blue eyes. Perhaps she's four inches shorter than Connor.

"No, I've been looking for someone. Do you stare at everyone who walks by?"

"Just about. My desk is by the window, and I sit around waiting for people who want to take geographic cures. Are you looking for someone who works near here? Maybe I can help. I've been here almost nine months."

The woman has an oval face with a pointed chin, and she watches Connor with the good humor of someone telling a joke. A strand of hair falls across her right eye, and she flicks it away. Connor likes how easily she talks to him but thinks if she's bored with her job, she must be talking to him out of boredom.

"What's your name?"

"Linda."

She looks at him inquiringly, expecting him to identify himself. Connor isn't sure whether he should use his regular name or a Portuguese name or some other name that he might like to assume, such as Rex or Woodruff. "Connor," he says.

"Are you Irish?"

"Not that I know of."

"Connor's often an Irish name."

"Then maybe I should change it."

"No, don't do that. I like it. But you don't seem Irish—your hair's too black."

"I could be black Irish," says Connor.

They both smile and look at each other for an extended moment. Then Connor says, "I'm trying to find a homeless man. I'm told his name is Fidget."

"Oh, I know him," says Linda brightly. "He often walks around asking for spare change. I've talked to him several times. I like him, but he smells. I think it's his feet. I haven't seen him today, but he might be along the street someplace. Why're you looking for him?"

"Do you always ask so many questions?" Connor, whose work with Bounty, Inc. exists on the shady edge of legality, has what we may call "functional paranoia." He's often suspicious of people he meets, especially those who ask questions. "I'd just like to talk to him about the accident on Monday."

Linda tilts her head slightly. She's tempted to ask Connor if he's a reporter, but she doesn't want to ask another question. "I heard the crash, but in the office I'm on the far side of where the motorcycle hit the truck, so I saw nothing, luckily. It must have been awful."

Connor nods as Linda folds her arms. "Are you getting cold?" he asks. "You should go back inside."

"I was just going up the street for coffee when I saw you. I'll get my jacket."

Connor's functional paranoia resurfaces. He considers walking away, but it would be rude. Anyway, he doesn't want to. Linda reappears wearing a half-length dark red jacket with a double row of silver buttons, which, on closer inspection, prove to be plastic. It's the sort of low-cost coat made to look like a high-priced coat.

"No hat?"

"They mess up my hair," says Linda, whose ragged cut looks professionally messed with one side longer than the other, which gives her diagonal bangs. "Do you think I'm pushy? Really, I was going out for coffee anyway. And Fidget knows me. I give him a silver dollar now and then. I always carry a bunch of them." She shakes her pocket, and there's a jingling noise.

"To give away?"

"It's much easier than making excuses or pretending I don't see people, though it costs more in the summer. I'm probably getting a reputation."

Connor can't think of a suitable response. "At least it's generous," he says.

"More practical than generous. It's like I'm paying for safe passage. But they're friendly enough, for the most part."

"No one bothers you?"

"Never. Fidget even told me about his tail."

"Tail?" Connor thinks he isn't sharing in a conversation so much as chasing after one.

"Like a Komodo dragon, or so he says. I've never seen it myself. It shows up when he's coming to from a blackout after drinking Everclear."

By now they've reached a four-story yellow brick building with the word HOLLYWOOD painted over the bolted-shut front door. Above are Palladian windows sealed with gray plywood. On either side of the windows, four brick pilasters, three stories high, resemble Greek columns emerging from the brick wall. A plain, classical frieze runs across the building below the roof.

"This's the Capitol Theatre," said Linda. "It's been closed for forty years. No sprinkler system, and no one wants to buy it. Supposedly it's very fancy inside. It's probably full of rats."

"Was it a movie theater?"

"For a while at the end, but it was built in the twenties as a vaudeville theater. It's where George Burns met Gracie Allen—isn't that romantic?"

The names are only vaguely familiar to Connor. "Hmm," he says. "It'd be nice to see what it's like inside. A bunch of those theaters from the twenties were decorated to look like ancient palaces. Is there a back door?"

"Off a parking lot, but it's shut up like these."

"There's got to be a functioning door someplace. People must go in and out."

"Not that I've seen, though that doesn't mean anything. It's just a dead building and probably haunted. Why're you interested?"

"No reason, I guess. Just curiosity. Well, I don't expect to see it in any case."

Connor and Linda continue up the street.

We should say that Connor is mistaken about never seeing the inside of the Capitol Theatre. It's like those times when a person says, "I'll never break my leg." The next day he falls down the stairs and breaks his leg. To claim certainty about a future possibility is risky business. Didi would claim that the tradiculous is at work again. For instance, if we brag we never get the flu, we'll get it by the weekend. But such claims rarely work in our favor. If we say we'll win a million dollars, we won't. This is how we know it's an example of the tradiculous, because if it weren't, then the negative and positive would show up fifty-fifty. So with Connor saying he doesn't expect he'll see the inside of the Capitol Theatre. It's a form of tempting fate, especially if the consequences are negative—that is, like awful.

"So if you don't work around here," says Linda, "what sort of work d'you do?"

Connor stumbles over his feet, which suddenly feel very large. Linda catches his arm. The feel of her touch startles him, as if they shared a metaphysical link, and perhaps this is what leads him to be truthful, or perhaps he's just tired of lying.

"I work for some people who collect money for phantom organizations that support phantom causes."

Linda has stopped, and they look at one another. Pedestrians divide and pass around them like a stream passing around a rock.

"What sorts of organizations?"

"They change. Right now it's Prom Queens Anonymous, Orphans from Outer Space, and the Holy Sisters of the Blessed Little Feet."

Linda laughs. She laughs so hard she has to lean against a building. Connor waits. He had expected censorious indignation, not laughter.

"That's wonderful," says Linda, still laughing. "What do you do with the money?" She wipes her eyes with a tissue. They begin walking again.

"We spend it, though Didi—he's in charge—gives fifteen percent to real organizations if they're vaguely similar to a phantom organization. For instance, we've also been collecting for Free Beagles from Nicotine Addiction, and Didi says some of the money goes to the Humane Society, but I'm not sure I believe him."

"Why not?" Once more Linda begins to laugh.

"His relationship to the truth is relatively elastic."

"I guess it'd have to be. Who gets money from Orphans from Outer Space?"

"Well, that specific organization brings in very little, so I assume he puts it in the general fund." Connor thinks that if he expanded his account of Bounty, Inc. to include the work of Vaughn Monroe and Eartha Kitt, she'd be certain they were nuts. *Maybe we are,* he thinks. *Maybe we're in some kind of alternate universe.*

Connor and Linda have reached the corner, and Linda stops. "This is as far as I'm going. I'll get a cup of coffee and take it back to the office. I'm already late."

Connor is surprised. He hadn't thought of her going. "Now? What about Fidget?" Besides being disappointed, he feels an element of grief. Just a touch. It's like a chill inside him, and the day gets a bit darker, though it's only midmorning. At first he doesn't recognize the feeling, a tiny mix of sadness and loss. We don't want to make too much of this. This particular element of grief is just a seedling.

"Either you'll find him or you won't, even if I come with you. Just keep going up the street." She sticks out her hand. "I liked talking to you."

"Don't tell the police."

Linda laughs again. "Of course not. Actually, I'd much rather work for you than for the travel agency. It sounds great."

Connor shakes her hand. She wears brown leather gloves, so, really, he has no idea what her hand feels like. The handshake contains no intimacy, but she has a strong grip. He imagines asking her to take off her glove, and he smiles to himself.

"What's funny?" asks Linda.

He shakes his head. "May I have your phone number?" The question takes some courage on his part.

Linda hesitates and then says no. "I don't think it's a good idea." How complex are the simplest of exchanges. Their faces express interest, but Linda thinks, *Should I?* And Connor had thought, *Why not ask her?* As for their emotions, there're a bunch of them, starting with Connor's disappointment, which leads to the worry that she finds him unattractive. Maybe she doesn't like his black hair or his dark eyes, or maybe his chin is too big. And Linda thinks, *Why do I always say no? Dr. Goodenough has been saying I need to take a chance. What am I afraid of?*

We know these situations. They've been repeated millions of times. Anna Karenina and Count Vronsky had similar exchanges, but they spoke in Russian, which makes it more interesting.

"Are you married?" asks Connor.

Linda shakes her head.

"Do you have a steady boyfriend?"

She again shakes her head and then says, "But I'm in the office every day. You can stop by whenever you want."

"Maybe I'll do that." He says good-bye, waits for the light at Golden Street, and then crosses. The element of grief within him has begun to sprout. He no longer has an interest in finding Fidget. But he won't give up; he'll keep looking. Bank Street, Tilley, Green Street, State, Starr Street, Pearl—Connor walks them all. By noon, with sore feet, he quits to get a sandwich.

We should understand that Connor is torn. First we have Eartha with her scientifically engineered breasts that include silver nipple bars with tiny rubies at the tips. Then there's Céline. Tight white shorts and a small white T-shirt, black eyes, a tangle of black hair. She might lack Eartha's warmth, might in fact be devoid of warmth, but her half smile made Connor shiver.

Then there's Linda with her glasses and her short, slanting blond hair and runner's body. Connor finds her very pretty, but he also likes her manner, her edge of irony and interest, and he liked her laugh and her response to Orphans from Outer Space. Well, such comparisons are complicated. Put these ladies on a wheel and put Connor on the hub and have them circling and circling, and Connor would be no more dizzy than he is now.

EIGHTEEN

Manny pulls his Subaru Forester up in front of the Hog Hurrah. To his left, a dozen shining Harleys are parked side by side like multicolored jewels waiting to be strung for a giantess's matinee necklace. "I could knock them over with a little push," says Manny. "Wanna see it?"

"Why would you want to?" says Vikström, getting out of the car.

"Just to add a few vitamins to the day. A little adrenaline." Manny's black eye has become a pale yellow with some bits darker than others.

Vikström decides not to answer. Looking at the row of Harleys, he sees a red one that looks exactly like a red one he'd seen in Fat Bob's garage. Actually the color is called Amber Whiskey. At the moment he assumes it's a coincidence.

The detectives stand on the sidewalk by Manny's car. They've spent three hours looking for Fidget without success. Now they want to talk to Lisowski. The doors of the Hog Hurrah are up, and biker types give them quick looks, though—considering what Lisowski said—they're more likely brain surgeons or real estate agents.

"You know what my wife did?" Manny asks in a stage whisper.

This sort of question generally drives Manny crazy, and if Vikström had asked it, Manny would shout, "How the fuck could I know what your wife did!"

Vikström says, "Please tell me." He suspects that Manny is at the very edge of an explosion, and he has no wish to ignite the fuse.

Manny stands with his legs apart. His overcoat is unbuttoned and shows his blue suit. The sun twinkles on his silver belt buckle with the dying Indian slouched forward over his starving horse. A flicker of suspicion crosses his face: Vikström isn't usually so polite.

"She gave a thousand bucks to a crook on the phone who promised to use the money to keep dogs from smoking cigarettes. You ever heard such nonsense? We had a fight, and I've got to sleep on the living room couch."

Vikström maintains his friendly expression. He decides he's being baited in a complicated way he has yet to understand. "Who knew that dogs were problem smokers? Is this what's been making you angry?"

"Wouldn't it make *you* angry?"

"We don't have a dog. How do the dogs buy the cigarettes?"

"They don't fucking buy them, nitwit," says Manny, raising his voice. "The dogs are in medical-research labs hooked up to machines that make them smoke. Yvonne says they have yellow lips, and she says the fucking check has already been cashed. She sent it to a post office box."

"All kinds of dogs?" Vikström notices that many of the ponytailed, middle-aged men in black leather vests have put down their tools and are listening.

"Fuck no, just beagles. Yvonne says they only use beagles because they're so bighearted, like our Schultzie. She says they use seventy thousand beagles a year."

One of the ponytailed middle-aged men whistles in surprise. Manny shoots him a look that says, *I could crush your head with my bare hands if I wanted.*

"So they're not *made* to smoke, they *choose* to?"

"First they're made, then they choose. They're addicted."

"What happens after?"

"Just what you'd expect—they're tossed in the trash."

A biker makes a sympathetic groan.

"Still," says Vikström, perhaps forgetting himself, "it's for a good cause."

"Fuck you! You never had a dog. Anyway, they're crooks. No charity gets money to make dogs stop smoking. They call themselves FBNA, Inc. That stands for 'Free Beagles from Nicotine Addiction.' I Googled it, and it doesn't exist." Manny lowers his voice. "And one more thing."

"What's that?"

"She said the guy on the phone sounded exactly like Vaughn Monroe."

"The singer? Isn't he dead?"

"He's Yvonne's favorite singer. We always sing his stuff at—" Here Manny glances at the ponytailed bikers, who listen as if hearing Shakespeare recited. Manny drops his voice even lower. "On our karaoke nights."

Vikström sees Milo Lisowski standing in the door of his office. As we've said, he has a glass eye, a wandering eye, or he suffers from strabismus, with each eye pointing in a different direction. We don't know which is correct. So even though Manny and Vikström are standing five feet apart, each thinks that Lisowski's stare is focused on him alone. *Why the fuck's he staring at me?* This thought comes to both. In truth Lisowski looks at a spot between them, or someplace else entirely, like up at the clouds.

"You been to the post office to check the mailbox?" asks Vikström.

"The wife wants me to leave things as they are. She says it's her money from her bank account, which is true enough. And there's the Vaughn Monroe stuff. She doesn't want me fucking around with Vaughn Monroe. It's almost a religious thing."

"So this's what's pissing you off?"

"Let's say it's not cheering me up."

"What about Vaughn Monroe?" asks Vikström.

"I don't give a fuck about Vaughn Monroe!" shouts Manny. "Fucking Vaughn Monroe died in 1973! No more fucking ghost riders in the sky for *him!*"

Vikström sees that ten ponytailed bikers stand in the doorway staring at the detectives. Some seem amused, some critical. Lisowski stands to one side. They all have expectant expressions as they wait to hear what the detectives will say next. Lisowski's can't be read. Vikström takes Manny's arm. "We need to talk to Lisowski and beat it unless you want TV trucks to start showing up. These guys are waiting for you to pop."

A minute later the detectives are in Lisowski's small office with its piles of papers, catalogs, repair manuals, newspapers, and several banana peels. Lisowski leans against his desk, and Manny stands in front of him. Vikström stands back by the door, thinking about lunch. The office smells of oil and bananas. Nobody says anything. Lisowski gets increasingly uncomfortable. His blue overalls are spotted with grease, and his wandering eyes are doing calisthenics.

"We just going to stand here?" says Lisowski, acting tough. "I'm going back to work." He takes a step toward the door.

Manny holds out a hand signifying stop. "We'd like to see your pistol."

"I don't know what you're talking about."

"The pistol you used to shoot up Fat Bob's Fat Bob: the bike that burned in front of his house. We picked up ten nine-millimeter casings."

"I haven't had a pistol for years."

"You got a permit for a Smith & Wesson 469," says Vikström. The news about Lisowski's pistol permit came back that morning. This is what led to the detectives' visit.

"The gun's in the house someplace. I don't know exactly where."

"You report it as missing?" asks Vikström.

"No, no," says Manny, "he means it maybe slipped between the cushions of his favorite chair. It could happen. It's one of the small ones, right? Three-and-a-half-inch barrel, shortened grip? It's probably somewhere under the rug, or—I know—you lost it in the wash like a stray sock." Manny bends over and sneezes. It's one of those joke sneezes invented around the time of the *Mayflower*: "Horse-shit!" Then he straightens up and gives a smile as thin as a crack in a teacup.

Vikström has heard Manny do this five hundred times, and his face is stony. "Why would someone shoot up the Fat Bob?" he asks.

One of Lisowski's eyes seems focused on the window looking into the garage, where two impact wrenches practice a duet. The other looks idly at the ceiling.

"Beats me," says Lisowski.

"Hey!" says Manny. "You got to do better than that. We're having a pleasant chat. We take you downtown, it won't be pleasant."

"I told you before," says Lisowski with some exasperation. "Fat Bob owes people money, and he's not paying. Lots of people are pissed at him."

"How much does he owe you?" asks Vikström.

"'Bout a grand."

"You said before it was a coupla hundred," says Vikström.

Manny interrupts, seeming astonished. "You blew up a guy's bike for a thousand bucks?"

"I told you, I'd nothing to do with it, but I bet whoever blew it up didn't think the bike would explode. He only wanted to put some holes in it."

"Just clean fun, right?" says Manny. "What happened to the money?"

"He lost it at Foxwoods. He thought he had a system."

"How many people does he owe money to?" asks Vikström.

Lisowski works hard to appear helpful and patient, but a muscle in his cheek twitches impishly. "I don't know. Ten, maybe twenty, maybe more. This goes back a few years. It adds up."

Manny points to the window and the garage beyond. "He owe money to any of those guys?"

"Dunno, you'll have to ask them."

"You own a green Ford?" asks Vikström, who already knows he doesn't.

"Not me. I got a Tacoma. White."

"A green Ford pulls up to Fat Bob's old house with two guys in the car," says Manny. "The guy riding shotgun is the shooter. He blasts the bike and they're gone. A day later some guys swipe bikes from the garage of Fat Bob's *new* place. Maybe the same guys. So, Lisowski, if you weren't driving the Ford, you had to have been the shooter. You blast the bike with your Smith & Wesson and leave lots of nine-millimeter shells.

During the shooting the bike explodes. Maybe it's an accident, but no court will buy that. In fact, because it exploded, it looks like terrorism. But you give us the gun and say who was driving the Ford, maybe we'll drop the terrorism charge. You ever been to one of those training camps in Afghanistan?"

Lisowski is pressed back against his desk. "Course not! I hardly leave the state except for Motorcycle Week up in Laconia. What d'you mean, Afghanistan?"

Vikström shrugs. "He's joking. He can be a funny guy. . . ." Vikström wants to ask Lisowski about the red Fat Bob out in front, but Manny keeps distracting him.

"By the way," says Manny, "you seen Fidget anywhere?"

"The homeless guy? What's he got to do with anything?"

"Just need to talk to him," says Manny.

Lisowski begins to tell them he hasn't seen Fidget, but then he says, "Someone mentioned they'd seen him coming out of a package store across town with a couple bags of stuff. Said he was practically dancing."

"When was this?" asks Vikström.

"I don't know, yesterday maybe."

"Who told you?" asks Manny.

Lisowski pulls thoughtfully at his nose. "That's what I can't re-member."

Manny and Vikström aren't sure they believe him. Then Manny gives Lisowski a card. "Call us when it comes back to you. Okay? And don't forget, we want the pistol or else." Manny opens the door.

"Wait a second," says Vikström. "That red Fat Bob out in front, you took it from Fat Bob's garage, didn't you?"

Lisowski opens his mouth as he constructs what he hopes will be a credible lie. But there's no point. The detectives can check the VIN number.

"I bought it from Angelina. She had the title. We're a number."

"A number?" asks Manny.

"We've been dating."

"Jesus Christ, and you're alive to talk about it?" Manny wants to ask if Angelina really has tangles of pubic hair from her thighs to her belly, but he can't get up the nerve, which seems unusual for Manny.

"Come on, let's go," Vikström tells his partner.

The detectives consider taking Lisowski downtown, but it wouldn't be worth the effort. The trouble is, with the FBI buzzing around, the main focus is on Sal and the casinos. They've no interest in Fat Bob or the motorcycles. Manny and Vikström still want to talk to Fat Bob and learn more about why Jack Sprat wants to kill him, but they don't think they can charge him with anything. And then there's Fidget.

Walking back to the Subaru, Manny's impressed that Vikström recognized the red Fat Bob, but he won't compliment him on his sharp eyes. Instead he says with a sigh, "Can't wait to get back to the box."

Vikström, whose mind is still on Lisowski, mishears. "You fight?"

"Hunh?" says Manny.

"You box? What's your weight?"

"Karaoke box, asshole, karaoke box!"

"Ah," says Vikström, who likes boxing and had thought that he and his partner might share a common interest.

During the day Vaughn and Eartha make their calls. We've heard these before, and not much difference is to be found from one to the next except in terms of gusto and a bit of ad-libbing. After all, they have a script. But here's one we need to mention: a call that Vaughn made in the morning.

He dials, and a woman answers. "Yeah?"

Frantic question. "Angelina, is Magsie right there by your side?"

Angelina notes the familiar voice. After all, her parents had lots of Vaughn Monroe's albums, not just *Riders in the Sky* but also *On the Moon-beam, There! I've Sung It Again,* and *Ruby,* with the Moon Maids and Moon Men. She's also stunned that yesterday she talked to Eartha Kitt about Prom Queens Anonymous and now she's talking to Vaughn Monroe. But first things first. "How'd you get this number?"

"Please, please, Angelina, no delays! Is Magsie in the house?"

"I think he's upstairs." Her voice contains a hint of uncertainty.

"Run go see! It's important! I'd be crushed if anything's happened!"

Angelina sets down the phone and hurries off. Although she thinks, *Nutcase, nutcase,* she wants to make sure Magsie's safe.

Two minutes pass as Vaughn puts clear polish on his nails. Then Angelina returns. "Okay, wise guy, Magsie's right here on my lap."

"Oh, thank goodness, thank goodness. The dog trucks are out, and they're gobbling up beagles all over town. I've seen fistfuls of fur in the gutters!"

"Gobbling?"

"They steal them from right under your nose and sell them to midnight labs for research. They make them smoke nonfiltered cigarettes! You must, must, *must* put your trust in FBNA! Your donation will be your pup's lifeblood."

"What's FBNA?"

"Free Beagles from Nicotine Addiction, Inc. It's all that stands between your pup and years of torment."

Angelina puts up a good fight, but at last she offers fifty bucks, and she might have given more if she weren't saving up for her face-lift, et cetera. Anyway, she's already contributed fifty bucks to Prom Queens Anonymous.

Vaughn reads from his script. "Am I to understand that your love for Magsie is worth only fifty dollars? Your dear pup has given you thousands of hours of love and devotion, and your fifty-dollar pledge adds up to a hundredth of a penny for each of those hours. To my mind that's a shocking admission. Tell me, Angelina, do you secretly hate your little dog?"

"Fuck you, you son of a bitch! You're lucky I can't twist your balls off!"

In his work Vaughn has heard this sort of anger before. What he listens for, however, are the choked sobs beneath the shouting. And he thinks he hears them.

"Please, Angelina, no personal attacks. It's Magsie's welfare that matters here. We need to speak calmly. What about one hundred?"

"It's fifty or nothing, shithead! Unless you want a motorcycle. I got a bunch of them, all Harleys. I'll sell you one cheap."

We shouldn't think that Angelina is a fan of motorcycles. Her life with Fat Bob has led to a serious hatred of Harleys, since she suspects he prefers the touch of his Fat Bob to her own caresses, which is probably true. But Fat Bob is at the edge of bankruptcy. He owes money to lots of people. And, as said before, Angelina holds the titles to the Harleys in the garage on Montauk Avenue. She doesn't hold these titles out of kindness; it's simple leverage. It lets her make Fat Bob jump through hoops.

"I'm sorry," says Vaughn, "we don't do merchandise."

They haggle some more. At last Didi signals to Vaughn to accept the fifty bucks. Time is money, and the conversation is lasting too long.

Then, before Angelina hangs up, she asks, "Tell me, d'you know Eartha Kitt?"

Vaughn Monroe rumbles with a sound comparable to distant, stampeding cattle. "The name's familiar, but I like male singers best, tenors and baritones. Does she live around here?"

"I'm beginning to wonder."

The day progresses. Connor has no luck in finding Fidget, so by late afternoon he's picked up the mail from the P.O. and stopped at a dozen houses where people have promised sums ranging from fifty to one hundred dollars. As said before, these actions spike Connor's anxiety to lunar levels, since each could lead to his arrest. But every so often Didi has called with another bunch of names. Soon Connor will head back to the Winnebago, but now he has time for one last visit: Angelina Rossi.

The name rings a bell, but Connor ignores the subliminal warning. And maybe Angelina's house looks familiar, but he's already visited many houses, and at the moment he is busily comparing the attractions of Linda and Céline. Each, to Connor's mind, has trunkloads of allure, so to compare them is serious work.

He hurries up the steps and rings the bell. Again he experiences a subliminal discomfort. There's the metallic rattle of locks being unfastened, and the door opens.

"You!" barks Angelina.

The scales fall from Connor's eyes, and he squeezes his expression into one of happy incredulity. "What a glad surprise!" His smile hovers at the cusp of lockjaw.

"I just gave you money yesterday!" says Angelina through the screen. "You're supposed to work for Prom Queens Anonymous. What's going on?"

Connor knows if he bolts down the street, Angelina will pursue him. Were he a dog, he'd roll over and pee a little. He laughs gaily. "Oh, I see your mistake. You think I'm actually employed by PQA, Inc. No, no, no. To save money for their prime target, these groups, with others, have formed a consortium to see to the gathering and distribution of funds. Occasionally I visit the same house five or six times."

Angelina believes none of this. "And what about Eartha Kitt and Vaughn Monroe? What kind of trick is that?"

"Charities employ many voices: Julie London, the Big Bopper, Lupe Fiasco. As for me, I don't like it, but management claims it lifts the comfort level of donors."

"So it's a trick!"

"No, no, no!" Connor feels sweat forming on his forehead on this otherwise cool day. "It's like a beautiful woman wearing perfume. Does she need the perfume? Can you call it a trick? Of course not. It only adds a touch of magnitude to the package."

Angelina keeps lobbing shells of grievance, and Connor dodges them. At last he says, "Do you have the check right now?"

Angelina looks steely, and Connor looks benign. In fact, Angelina tries to look generous, because she's formulated a plan, while Connor tries not to show panic. Each sees the deception of the other.

"I don't have it right now," says Angelina, "but I'm expecting it soon. Would you like to come in and wait?"

Connor's benign expression acquires hints of terror. No way will he enter Angelina's house. He glances at his watch and makes a sad face. "I have several more appointments. Could I come back around seven?"

"I've just baked brownies," says Angelina, who has never baked anything sweet in her life. "I'm sure they're still warm. I bet you'd like a couple with a cup of coffee." She pushes open the door.

"We're on a pretty tight schedule. Save the brownies for later. Shall we make it seven o'clock?" He tries to back down the steps without falling.

We don't know if Connor's education included the tale of Medusa with her rattlesnake ringlets and knack of turning men to stone, but he suspects Angelina's skills fall in that area of expertise. He also knows she intends to call the police. He walks quickly to the Mini-Cooper, almost a run. He'll deposit the checks he's picked up during the day in the FBNA account and return to the Winnebago.

C onnor is driving back to Brewster when his cell phone tweedles. It's Vasco.

"What the fuck are you doing, Zeco?"

Connor imagines many possible answers, but he says, "Driving back to the Winnebago." It's sunset, and the sky is red behind him.

"Not now, you silly fuck. What do you mean going over to Céline's? You got to stay away from there. You'll get yourself hurt. Chucky's furious."

Connor is more angered at being called a "silly fuck" than interested in why Chucky might be furious.

"She invited me. She's upset."

"You think she's a grieving widow? Sal Nicoletti's name is Danny Barbarella, and he's from Detroit, like you said. The whole thing's an FBI setup. Céline's an escort hired to play a part. No wife, no kids, it's all bullshit. Stay away from her."

"She called, and I went over. That's all. I feel sorry for her."

"You're caught in something too big for you. Shall I tell her you're a cheap little charity con man? How's she going to feel when she learns you're the one who outed Danny? Céline stood to make a good chunk of money from this charade. How'll she like it when she hears you fucked it up?"

Connor hears slot machines jangling in the background and doesn't answer. He wants to think his brother is lying, but he doesn't know why Vasco should lie.

"There're guys that don't like you, and Chucky's at the top of the list. He hurts people. It's his job. He wants you to find Fidget and to stay away from Céline. You go to her house again, bad things will happen. I'm just passing on the message."

NINETEEN

Manny drives down Eugene O'Neill Drive, three lanes heading into town. It's Thursday afternoon. He and Vikström are coming from Lisowski's Hog Hurrah. Their disappointment isn't as bad as broken toothpicks in a toddler's Christmas stocking, but it's disappointment nonetheless. As for Eugene O'Neill, Manny believes he was a former New London mayor, but he's not sure. He could ask Vikström, who knows that sort of thing, but he doesn't want to give Vikström the opportunity to be right. Better to be wrong and silent than to see Vikström smirk. Merely the chance of this, for Manny, is an irritant.

"I just can't fuckin' believe," says Manny, "that Lisowski is banging Angelina. He didn't even have any black-and-blue marks."

"Maybe they're still at the hand-holding stage," says Vikström.

"You kidding? She's a crocodile. They don't nibble—they gulp. One bite and he's gone. He's lucky to be alive. She's walking *vagina dentata.*"

"Vagina what?"

"Pussy with teeth. It's Latin—the Romans had it. That's why their empire fell."

Manny's brain is moving too fast for Vikström. "Has it occurred to you that Lisowski might have busted into Burns Insurance and stolen Fat Bob's computer?"

"Say more." *Uh-oh, here's Vikström being right again,* Manny thinks.

"It happened Monday night or early Tuesday morning when most people thought Fat Bob was dead. Angelina might want the computer to see if Fat Bob had any hidden money or other stuff she could get from him. She wouldn't break in herself, but if she and Lisowski were 'a number,' she might get him to do it. Like, who else would do it?"

Manny is silent, then says, "Fat Bob might do it himself to hide his tracks, or a thug from the casino might do it to see if Bob had any 'hidden money,' as you say."

"Sure, those are possibilities, but Lisowski had already shot up Fat Bob's Fat Bob. He might have broken into Burns's place around then or later."

"So how do we hang it on him?"

"That's the trouble, I don't know. But if we get a hold of his pistol and ballistics can tie it to the shells we found around the shot-up Fat Bob, then that's a start."

"If, if, if," says Manny. He hates disappointment. It's often with him twenty-four hours a day. So when it shows up, he takes it out on Vikström, his special target.

Vikström, on the other hand, meets disappointment philosophically, or what he calls philosophically, meaning they'll find their answers soon or, conversely, they won't. And in two or three days, the disappointing event or person or fact will be buried under the weight of a dozen new cases.

Looking out the passenger window, Vikström thinks that proving Lisowski shot up Fat Bob's Fat Bob would mean getting search warrants for the Hog Hurrah and Lisowski's house to look for the pistol. But their supervisor, Detective Sergeant Masters, would never sign off on it. He hears her saying, *Is this another one of your hunches, Detective?* And he imagines her sarcasm dripping like fat from a cheap steak. Anyway, the pistol might be at Angelina's—or simply elsewhere—and they'll never find it.

At the moment the detectives are on their way to talk to Angelina, which does nothing to improve their mood. They again want to ask her about Fat Bob and where he might be found. And they may ask about Lisowski and his pistol. Vikström believes that Angelina won't be as angry as she was the other night, which will make her easier to talk to. So the visit is Vikström's idea. Manny has no wish to see Angelina again. His annoyance with Vikström is like semi-molten magma bubbling near the surface.

Out of the blue, Manny says, "I've been meaning to tell you: you don't want to pronounce it like 'okeyDOkey' or 'upsy-DAIsy.' It's not like that. Only beginners pronounce it 'kar-ee-O-kee.' The real pronunciation is 'KAR-e-o-KEE.' That's how the Japanese pronounce it, and that's how we should pronounce it."

Vikström feels he's been struck in the head by a sock full of wet sand. Where had this attack come from? "*You* always pronounce it 'kar-ee-O-kee.'"

"That's because I don't want to be accused of showing off. How's it going to seem if the only ones to pronounce it correctly are me, the Japanese, and maybe a few Koreans? So you've got to start saying it right."

Vikström begins to protest but asks himself, *Is it really worth it?* "You mean like 'CARE-e-o-KEY'?"

"That's not bad, but it's still not correct. You got to hit the first syllable like 'KAR,' more of a *K* sound than hard *C*; and 'KAR' is pronounced somewhere between 'KAR' and 'CARE.' Let's hear you do it."

Vikström begins to feel sullen, but he gives it a try. "KAR, KAR, KAR!"

"That's good, but not good enough. Say 'KAR, KAR, KAR!'"

"For Pete's sake, that's what I said!"

"No, you're slipping off the diphthong. Look, don't get pissed I'm trying to help. You'll have to practice it at home till you get it right. Now for the hard part. It's not 'KAR-e-o-KEY.' It's 'KAR-e-o-KEEEEE'! Try it."

"CARE-e-o-KEE!"

"Better, but it won't win no cigar. Hit that last syllable hard."

Vikström feels trapped in Manny's irritating game as he might feel trapped in a jail cell. "CARE-e-o-KEEE, CARE-e-o-KEEEEE!"

The Subaru has stopped in Angelina Rossi's driveway. Angelina's on the front porch; she looks at Vikström as if he were fighting his way out of his human form into something Martian. She's not sure whether to run into the house and call the police or to pretend that she's suddenly gone deaf and has heard nothing.

Vikström sees Angelina on the porch with her eyes squeezed half shut and her mouth half open. He turns to Manny. He doesn't shout, but he grinds his teeth.

"That's much better," says Manny, getting out of the car. "We'll do the whole thing again later."

"Fat fucking chance," mutters Vikström as Manny slams the car door.

Soon Vikström and Manny stand in Angelina's living room while she hovers in the doorway of the kitchen—a possible escape—and her beagle, Magsie, dances in front of the detectives barking its little heart out. Angelina wears tight jeans and a dark turtleneck sweater—lingering echoes, perhaps, of having been a prom queen.

Vikström's afraid he'll have to kick the dog if it attacks.

Manny says, "We got one of those. Call it Schultzie. Cutest thing in the world."

Angelina chooses not to be diverted from the main subject. She nods toward Vikström. "Why was that guy screaming in your car?"

Manny holds up a finger. "Not screaming. Shouting. There's a difference."

Angelina isn't satisfied. "I should call the police and get a conjunction."

Vikström tries to bend his features into a warm smile. "We'd like to ask a few more questions about Fat Bob. You have any pictures?"

"I burned them, like I told you last time. I burned everything, even burned his jockstrap. Whyn't you lock up the con men who want to steal my pup? The guy was just here for the second fucking time trying to get my money. I just called 911. That's why you showed up, right?"

Manny and Vikström have heard nothing about the 911 call. Manny says, "I was just getting to that. We came personally to make sure you were safe."

"They called me and called my ex, and we've both got unlisted phones. A woman called about giving money to Prom Queens Anonymous. I Googled the name and couldn't find it. And the guy who called today had a voice like a famous singer."

"Vaughn Monroe," says Manny.

Vikström's surprised. "How'd you know?"

Manny chooses not to say. "I've had my eye on him. Were you told to send the money to a post office box in New London?"

Angelina nods. She finds Manny a reliable sort of fellow, unlike the other one.

Vikström feels unsteady on his legs. "How d'you know this stuff?"

Manny shrugs. "Elementary multitasking."

"The guy who came to the house, I told him to stop by later for my check. That's why I called 911, so you could catch him."

"Good thinking, but I doubt he'll show. We'll stake out the post office."

Vikström keeps his mouth shut. Manny and Angelina have exchanged a look, which is not sexual but has marked them as platonic soul mates.

"Can you describe the guy?" asks Manny.

"He was young, tall, and he had a tan—"

"Ah," interrupts Manny. "We know him—Connor Raposo. Very dangerous. Do you feel safe? We could put you up in a hotel with a guard."

Manny shows no surprise that once again they've come across the young man with the tan, but Vikström is stunned. He's torn between being impressed and disgusted by his partner. No way could Manny get permission to put Angelina in even a cheap motel. He begins to speak, but he sees that Manny and Angelina are communicating in a nonverbal region somewhere high above him, one from which he's excluded. Maybe it's not a bad thing, Vikström decides.

"I'm okay here." Angelina opens the door to the hall closet and stands on her tiptoes, reaching into the top shelf. Her tight jeans creak. "I have a weapon." She pulls down a vicious-looking long stiletto. The detectives feel little surges of adrenaline.

"It's a Chinese folding spike bayonet. Daddy brought it back from Korea. He was a marine. He said I could use it against scumbags." The bayonet is fifteen inches long and looks like a fat needle.

"That should do the trick," says Manny.

"I should've grabbed it when that guy came to the door," says Angelina, "but I didn't want to turn my back on him. I could've stuck him."

Manny and Angelina again look fondly at one another, but again it's platonic. It's a beagle owner's kind of fondness.

Vikström, on the other hand, feels a burst of sympathy for Connor. Maybe *he* can't picture Connor stuck with a Chinese bayonet and bleeding all over his black Bruno Magli slip-ons, but *we* picture it well enough.

"So where can we find your ex-husband?" says Vikström, feeling impatient.

Turning in unison, Manny and Angelina give Vikström identical looks of annoyance; when they turn back to one another, their features soften.

"Tell me," says Manny, "what are your feelings about karaoke?"

"No!" shouts Vikström. "What about Fat Bob and the guy with the tan?!"

Angelina ignores him. "Really, I've never tried it, but I've always thought it looked wonderful. My ex, the fuck, didn't like music."

"What a pity," says Manny. "My partner doesn't like music either." Angelina and Manny assume identical frowns.

"These partnerships look so good at the beginning," says Angelina.

"Say, you know what?" asks Manny, as if he's just discovered anti-matter. "They got karaoke apps on smartphones. I got one right here." Manny digs an iPhone out of his back pocket. "We could try a song. It would get you started!"

"Oh, I'd be too embarrassed." Angelina blushes. It's probably her first blush since junior high school.

Vikström stands in the entryway. He's appalled.

Manny jabs buttons on his phone. "It'll just take a second. You say you like Vaughn Monroe?"

Angelina doesn't deny it.

"The words'll scroll past on the screen. Sorry the speaker's so shitty." Manny holds the phone in front of Angelina's nose. "See? Here it is. We'll sing together."

Angelina leans forward. Though shy, she doesn't want to miss this chance. The music starts; the words appear. Manny and Angelina stand so close that Manny's right ear vanishes within her tangles of black hair.

"An old cowpoke went ridin' out one dark and windy day.
Upon a ridge he rested as he went along his way.
When all at once a mighty herd of red-eyed cows he saw,
A-plowin' through the ragged skies and up a cloudy draw. . . ."

Vikström backs against the front door. He's afraid he'll shoot them both out of psychotic aggravation. We know what happens with temporary lunacy. People get weird. Angelina's voice is a high soprano. It's not bad, but it's untaught. When she strains for the high notes, her face looks like a bruised fist.

Manny turns toward his partner and winks. Vikström is confused. Then he realizes that what seemed Manny's madness is in fact strategy. He's concocted the whole charade, standing arm in arm with Angelina, caterwauling. He's softening her up and driving Vikström nuts at the same time.

But Vikström wants no part of it. He buttons his coat. "Finish this quick. I'll wait in the car."

Sitting in the shotgun seat of the Subaru, Vikström rests his head against the headrest and puts on his dark glasses—a cheap pair with heavy tortoiseshell frames whose lenses distort the world as completely as an antique pane of glass. The afternoon sun gives a little vibrancy to his thinning blond hair, but, like much else, it's an illusion.

Vikström digs out his cell phone and calls his fellow detectives, Herta

Spiegel and Moss Jackson, who are supposed to be looking for Fidget. But Herta doesn't pick up, and Moss has called in sick. He's got a bad case of psychosomatic flu.

That Manny was trying to drive him nuts is, for Vikström, no surprise. In fact, if a day passed *without* Manny's trying to drive him nuts, that would be—Vikström pauses at the brink of metaphor—something to write home about. But it's only a surprise if Vikström thinks of Manny as a police detective. His conduct is surprising for a cop. But is it surprising for a karaokean, a practitioner of the art of karaoke?

Such is Vikström's idle thought. The sun through the windshield is warm, and Vikström has reached one of life's little forks in the road: nap on one side, cogitation on the other. So if Manny's behavior is unsurprising for a karaokean, it suggests his behavior is personality-driven rather than his personality being behavior-driven. If personality is the cause and not the effect, then this is a whole new understanding. And what seems clear—and this is the target of Vikström's thought—is that personalities are flexible. One can pick and choose. One can be a cop one day and a phony songster the next. At any moment one may have a number of personalities vying for one's attention.

Is this schizophrenia? Vikström thinks not. If a person has no control over these shifts, it might be a bad sign, diagnostically. But if one could choose, then the shift would be hardly more significant than the daily changing of a necktie. Of course, people might be afraid of these shifts; they might cling to what they think is their true personality out of fear of being booted into the unknown. But Vikström doubts that the shifts would be sudden. In Manny's case, he gradually became drawn to karaoke, and, also gradually, a karaoke self joined his cop self. And Manny has other, lesser personalities, such as being a jokester and being fixated on beagle pups, which have nothing to do with singing and arresting bad guys.

Moreover, to be a karaokean can mean taking on another man's personality—someone like Frank Sinatra, Vaughn Monroe, or Prince. So Manny can first shift to his karaoke personality and then shift to his

Elvis Presley personality or whoever. Manny's erratic behavior, Vikström decides, is simply a result of shifting to other levels of personality: Manny/cop/beagle lover/karaokean/Elvis. No wonder it's so difficult to catch the bad guys. Psychologically speaking, they have many places to hide.

Likewise, Angelina's disagreeableness and threats of physical violence don't come from being a New London housewife, far from it. They come from being an unfulfilled prom queen. And for Angelina to be a prom queen once in her life means to be a prom queen forever, which means being frustrated forever. Yet, to counter this behavior, she's also a beagle lover, which calls up a third personality: one that's sweet, generous, and loving.

These thoughts, which began as idle speculations for Vikström, now seem a pathway through life's byzantine corridors. Never mind that he's banging on the back doors of behaviorism. He's never heard of John B. Watson or B. F. Skinner; his ignorance in these areas remains as virginal as an uncut birthday cake. And the identity shifts that Vikström has diagnosed are not brought about by bed-wetting or sexual abuse. Rather, they're personality-driven choices intended to satisfy deficiencies we see as limiting our lives; they're reactions to those limitations. As for the rat that hits the little bar and gets a treat and then hits it again and gets another treat . . . well, the third time he might scamper to the back of his cage and think, *I'm fuckin' tired of being nickeled and dimed!* That's personality.

We might suspect a certain whimsy in Vikström's speculations, but the more he reflects, the more serious grow his thoughts, until he sits up so quickly that his cheap sunglasses slide down his nose. *And who am I?* he asks. Surely he's not the same person at home as he is at work. And he might have other personalities. If his fear of heights comes neither from his cop self nor from his domestic self, then perhaps he has a third self deep within him, a timid self who is too timid to confess his timidity and is a famous Swedish detective who hates heights.

This is as far as Vikström gets this afternoon. Having reached a scary place, he steps back from speculative thought for the day. Gratefully, he sees his partner leaving Angelina's house. Manny pauses in the doorway to clasp Angelina's hand: the karaokean and the prom queen. She leans forward to kiss his cheek. Vikström thinks he might vomit.

But let's continue our digression for a few moments more. If Didi Lobato were in the backseat of the Subaru, he'd tap Vikström's shoulder and explain about the tradiculous. It's not funny that Vikström has the subpersonality of a Swedish detective with a fear of heights. It's tradiculous.

So Didi would tell Vikström to relax. This business of shifting identities is as common as bunions. Look at Eartha and her implants, Vasco and his rented Rolex. *Where's the harm?* Didi might ask. But does Didi know who *he* is anymore? Might he think his identity is more authentic than Fidget's? That perhaps is the most tradiculous thing of all: Didi is convinced he's been spared this plague of shifting identities, as do others we've mentioned. But they're mistaken.

Even so, there are exceptions. This is why our own Vaughn Monroe is so worrisome to Connor, Didi, and Eartha. When asked who he is, Vaughn might say, "I used to be past-tense when I was nervous, but that was when necessity became the mother of convention and I let the gift horse sleep in the house. So I was forced to wrestle the toothy allegories, and today I'm a suppository of knowledge. No more soiled gold rings, I say! Illiterate the enemy!"

Vaughn's speech carries a patina of sense, which is more worrisome than actually making sense. And as Vaughn's words, those great communicators, turn to Jell-O, Connor might fear he's losing another degree of existential clarity. "Is it me?" he'd ask. "Am I the only one who can't understand him?"

So Vaughn is always Vaughn, and his apparent suprapersonality of Vaughn Monroe is merely glitter. Vaughn claims to be everyone and no one, to be all names and none. "After all," he'd say, "the plausibilities are endless in a doggy-dog world."

But Vaughn isn't the only person with a single personality. There's also Chucky, the oversize offensive-tackle type we've seen at the casino and who is Vasco's boss. In fact, he's boss of a bunch of people. This has nothing to do with seniority or rank. He's simply "Boss"—it's his job title, and if you disagree, he'll hurt you. Call him Mr. Pain. It's who he is when he wakes in the morning till he goes to sleep at night. He is a freelance pain distributor. So there's always a lot of space around Chucky, and people avoid eye contact.

We haven't seen much of Chucky, but he's out there. He's been strolling around and making his arrangements about Sal and Céline, maybe even about Fat Bob and Marco Santuzza. He's a worker, and he leaves a big footprint. So even if we haven't seen him, he's been busy. But he has a weakness. He loves gold. And when he ran up the stairs to Sal's office and found Sal's sprawled corpse with the plastic flower stuck in his forehead, he was seriously pissed that the gold was gone.

B ut we've left Manny Streeter on Angelina's front steps as she's kissing him on the cheek, a platonic kiss. Before he turns away, they squinch their eyes at one another as a sign of nonphysical intimacy. Now Manny hurries to the Subaru, throws open the driver's door, jumps in, inserts the key, and fastens his seat belt.

This is when Vikström asks, "Have you ever thought that nobody's really what they seem?"

Manny freezes. "Run through that again?"

"I mean, you know, a person seems like one person and then seems like a second person and then seems like a third person and then—"

Manny half turns. "You calling me a hypocrite?" The Subaru's 2.0-liter turbo screams to indicate his outrage. In such a way is man linked to machine.

TWENTY

It shouldn't be thought that Manny spent all his time with Angelina talking about pups and karaoke. No, he also picked up useful bits having to do with their investigation, though both detectives feel, with a bit of chagrin, that the word "investigation" is an overstatement.

Backing out of Angelina's driveway, Manny laughs an unfriendly laugh. "Lisowski's telling the truth. He's been balling Angelina. So I say to her, 'I didn't see any black-and-blue marks.' And she says, 'I only leave marks where they don't show.' Poor Lisowski's a walking contusion. What I got around my black eye, he's got round half his body. So I says to her, 'Was it hard to get Lisowski to steal Fat Bob's computer from Burnsie's office?' That surprised her. So I adds, 'This's just between friends.' It's like fuckin' Shakespeare. She gives him a choice between 'the delights of the bed'—her phrase—or get booted out the back door. And she tells him she'd also tell the cops, meaning us, that she saw him taking potshots at Fat Bob's Fat Bob till it blew up. So I ask her, 'You been hiding Lisowski's pistol?' But she said no, and I believe her. So tell me, Benny, am I a genius or am I a genius?"

Vikström wants to say, *You were lying to her. You were leading her down the yellow brick road.* Instead he says, "You're a genius." But the words leave a sour taste in his mouth.

"Another thing," says Manny. "You know those bikes that been disappearing from Fat Bob's garage? Lisowski's been shopping them for Angelina. She's got the titles, so technically they're hers, even though she promised Fat Bob she'd keep them safe from the bank. But she says she wants to look like a prom queen again and that takes lots of expensive reconstruction. And this is the part I like: She's selling them cheap just to piss off Fat Bob even more."

Vikström doesn't call Manny a genius again. He's distracted by the fact that his partner isn't driving into town toward the police station but toward I-95.

"Another thing, Caroline Santuzza called Angelina."

It takes Vikström a moment to recall the name, but then he says, "What about?"

"First she tells Angelina that Giovanni Lambertenghi plans to shoot Fat Bob."

"Who the fuck's Giovanni Lambertenghi?"

"Jack Sprat. What've you gone soft in the head? He's been zooming around town on a red scooter. We rousted him right on Bank Street."

Vikström is more worried that Manny has pulled onto I-95 and is heading toward the bridge. But he manages to ask why Jack Sprat wants to kill Fat Bob.

"He thinks that Fat Bob set up Santuzza's death to get out of paying him the money he owed him. It makes sense, right?"

It's rush hour, and traffic is thick. Vikström sees the bridge looming in the near distance, as menacing as Godzilla in a reclining position. "But his bike was destroyed. It had to be worth fifteen grand."

"Nah, he'll get insurance money for the bike. You closing your eyes, Benny?"

Vikström tightens his stomach muscles to ready himself for an attack of the phantom icy hand that's about to grip his guts. "No, no, of course not." He tries to keep his voice calm, as if he were asking, *What's for lunch?*

Manny's not fooled. He jerks the wheel to make the Subaru swerve. "I sure hope I don't crash over the side this time. Ha, ha, ha."

Vikström's body is as tight as a miser's purse. "Was there a second thing?" To his right, way down in the troublesome waters, he sees the Long Island ferry setting out for Orient Point. He shuts his eyes.

"Yeah, Caroline said Marco had a visit a week ago from a big, bulky

guy in a hoodie. She'd never seen him before, and Marco didn't introduce him. In fact, Marco told her to wait in the kitchen. It could be the
same guy in the hooded sweatshirt who Dr. Goodenough saw jump out
of the Denali and disappear, the guy who jumped out before the hit man."

Vikström hardly pays attention. He's totally focused on the water
down below. "Where the fuck we going?" He hears a pathetic squeak in
his voice.

"Angelina says Fat Bob's got a biker friend named Otto who lives
halfway to the casino on this side of Ledyard. That's where he's been
staying. We'll be there in ten minutes. You okay?"

"Course I'm okay." Vikström's eyes are shut tight. "Who said we
could prowl around across the river? It's out of our territory."

"Just want to take a peek, that's all."

Angelina Rossi has told Manny that Fat Bob has an old high school
chum—"a real loser"—who lives in a faded, postwar subdivision off
Center Groton Road. "His name's Otto something, but you'll see his
house. You can't miss it. It's up against the woods—a fixer-upper. Otto's
been there forever."

Vikström opens his right eye half a crack. "You think Fat Bob will be
there?"

"It's a lead, that's all," says Manny. "They're both bikers."

"Half the world are bikers."

Manny gives the Subaru another spiteful swerve. "Don't get all
fuckin' philosophical on me, Benny! And stop that la-la-la shit!"

Recently Vikström has read that close to the country's biggest bridges
live people who drive the terrified across those fragile structures span-
ning the abyss: Good Samaritans who offer their services for a price. But
the I-95 bridge is too short to support such a career. What a pity.

The house, a bungalow, is on Hill Street. Rusted car parts decorate
the dead grass. The trees are leafless, but an evergreen stands to the left
of the driveway. It's still festooned with Christmas lights, as if Otto were
keeping his hopes up. No car is in the driveway, but it might be in the
garage. It's five-thirty, and the sun is going down.

Manny cuts his engine. "You want to take this one?"

"Let's do it together," says Vikström, staring at the house.

"Makes you nervous, doesn't it? I don't blame you."

"I'm not nervous. It's just part of our job description: doing things together."

"It's not our business to do it together if we're outside city limits. I'll wait here. These banged-up bungalows are a little creepy."

"What d'you mean, 'creepy'?'

"There's a silence about them."

Vikström listens. "What kind of silence?"

"You remember that poem about folks living lives of noiseless distraction?"

Vikström opens his mouth, then closes it. He climbs from the Subaru.

"Any last messages for the wife?"

"Fuck you," says Vikström.

The subdivision is probably full of navy or ex-navy, stand-up guys who start drinking early in the afternoon. In the backyards of a few houses are small boats covered with blue tarps. Vikström walks to the front door. The roof's overhang sticks out about four feet from the house, to protect the postman from the elements when he delivers the bills and junk mail. Vikström rings the bell; he hears a tinkling from inside. He's nervous, and he knows he wouldn't be nervous if Manny had kept his mouth shut. He rings the bell again. In the front seat of the Subaru, Manny leans back as if to take a nap. Then Vikström glances at his feet, jumps, and nearly falls. He's been standing in a puddle of blood. Manny starts laughing from the car. Vikström calls to him, "There's blood here!"

Manny scrambles out of the car and hurries to the house. The pool of blood is mostly dry, about a foot long and shaped liked Florida without the panhandle. As he reaches the porch, a silver 159 Interceptor with a discreet light bar and a toothsome front crash bumper turns in to the driveway behind the Subaru. The car has no markings, but Vikström knows it right away. He takes his police ID from his jacket pocket. Manny turns, sees the state police car, and takes out his ID as well. A trooper in a gray Stetson gets out, his slow movements meant to show professional composure and superiority in the presence of local cops. His passenger gets out more quickly—a balding, middle-aged guy. His gray work shirt is spotted with blood, and his left arm is in a blue hospital sling.

"You catch 'em?" shouts the balding guy.

"You mean Fat Bob?" asks Vikström, still on the steps.

"No, not him, the other ones. Fat Bob lit out on his bike, straight through the backyards. Lucky he didn't get gagged on a clothesline."

"You're Otto?" says Manny.

"Bob stayed here a few nights. I didn't know the cops were looking for him. 'Cross the river I don't hear nothing."

The trooper stands looking up at the winter trees. He's nodded to the New London detectives to concede their legitimacy: a grudging nod. Manny thinks all troopers look the same. Maybe it's the hats. How do they tell one another apart?

"So where'd the blood come from?" asks Vikström. "What's going on?"

"I got pinked," says Otto. He makes a gesture with his thumb over his shoulder toward the trooper. "He brought me back from the hospital."

At ten o'clock that morning, a black Denali pulled in to Otto's drive-way and tooted its horn. Fat Bob was asleep in a spare room, and Otto went out onto the porch. The driver got out and said he was looking for Fat Bob. "Nope," Otto told him, "I haven't seen him for a coupla weeks." Then the passenger got out. The men were around forty, nicely dressed and physically fit. Otto made a point of this. "They looked like they worked out a lot. I mean to start doing that myself. I'm a winter gainer, and my wife's repugnated by it." Was there anything else that struck him? "They looked like guys who wouldn't care shit about a good joke."

The men responded to Otto's statement about not seeing Fat Bob by saying they wanted to come in and look around.

"I told them, 'No way.' They weren't official. I mean, they were just guys. Even if Fat Bob hadn't been inside, I wouldna let them in. Like, my house's my house, don't you think?"

Ignoring Otto, the men walked toward the porch. So Otto stepped inside to grab a shotgun. And why did Otto have a double-barreled shotgun leaning against the wall inside the door? So he said he always kept it there. He liked to play it safe.

When Otto stepped onto the porch again, he heard Fat Bob's motorcycle start up behind the house. The men ran back to the Denali. Brandishing his shotgun, Otto shouted at them to stop.

"Guy didn't give any warning. Just raised this pistol and fired. Startled me so much I pulled the trigger. I wasn't aiming or nothing. The shotgun kicked back out of my hand, and I did that." Otto points up at the overhang to indicate a ragged hole about a foot and a half across. "So I went down. I didn't need to go down, like the bullet only hit my arm, but what's the point of staying on my feet? I mean, Fat Bob was already tearing through backyards on his hog. It wasn't like I was protecting him anymore. By the time the two guys got into the Denali, Bob was out on the road. Now I got this fucking hole in my overhang. You think insurance'll cover it?"

A neighbor called the cops, and soon three squad cars showed up.

"I hadn't meant to call them myself. Anyway, I'd nothing to say. Shit, my neighbor had more to say than me. He wanted to tell a whole story. He's like that. But he didn't get the plate number of the Denali, though he said it didn't look like Connecticut. And he couldn't say any more about the two men than I've said myself. A statie took me to the hospital, and a statie brought me back. They kept asking about that smash-up in New London, but I didn't know anything about it. They asked all sorts of shit, and after a while they got tired asking."

"So what'd the two guys want?" asks Manny.

"They didn't tell me. They wanted Fat Bob, that's all."

"What for?" asks Vikström. "Take a guess."

"I figured Bob owes them money."

"Who d'you think they're working for?" asks Manny.

"I figured they're working for themselves."

"Nah, they're just soldiers," says Manny as he taps Otto on the chest with one finger. "They work for someone bigger, someone big enough to make you keep a shotgun right beside the door. Give me a name."

Otto looks stubborn. "I don't know what you're talking about."

Manny keeps insisting and Otto keeps denying until Vikström interrupts to ask Otto if he knew Milo Lisowski and the Hog Hurrah. Otto says he heard of the place but he'd given up his bike years ago after a crack-up. "Pitched into a ditch and busted a leg. You can't hang around a bunch of bikers if you're driving a Chevy. You start getting chilly looks. But Bob kept bitching about Lisowski, said he'd been taking his bikes, thinking Bob was going to get killed. Bob called it pillaging."

By now it's dark. The state cop and his silver Interceptor are gone. Vikström gets Otto's last name—Schwartz—and a phone number. He asks Otto if he knows Marco Santuzza or Pappalardo or Jack Sprat. He doesn't. Otto says he only knows some navy guys. They play poker Wednesdays. Vikström and Manny look at one another—itself a rarity—and shrug. They know that Otto has another name he's not revealing: the man who'd hired the two guys in the Denali. They walk back to the Subaru. Both know they need to talk to the FBI guys, but it can wait till morning.

"Pillaging," says Manny. "You can arrest a guy for that."

What's too much of a good thing? For Didi it's knowing that Angelina Rossi was called twice: once for Prom Queens Anonymous and then for Free Beagles from Nicotine Addiction. This might fall under the category of the tradiculous, but Angelina has acted suspiciously by asking Connor to return later. This fools nobody, and for Didi the police and the tradiculous fit together as nicely as thumbtacks and ice cream. So he decides to stop the phone calls until he thinks it's safe to continue.

It's Connor who brings the news that Angelina has been "double-dipped," as Didi calls it. Neither Didi nor Eartha likes its possible consequences, while Vaughn says, "I find myself unable to associate myself with that thesis." But it's not clear if this is agreement, disagreement, or something else. And since Vaughn sits on the floor with his back to them as he fusses with his yellow sheets of paper, it's not clear that his statement concerns the others at all. His short, peroxided hair gleams in the overhead light—a small light beneath the larger one.

Though Connor was the one to bring this news, his mind is on Vasco's call and his warning to stay away from Céline. Connor doesn't want Céline to know he told anyone that Dante Barbarella was living in New London under the name Sal Nicoletti, but if she *has* to know, Connor wants to be the one to tell her. This means driving back to New London and ignoring his brother's warning that "very bad things" will happen if he sees Céline. Those bad things are a subheading under the main heading of "Chucky."

Again we ask if Connor is brave or a coward, recalling that his only fistfight was in ninth grade, and he was losing when it was broken up. That was twelve years ago, and since then nothing's happened to make Connor a better fighter: no kung fu classes, no karate. In fact, he's better at almost everything *except* fighting. Connor, however, feels it's not about fighting—it's about Céline, and if a few bruises are the price he has to pay to see her, it might be okay. But he's not going to tell Didi or Eartha, who will try to talk him out of it. This suggests that Connor has doubts, though he claims to have no doubts. How difficult are these emotional mix-ups that inhibit Connor from exploring the consequences of self-deception.

Didi opens the envelopes that Connor brought from the post office. It's a job Didi likes to do himself; it lets him imagine that the foolishness is worth the trouble. Eartha sorts the checks. At times a dog lover or former prom queen sends cash, always a special pleasure. It's only a pity they *all* don't send cash.

"By the way," says Didi to Connor, "your brother called. He said you been hanging around that woman whose husband was shot the other day. He said it'll lead to serious trouble. You're not doing that, are you?"

Connor's back is turned; otherwise his face might provide an ugly admission. "Of course not!" he says, loud enough to imagine he's convincing. In fact, he intends to drive back to New London in just a few minutes, but he wants to change his shirt, brush his teeth, and put on a drop of Didi's cologne, which is called Tough Guy.

Vaughn looks up with one of those expressions that Connor can never interpret and says, "You describe one of life's internal vulgarities."

The gleam of Vaughn's peroxided hair under the ceiling light hurts Connor's eyes as he tries to sort through Vaughn's possible meanings. At last he asks, "You expect me to answer that?"

"Any pro-boner work often causes dysentery instead of thanks."

Connor sees Didi and Eartha looking at him thoughtfully. He wants to ask if they know what Vaughn is saying, but he's afraid they do. "I gotta go pee," he says.

Didi watches Connor walk by. He knows that Connor intends to see Céline despite his warning, though he doesn't know Céline's name. Who she is and why Vasco would be worried about it doesn't concern him, although it should. Didi sees himself as living in another world; he believes he lives in the Winnebago as if in the shell of a fast turtle, a kind of rocket turtle. If there's a problem, he can speed away. Here again we see one of Didi's weaknesses: If he believes that something is true, it must be true. Didi is more concerned that Connor is lying. It means their partnership—though of course it isn't a partnership—is coming to an end. Pity.

To cheer himself up, Didi keys in a number on his cell phone. A woman answers. "Yeah?"

"Is this Angelina? Angelina Rossi?"

"And who the fuck are you?"

"Wait! For both of our sakes, look out the window and into the sky." Didi's voice is as smooth as warm molasses. *This is what I was born for,* he thinks.

Angelina protests, Didi reassures. Angelina makes rude remarks, Didi is sweetly repentant.

After a brief silence, Angelina says, "Okay, I did it. So what?"

"Could you tell me what you saw?"

"Darkness. Fuckin' darkness and some stars."

"Ah," says Didi, "I thought so. Did any of those stars seem to be falling?"

"You mean like a shooting star? Yeah, maybe one."

"Angelina, bear with me. It wasn't a shooting star."

Angelina makes the rasping, throat-clearing noise of a smoker. "So what was it, wise guy?"

Didi's voice is muted velvet. "Angelina, it was an orphan from outer space."

"Say what?"

"Orphans from outer space. They're out there wandering the back nighttime streets or trapped in halfway houses of desperation, and they need our help."

"Fuck you, asshole!" She cuts the connection.

Didi turns to Eartha. "She hung up on me." This, for Didi, is a minor letdown and a masochistic pleasure.

Vaughn asks, "And who are the orphans of inner space? Are they, too, pigments of your imagination?"

From her place at the table, Eartha reaches out and puts one hand over Didi's. Along with her jean shorts, she wears a magenta crop top with spaghetti straps. "Yeah, people hang up on me all the time. Win some, lose some. You can't let it mess with your thinking." She laces her fingers behind her head with her elbows akimbo, then arches her back, forcing her breasts upward to distract Didi from minutiae.

Connor pauses on his way out of the bathroom, where he's brushed his teeth, combed his hair, and doused himself with Didi's Tough Guy cologne to prepare for the evening ahead. He ponders Vaughn's question: "Who are the orphans of inner space?" As with others of Vaughn's remarks, it simultaneously made sense and no sense, except, as Connor recalls, Vaughn is an orphan: the son of Gone and Goner.

TWENTY-ONE

t's past seven, and the houses on Glenwood Place are sporadically lit. People are having dinner, TVs flicker, a door slams. Connor parks the Mini at the curb and walks up the sidewalk to the front steps of Sal's—now Céline's—house. There's no warm glow of a porch light to welcome him, but a light's burning somewhere in the back. No car is visible. Connor keeps his mind blank, not only to avoid fantasizing on what lies ahead but also to avoid thinking about his brother's warning, which means not thinking about Chucky. He imagines he's being watched by people in surrounding houses. He imagines them shaking their heads and saying to their spouses, *There goes another dumbo.*

Connor rings the bell. After a moment the porch light comes on and he hears locks being unlocked. Then Céline stands before him behind the storm door. She wears a green Moroccan caftan with gold buttons and gold lacing decorating the high collar. Her lipstick is a darker green; her black hair is parted in the middle and hangs past her shoulders. She looks at Connor with her head tilted.

Slowly, Céline opens the storm door. "You find Danny's gold?"

"Danny?"

"Sal. Do you have the gold or not?"

"A homeless guy has it: Fidget. I've been looking for him all day. I'll find him tomorrow morning for sure."

"What makes you think so?"

"I've got people looking for him." Connor is referring to Linda rather than to an army of volunteers. "Is it true you weren't married to Sal?"

Céline's laugh is like fingernails on sandpaper, expressive more of mockery than of delight. "Not only wasn't I not married to him, but Sal wasn't even Sal. The whole business was meant to keep Danny hidden until his trial in Detroit."

Despite knowing this, Connor hadn't wanted to believe it. "You're an escort?"

"I was hired to act out a part. It was like a bad play. But Danny attracts too much attention. They should've sent him to Guam."

Standing just inside the door, Connor again tells himself that he's the one to blame: it's his fault Sal was killed. First he gets Sal shot, and then he pursues Sal's wife, who turns out not to be Sal's wife but an escort. Connor's appalled by his behavior. Was it for this he left Iron Mountain? But though he's appalled and has a long list of insulting names to hurl at himself, he's excited to be where he is. He may not like Céline's green lipstick, but he finds her beautiful, and he stares at her as a starved Great Dane might stare at a flank steak.

She, on the other hand, stares back as she might stare at a superfluous purchasing option: another pair of cheap flat shoes. "So why are you here if you couldn't find Fidget?"

"I wanted to see you," says Connor.

Céline wears a bemused expression to go with her slightly tilted head. "And what do you see?"

Unluckily, Connor's mind goes blank. But no, that's not true. Springing to his lips, as it were, are romantic lines from famous movies.

Such as: *Well, it was a million tiny little things that, when you added them all up, they meant we were supposed to be together.*

And: *I'm just a boy, standing in front of a girl, asking her to love him.*

And: *I came here tonight because when you realize you want to spend the rest of your life with somebody, you want it to start as soon as possible.*

And: *You should be kissed, and often, and by someone who knows how.*

And: *We'll always have Paris.*

But Connor lacks the nerve to say any of this. Instead he shrugs. *How pathetic!* he thinks.

Céline twists her face into an *I want to spit* expression. "You've got a lot of nerve to come back here without Danny's jewelry."

Taking strength from all the romantic lines he didn't say, Connor walks past Céline into the living room with its beige carpet and beige furniture, muted gray lampshades, and a seascape of racing sailboats over the mantel.

"So this stuff is rented?" He tries to sound assertive.

Céline faces him again and lights a cigarette. "Even the mice. So if you don't have the gold, what do you want, or are you just going to stare at me?"

"No, of course not. I thought we could talk." This, to Connor's way of thinking, is a mindless euphemism.

"You want a drink? It might quiet your nerves."

Connor didn't realize his nerves were so obvious. "That'd be great."

"Scotch?"

"Perfect."

"Anything in it?"

"Just scotch."

Céline leaves the room. The swaying of her hips under her caftan strikes Connor with the force of lightning knocking a squirrel off a high branch. He also wonders why Céline has decided to play the perfect hostess. He hears her talking on the phone in another room, but he can't make out the words. More time passes.

As he waits for his scotch, Connor studies his surroundings. It's like a bad stage set. What was her life like with Sal—did they have sex?—and what was her life like before that time?

But when Céline returns, Connor's musings vanish. She wears a white, ankle-length, sleeveless nightgown of pleated chiffon with a deep V-neck and needle-lace straps. We say this because the translucence of the gathered pleats takes all of Connor's attention, especially the shadowy display of her dark nipples. Her skin is only several tads darker than the white of the fabric. As she walks, the chiffon's pleats eddy around her.

Echoes of her suppleness, thinks Connor, still caught up in the world of romantic films. She hands him a crystal whiskey glass of scotch. Light flickers on the facets of the cut-glass surface. Only a reading lamp by the sofa illuminates the room.

"What do you want to talk about?" she says matter-of-factly.

Connor's mind moves as fast as cold molasses. "Who were you talking to?"

Céline gives a little smile. "I'd just ordered a pizza, and I called to cancel the order. You don't want to eat pizza, do you?"

Connor shakes his head and tries not to stutter. "Who . . . who d'you think shot Sal?" The question doesn't interest him, but he can think of nothing else to say.

"Connor—that's your name, isn't it?—I'm a bit player. I got a check when I started, and I'll get another tomorrow. Now can we talk about something else?"

"Like what?"

"Like would you like to undress me?"

Connor is afraid he'll fall down, but surely that's an exaggeration. Still, his view of the room is jittery, and his legs feel weak. If he spoke, he'd say, *Wow, that'd be cool!* And so he says nothing. He takes a step forward.

Céline holds out a hand to stop him. "Let's slow it down a little. Would you like some music? What do you think would go best?"

"No music."

Céline walks to a small table by the beige couch. She opens a drawer and takes out a blue velvet box about the length of a finger. Walking back, she hands the box to Connor and steps away. "Open it."

Connor juggles his glass of scotch and the blue box, afraid of dropping both. He drinks his scotch, coughs loudly, and puts the glass on a table. Inside the box is a pair of gold-plated cuticle scissors with curved half-inch blades.

"Use those."

"These?"

"Start cutting at the bottom and work your way to the top."

"But it'll ruin the nightgown."

Céline gives a minuscule shrug. "I have others."

The scissor handles have two loops of unequal size, the larger being for Connor's right thumb. Both are too small for him. The scissors fall to the rug. Does she have bigger scissors, like garden shears? He lifts the scissors and wedges his thumb into the appropriate loop. "Tight fit," he says. He bends over to catch the hem of the nightgown; then he gets on one knee. He glances up, but the alpine projection of Céline's breasts blocks her face. Connor gathers the fabric and attacks the hem with the curved blades. The fabric bunches, and nothing happens.

"Do it slowly," says Céline. Her tone suggests mild interest. "If you stick me with the scissors, all bets are off."

Connor pinches a bit of the fabric between his left thumb and index finger and another bit between his left ring finger and pinkie. This is not done easily. He sets the half-inch blades against the hem and squeezes. The hem separates. Connor experiences a droplet of joy. He attacks the fabric again, and it bunches. Once more he holds the fabric firmly and cuts a quarter of an inch. The house is silent except for the sound of cutting, which is no louder than a tail feather falling from a passing sparrow. Only Connor can hear it. The curved blades of the scissors bend to the left.

Glancing at Céline rising above him, he feels as if he were taking a teaspoon to dig up the Matterhorn. He readjusts the scissors to cut to the right, then to the left again. He zigzags upward one inch. He imagines the heat of her body beneath the chiffon. Connor begins to sweat. He changes his position so he sits on the floor. He's cut a little higher than Céline's anklebone, and the fabric keeps bunching. By the time he reaches her knees, he feels as though an hour has passed, but of course it's only been a few minutes. He looks up, and again he sees the dark shadows of her nipples.

"Hard work." A drop of sweat rolls down his forehead; he wipes his brow.

Céline doesn't respond. He pulls back to see her face; she's looking idly at her watch. *At least,* thinks Connor, *she's not reading a book.*

Connor switches the scissors to his left hand and drops them to the rug. They are right-handed scissors, and his left thumb won't fit in the loop. He switches back again. He's getting a blister on his right thumb.

"Do you mind if I smoke?" asks Céline.

"No, sure, go right ahead."

Céline takes a cigarette from a pack of Salem Slim 100's and lights it with a silver table lighter. "Helps pass the time." She blows smoke toward the ceiling.

When Connor reaches her thighs, he gets back onto one knee, which puts his eyes just above the dark shadow where her thighs terminate. This is revitalizing. He pushes forward, and the fabric bunches. He slows down and readjusts the zigzag. As the scissors rise, so does his sexual desire. He'd like to ask for a glass of water but says nothing. The scissors snip another inch.

"I'm getting the hang of it," says Connor.

Céline doesn't answer. Looking up, Connor sees she's studying her nails, which are also green. She's his height, about six feet tall. From his present position, she looks ten feet tall. With the increase of his sexual desire, the fabric seems to bunch more frequently, and he wants to rip the damn white nuisance off her body. He cuts another quarter inch. The darkness of her pubic hair is six inches from his nose. He wonders if he might have a heart attack. Perhaps many of the heart attacks described in newspaper obituaries were caused by games like this. He takes a moment to breathe deeply. Céline's pubic hair has been shaved into a diamond shape, and Connor focuses on the tight black curls.

"You know, Céline's a beautiful name," he says, trying to distract himself from the mound of curly hair. "I really like it." He readjusts his pants.

Céline stubs out her cigarette in a green ashtray. "My real name's Mabel."

Connor stops readjusting his pants as his tumescence deflates. "Oh?"

"My folks called me 'Maybe.' Are you going to be there all night?"

"Slow but sure, that's the best approach." Connor hardly knows what he's saying. *Mabel!* he thinks.

"Which do you like better, Mabel or Céline?"

"I'd gotten used to Céline." He sees that Céline has a belly-button ring with a small blue stone.

"I'm pulling your leg," says Céline with a giggle. "That's not my name."

Connor exhales. "So what is it?"

"Shirley."

"You're kidding." He sees that she's again looking at her watch. From below, her grin appears carnivorous. "You play that trick on a lot of men?"

Another giggle. "Some get mad. I was born Shirley but changed it to Céline in high school. It's all legal. My mom signed the papers. So I'm really Céline."

Connor feels reassured. "That's what I did. My parents named me Juan Carlos, and I changed it when I graduated from high school." He resumes cutting.

"Did people call you Zeco?"

"Yeah, how'd you know?" The loops of the scissors have made deep indentations around Connor's index finger and thumb.

"I know things."

Connor wonders if she could have heard this from Vasco, but how would she know Vasco? "You know Vasco?"

"Never heard of him."

"Where d'you get the beautiful nightgowns?"

Connor feels rather than sees the slight shrug of Céline's shoulders. "Oh, you know, boyfriends."

He has cut through three-quarters of the nightgown, and when he leans forward, he sees the cantaloupe undersides of Céline's full breasts. He snips more quickly, only to have the fabric bunch again.

"Don't you think we have enough?" asks Connor. "It's basically open."

The cheap beige carpet digs into his knees. Céline arches her back, which raises the bottoms of her breasts out of Connor's view. He's impressed he can feel bored and sexually excited at the same time.

"You've got to go to the top." Céline runs her fingers through her black hair and studies the ceiling. Given a change of clothes, she could be waiting for a bus.

Connor reaches a difficult section: three inches of ornate needle lace rise from the bottom of the deep V-neck. He's unsure whether to cut it strand by strand or force the scissors through by spreading the fabric with his fingers. He crouches to approach the dangerous area more directly. In silhouette he resembles a gorilla. He recalls the old days when he and his girlfriends simply held hands.

Connor has just cut through a bit of the needle lace when Céline says, "Did you just hear a car door?"

Connor pauses, catching the anxiety in her voice. "Opening or closing?"

"Both."

Connor cuts faster, but the needle lace bunches. He listens again but hears nothing.

The doorbell rings. In his surprise Connor jabs Céline's right breast with the scissors. She screams. This is followed by someone pounding.

"Céline!" shouts a man's voice.

"It's Chucky," whispers Céline.

Connor has a sudden realization. "You called him, didn't you?" He grips a handful of white fabric so Céline can't pull away. He's unaware of doing this.

"I had to. He'd hurt me if I didn't. He told me to keep you here." Céline says this all in a rush.

The scissors have nearly reached the top of the needle lace. Only a few snips left. Connor still holds the nightgown. He notices a speck of blood from where he'd stuck her with the scissors. At last he lets go. He drops the scissors to the rug and readjusts his pants. Céline stumbles back, rubbing her snipped breast.

More hammering: the door shakes in its frame and cracks.

"Look, you're a nice boy," says Céline, "and you have a nice face. It'd be a pity to have Chucky destroy it. He wants to turn it to hamburger."

Perhaps Connor had thought that Chucky might wait patiently on the sofa until he, Connor, had finished his business. We'll never know. Connor heads for the back door, picking up his coat from the beige sofa.

Turning, he says, "Chucky calls me Zeco, doesn't he?"

Céline nods. "Use the bedroom window," she whispers. "He'll have one of his thugs at the back door."

Connor veers toward the bedroom. As he reaches the window, he hears Céline shout, "All right, I'm coming! Give it a break, already!"

Pushing out the screen, Connor scrambles over the sill and hurries into the night. The sky is clear, but there's no moon. The stars are bright and full of questions.

TWENTY-TWO

In Connor's dream a pileated woodpecker hammers on his forehead. In real time it's the knuckle of Didi Lobato's right index finger. Over the space of a second, Connor shifts back and forth between dream and reality, attempting to preserve the dream from the greater annoyance that reality offers. In this he fails.

"What the fuck happened to the car?" shouts Didi.

Connor's eyes remain shut. He has a mental image of the smashed windshield of the Mini-Cooper and a large stone resting on the passenger seat. He'd found the damage after running from Céline's house to where he had parked the car on Glenwood Place. Then he'd hardly paused to brush the glass from the driver's seat as he started the engine and accelerated away at full speed with the wind beating against his face like the onset of repressed memory.

But since Connor didn't see anyone hurl the stone, he's able to say, "I've absolutely no idea. It was like that when I found it."

Didi steps back from Connor's bed. "You're lying. You went to see that woman, Céline. You were told not to see her."

"I wasn't there long." Uttering the words, he knows it's an absurd excuse.

"A nanosecond would have been too long." Didi is on the edge of berating his nephew. He wants to tell him he's "jeopardizing their endeavor" and "sabotaging the basic principles of Bounty, Inc." Instead he says, "You've disappointed me. You lack the tugo spirit."

Connor feels his stomach knot. He sits on the side of the bed wearing a white T-shirt and his undershorts. Eartha stands by the stove making coffee. Vaughn sits cross-legged on the floor with one of his yellow pads. His oversize sweatshirt makes him resemble a beanbag. They, too, look disappointed. Connor can't think of an excuse that has any bite to it. Yes, Céline had told him to come over right away, but where were his priorities?

"Did you at least fuck her?" asks Didi sarcastically.

Connor shakes his head. "She gave me some manicure scissors and told me to cut off her nightgown from bottom to top. It's harder than you might think."

"Oh, yeah," says Eartha, "I've done that. Gets boring after a while. Manicure scissors are no good. You need fingernail scissors—they got a bigger blade."

Vaughn's normally blank face refashions itself into a squeezed, sympathetic expression. "You're the victim of impecunious dreams."

"You get all the way to the top?" asks Eartha, bringing Connor a cup of coffee.

Again Connor shakes his head. "Someone started hammering on the door. She said it was Chucky."

"That, too," says Eartha, "I've done that. It's part of the routine. The arrival of the stranger. You're sure it was Chucky and not FedEx?"

"A black GMC Denali was in the driveway. I'd parked the Mini-Cooper on the street a couple of houses away. I just ran."

"Like an escape goat," says Vaughn.

We might think that Connor is as full of shame as a sock is full of a foot, but his main concern is that Céline will learn from Chucky that he's the one who told Vasco about recognizing Sal Nicoletti, meaning that first action was the beginning of all else. Céline said she didn't know Vasco, but it didn't matter. Connor told *someone*, and two days afterward Sal was shot and a plastic rose was stuck into his forehead. And the reason Connor told Vasco was he didn't want his brother to think he was boring. How ridiculous! But eating away at Connor's feelings for Céline is his new awareness that he was looking for Sal's jewelry not for Céline but for Chucky. Céline was only Chucky's pawn.

"I'll get the windshield fixed this morning," says Connor, formulating another reason to return to New London.

Didi pours himself a cup of coffee. "We're done here. It's over. Vasco called to warn me about Chucky. He wants us out of here. We'll empty the New London mailbox and leave. I'd hoped to stay another two weeks. This is your fault, Connor."

Eartha protests. "You're the one who called Angelina Rossi about Orphans from Outer Space," she reminds Didi. "And she must have told the cops about Connor. What will you do about that?"

Didi sips his coffee and looks out at the ocean. "I have a plan," he says.

Connor's swimming goggles have blue lenses, which give a little vigor to the late-winter landscape. He bought them in Brewster at a sporting-goods store, and as he drove out of town, the startled looks he got from the drivers of oncoming cars and pickups led to abrupt swerves—but luckily no smash-ups. As it turned out, he was unable to replace the windshield of the Mini-Cooper in Brewster unless he could wait until Monday, which wasn't possible. His options, as he learned through some phone calls, were to drive north to Warwick or south to New London, where he was going in any case. The goggles protect his eyes from the blasts of cold air that buffet him through the empty space where the windshield used to be. He also wears a blue ski cap, a blue windbreaker, and a green-and-yellow scarf wrapped three times around his head. The temperature outside the car is in the low fifties; inside the car in the area around Connor's nose, the windchill is below freezing.

Connor heads south on Interstate 95. The heater is on full blast but has little effect on his face though he keeps his speed at a modest forty-five. Twice he stops to thaw out his nose. His punishment's only virtue is that he feels he deserves it. He'd lied to Didi and ruined the current prospects of Bounty, Inc. He'd told his brother about Sal, which most likely led to his murder. He'd played the fool with Céline and, worse, might play the fool again if the chance arose. So he suffers from the onslaught of wind and takes pleasure in his suffering.

It's nine-thirty when he reaches the auto-glass shop on Broad Street in New London and almost ten-thirty by the time the windshield is replaced. He pays with one of Didi's credit cards. Possibly it's bogus. Then he drives back across town to Céline's house, telling himself that he's curious, though he remains vague about the specifics. It's simply free-floating curiosity. He keeps the car heater roaring full blast until he begins to sweat. It's like a belated blessing.

When he turns onto Glenwood Place, Connor receives a shock. A large white truck is backed into the driveway, and on its side are the words MURPHY'S RENTALS, along with a New London address and phone number. Two men in gray overalls carry a beige couch from the house to the truck. Two more men edge past them back into the house.

Connor pulls to the curb and jumps from the car. His first impulse is to tell the men to stop what they're doing. They've no business taking away Céline's furniture. They have to put it back. He won't do this, of course; it's just an impulse. But he runs to one of the men and asks what's happening.

"It's all going back to the warehouse," says the man, pushing the couch into the back of the truck. He's tall, muscular, and no-nonsense. "That's where it goes when folks are done with it."

"Where's the woman who lived here?"

"She took off this morning with two suitcases. Cab picked her up."

Connor hurries to the house and reaches the door as two more men emerge with a beige easy chair, turning it first one way and then another so they won't knock its wooden legs against the doorframe. Connor waits and then runs inside.

Half the furniture is already gone. The bedrooms are empty. Connor opens one of the closets, but the clothes are gone as well. He sniffs. He detects a sweet smell that he decides must be Céline's perfume. His knees wobble with desire. But the sweet smell is a Chanel cologne for men called Égoïste Platinum: Sal Nicoletti's favorite.

In the kitchen two women in gray overalls pack the dishes and silver-ware. The refrigerator is already empty.

"We'll be done in another half hour," says one woman. "You movin' in?"

Why not? thinks Connor. He could rent the house and rent the bed in which Céline had slept. He could eat off her dishes and use her silver-ware. But Connor's romanticism has its limits.

"I'm just looking," he says.

"It's a rush job, so we figured someone wanted it right away." The woman puts her hands on her hips, stretches backward, and grunts.

Connor spends twenty minutes searching the house. Maybe he's looking for one of Céline's intimate articles of clothing or one of her black high-heeled shoes. He imagines finding a letter addressed to him personally, in which she apologizes for the previous evening and includes a phone number where she may be reached. She'll wait for his call. These thoughts zip past like flies and are gone before he can swat them away. They embarrass him. *Cut it out!* he tells himself. It's just as well she's gone. He's not infatuated; he was hypnotized. It's like being drugged. After all, her real name was Shirley. The creature known as Céline was a phantasm. In real life, as Eartha had once told him, Céline was some-one who scratched and farted. She had no conversation. She only gave commands.

Maybe this is exaggeration. Maybe back in Detroit, Céline is a Cub Scout mom. She was offered serious money to move to New London to pretend to be a creep's wife, and jumped at the chance. Connor knows nothing about her, and he must stop thinking about her. Even Eartha—or Beatriz, whatever her name is—has greater actuality, despite a plastic surgeon's nips, tucks, and additions. At least she speaks truthfully to Connor, even if she doesn't speak truthfully to anyone on the phone.

Connor pauses in the empty living room and considers Linda, the young lady who works at the travel agency. Yes, yes, we see where these thoughts are going as she begins to blossom in his mind. If Didi were here, he'd urge Connor to slow down. It's unlikely that Linda is a secret serial killer, Didi might say, but you know nothing about her. Nearly everyone is on his or her best behavior when we first meet. It's only later that the rough spots emerge: the bad habits, insecurities, and secret angers. But Connor's alone at the moment and able to avoid Didi's cautionary messages. In this he's fortunate. It's sufficient that his thoughts about Linda are strong enough to nudge Céline from the forefront of his brain. He won't forget about her—it's too soon for that—but she's moved back a few steps. Is Connor ridiculous? Surely he's no more ridiculous than most young men with romantic natures and healthy libidos. Indeed, there are days when Connor doesn't think of sex more than two dozen times, days when he's efficient and hardworking and his intelligence is able to crawl out from underneath his fantasy life and show its muscle.

The movers are nearly finished. Two men carefully take down the seascape from the living room wall. In a day or so, it will grace the wall of another rental. Connor hears a breaking noise from outside that he can't identify. A man shouts, "Hey you, cut it out!"

Running to the window, Connor sees someone bashing the new windshield of the Mini-Cooper with a golf club. Idling behind the Mini-Cooper is the black Denali.

By the time Connor gets outside, the man has completed his work. The windshield is in a thousand-plus pieces. "I told him to stop," says one of the moving men. "Should I call the cops?"

Connor doesn't respond. The guy with the golf club gets back into the Denali. Without thinking, Connor runs toward him. Who knows what he hopes to do? Among his confusing thoughts, not one has yet crawled its way to the top.

The moving man calls to him. "I wouldn't do that if I were you!"

A rear window of the Denali opens, and Chucky looks out. His smile is as friendly as a spider bite. He sticks out his hand and makes a peace sign. Then, with the same two fingers, he taps his throat, as if to say, *You're a dead man.* Connor comes to a halt.

Fidget lies stretched out in a tub of tepid water with his bony knees poking above the surface like twin Ararats. He thinks it's time to give the hot-water tap another twist to increase the temperature a few degrees, but if he leans forward, he'll disturb the gold necklaces arranged becomingly on his chest. Fidget's chest is more sunken than thin, and the necklaces nicely fill the declivity. So he's torn, but if he does nothing, he'll grow cold. He remains still for another minute to further admire the golden twinkling, as he delights in the smallness of his present dilemma. He has gold, vodka, and food. What more can the world offer?

This is when Fidget hears the opening of the garage door, followed quickly by the sound of a motorcycle being revved up. The 1690-cc air-cooled twin-cam 103 engine and Tommy Gun 2-1-2 exhaust of the Fat Bob would be noisy even in Times Square, but within the garage they're thunderous. Terrified birds fly up from the bare branches. The surface of Fidget's bathwater ripples.

At other times Fidget might feel anxiety about possible intrusions, but he's inside a fortress. The doors and downstairs windows are covered with plywood, and no one can enter. Eventually he might worry about how to get out, but not today. The outside world is not his concern.

If Fidget cared to disturb his comfort and look from the window, he'd see a black Fat Bob hurtle out the driveway and accelerate down the street. But he sees nothing. His attention is focused on sliding forward as slowly as possible so he can turn on the hot-water tap and solve his only significant problem: tepid water. As his knees disappear, his nugget rings, gold bracelet, and gold Rolex break the surface and sparkle a sentimental greeting. He admires them fondly as he adjusts the tap and the water heats up. When a nearly unbearable warmth is reached, he closes the tap, leans back, and readjusts the gold chains across his chest. The rings, bracelet, and Rolex disappear as his knees rise like baby Alps, or were they Ararats? Fidget sighs.

An hour passes. Perhaps Fidget dreams—we have no information about this—but when he wakes, the water is again tepid. Such a nuisance. Slowly, he pushes himself upward to turn on the hot water. But over the sound of the splashing water, he perceives another noise. A car has pulled in to the driveway. Should he investigate? He thinks not. Still, he hears voices: a conversation that becomes audible as two men walk toward the rear of the house.

First voice: "Back door's sealed up, too."

Second voice: "What about the garage?"

We have heard these voices before. Manny and Vikström are paying a visit to Fat Bob's small house on Montauk Avenue to make sure it's shut tight.

Manny: "What I don't fucking see is why the black Denali is after Fat Bob."

Vikström: "He owes people money. The Denali's probably an enforcer trying to collect on past-due debts."

Manny: "So the Denali works for the casino?"

"No way," says Vikström. "The casino doesn't need enforcers. But someone *at* the casino might make a private bet with someone else at better odds. The betting doesn't have to be on a table game, though. It can be on how long it takes a fat guy to walk to the men's room. The casino only supplies suckers willing to make the bets and hustlers willing to take them up on it."

As the detectives talk, Fidget idly listens from above. He wishes they'd leave so he can return to his aquatic dozing, but he'll be patient. After all, he knows their voices. How could he not after so many years of receiving their negative attention?

"The problem for the hustler," Vikström continues, "is how to collect on the debt. So he might use an enforcer. In this case it's maybe the guy in the Denali."

"But you don't know this." Manny chuckles to suggest that Vikström rarely knows what he's talking about and is just spouting hot air.

"I don't know squat. I'm only saying the guys in the Denali are probably trying to collect money."

Manny's about to say, *Squat don't count.* Instead he's distracted. "For fuck's sake, the Fat Bob's gone! That's five gone in a week!"

The violent segue is caused by Manny looking into the garage and realizing that the last of the Harley Fat Bobs—the black one—has vanished.

Vikström peers over his partner's shoulder. "I thought the garage was supposed to be secured."

"They only secured the house, the lazy fucks. I bet Lisowski took it."

"Maybe," says Vikström, "and maybe not."

Around one o'clock Connor sits at the bar of the Exchange on Bank Street waiting for his lunch: a hamburger with Swiss cheese and mushrooms and a side of french fries. He drinks a Corona. Given his druthers, he'd drink a dozen.

A new windshield for the Mini-Cooper is being delivered from Hartford. The manager at the New London auto-glass shop has said the car will be ready around four. He's dying to ask Connor why his windshield was smashed twice in a twelve-hour period, but he bites his tongue. After all, Connor might be returning often. The walk to the Exchange took Connor half an hour and confirmed what he already suspected: his Bruno Magli slip-ons are too loose and chafe his Achilles tendons.

Didi, when Connor calls to tell him what happened, says, "Why the fuck did you go to her house? It's not just you that Chucky's mad at. Your brother says he thinks we're out to steal some goddamn jewelry. At least pick up the mail!"

Connor decides to wait till after lunch. He dislikes being yelled at. Pure petulance on his part. But he's increasingly reluctant to be part of Bounty, Inc., and this feeling has grown to the point that all he wants is to see how many Coronas he can drink before passing out. But he'll refrain. We may have noted that Connor suffers from a complex mix of responsibility and irresponsibility, leading to alternating impulses that cancel one another out. Warring good and bad angels, people say. Whatever.

Before reaching the Exchange, Connor stopped at the travel agency a block away to see Linda, but a note taped to the glass said she'd gone to lunch. The one fact he knows for sure is that she isn't having lunch in the Exchange.

At this moment a man takes the stool to Connor's right and jostles him with his elbow as he removes his leather jacket. "My fault, my fault!" says the man.

Connor didn't see the man enter, but he realizes it's Fat Bob even before he notices the motorcycle tattooed on his left forearm. However, he's not in the best of moods and says nothing.

"You seen a little red guy around here?" asks Fat Bob.

Connor thinks it's a racist remark. "Are you referring to a Native American?"

"No, no, a little red guy. Red hair, red face, rides a red scooter. Wants to shoot me."

Connor wonders if his assumption of racism is in fact an indication of his *own* racism. "He's the man who was chasing you yesterday morning past the train station? I haven't seen him today. Have you seen Fidget?"

"The homeless guy? Not recently. The cops probably arrested him again. Why're you interested?"

"Just curious. Why's the little red guy want to shoot you?"

"Just a misunderstanding. Anyway, he's a nut job. Calls himself Jack Sprat."

A waitress brings Connor his hamburger with Swiss cheese and mushrooms and his french fries. Fat Bob nods at it. "Get me one of those suckers, will you?" he says to the waitress. "And a Corona."

"I thought the cops were after you," says Connor.

"Them and all the world," says Fat Bob with a touch of melancholy. "How's the lying going? Making improvements?"

"I don't seem to get better."

"Yeah, Angelina said that. She said you'd stopped by twice collecting money for ex–prom queens and smokin' beagles. Seems like a hard way to make a buck."

Connor's surprised. "How d'you know it was me?"

Fat Bob reaches over and takes several of Connor's fries. "She described you: tall, black-haired guy with a tan. Said you were an awful liar."

"She called the cops on me."

"Yeah, she does that to everyone. Don't take it personal. Just stay away from her and you'll be fine. Right now she's been selling my bikes. I'd been storing them out at my place on Montauk Avenue. It's driving me crazy. She wants money for a face-lift, says she wants to look like a prom queen again. Someone on the fuckin' horn's been telling her she owes it to herself."

"Why'd she call you? I thought she hated you."

There's a pause as the bartender appears. He's a round, middle-aged man with a shaved head and a stained white apron. He puts a little cardboard coaster advertising Guinness in front of Fat Bob and a bottle of Corona on top.

"She gets a charge from turning the blade. Like, she calls when she sells one of my Fat Bobs cheap. I mean, she'll sell a bike worth fifteen grand for five thousand."

"Scary."

Fat Bob sprinkles salt on Connor's fries and takes a few more. "She's got this guy who runs Hog Hurrah helping her: Lisowski. Says I owe him money. You mind if I put ketchup on these suckers?" Fat Bob squirts dollops of ketchup on Connor's fries.

"Go right ahead," says Connor. "So why are the cops looking for you?"

Fat Bob sighs. "You know Marco?" He takes a few more french fries. Connor shakes his head. "I only saw him . . . after."

"I'm bummed he got killed, I really am. But it wasn't my fault. I offered him my bike, and he took it. I mean, it was like a test-drive. He said he wanted to buy it."

We can't say how much Fat Bob believes this. He owed Marco money as he owes everyone money, and he might have offered Marco a cheap price on the Harley and urged him to take a spin. *Ride it to work today,* he might have said. *You'll love it.* After all, on that Monday morning the weather was beautiful, and at that time Fat Bob still had five other Fat Bobs in his garage on Montauk.

"Did you have an appointment to meet Sal?" asks Connor, taking a guess.

"Hey, look at it this way: If I'd ridden that bike into town, I'd've been smashed to pieces just like Marco. I'd put money on it."

"Someone hates you that much?"

Fat Bob rubs his chin, a thoughtful gesture with a touch of irony. We should say that Fat Bob is one of those fellows who could shave two or three times a day, so thick is his beard, and now, at lunchtime, his heavy cheeks and chin are darkened by incipient stubble. Indeed, when he rubs his chin, there's a sound like a cat scratching in its litter box, but very faint.

"The ex-wife might stick a knife in me if she wasn't afraid to get in trouble, like jail. But she calls to say people keep asking if I'm dead yet. They want my stuff, and they're ripping off my bikes. I'm fuckin' broke. And I lost my job at the casino. They said I had a conflict of interest. Like I wanted their money."

The waitress brings Fat Bob's hamburger with Swiss cheese and mushrooms and his french fries. He and Connor engage in some companionable chewing until Connor asks, "So you'd seen Sal upstairs when you were visiting Marco?"

"We'd talked." Fat Bob lifts the bottle of Corona to his lips and drinks. He wipes his mouth with the back of his hand.

"You know his real name was Danny Barbarella?"

Fat Bob lowers his voice. "Dante, he liked to be called Dante. I met him once in Detroit, and then I read about the court stuff. What a fuckup. He sure wasn't any good at hiding himself. He should've gone to Guam."

"That's what his wife said."

"Yeah, it was the general consensus. He was too fuckin' easy to spot."

Sal, we can say, had his weaknesses, and a big one was vanity. He loved his rockabilly pompadour, but if he'd lopped it off in favor of a crew cut, he might be alive today. And the gold chains, rings, brace-let, gold Rolex, and Montegrappa St. Moritz Limited Edition Woods eighteen-karat-gold rollerball pen drew attention. Sal saw this as part of his fundamental self; his very essence was mixed in with his pompadour and bling like hair gel.

"I told him he should be more subtle," says Fat Bob. "But he thought I wanted his stuff—his Rolex and gold chains and stuff. He thought I was threatening him."

"And were you?"

"Just a little."

"His wife said his jewelry only amounted to about five thousand."

"You kidding? The Rolex alone's worth over fifty. I could sell it for twenty-five in a heartbeat. Anyway, she wasn't his wife."

Connor sipped his beer. "Why would he want to kill you? Did you try to get money out of him?"

Fat Bob put a hand over his eyes. "Did Angelina tell you that? I might have tried to touch him for a little loan, I can't remember. But for fuck's sake, I'd never threaten him. Anyway, he didn't give me a dime."

Connor doesn't believe this, but he won't challenge it. "You know Chucky?"

Startled, Fat Bob slops a little beer on his shirt. "Jesus, I'd never bor-row money from Chucky! He'd shoot me in the foot if I was no more than a day late in paying him back. And that'd be just the start. You met Chucky?"

"Once or twice."

"Don't go near him. He likes scaring people. Fuck, he scares me all the time."

"What's he have against you?" Connor considers what might have happened if Chucky had caught him with Céline the previous evening. Ruefully, he recalls her nakedness beneath the nearly severed nightgown.

He'd less than a half inch left of needle lace to cut when Chucky had started pounding on the door.

"Nothin', nothin'! Well, he knows I'd seen Dante in Detroit. He knows I knew Dante and Sal were the same guy, so he might think I figured he'd whacked him. But I'd never be that dumb. As far as Chucky is concerned, I keep my mind blank."

"So Chucky shot Sal?"

"No way, it was an outside job. At most Chucky was a kind of facilitator."

"Did you tell Chucky you'd seen Dante in New London?" This is Connor's big hope: that he can blame Fat Bob for spreading the news that Dante Barbarella was hiding in New London. It would let Connor off the hook about outing Sal to his brother, meaning Sal had already been outed. What a colossal relief it would be!

Fat Bob chokes, coughs, and spits up a bit of burger. "Fuck no! I never go near him. You go near Chucky, then some way or other he takes a piece of you. He likes to own people."

Perhaps Fat Bob is not entirely truthful. After all, two guys in a Denali came looking for him at Otto's place near Ledyard. Maybe they only wanted to chat, but as we know, when Otto showed them his shotgun, one of them pulled a pistol and winged him in the arm. It suggests that Chucky may have a fatal agenda as far as Fat Bob is concerned. But Connor isn't privy to this information.

"Chucky and Marco had some deal going," says Fat Bob, talking and chewing at the same time. "I don't know what it was, but I saw Chucky up in Marco's office. Whatever it was, it scared Marco, but Marco was more scared of Chucky than he was of what Chucky was scheming. At first I thought Chucky'd killed Marco, but I was wrong. I mean, it was an accident Marco got killed, no matter what others say. And it was Sal that did it, not Chucky."

"D'you know Céline?"

Fat Bob shakes his head. "Who's that?"

"She was living here with Sal and pretending to be his wife."

"Oh, yeah, Shirley—hot, hot, hot! I didn't see her here, but I saw her in Detroit. Wants to be a torch singer but can't carry a tune. Maybe it doesn't matter."

Connor's inner voice shouts, *Shirley, Shirley, Shirley!* His outer voice asks, "Is she involved with Chucky?"

"Nobody wants to be involved with Chucky. If she's mixed up with him, it's because he's got some hold over her."

We shouldn't think Connor dislikes the name Shirley. He can rattle off the names of many famous Shirleys: Shirley Temple, Shirley Mac-Laine, Dame Shirley Bassey, and Shirley the Girly, a drag queen he knew in San Diego. But once he'd wrapped his heart around the name Céline, other names were only barking noises.

The bartender reappears and taps the bar to get Fat Bob's attention. "Bob, hey, Bob, you wanted me to keep an eye peeled for Giovanni. He's out front."

Fat Bob jumps off his stool. "Shit, I hate to leave food on my plate," he tells Connor. "You finish it if you want."

Connor looks toward the front door and then turns to ask Fat Bob the identity of Giovanni, but Bob's running down the back stairs that lead to Water Street. A moment later Jack Sprat darts into the Exchange, and right after that, Fat Bob's noisy Fat Bob starts up down below.

TWENTY-THREE

Mailboxes—it's an indication of Connor's growing reluctance to be part of Bounty, Inc. that he's dragged his feet in getting to the New London post office, but after all, the new windshield for the Mini-Cooper won't be ready until four and at the moment we write, it's only two. But the growing reluctance needs another look. Maybe it began on Monday with his shock at Marco's death, though we should call it murder, even if Connor didn't know it at the time. Or it could have begun later when he saw Céline in her T-shirt and white shorts: a definite body blow. Or maybe it was when Connor told Vasco that he'd spotted Sal near the scene of the accident and recalled seeing him in Detroit. But it wasn't just the recklessness of telling Vasco that mattered, it was Vasco's response: a sudden attentiveness.

To simplify, ever since Didi Lobato parked the Winnebago on the Hannaquit Breachway outside Brewster, events have raised Connor's reluctance to be part of Bounty, Inc., and caused his sense of security and sense of self-worth to receive ever harder knocks on their metaphoric heads: the very reverse of the stultifying boredom he'd felt in his last months as a slot attendant at the Viejas Casino, thirty-five miles east of San Diego. But Connor has begun to feel fragile. It's not just big events like Sal's murder that cause him to question what he's doing—even small events make him nervous, as when Angelina invited him into her kitchen to partake of a plate of brownies. Maybe the brownie was just a brownie, but Connor was glad to escape in one piece.

Then, this morning, when he made his way from the RV to the dam-

aged Mini-Cooper, Vaughn came running after him. Connor hesitated—
more of a flinch than a pause.

"You know who I really am?" called Vaughn. The sunlight seemed
entangled in his golden blond hair; his freckles twinkled.

"You're Vaughn." Connor was in no mood to fool around.

"Yes, that's a reasonable preposition, but I don't unkind what I'm
called."

"You mean 'mean.'"

"Left."

"Right," corrected Connor. "So who are you?"

Vaughn glanced behind him, then ducked down to look under the
Winnebago. Getting up, he lowered his voice to a whisper. "I'm an orphan from outer space."

Connor wasn't sure he'd heard correctly; then he was sure he had. He
opened his mouth to speak but thought better of it. Vaughn smiled
brightly, and his lips seemed pinker than usual. Connor nodded and
hurried to the Mini-Cooper. Some subjects, he thought, were better left
untouched.

Connor's brief exchange with Vaughn produced another upward tick
in his disinclination to continue with Bounty, Inc. He'd be hard-pressed
to define it, but he worries, and perhaps maturation is no more than the
accumulation of worry. This in itself is important. Though Connor is
twenty-six, he begins to feel old. (Contrarily, that's why Fidget in his tub,
as his worries are soothed away, begins to look younger.)

After lunch, as Connor enters the post office, he again recollects
Vaughn's claim and thinks, *I need to drop everything and get the hell out of
here.* Connor can't explain why, but it's another bump upward in reluctance. Of course he doesn't believe that Vaughn is actually an orphan
from outer space, but neither is he one hundred percent positive that
Vaughn isn't. This in itself is worrisome.

As he nears the post office box, Connor spots Detective Manny
Streeter leaning against the wall and studying the ceiling. Connor turns,

meaning to escape, but Benny Vikström stands in the doorway. Possibly, if Connor hadn't been brooding about Vaughn, he'd have seen the detectives earlier and right now he'd be running down the block. Instead he veers toward the phony box, not the one with the money but the one with Didi's postcards. The detectives veer after him and wait.

We've already mentioned the box with the postcards sent by Didi, but what we haven't said is that the postcards are addressed to Connor. Since Connor was the person most likely to open the box, it made sense to Didi to use Connor's name. But he should have told Connor about his intentions.

As Connor removes a fat wad of postcards, a hand reaches over his shoulder and seizes them. "I'd like to take a look at those, young fellow," says Manny. Connor spins away and promptly bumps into Vikström, standing on the other side of him.

Stentor, the Greek herald in the Trojan War, is said to have had a voice as loud as fifty men. When Manny reads the first postcard, his voice isn't as loud as that, but it's stentorian nonetheless. "'Dear Connor: The baby has your eyes. He's yours, I know he's yours. Send money, we have nothing. Your devoted Brenda.'"

Manny gives Connor a push. "You're a real scumbag, aren't you?" He reads another card. People nearby stop to listen. "'Dear Connie: Dad and me think your sex-change plans are a bad idea. We like you best as a girl. Love, Mom.'"

Manny and Vikström give Connor a long look. "At least they did a fair job of it," says Manny. He reads a third. "'Connor: Did you remember to let the dog out of the house when you left California?'

"What kind of dog?" asks Manny.

Connor shakes his head. "I don't have a dog."

Manny's indignant. "You mean it went and died on you?"

"No, no, I haven't had a dog since junior high school."

Then, among the ten or so people who are listening, Connor sees Linda. She stares at him inquiringly, as if thinking new evidence has been revealed, though not evidence of a positive nature. Connor wants to signal it's all a mistake, whatever "it" may be, but he's afraid Manny and Vikström will ask her questions.

Manny reads another postcard. "'Dear Connor: You too are an orphan from outer space. Best wishes, Vaughn.'"

Connor doesn't scream—he's too mature to scream. But the thought crosses his mind.

"You've no right to read my mail," he says.

"These're postcards," says Manny. "Anyone can read them free of charge."

And Vikström thinks, *I wonder if that's really true.* He takes the postcards from Manny and studies them. "They all have the same handwriting."

Manny takes them back. "Without a specialist it's hard to say." Then, to Connor, "I bet you wrote them yourself. You're some kind of weirdo. Don't you have any regular friends?"

Various semi-witty remarks flit across Connor's cerebral cortex, but he only shrugs. Any explanation would take a week to recount.

"You were seen coming out of Sal Nicoletti's office the other morning," says Vikström. "You want to tell us why you shot him?"

"He was already dead when I got there." Connor's voice is a pathetic squeak. He snatches another glance at Linda, who gives him the same curious stare.

"Then why didn't you report it?" says Manny.

"I was scared. I just wanted to leave." Connor, in fact, had never considered calling the police.

Manny and Vikström know perfectly well that Connor didn't shoot Sal, and they know he didn't steal Sal's bling. What they don't understand is how Connor fits into "the big picture," as Manny likes to say, and the comic postcards don't help.

"Where's the other post office box?" asks Vikström. "The one with the checks."

"What're you talking about? This's the only box I've been renting."

As has been said often, Connor is a terrible liar. His eyes get all strange and whirly. They're doing it now. Manny and Vikström are impressed by the display of ocular pinwheels, but not for long.

"Okay," says Manny, taking out his handcuffs, "we're going for a trip."

Connor presses his back against the wall of boxes. "But what have I done?" Linda is still watching him.

"That's what you're going to tell us," says Manny.

Connor is spun around before he can protest. He wants to tell the detectives to wait. He wants to say, *Can't you just hang on and let me tell that pretty woman it's all a mistake?* As he's bundled out the door like a parcel with feet, he snatches a final glimpse of Linda. She gives him a little wave.

M anny and Vikström are arguing. They're in the detectives' office, and Connor's in a small interview room, waiting. It's an hour later.

"The fuck you say," says Manny. "He could be the killer for all we know."

"Except you know he isn't." Vikström knows their argument has become not so much about Connor's criminality but has morphed into another chapter in Manny's attempts to make Vikström appear mistaken and foolish. As for Connor, they have an address in San Diego, a California driver's license, an ID card from Viejas Casino, and no evidence of a criminal record. When they asked where he'd been staying, Connor said, "With friends," and mentioned his brother. He told the detectives he'd met Sal Nicoletti at the time of the accident and they'd talked several times. He described going to Nicoletti's house that morning to speak to Céline but learned she'd moved out and the rental company was taking away the furniture. This is news to Manny and Vikström.

"He obviously scared her, and she got the fuck outta town," says Manny. "No telling what dirty thing he tried to make her do. Too bad she gave up the shotgun."

"You've no proof of that."

"Maybe not, but it fits the patterns. Look how he was trying to weasel money from Angelina. Good thing she kept him out of *her* house. No telling what crimes a sex fiend like him would have committed."

"Sex fiend?"

"You can tell by his eyes that he's a degenerate. No telling what his secret sex history might be, but it's bound to be perverse."

Vikström wants to say, *If you say "no telling" one more time, I'll . . .* Instead he says, "He claims he never went to Angelina's."

"Look at his eyes! I thought they'd pop from their sockets. He's a congenital bad liar, like what he said about Céline and Fidget. Why should a beauty like Céline be interested in a scumbag like Fidget?"

"She knows he took Sal's jewelry."

"You're right: the fuckin' bling. That's the fuckin' elephant in the room. We got to find Fidget before he gets whacked. Shit, he might be whacked already."

Manny also asked Connor about his "friendship with Fat Bob." Connor, regrettably, answered by saying, "Friendship? I hardly know him!" It's the word "hardly" that was regrettable.

They'd been sitting in the interview room: gray table, gray plastic chairs, gray walls, and a pane of two-way glass. On a scale of one to ten, its charm level was subzero. The only artwork was a No Smoking sign. It wasn't by Andy Warhol.

"So you knew him," said Vikström.

"I don't know him," said Connor. "I ran into him at a bar."

"That's knowing," said Manny.

"It was coincidental. We were having lunch. He sat on the next stool."

Manny shook his head. "That's not good enough. You could have moved."

"Don't I get to ask for a lawyer?" Connor's grasp of legal subtleties comes entirely from TV's *Law & Order.*

"This is a friendly chat," said Vikström. "You only get to ask for a lawyer when it's unfriendly."

"Of course," said Manny thoughtfully, "lots can happen between the asking and whenever the lawyer shows up."

"Lots of unpleasant stuff," added Vikström, lowering his voice a little.

"Let's hear about Fat Bob and Sal," said Manny. "They were buddies, right?"

So Connor told them that Fat Bob had seen Sal in Detroit once or twice and knew about the court case. "But they weren't friends," Connor insisted. "He only recognized him one day when he was visiting Marco at his office."

"You mean he tried to blackmail him," said Manny.

"I don't know that." Once again facial evidence showed Connor impeded by a challenged communication skill—that is, Manny and Vikström perceive the lie.

"And now he's hiding from the police because of the blackmail," said Manny, who knew this was one of the smallest of Fat Bob's complicated motivations.

"I know nothing about that either. He says people want to kill him."

"Like who?" asked Vikström.

"Giovanni somebody, for one."

"Jack Sprat," said Manny. "Who else?"

Well, it took a few more questions, but eventually Connor mentioned Chucky, though even mentioning Chucky's name scared him.

"Who's Chucky?" asked Vikström.

That was an important moment. Neither detective had heard about Chucky before. Know-how is knowing what questions to ask, and Vikström had asked a big one. But he didn't know it yet.

"He's a big guy who hangs out at the casino. He scares people."

"How big?" asked Manny.

"Broad shoulders, tall, big arms. He looks like an offensive tackle."

"And Fat Bob owes him money?" asked Manny.

Connor shook his head. "He says he'd be too scared to owe Chucky money."

"Then why's he hiding from him?"

"I don't know."

Again the detectives saw the lie.

"So when did you last see Chucky?"

"This morning when I was leaving Céline's."

A small spark ignited in Vikström's brain, but it's the wrong spark, or rather it's not the primary spark, which would be to ask what Chucky was doing at Céline's. Instead he asks, "What kind of car's he got?"

Connor didn't give these answers easily. We've mostly omitted the denials, complaints, and foot-dragging. At last he said, "He was in a black Denali. But Chucky's not the kind of guy who drives himself. He gets driven."

"Ah," said Vikström.

Manny smiled at Vikström, another rarity. "Those two guys at Otto's were working for Chucky."

And once more Vikström said, "Ah."

But their sense of accomplishment might have been greater if they'd asked why Chucky had been at Céline's, which might have led them to realize that Chucky was looking for Fidget and the jewelry that Fidget had pilfered from Sal's corpse.

So now we return to the present moment, with Manny and Vikström in the squad room leaning back in their chairs with their feet on their desks and cradling their heads with knitted fingers. Connor remains in the interview room. It's five o'clock. They are waiting for the FBI agents Orville Percival and Henry Lascombe, otherwise known as Percy and Hank. Let *them* deal with Chucky, they think. In fact, Manny and Vikström have little choice.

"Then what's this business with Chucky," says Manny, "if Fat Bob doesn't owe him money?"

"It means Fat Bob knows something that could hurt Chucky."

"Like what?"

"Maybe Chucky knows that Fat Bob was trying to blackmail Sal."

"It's got to be more than that."

"Maybe Chucky knows something about Sal getting whacked."

"More than that."

"Maybe Chucky lined up the whacker."

"Jesus, Benny, you don't say 'whacker,' you say 'shooter.' . . ."

The detectives' promising dispute on correct usage when discussing the criminal netherworld might have lasted another instructive hour, but at that instant their chat is cut short by the FBI agents Percy and Hank, who enter the room with the evident aversion of two men entering the environs of an open latrine. This was their ongoing joke.

"Good to see you guys hard at work," says Percy.

"Don't bother to get up," says Hank.

The agents chuckle a humorless chuckle. They're similarly dressed in suits of different shades of gray. Manny and Vikström remain with their feet on their desks. They decide not to feel intimidated.

"That escort who's pretending to be Sal's wife," says Manny. "What was her name? Shirley something? Anyway, she's gone missing, and we'd like to talk to her. You know where she might be?"

Doubtless the agents know about Céline's departure, but they don't show it. Their cheeks are pink, and their short hair is freshly trimmed. Their appearance differs from that of a male mannequin in the display window of an expensive men's shop only in the area of the lips: a slight smile with Percy, a slight sneer with Hank.

"What do you want to talk to her about?" asks Percy.

"You're not overstepping your prerogatives, are you?" asks Hank.

"Getting too ambitious?" asks Percy.

Manny swings around in his chair, and his feet hit the floor with a thump. "Just answer the fucking question."

The agents give him a look that's supposed to make Manny shrivel up like a wasp squirted with lighter fluid, but he doesn't. "Her assignment has been completed," says Hank. "She'd no reason to stay here."

"So she went back to Detroit?" asks Vikström.

"We don't see how that concerns you," says Percy.

"She's mixed up with the theft of Sal's jewelry," says Manny.

"Small potatoes," says Hank.

Vikström and Manny consider various responses. After all, Céline or Shirley was living with a guy who was murdered right downtown on Bank Street. But they can also anticipate the agents' reply: *It's a federal issue.*

"So who put the fucking flower into the fucking bullet hole?" asks Manny.

Percy shakes his head. Hank inspects his fingernails.

But Vikström has begun to wonder why Chucky had been at Céline's that morning. What was their connection? He sits up in his chair. "Give us Chucky."

The two agents blinked loudly.

"Who's Chucky?" asks Percy.

"He's the guy with the Denali. He smashed up a local man's windshield."

"On purpose," adds Manny. "It's an expensive windshield. That's a felony. He did it twice."

The agents move toward the door. "You guys are off your leash," says Hank.

"What leash?" inquires Vikström.

"Hey, hey, wait up," says Manny. "Let's not get personal. You guys like to come over to my place tonight, do some karaoke, knock back a few beers?"

The door clicks shut. The several million dust motes activated by the agents' brisk departure begin to settle.

"Fuck me," says Manny. "That went well, don't you think?"

"Forget about the windshield," says Vikström. "Why was Chucky at Céline's this morning?"

"Maybe he wanted to ball her."

But Vikström isn't thinking straight. He should be focused on the connection between Céline and Connor, meaning Chucky and Connor. He should be thinking about Fidget. Instead his fears are focused on the department's Mountain Bike Patrol. He remembers an old bike in the back of his garage. Maybe it's time to drag it out, spruce it up, and get his leg muscles in shape.

One last little bit before the chapter comes to a close. Manny and Vikström are in the Subaru Forester on their way to talk to Angelina Rossi as they try to build a case against Connor, who is in the backseat staring out the window. This time he hasn't been handcuffed. The detectives have decided he isn't a flight risk. Connor asks himself if he should find this mildly insulting.

Manny and Vikström believe that in the New London post office is a second box full to bursting with checks and hard cash that suckers have sent to Bounty, Inc., though the actual name Bounty, Inc. is unknown to them. They also believe that Connor is mixed up with Sal's death, Céline's departure, and Chucky's indefinite presence. And they suspect that Connor and Fat Bob are in league in some way. They claim to understand all sorts of incriminating particulars, which in fact they don't understand. But to build a case, they must start with Angelina. She has to identify Connor as the degenerate scammer who demanded she fork over hundreds of dollars, twice. Mercifully, as she earlier told Manny, she'd been able to fight him off.

But Angelina is in a bad mood. She's been giving Magsie a bath, and at times he nips. For some dog owners, this is tantamount to betrayal—a brutal attack from their dear pup—but she won't strike him. Instead she shakes her finger very hard and says she'll withhold his cookie. This is when her doorbell rings. She ignores it, and it rings again. A few seconds later, it rings a third time. Now she has to remove Magsie from the tub when he's incompletely washed and rinsed. This means gripping him tightly in a towel so he won't escape through the house, making a mess. And Magsie hates being gripped tightly in a towel. He snarls and snaps. Angelina could turn this into a story as long as *War and Peace*, but we won't. She reaches the door with Magsie clamped under her arm and flings it open.

Manny stands on the stoop facing her with an affectionate smile. Vikström and Connor are a few feet behind.

"We caught him," says Manny. "I found the guy who was harassing you. This is him, right?" He beams and points back at Connor.

Angelina squeezes her bad pup a little harder, and Magsie makes a noise like "Ooof!" She focuses on Connor. "I've never seen that man before in my life!"

TWENTY-FOUR

The maroon desk chair with wraparound back and padded armrests has wheels that easily slide on the tile floor, forcing Connor to keep one hand gripping the edge of Linda's desk so he won't skate across the office, which happened when he first sat down. And as is the case with many old buildings on Bank Street, the floor here is slightly tilted.

"Why do you think Angelina said she'd never seen you before?" asks Linda. "You can't just decide she's crazy. Maybe she likes you." She wears a man's white dress shirt with a button-down collar. The top two buttons are open, revealing a substantial wedge of pink flesh. Connor tries not to stare at it. In this he's only partly successful.

"That's absolutely impossible."

"Nothing's impossible."

Connor has been describing his difficulties, which began with telling Linda about his visit to Céline's, though he doesn't mention the contest between Céline's nightgown and the cuticle scissors. Then came the double smashing of the Mini-Cooper's windshield, his lunch with Fat Bob, why the two detectives had arrested him at the post office, and why he'd been set free. The last he blamed on madness or luck—nothing rational.

"Okay, maybe she's not crazy, but I can't think of a better reason. The cops practically fell off the porch. They accused me of bribing her, but I hadn't gone near her again. She's scary." As if in emphasis, Connor's chair skates another foot or so away from Linda's desk, and he has to dig his heels against the tiles to bring it to a stop. He rolls back and tethers himself to her desk with his right hand. Linda grins. Connor thinks that somewhere in this nonsense is a metaphor about his approach-avoidance conflict with beautiful women. It's six o'clock, and they are alone in the office. The only light comes from Linda's desk lamp and the streetlamps out on Bank Street.

"Perhaps someone else is bribing her," says Linda.

"Possibly, but I can't think who'd do it." This is a lie, and Linda gives Connor a long look. "Okay, okay," says Connor. "My Uncle Didi might have bribed her. He thought we'd end up in jail. Then he said he had a plan, though he didn't say what it was. He likes being secretive."

Manny and Vikström had driven Connor back to the New London police station from Angelina's. Vikström had remained silent. Manny had said, "You're fuckin' lucky," twenty times. When Connor at last got out of the car, Manny said, "I'm going to be working hard to put your ass in jail, so you better clear outta town." Connor called a cab to take him from the police station to the auto-glass store to pick up the Mini-Cooper. Then he drove back to Bank Street.

Half serious, Linda shakes her head. "I don't see why you keep calling people and scaring them about their dogs. No wonder Angelina was mad."

"It's not just dogs," says Connor defensively. "And I don't do the calling—I just collect the money. It's a family business."

"Some family. Prom Queens Anonymous and Orphans from Outer Space. What was the other one? Oh, yes, Free Dogs from Nicotine Addiction. Are there more?"

"Not dogs, *beagles*. It's breed-specific. Bounty, Inc. has lots of phantom organizations. Didi also wanted to use Victims of Roadkill Gastronomy, but we voted him down. It didn't seem serious enough."

"Unlike the others," says Linda, beginning to laugh again.

"Right."

"And people give money to Orphans from Outer Space?"

"It's not a big moneymaker. Didi's more interested in the process than the money, though he likes the money. And he says the pitch is more important than the actual cause. He claims he once raised a hundred bucks for Organ Grinder Monkey Retirement Ranch, Inc. and fifty for Halfway Houses for Homosexual Horses."

"You all must be crazy," Linda says with severity and delight.

"People believe in crazier things, like the ones who deny climate change. Reason and proof have hardly any influence over people's belief systems."

"Does Didi say that?"

"How'd you guess? You probably think we're crooks."

Connor is struck that away from the Winnebago the business of Bounty, Inc. seems vaguely subversive, a manic tomfoolery, originating in Didi himself. But Didi is also serious, though his seriousness derives from a mix of nihilism, anarchism, and his belief in the tradiculous. Or, as Connor has thought, Didi may simply be mad.

"Well, you may be crooks, but it seems wonderful," says Linda, laughing.

Connor shakes his head. "It's getting too dangerous. After all, I was nearly arrested. I need a new geographical cure, one that comes with the guarantee that I won't be killed."

"My company specializes in geographical cures," says Linda.

"I don't want a round-trip. I want to go someplace and stay awhile." On the far wall, travel posters of the Greek islands offer themselves up as options. Another poster displays the towers of Sintra. *I could escape to Lisbon,* thinks Connor. But he has no money.

"By the way, have you seen Fidget?" Connor now accepts it was Chucky who wanted the gold, not Céline. She'd only been following orders. And he knows that Chucky's surely out there right now looking for it. But Connor thinks if he himself is the one to find Sal's jewelry, he might get a reward. After all, Fidget can't sell the gold, he can only hoard it. Connor has lots of reasons to think it's okay to take the gold from Fidget. But he doesn't believe any of them.

"He seems to have vanished. But someone else is looking for Fidget."

"You mean the police?"

Linda shakes her head. "No, some men in a black SUV with tinted windows. Do you know who they are?"

"I've no idea." Connor tries to keep his face rigid while Linda looks at him doubtfully. But he doesn't want to explain about Chucky. And he doesn't like to think what Chucky might do to Fidget.

"I'm surprised you haven't seen them, since they've been driving around. But I also have a treat for you. At least I hope it's a treat."

"Like what?" says Connor suspiciously.

Linda's smile seems always present at the edges of her lips, ready to emerge. Now it spreads across her face. "It's not scandalous, if that's what worries you."

"I don't worry about anything like that," says Connor quickly. "I'm curious."

As Linda grows serious, her smile retreats. Connor thinks she wears no lipstick, which he decides he likes, but in fact she wears a small amount of lip gloss of a shade called Pale Pink. Whatever she wears or doesn't wear, Connor finds it vastly superior to the green lipstick that Céline wore the previous evening, called Manic Panic Green Envy Metallic Lipstick Goth Deathrock.

"You said you'd like to see the inside of the old Capitol Theatre that's been closed for forty years."

This was nothing Connor had expected. "I would. Did you get a key?"

"No, but I met a man who knows who he can ask for one."

She tells Connor she'd been in the parking lot behind the theater, examining the theater's bolted back door. Trash and empty bottles had been scattered in front of it, making Linda think it hadn't been opened for years.

"A man asked what I was doing. I thought he was a plainclothes policeman, but he said he worked for the historical society. I told him my friend Connor and I would like to see inside, that you were a writer and wanted to take some pictures."

Connor's on the brink of chastising Linda for lying, but he's a poor example of truth telling. It isn't that Connor doesn't lie, it's that he's bad at it. Were he any good, he'd be making fake phone calls along with Eartha and Vaughn.

"I don't have a camera," says Connor, mildly relieved.

Linda opens a lower drawer of her desk and takes out a Panasonic Lumix. "But I have one." Seeing that Connor seems hesitant, she asks, "What's wrong? I even bought two flashlights." She takes two small flashlights from her desk, one red, one blue. "Which do you like?"

"The guy was just hanging around in the parking lot?"

"His car was parked there."

"Did you see what kind it was?"

"No, he just pointed behind him. What's bothering you?"

"Nothing, nothing. So this man has a key?"

"He has to get it from someone else. He said he'd call me."

Connor isn't sure if he's hesitant about this man in particular or if the events of the last few days have made him hesitant about everything. But he sees that Linda wants to investigate the theater, and he doesn't wish to disappoint her.

"Well, okay then," he says. "Let's do it."

Dr. Hubert Goodenough leans back in his chair and smiles at the two men sitting on the couch. It's a friendly smile, a kindly smile. It's five o'clock, and the sun is setting, but Manny and Vikström still aren't done for the day.

"So how does it make you feel?" the doctor asks Vikström. "To share your name with a famous Swedish detective?"

"Great," says Vikström tonelessly. "It feels fantastic. I'd write him a letter if he weren't some made-up asshole person on TV."

"Don't mind him," says Manny. "He's actually quite proud."

Vikström gives his partner an evil look and turns back to Dr. Good-enough. "Tell us again about the guy who got out of the Denali first, the one in the hoodie."

Dr. Goodenough knits his fingers together and rests his chin on top as he stares at the rug. It's a professional pose he's used a thousand times to indicate deep thought, but in fact he wishes the detectives would leave soon so he can get home to dinner. What will his wife make tonight? It's their Russian evening, so it might be beef Stroganoff or chicken Kiev.

"I hardly saw anything," says the doctor. "A large man jumped out the back and ran across the street. He was somewhere beneath me, and I couldn't see him. He wore a dark hoodie with the hood up. He seemed big, that's all I can say."

"What'd he have on his feet: boots, dress shoes, or running shoes?" Manny tries to speak politely, but there's an edge to his voice. Fuckin' shrinks are supposed to have sharp observation skills, and this one doesn't even know how big is big.

"I don't recall his shoes. I expect they were dark. Dark shoes, dark pants, dark sweatshirt."

"By dark do you mean black?" asks Vikström.

"Not black, I'm sure of that. Perhaps dark blue or charcoal gray. I really don't remember. I'm sorry."

Vikström notices white crumbs on the rug, lots of them; the more he looks, the more he sees. He's surprised the doctor is so messy.

"Could he have come back across the street and gone upstairs?" asks Manny. "And you maybe didn't see him?"

Dr. Goodenough changes his position, leans back, and stares up at the ceiling. But don't let him fool you. He's still thinking about beef Stroganoff and chicken Kiev, except now he's also added the possibility of cabbage rolls with mushroom sauce.

"Absolutely it's possible. I'd turned away to dial 911, and then my patient accused me of not listening to what he was saying. I reassured him I'd heard quite well. So he asked what he'd said. I said he'd been speaking of squeezing loaves of white bread, because that's what he always talks about. But this time I was in error. He'd been talking about English muffins. Quickie squeezes, he called them. So it was ten minutes before I looked out the window again, and that was when the police arrived. An elephant could have crossed the street and gone upstairs in that length of time."

Five minutes later, as the detectives are descending the stairs, Manny says, "This Chucky guy's getting important. He's probably the one in the hoodie who got out of the Denali and crossed the street."

Vikström can't disagree. "So what do you suggest we do?"

"I got bad news for you. We've got to go to Groton. We've got to cross the bridge. We've got to talk to Caroline Santuzza."

Vikström, as they drive toward I-95, offers reasons why a trip to Groton is a bad idea. For instance, it's cruel to interrupt Caroline's healing process, and again comes the claim they're trespassing on the Groton police department's acreage. Maybe they can just call a Groton detective and ask him to have a chat with Caroline.

Manny shoots down Vikström's arguments like popping balloons at a kiddie birthday party. "Just a few questions, Benny. We'll only be there ten minutes."

Vikström doesn't respond. He knows they need to talk to Caroline Santuzza, but he doesn't plan to admit to Manny that he's right. It would bring about unending contention, with Manny saying, *Well, I was right about that other thing, so I must be right about this thing.* It's happened often, and Vikström's sick of it.

"Have you ever thought . . ." says Manny. Here he pauses to give Vikström time to flinch and intensify his sense of dread. "Have you ever thought," Manny repeats, "that instead of hiding your head and going la, la, la as we cross the bridge . . . have you ever thought it might be more effective to name all the women you've fucked? You could say, 'Well, first there was Alice, and then there was Harriet, and then there was Giselle.' And with each name you could raise a finger to give the act of fucking that person more authority. Have you ever thought of doing that?"

Vikström explodes. "You son of a bitch, if you weren't driving, I'd throw you out of the car!" Actually, Vikström and Maud were married at nineteen and twenty. Before that, Vikström had sex with only one other woman, and it was a disaster.

"What, what?" says Manny pulling onto I-95. "I give useful advice and you threaten me? Don't you see I got your best interests at heart, that I'm forgiving you for months of abuse?"

"Shut up," says Vikström. "Don't say another word." They're now on the bridge, and Vikström glances at the flimsy black iron railing dividing him from the abyss. He shuts his eyes. Manny begins to whistle. It's a Vaughn Monroe song called "There! I've Said It Again," but Vikström doesn't know this. Manny begins to sing quietly, "'I love you, there's nothing to hide. / It's better than burning inside. / I love you, no use to pretend. / There, I've said it again.'"

"Give me your honest opinion," says Manny. "Whose version of this song do you like best? Vaughn Monroe, Bobby Vinton, or Sam Cooke?"

Vikström imagines breaking Manny's fingers one by one.

"Ha," says Manny. "We're over the bridge. I distracted you. You didn't even notice we were crossing the bridge. Believe me, Benny, I'm looking out for you. I'm in your corner."

Only one car is in the driveway when they reach Caroline Santuzza's house on Godfrey Street: a dark Chrysler PT Cruiser that must be a dozen years old. In front of the Chrysler is a red scooter.

"Ah," says Manny, "Giovanni Lambertenghi is in residence."

Vikström knocks on the front door; after a moment he rings the bell. A woman's voice from inside shouts, "Hold on to your horses, will you?"

Manny and Vikström wait on the small porch as Caroline Santuzza unlocks the door. They can see her through the glass with a red towel around her head.

"Don't let the cats out!" she shouts.

A large black tomcat bullies its way through the opening door and darts between Manny's legs. He stumbles and grabs Vikström's shoulder, then lets go as if the shoulder were hot. No way does he want to feel obliged to Vikström for keeping him from falling.

"Jake, Jake!" shouts Caroline. She turns angrily to the detectives. "You let him out, so you go find him!"

Manny says, "We have a few more questions to ask. It won't take more than a minute. Sorry about the cat. Can we come in?"

Caroline Santuzza crossly stands aside to let them enter. She's a big woman wearing a pink Mother Hubbard, and the detectives have to brush against her as they pass. Manny thinks it's like brushing against a giant marshmallow.

"Marco's funeral's tomorrow morning at ten o'clock." She follows the detectives into the living room. "I don't want you guys to be there, no way."

"Wouldn't dream of it," says Manny. "Did you solve the head problem?"

Caroline glares. "It's in the box. They couldn't attach it, but it's between the feet, so I got a shorter casket. It was cheaper."

"Good thinking," says Manny.

Looking around the living room, Vikström counts eight cats, three more than last time. The couch and two armchairs are ripped to shreds, so it's difficult to determine their color.

"I wonder if you can tell us more about the man who visited your husband," asks Vikström. "You said he was wearing a hoodie."

"I didn't like him," says Caroline. "He made Marco tell me to go into the kitchen. Marco was afraid of him."

"What did he look like?" asks Manny.

"He was wearing a hoodie, like I said. I didn't see much more than that. And he was big." She nods at Vikström. "Taller than you. He had great big fat hands."

"Did you hear his name?" asks Manny.

"Marco didn't introduce us."

"Could it have been Chucky?"

"Like I said, we weren't introduced."

"What did he want?" asks Vikström.

"He was paying Marco to do something. I don't know what. Marco didn't want to do it, but it was a lot of money. I asked him about it afterward, but he wouldn't say anything. He was scared."

"Anything else?" asks Vikström.

Caroline shakes her head. "Maybe Giovanni knows more. Marco talked to him a little. Should I call him? He's upstairs in his room."

Caroline goes to the foot of the stairs. "Johnnie, some guys want to talk to you! Get down here, will you?" She turns to Vikström, slightly embarrassed. "He's been playing Killzone 3 all day. Yesterday it was Mortal Kombat. Some days he never comes downstairs. You should hear the noise!"

"He should try karaoke," says Vikström. He hears Manny growl behind him.

Jack Sprat is as they saw him before: red hair, red-freckled face, and a red shirt. He also wears blue jeans, but if they came in red, he'd prefer them.

"Hunh?" he says. His red eyes are perhaps a result of all that video gaming.

Manny asks about Marco. Jack Sprat stands on the first step of the staircase, which makes him as tall as Vikström, who thinks that Jack Sprat looks like a force of nature rather than a thinker, one of those forces of nature that rips through towns in the Midwest without apology.

"Marco called him Chucky, but they weren't friends," says Jack Sprat. He looks at the two detectives with dislike. "He was paying Marco to do something. I don't know what, but it was something in Marco's building downtown."

This is about all the detectives get. Jack Sprat says Chucky's hoodie was dark blue and he wore black motorcycle boots. He also mentions Chucky's big hands.

More out of curiosity than to rile him up, Manny asks if Jack Sprat still thinks Fat Bob was responsible for Marco's death.

Jack Sprat sputters with anger. "Fat Bob made Marco take the bike. Marco didn't want it, didn't want to ride it. Fat Bob knew the guy was downtown waiting to signal Pappalardo to back up. Marco and Pappalardo were buddies. It drove him nuts to think he'd killed Marco instead of Fat Bob. So that's murder. Fat Bob murdered him."

"But you can't prove it," says Vikström.

Jack Sprat sputters some more. "I knows what I knows."

TWENTY-FIVE

Consider a king-size lazy Susan thirty-six inches across. It's turned by an electric motor, though not too fast. We don't want anybody to fall off. The man standing on it is naked, but to avoid giving offense we place a flashing swirl of light over his genitals, something like the visual distortion superimposed over the faces of the innocent on TV news shows. The effect of the flashing swirl is to draw attention to the genitals at the same time it conceals them.

The man has flat feet and pink, tuberous toes resembling fingerling potatoes of the sort called Russian bananas. The nails need trimming. The ankles are swollen; perhaps the man spends too much time walking around. The calves are muscular and darkened with leg hair extending from the metatarsus to the knees, which are puffy and bear a resemblance to twin Winston Churchills, minus the nose. The thighs are as thick as the waist of a ballerina. Here the dark hair evident on the calves is more abundant, giving the thighs a chimpish aspect. The buttocks are brawny, while the circumference of the hips, belly, and hairy chest are equally round, making the entire torso resemble a fifty-five-gallon drum. The extra-large scapula and clavicle extend from the chest, letting the arms hang down like fat kielbasas ending in soft, seemingly bloated hands, the backs of which are shaved to accentuate their whiteness.

The man's neck is short, meaty, and nearly nonexistent: a pedestal on which a basketball-shaped head seems insecurely balanced. A small chin protrudes like a carbuncle. The mouth is thin-lipped, with many small teeth, more than seems normal. Fat cheeks and a nose like an oversize thumb, once broken and badly reset. Swollen and seemingly bone-less cheeks with old acne scars; dark, hooded eyes that may or may not be looking at you—surely it's the massiveness of the head that makes the eyes seem small—dark eyebrows and a large rectangular forehead like a car bumper. The thin, dark hair shows an almost touching vanity, with tufts of it stuck down as if glued upon the vulnerable, denuded areas. The oddly delicate and parchment-colored ears resemble midnight moonflowers.

This is Chucky.

We've said before that he has a single personality, while others we've met have multiple personalities and shifting identities. Robert Rossi ver-sus Fat Bob, Eartha versus Beatriz, Céline versus Shirley, Connor versus Zeco. We could go on. But Chucky is only Chucky, an enforcer, a facili-tator, and a bully. His ambition to be a bully began in his crib when he pushed his stuffed animals around; in kindergarten he broke the heads off his toy soldiers; then, through his school years, he refined his skills. He fed on the defenseless as a whale feeds on plankton. He bulked up. He became monosyllabic. He didn't graduate.

We've also spoken of people having a dominant emotion: disappoint-ment for Manny, resentment for Angelina, revenge for Jack Sprat, while Connor's dominant emotion is confusion, if indeed confusion is an emo-tion, which he often articulates with the phrase "Just who am I?"

Chucky's dominant emotion is a lust for power. He'd never ask, as Connor asks, "Just who am I?" He feels he knows exactly who he is, and he'd be glad to explain it to you either verbally or physically, preferably the latter. But Chucky was not born Chucky. As with others we've met, he changed the name his parents gave him, which was Holcombe. But in third grade he decided that Holcombe wasn't a credible name for a bully, and so he became Chucky. He's never regretted the decision.

Along with his dominant emotion, Chucky has a fatal flaw. He loves gold; he loves it as a dragon loves gold, as something to sit upon rather than spend. It was Céline who told Chucky that Sal Nicoletti was Dante

Barbarella. She sold him the information after Sal slapped her. Céline also told Chucky about Sal's gold: the rings and necklaces, the cuff links and bracelets, but especially the Rolex Oyster Perpetual GMT-Master II with an eighteen-karat yellow-gold case and an eighteen-karat yellow-gold bracelet, plus a sprinkling of diamonds, sapphires, and rubies. She also told him about the Montegrappa St. Moritz Limited Edition Woods eighteen-karat-gold rollerball pen, though Chucky can barely write his own name. But having heard about them, he wanted them all.

So Chucky sold the information about Sal to some gentlemen in Detroit, and they contacted a nameless fellow in Cincinnati who agreed to do the removal work for financial considerations. Chucky was also asked if he'd like to do the removal work, but Chucky isn't a killer. He might beat a person to a splop of jelly, but at the end the person was usually alive. Indeed, Chucky might beat the same person five or six times, allowing for periods of recuperation between each application.

As a facilitator, Chucky arranged to pick up the shooter from T. F. Green Airport just south of Providence, drive him to New London, and drop him off on Bank Street outside Sal's office. Then, when the man finished his work and came back downstairs, he'd be returned to the airport.

But Chucky's desire for Sal's gold led him to a concurrent plan that involved Marco Santuzza. A few perceptive readers may already have deduced this. Marco would wait by the door of his office till the shooter left. Then he'd hurry to Sal's office, remove Sal's jewelry, putting it in a small black bag, and run back to his own office. Altogether it might take him two minutes.

But Marco didn't want to do this. Maybe he was squeamish about removing the rings from Sal's dead fingers. Maybe he was afraid of being caught by the police. We've never really met Marco, so it's difficult to understand his reasons. For us he was only a shadow shooting past the window of the shoe-repair store.

So Chucky offered Marco a thousand dollars. Marco, though tempted, was hesitant. Then Chucky threatened to turn Marco into a splop of jelly. This is Chucky's threat of choice: "I'll fuckin' turn you into a splop of jelly." So Marco agreed to divest Sal of his jewelry as described. Later in the day, after the police had done their work, Chucky would collect it. This seemed like a fine plan for all concerned, though Marco continued to have doubts. However, he was being paid and his face would remain in one piece.

Unluckily, two days before Sal was to be shot, Fat Bob lent Marco a Fat Bob to drive to his office, and that was that. Leon Pappalardo backed up his dump truck, and Marco was mushed.

Chucky was furious, but who could he punish? Certainly he suspected Fat Bob of a hidden agenda, and Chucky meant to engage him in his favored nonverbal communication—biff, bam, boom. But although Fat Bob might have given his bike to Marco for devious reasons, he knew nothing about Chucky's plan to filch Sal's bling.

So what could Chucky do? He employed two thugs, but he trusted neither to remove Sal's gold. Thus he was forced to fetch it himself. He jumped out of the Denali before the shooter, crossed the street, waited for the shooter to return to the Denali, and then meant to hurry upstairs to remove the rings, et cetera. But Fidget went upstairs first, occupied himself for a few minutes, and came rushing back down. Then Connor went upstairs and came rushing back down. And perhaps other people were nearby on the sidewalk who made Chucky hesitate, or perhaps there was traffic. Whatever the case, when Chucky went upstairs, Sal's jewelry and the Montegrappa rollerball pen had vanished. We expect he roared and shouted, but when he was done, he ran back down to the sidewalk. He looked for Fidget and Connor, but they were gone.

By then the Denali was on I-95 heading north. Chucky was ready for this and had another car parked a block away, off Golden Street. And Chucky saw himself as being disguised—that is, he was wearing a dark hoodie. But Chucky is a big man, and a gorilla wearing a hoodie still looks like a gorilla. So much for the disguise.

Y ou ever tried singing?" says Manny. "You know, like, in the privacy of your own shower? Even humming a little tune?"

Vikström cringes. He's been filling out overdue reports while Manny plays cat's cradle with a loop of string. They are in their office, and it's after seven.

"Come on, tell me," says Manny, "you must of sung sometime."

Vikström lowers his head and keeps writing.

"Like, as a kid," says Manny. "Kids are always singing. *Sesame Street*, you watch *Sesame Street*?"

Vikström turns his chair slightly so he can't see Manny's face.

"You remember their theme song? 'What Are the Directions to Sesame Street?' You must have sung that. Sometimes we do it in the box— that's 'karaoke box' to you." Manny laughs.

Vikström knows that Manny knows that's not the real name of the *Sesame Street* theme song, and he wants to shout it out: "Can You Tell Me How to Get to Sesame Street?" Instead he clenches his teeth until they moan.

"You sing along with those great characters? Squirt and Bernie, Oswald the Grouch, and Fat Bird?"

Vikström snaps his ballpoint pen in half. "What're we going to do about Chucky?" His question emerges as a loud hiss.

"Got to find him first, right? Stands to reason."

"After we find him."

"Then we have a chat."

"What can we charge him with?"

"Shit, Benny, you know that as well as I do. We can suspect him of all sorts of stuff, but we can't charge him with squat. Like, he's bound to be connected to the guy in the Denali who shot Otto in the arm, but try proving it, that's what I say."

"And Lisowski?"

"Ditto. We'll never find his pistol."

"And Fidget?"

"He'll probably turn up dead. He's carrying too much treasure to stay alive for long. Shit, he's probably dead already."

Several policemen have been checking package stores, looking for the store where Fidget might have made a large purchase. But Manny and Vikström have yet to hear from them.

Likewise, policemen have been checking motels looking for Fat Bob, but so far there's no trace of him. As Manny has said, "He's probably got a broad someplace, or maybe Jack Sprat has already shot him."

"What about Connor what's-his-name?"

"The charge, Benny, what's the charge? Angelina fucked us on that one."

"And the FBI guys?" asks Vikström.

"Maybe they're still tiptoeing around, or maybe they've gone home. Maybe their job ended when Sal got whacked."

"Don't you think there's too much we don't know?"

Manny is cracking his knuckles one at a time and slowly. It's a sound that sets Vikström's teeth on edge. He's positive Manny knows this.

"That's life, right?" says Manny. "How often have you been satisfied with how much you know? Like never, right?"

Vikström is about to say, *Don't go all philosophical on me,* which Manny often says to him, when the phone rings. Manny picks it up. "Yeah. . . . Yeah. . . . You're fuckin' kidding me! . . . Okay. . . . Okay. . . . We're on our way."

"Someone's broken into the Capitol Theatre," says Manny.

It takes Vikström a moment to gather his thoughts. "But it's closed."

Manny jumps up and lifts his hands as if preparing to catch a large ball. "That's the fuckin' point, Benny! The theater's been closed for forty fuckin' years!"

Linda drops her flashlight. It hits the floor, goes out, and rolls down several steps. "Rats," she says.

A prey to mild rodent phobia, Connor hastily sweeps his light in a circle around him before realizing she's only voicing a mild curse. "I see it. It's by the wall." Had he heard scurrying noises? Perhaps he's mistaken.

They're ascending the narrow corridor next to terraced loge seating on the right side of the theater. The boxes are empty; all the seats were taken out years ago. Plaster flakes off the walls, and they try not to brush against it as they climb. The air feels old, with a damp, musty smell flavored with rodent droppings. Connor and Linda have come in through the back, across the stage, and passed under the proscenium arch to reach the stairs to the balcony: their destination. Shreds of purple velvet curtain hang from the round arches above the celebrity boxes. High above, the ceiling is a smudged shadow with ragged hints of great images, perhaps Roman gods, that seep bit by bit into the empty theater. Their flashlights are too weak to show the main floor, the stage, or the terraced loges on the opposite side of the dark vacancy. Now Linda's light is broken. Connor, who finds his own emotional state endlessly fascinating, wonders if he's frightened. But it's not fear he feels, at least not yet; rather, he's as tense as a stretched rubber band. He begins to regret their adventure. The theater's like a great tomb.

"My iPhone has a light," says Linda. The cell phone in her hand begins to glimmer. "It's pathetic, but at least I can see my feet."

The man from the historical society had introduced himself as Jasper Lincoln. Connor, having a certain familiarity with bogus names, was skeptical. Letting Connor and Linda in by the back door, Lincoln had said he'd wait there for their return. "I'm allergic to dust," he'd explained. "But you'll be delighted by the interior. It's pure Egyptian." He wore an apple green sport coat, had a long Lincolnian face, and was probably about forty. "Just rap on the door when you're done, and I'll open up. I promise." Then he laughed in a way that made Connor's palms begin to sweat. But Linda had already passed through the door, and so Connor followed. The sound of the door slamming shut reverberated through the hallway. Connor had been mildly surprised that Jasper Lincoln hadn't inquired how long they would be.

Linda continues up the sloping corridor. She wants first to explore the balcony and then take the stairs down to the front entrance and box office. Lastly they'd return through the bare auditorium to the small orchestra pit and perhaps investigate the actors' dressing rooms. Connor sees her thoroughness as a virtue, but he worries about what might lurk behind the farthest range of their vision. He regrets the loss of her light and worries that his own batteries might fail. As far as he's concerned, the cell phone flashlight is useless.

They've just reached the balcony when they hear the rear door bang open. Perhaps Jasper Lincoln means to join them after all. Heavy footsteps cross the stage, and a booming voice calls out, "Zeco, I'm going to break your face!"

Connor is almost surprised by how unsurprised he feels.

"Who's Zeco?" whispers Linda.

"I'm Zeco," says Connor.

"I thought your name was Connor."

"It *is* Connor, but it's a long story."

"So you have *two* names?"

"Get down, get down!"

A bright light sweeps across the auditorium. Connor crouches behind the balcony railing and pulls Linda after him.

"The floor's filthy," she says. She starts getting up. "Who's down there?"

"His name's Chucky. Please, don't let him see you."

"Zeco, I'm going to hunt you down like a rabbit. I'm going to hurt you! If it weren't for your brother, you'd be dead."

"Does he always talk like that?" asks Linda, speaking with a tone of scientific curiosity. "He sounds like the Big Bad Wolf."

"Get down! He's serious."

Linda crouches behind the railing. "I like the name Zeco. It's exotic."

"Please," says Connor. "It'll be awful if he finds us." He sees Linda fussing with her phone. "What are you doing?"

"I'm calling 911. And this doesn't look a bit like Egypt!"

Connor is appalled. "You can't do this. He'll kill us!"

But Linda is already talking into the phone.

The balcony railing consists of iron scrollwork panels with open areas that brighten and darken as Chucky's light passes across them.

"The police are coming," whispers Linda.

"You shouldn't have done that. They'll arrest me."

"Why should they arrest you again?"

"It's a long story."

Linda makes an exasperated noise. "Why's everything with you a long story?"

Chucky's light stops swinging back and forth, and its beam throws shadows of the scrollwork across Connor and Linda. "I see you, Zeco, you and your girlfriend. I'm looking forward to this."

Connor tries to make himself smaller as he hears Chucky's heavy boots plod heavily across the floor. Then he sees Linda has jumped to her feet. "Get down, get down," he whispers. What a nuisance that the innocent lack a guilty conscience. It robs them of their susceptibility to terror and trades it for indignation.

Linda ignores him. "All right, Mr. Chucky!" she calls out. "I've just called 911. The police will be here in two minutes. I've told them about you!"

We must pause to consider Chucky's response. He had imagined Linda to be curled up in a terrified puddle on the floor. It never occurred to him she might call the police. It seems somehow underhanded. Mostly when Chucky menaces people, they collapse and weep. It would be silly to say he thinks Linda is not playing by the rules; nevertheless, he finds her response unfitting. Bullies expect their victims to feel bullied. Linda has let him down. Of course his response isn't rational, but it's not rationality that has brought Chucky to where he is today.

"Do you hear the sirens, Mr. Chucky? Here they come!"

Chucky's light abruptly shifts from the balcony railing, and his big boots clomp away toward the back.

"D'you realize how furious he's going to be?" says Connor, impressed.

But Linda isn't paying attention and seems to be listening for something far away. "He's left the door open," she says. "I'm afraid it's time to go."

As Vikström jogs across the parking lot to the back door of the Capitol Theatre with Manny a few steps behind him, he wonders if he should preserve his resistance to the possibility of singing. Although dismayed by the idea of standing on a stage and caterwauling "Riders in the Sky," he thinks it might, in the long run, make life easier. The sniping could disappear, friction would be reduced. It's not that he wishes to make Manny a friend; rather, he desires the comfortable neutrality that Vikström believes to be the foundation of any good partnership. Isn't that worth the mortifying self-abasement of singing about a lone cowpoke?

Up ahead Vikström sees two uniformed officers standing on either side of a smaller person by the back door of the theater. The smaller person is Linda, and both detectives find her familiar. Actually, they'd seen her in the post office earlier in the day when they handcuffed Connor and marched him from the building. But they won't remember this. Instead, when Linda explains that she works at the travel agency, they'll assume they saw her there or near there or perhaps through the window. Even though this is perfectly reasonable, it doesn't happen to be true. Perhaps it's of no consequence, but if they recalled seeing Linda at the post office, they might also recall that she'd given Connor a small wave.

Vikström and Manny are normally very good at traveling up or down the chains of causality required by police work, and conceivably, by concentrating on Linda, they might move step-by-step back to the moment when they saw her in the post office, et cetera. Instead they are sidetracked by one of the uniformed policemen describing a vehicle that moments before exited the parking lot at high speed.

"It was a dark Yukon Denali, maybe black, maybe dark blue. We didn't see the plate number."

"Chucky," says Vikström.

"Ahh," says Manny.

And so the detectives don't inquire about Connor, who is crouched down just inside the theater, waiting for the police to leave.

One policeman has put in a call to the station about the Denali, and most likely other police cars are attempting to find it, but in this they won't succeed. The Denali is already crossing the I-95 bridge heading north, while Chucky is in the backseat shouting, "Fuck, fuck, fuck!" This is how he calms himself.

As for Linda, she's told the uniformed policemen that when she was passing through the parking lot and noticed that the back door of the theater was open, she decided to investigate. After all, she has the little flashlight on her cell phone.

She repeats this to Manny and Vikström, and perhaps she flirts a bit and appears mildly girlish to suggest the innocence of her curiosity. But then, she says, to her horror, a man followed her into the theater and the door slammed shut.

Vikström thinks the young woman is pretty and believes her; Manny thinks she's shrewd and has his doubts.

"What happened next?" asks Vikström.

Linda looks up at the two detectives and wrinkles her brow as her portrayal of breezy audacity shifts to enact female vulnerability and distress. "He laughed," she says, lowering her voice.

"Laughed?" Manny and Vikström say this more or less together.

"A loud, deep laugh. He said I was his little rabbit and he was going to catch me. That's when I called 911. I was frightened."

Vikström assures Linda that she did the right thing. Manny remains silent; he feels there's more here than meets the eye. But both detectives believe they have no reason to hold her.

Traffic is noisy on Bank Street, and perhaps there's another train. Or perhaps the hearing of the two detectives isn't as keen as it once was.

Whatever the case, they don't catch the single ring of Connor's phone just inside the door of the theater. Connor smothers it against his jacket as he answers it.

"You're messing up again, little brother. Get out here now."

"Where do I meet you?" It wouldn't occur to Connor to refuse.

"I'll call you again when you're on your way."

TWENTY-SIX

Connor once more sits in a leather banquette in the Scorpion Bar: the tequila, skulls, barn board, and glitter. It's nine-thirty, and the bar is getting full. Scantily clad Scorpion girls prowl the catwalk, while a tall blonde on the mini-stage flings and thrusts her body to recorded music made up of explosive chords, drums, and a tenor seeking erotic eruption by screaming, "Yeah! Yeah!" There's no sign of Vasco.

Then Connor realizes he knows the blonde, though the last time they met she had black hair. But the endless legs are tip-offs. Wrapped in a tiny black halter top emblazoned with the image of a scorpion, her breasts seem ready to explode through the fabric as she flicks her hair in circles and kicks up one leg after the other. Her fur boots prance as if crushing an army of fire ants. Connor finds nothing sexual about her dance; it's like the serious labor in a YMCA exercise class, and beads of sweat fly from her forehead. Still, he's instantly on his feet and moves toward her.

What he means to do is unclear, and perhaps we'll never know, because abruptly someone grabs his arm. It's Vasco.

"Hold up, Zeco. You're wasting your breath."

Connor continues to pull. "I need to talk to her."

"There's no point. Céline has gone back to being Shirley, an unwed mother with a pimply thirteen-year-old who divides his time between jacking off and smoking reefer. Forget about her."

Part of Connor wants to push toward the stage. Another part wants to give it up. Renunciation wins, and Connor relaxes. Vasco leads him back to the banquette.

"You that crazy about her, little brother?" Vasco raises his voice to be heard over the music. He sits down on the banquette with his legs stretched in front of him. Connor sits at the small table on Vasco's left.

"I really don't like her. It's some kind of hypnosis. In fact, I met a woman in New London I like better." Connor had driven Linda to her apartment on Cedar Grove after the police had gone. She'd invited him in for coffee, but Connor had to get to the casino to meet his brother. He had conflicted feelings about this.

Vasco shows his teeth. It might be a smile; it's hard to tell. "Stick with the sane ones. They last longer." He again wears a gray-on-gray pin-striped suit with a vest and a black silk shirt, but his silk tie is bright scarlet.

A cute waitress sets a glass and a bottle of Pellegrino in front of Vasco. "Here you are, Mr. Raposo." She gives Vasco a wink and drifts away.

Vasco squeezes a bit of lemon into his glass. As pretty young women walk past, he follows them with his eyes without moving his head. "Chucky called me just before I called you. He wants you dead."

Connor wants to ask what for, but it's a pointless question.

"Possibly I talked him out of it by saying you still might find the homeless guy with Sal's gold. You think it might happen?"

"I haven't had any luck so far." Connor considers the fact that some-one he hardly knows wants him dead; presumably he wants Fidget dead as well.

"Chucky found out the homeless guy made a bunch of purchases at a package store on the south side: vodka and snack food. So he must be holed up somewhere."

"I'd never turn Fidget over to him. Chucky would kill him."

Vasco shrugs. "That's your choice." He goes back to watching the girls walk by, an activity he calls "appraising the talent."

Connor studies his brother's black and betasseled alligator loafers with a bit of envy. He's tempted to tell Vasco that the hand-me-down Bruno Maglis gave him blisters, but he sees the complaint for what it is: a childish shot at grievance already doomed to failure. When Connor entered first grade, Vasco was entering seventh; when Connor entered seventh, Vasco was entering college. Always, it seemed, Connor was scrambling to catch up. That, too, was doomed to failure. Once, when Connor was ten, he asked his sixteen-year-old brother for assistance in thrashing a bully who'd bloodied his nose. "Can't help you, little brother," Vasco had said. "Try hitting him with a brick." So Connor tried the brick method, missed, and wound up in the principal's office. Still, the bully never bothered him again.

"Why did Chucky set up that game at the theater?" asked Connor. "What was the point of it?"

Vasco tilted his head back and laughed. Then he straightened his tie. "It's Chucky's version of role-playing. He likes violent games. He only wanted to scare you and maybe break some bones. But having your girl-friend call the cops pissed him off. So, personally, I think you'd better leave town. I already called Didi and told him the same thing. Chucky doesn't like refusals. He's been mad at you ever since you showed up with the news that Marco had been killed."

"But I'd nothing to do with that."

"You were the messenger. For Chucky it's not an excusable offense. He thought taking the Rolex and stuff from Sal's corpse would be easy. Then Marco gets killed and Chucky keeps running into you and you make it all more complicated. He knows you're aware of his involvement with Sal's death, and he blames you for dragging in the New London police. He also thinks you've been talking to the FBI, telling them he was the one who hired the shooter."

Connor feels a chill. "You know that's not true!"

Vasco glances at his watch, a different Rolex from the one he had earlier in the week, a more economical Submariner, no jewels, no gold, no color, and made in China. But to Connor it looks like the real thing. "Guys like Chucky are paranoid," says Vasco. "It helps keep them out of prison. Chucky doesn't like how you're hanging around. He doesn't like how you seemed friendly with Sal. Then you were stalking Céline. . . ."

"Stalking?"

"That's what he called it. So he told Céline to make you find the homeless guy, and you fucked that up as well."

Connor's chill increases. "I couldn't find him!"

"Maybe, but Chucky's got a whole story worked out about how you want Sal's jewelry for yourself. That's why you'd turn him in to the cops—you want the bling."

"Good grief, how much of it *is* there?"

"Enough to kill for. Isn't that the point? Right now all Chucky wants is to get the jewelry, grab Céline, and get out of town."

Connor experiences a pinprick of disappointment. "Are they lovers?"

"Chucky's not the loving type. It's a physical thing."

Connor feels another pinprick. He turns toward the mini-stage, trying to see Céline, but she's gone. A cover band has begun to play "Proud Mary," and Connor has to raise his voice. "Did you know about Sal when I talked to you last week?"

"Sure I did. The shooter had already been booked."

"Then why were you surprised when I told you about him?"

"That's not how it went. I was surprised about Marco Santuzza, not Sal. I thought the dead guy was Fat Bob, not Marco. And I knew that Marco being dead would mess up Chucky's plans."

The great weight pressing down on Connor's head all week is suddenly lifted, and he feels minimally buoyant. He hadn't outed Sal after all. "Why didn't you say this when I accused you of telling somebody about Sal? You know how guilty I felt?"

Vasco sips his Pellegrino. "It could complicate my relationship with Chucky, and I figured you could deal with it."

A typical and exasperating answer, Connor thinks. "When did Chucky learn about Sal?"

"A week ago more or less. Céline tried to sell the information to Chucky, who she'd known in Detroit. She said Sal slapped her for trying on a bracelet and chain. She didn't like getting slapped."

"And Chucky paid her?"

"I doubt it. But they must have come to an arrangement, because he's now fucking her. Maybe he just scared her. He's good at that." More women are passing their table, and Vasco returns to appraising the talent.

"So you work for Chucky?"

Vasco gives his brother a look of token contempt. "I'd never work for Chucky. It's not safe, and I don't want to get too close. Let's say I'm a consultant."

"But you knew that Sal would be killed. You could have told the police."

"That's true. And the police would tell the FBI, and the FBI would move him to another dumb town, and after a bit Chucky would learn I was the one who went to the police. Chucky's good at finding out stuff like that. No thanks."

Vasco's actual position was still unclear to Connor. "Isn't it dangerous for you to talk to me?"

His brother laughed his humorless laugh. "It's difficult. I'm trying to protect you from Chucky, but I also have to give Chucky information about you. In fact, he told me to talk to you. As I said, he wants you to leave town. Like immediately. That's what he told me. But what he really wants is to have you killed. He doesn't trust you not to talk to the police. Didn't the police pull you in this afternoon?"

"Yes, but it had to do with Bounty, Inc. It didn't concern Chucky."

Again came the humorless laugh. "Chucky finds Bounty, Inc. confusing. You see that guy over by the bar? He's one of Chucky's thugs. No, no, more to your right. He's got on a green jacket."

Connor catches sight of Jasper Lincoln from the New London historical society among the crowd at the bar. But of course Connor no longer thinks he's from the historical society or that his name is Jasper Lincoln. The man with the apple green jacket leans back against the bar and stares at Connor: a gaze that's blank and pitiless as the sun, as it were.

"Jasper Lincoln," says Connor.

"A nom de guerre. Chucky calls him Jimbo, but I doubt it's his real name."

"What's he want?" The man is still staring at him, and Connor looks away.

"He's here to keep an eye on you and to keep Chucky informed of your whereabouts. And I suppose he's keeping an eye on me as well. In any case, he saw the cops pull you out of the post office today. Chucky didn't like that."

"How'd he know I was here?"

"I told him. You see how complicated things can be? Chucky said to get you out here, and then I told Jimbo where I was meeting you. What choice did I have?"

"You could have said something to me."

"I'm telling you now. I'm also telling you that when you leave here, he'll be following you. Just be cool with it and you won't get hurt, I think."

"But what have I done?" *The whole business is crazy,* Connor thinks.

"Jesus, Zeco, don't you get it? You've been in the way, that's all. You've been in the way, and now you've got information that could put Chucky in jail."

"Even if I promise to keep quiet?"

"Chucky'd never believe it. He's not the believing type. So when will you be leaving town?"

"We need to check the post office for mail tomorrow morning."

Vasco gets to his feet and throws some bills on the table. "Okay, we're done. Just go immediately to that little car of yours and get seriously lost."

"How'd you know I had a Mini-Cooper?" Connor gets up as well.

"Get real, Zeco. Everybody knows it: Chucky, Céline, Jimbo, all sorts of people. You've never been subtle in your life, and that constitutes a problem. And, believe me, I don't want to be dragged into your problems."

We sympathize with Vasco. His business, if it can be called that, is to be unflappable, to supply his patrons with information and keep his eyes open. He's a consultant, a resource, and he doesn't talk: his mouth stays shut. But mostly he must be unflappable and unconcerned about the legality of his clients' conduct.

What Vasco's really like, we don't know. He seems to have no vices except for women, and his composure and self-control appear impenetrable. He has no friends and no home except for hotel rooms, and who he is when he locks his door at night is a mystery. Does he watch television, surf the Internet, or write long letters to his great-aunt in Lisbon? We don't know. In fact, if we were told he stands all night in his closet like a robot, humming and clicking until a radio signal sets him in motion again, we wouldn't be surprised.

But now his brother appears. Vasco never asked Connor to visit Connecticut. He simply called out of the blue and claimed his fraternal rights, meaning he wanted to get together. What's worse, Connor brought Didi, Vaughn, and Eartha. He brought a circus. Vasco's had little contact with Didi over the years, but it's enough for him to ask if Didi is a nutcase, a loose cannon, or both. The difficulty is that Didi's actions can't be predicted, and so Connor's actions can't be predicted either. What's Bounty, Inc. anyway? Instead of a real financial enterprise, it's a toy to keep Didi amused.

It was pure chance Connor visited the Bank Street cobbler just at the time Marco got mushed against a dump truck. And it was pure chance that Connor met Sal as they waited for their cars to be freed. Didi might tell Vasco, *Everything happens for a reason* or *There are no coincidents*, but he didn't say it because he believed it. Rather, he wanted "to destabilize Vasco's inner calm." Destabilizing inner calm is one of Didi's great pleasures. And this, we realize, would destabilize Chucky's inner calm, which has a high volatility rating. In fact, we might say that Chucky *has* no inner calm. He has only different degrees of suspicion and anger.

If we sat down with Chucky and explained the nature of Bounty, Inc., he wouldn't know how to respond. He'd think we were playing a trick. And if we told him about Orphans from Outer Space, he might have a breakdown. Chucky has precise definitions about the world and those who inhabit it. They may be narrow definitions, but they're exact and don't allow for foolishness. Mistrust and paranoia are the closest Chucky comes to having an imagination. This makes him good at what he does, but it's a niche profession with a problematic future.

So it was important to Vasco that Chucky not learn about Bounty, Inc. This, however, made it necessary that he talk to Didi during the week, which was when Didi made such remarks as "What goes around, comes around," remarks intended not to express an article of faith but to irritate. However, at least on Thursday, Vasco was able to warn Didi what might lie ahead Chucky-wise, and Didi began the work he described as establishing an escape hatch.

But we get ahead of ourselves, because at the moment Connor is leaving the Scorpion Bar with a rising sense of dread. He hurries down a hallway as high and broad as an airport concourse with restaurants and shops, but it's glitzier and no one is flying anywhere, except in the Technicolor imaginations that casinos encourage.

Behind Connor and just exiting the barn-board-adorned Scorpion front door is Jimbo or Jasper Lincoln in that apple green sport coat, and while Connor hurries down the middle of the hallway, Jimbo slides forward along the wall. Back in the bar, Vasco still stands by the small table with the half-finished Pellegrino. His usual composure is absent, and, instead he looks thoughtful and perhaps worried. We mention this because Vasco never looks worried. But now he, too, leaves the bar and turns down the hallway after Jimbo and Connor.

Well, we can't describe Connor's entire journey from the bar to his Mini-Cooper. It's a long way, as might be expected in a place that houses fifty-five hundred slot machines, to say nothing at all of the other varieties of noisy fun. The people we pass drift this way and that, stricken with sensory overload, though no one seems to be feeling the good times advertised on TV. Escalators, elevators, hallways with Connor in the lead, and then Jimbo some distance back and Vasco some distance behind Jimbo.

When Connor at last exits the long hallway onto the rooftop level of the parking garage, we rise above him, though we're a little out of breath.

It's a cold night with a clear sky and many stars. Behind us we can hear, faintly, a mix of music as various bands in various venues entertain the crowds. From where we look, the tops of the parked cars and SUVs, in their orderly rows, resemble dozing, multicolored turtles. And there's the small blue roof of Connor's Mini-Cooper in the sixth row, tucked between two hulking SUVs near the rooftop's opposite wall.

Connor isn't running, but almost. He's probably seen Jimbo some distance behind him because of his apple green sport coat, but he hasn't seen his brother. What we see that Connor can't is another man standing between the Mini-Cooper and a blue Grand Cherokee Overland. It's not quite the same blue as Connor's car, but there's enough of a resemblance to make the two vehicles look like a father and son waiting for what comes next, just as the man standing between them waits for what comes next. We don't know this man, but we might recall that he's the man who a day ago shot Otto in the arm, a wound from which Otto has nearly recovered, except for a little understandable stiffness. Otto said that the man was about forty, physically fit, and nicely dressed, and looking at him from above we can see this is true, though from our superior position it's difficult to see his face. And he occasionally stamps his feet, not from petulance but because he's cold.

Now the man in the apple green sport coat hurries through the door and onto the roof of the parking garage. We may realize at this point that he, too, was at Otto's, though he did no shooting, and that he's the associate of the man standing between the Mini-Cooper and Grand Cherokee Overland. One man pursues and the other man waits, while Connor hurries along between them. Although we wish him well, we also feel concerned, not to say pessimistic.

Connor is about two rows from his car when he abruptly notices the man who is waiting. He veers to his left, probably with no specific destination in mind, only wishing to escape. But as Connor turns, he sees the man in the apple green sport coat running toward him.

Well, what's left to say? We see Connor zigzagging between the parked cars as the two men draw closer. We could surely drag this out, because the chase goes on for another two minutes, but in the end, sadly, Connor is caught. Worse, the man who was waiting throws himself at Connor and hits him several times—once in the face and once in the stomach—while the man in the green jacket shoves Connor back toward his associate so he can hit Connor more easily without straining. And the two men are shouting. We're too far away to hear the specific words, but they are angry and threatening. Perhaps we can imagine what's being said.

We've mentioned before that Connor isn't a fighter, but he vigorously flails his arms, and—this is important—purely by accident he hits the man in the green jacket, the man called Jimbo, squarely in the nose.

The thugs step back. They're indignant. Just as Chucky felt offended when Linda called 911, so the thugs are offended when Connor refuses to suffer punishment meekly. It seems unfair, though what's unfair to a thug might seem fair to everyone else. "You'll regret that," says Jimbo as he wipes blood from his nose with the back of his hand. He stares at it in wonder. Perhaps he's never seen his own blood before and he's surprised it's the same color of the blood of his many past victims. But the job the thugs are meant to carry out is to exact punishment, and Connor's refusal to accept it meekly means they must exact greater punishment. Ask the thugs and they'll say that Connor brought this on himself.

With a strengthened sense of purpose, they step forward, grab Connor by the arms, and drag him toward the edge of the rooftop parking garage. Connor protests by kicking his feet at the other men's legs, but this offends them even more. The garage is several stories high, and the thugs mean to throw Connor over the side. To their minds—dim though they may be—this won't inevitably kill him. He might land on the ground or on the sidewalk. He might land on his head or on his feet. It's up to Fate, meaning they don't feel they should be blamed for whatever happens.

Fate, however, intervenes sooner than expected. Just as the men struggle to lift Connor over the side and send him on his way, there's a gunshot, as there's often a gunshot when a hero needs to be saved. We've nearly forgotten about Vasco, who stands five feet away with a small pistol. The thugs drop Connor, who falls to the concrete surface of the parking garage.

A moment of silence follows as the four men do a little heavy thinking. Then Jimbo says, "He won't do nothing. He's too scared of Chucky." They again pick up Connor, who feels stunned from his short drop, and begin to wrestle him over the side.

There's another gunshot, and the thug in the green jacket yelps. "He fuckin' shot me in the foot!" He hops up and down on his right foot.

"Your knee is next," says Vasco.

He tells the men to put their hands on the wall; then he tells Connor to check for weapons. Both carry pistols. Connor throws them over the wall, maybe thinking they'll follow the same trajectory he'd have followed if Vasco hadn't arrived in time.

"Get their cell phones," says Vasco. He sounds a little depressed.

Two cell phones are thrown over the wall.

"Chucky'll kill both of you for this," says Jimbo. "He'll kill you slowly."

"Throw their wallets over the wall," says Vasco. He doesn't need to do this. He does it out of spite.

Vasco marches the thugs to Connor's Mini-Cooper, tells Connor to start the engine, and then, when it's revving loudly, he jumps into the passenger seat. "Let's go!" The thugs disappear in the rearview mirror, and Connor drives toward the exit.

"Where're we going?"

"My hotel," says Vasco.

Connor drives down Trolley Line Boulevard and very soon pulls up in front of the Two Trees Inn. "What are you going to do?" he asks Vasco.

"Get my suitcase."

"You're leaving?"

"Didn't you hear what the guy said, little brother? Chucky will kill me. You think he was making that up? I told you to leave me alone. Now

I got about two minutes to get out of here, and maybe even that won't be enough. Don't wait till tomorrow, Zeco. Leave now!"

Vasco jumps from the Mini-Cooper and runs for the door of the inn.

"You'll call me?" shouts Connor.

Without turning, Vasco raises an arm. He could be waving in agreement, he could be waving *Fuck you*, or he could be waving good-bye. We just don't know.

TWENTY-SEVEN

Sitting in a lawn chair on the hill between the Winnebago and the ocean, Vaughn ponders a sky packed with stars. Neither moon nor clouds are visible, and it's about eleven o'clock. An overhead light above the driver's seat in the Winnebago twenty feet away seems the only light in a dark world; it settles a dim glow on the back of Vaughn's black sweatshirt and on the late Marco Santuzza's motorcycle cap. In Vaughn's left hand is a piece of cardboard of the sort that comes with a shirt from a dry cleaner's. In its center is a square hole no bigger than a quarter. Vaughn's right hand holds a yellow No. 2 pencil, and on his lap is a yellow legal-size pad of paper. He lifts the cardboard to the sky, keeps it still for a minute, and then writes on his pad. Then he raises the cardboard again, and the process repeats.

Headlights slowly approach along the gravel access road to the Hannaquit Breachway toward the RV campground. They don't belong to Connor's Mini-Cooper or to Didi's gray Ford Focus rental. We expect no one to be surprised when we say they belong to the black Yukon Denali: the ubiquitous vehicle we've seen before. The headlights sweep across the Winnebago as the Denali comes to a stop. Two men get out. One has a limp and walks with a cane. This is Jimbo, whom Vasco shot in the foot. Actually, his middle toe was blown off, and no trace was found when the shoe and sock were removed, apart from a little mush. So Jimbo is in a rage about life's unfairness. He looks for someone to punish.

His associate is a man we first heard about at Otto's house, though we haven't been properly introduced. He goes by the name of Joesy, but again we've no evidence that's his real name. This mix of names is an ongoing leitmotif, the choice of folks not rooted to the quotidian by charge cards, mortgages, and taxes. Maybe the illusion of anonymity makes them think they need not be accountable, letting them slide through life as on a secret errand.

Joesy carries a flashlight and swings it back and forth in an arc. He and Jimbo walk softly, even though they believe no one's at home. This is because they're up to no good, and their silence is due to a transferred sense of disquiet. Joesy pauses to focus the light on something written on the side of the Winnebago: HERE LIVES AN ORPHAN FROM OUTER SPACE!

The two men study it, and then Jimbo says, "What's that supposed to mean?"

"It means whoever lives here," says Joesy, "deserves what he's going to get."

Moving along the side of the Winnebago, they find the front door open. It's then that Joesy's flashlight settles on a vague shape sitting in a lawn chair. Although the shape must be aware of the light, he doesn't turn. Jimbo and Joesy aren't sure how they feel about this. Maybe the person is sleeping.

Joesy approaches the chair, and Jimbo limps behind him. Then Joesy stops and waits to be acknowledged. Instead the figure, who we know as Vaughn, again holds the cardboard up to the sky, mutters something, and writes a number on his yellow pad, now illuminated by the flashlight.

"Whatcha doin'?" asks Joesy. He sounds truculent, but then he always sounds truculent. Perhaps he imagines that Vaughn will be startled by the interruption, but Vaughn is as calm as ever.

"Counting stars," says Vaughn, again holding up the piece of cardboard. Then he mutters to himself, writes something down, and raises the piece of cardboard.

"Anybody inside?" asks Jimbo.

"Absence makes the heart wander." Vaughn speaks in a monotone, so his voice sounds robotic. Still, it's the rippling baritone of Vaughn Monroe, and Jimbo, whose parents might have listened to the famous crooner, feels a mild frisson, which he attributes to the likelihood of his getting a cold.

The thugs study Vaughn's motorcycle cap as they consider their options. At last Joesy says, "How the fuck can you count stars with a fuckin' piece of cardboard?"

Vaughn turns slightly. "It's an alimentary conundrum. I spot the platen at the bottom left of the sky, violate the stars within the orifice, fight down the sum, traffic the platen to the next significant area, again violate the stars, fight down the sum, traffic the platen to the next area, violate the stars, fight down the sum, traffic the cardboard—"

"Stop!" say Jimbo.

A long silence follows.

"Maybe he's fucking with us." Joesy keeps the light pointed at Vaughn's head.

The thugs have, unwittingly, allowed themselves to be sucked into the vortex of Vaughn's inner world and aren't sure how to escape. Of course, they don't articulate this to themselves, and instead they mistake their concern for a slight headache.

"Got any aspirin?" says Jimbo.

"Maybe we can find some inside," says Joesy.

"So who are you?" asks Jimbo gruffly.

Vaughn smiles up at the intruders. "I'm an orphan from outer space." He returns to counting stars.

The thugs consider the chance that this might be true. Both, in fact, are strong UFO believers. Then Jimbo says, "Nutcase."

"Wacko," says Joesy.

"Come on, we got stuff to do."

Jimbo and Joesy have three tasks: first, to make sure Sal's gold isn't hidden within the Winnebago—surely a long shot. Second, to destroy everything they can destroy as punishment to Connor for getting in Chucky's way. The third is to bring everyone they can find back to Chucky. For any self-respecting thug, this is child's play.

Vaughn remains in his chair on the crest of the hill, but as crashing noises erupt from inside the Winnebago, he begins to lose track of his counting. He looks back over his shoulder, puts down the pencil and pad of paper, and gets to his feet. Dishes are being broken, heavy objects are being thrown, a window on the slide-out is smashed, clothes are tossed out the door.

With each sound, Vaughn grows more disturbed. He hurries to the Winnebago. "Don't touch my yellow pads!"

Abruptly, a pile of pads is thrown through the door. "Nix, nix, nix!" shouts Vaughn. He begins picking them up; some have sailed a dozen feet or so. He runs from one to another. "Nix, nix, nix!" More pads are flung through the door, and the wind blows several down to the water. Vaughn agitatedly gathers them up until he has a pile pressed to his chest. He puts them on the ground and places the lawn chair on top of them. "Nix, nix, nix!" he shouts again. A TV flies out the door. Vaughn lifts his hands to his head, runs to the Winnebago, and dashes up the steps. Almost as soon as he vanishes inside, he comes tumbling back down. A thug has hit him. He again runs up the steps and is knocked back down. He runs up the steps a third time, but this time Joesy appears at the top, grabs Vaughn, and pushes him away.

"You're as cruel as a cucumber!" shouts Vaughn. His voice trembles.

"Stay outta here!" shouts Jimbo, jumping down to the ground.

Joesy appears at the door. "Maybe we should shoot him."

Jimbo thinks about this. "We weren't told to shoot nobody."

"We could shoot him just a little, like you—like in the foot. Nothing drastic."

"No can do. We can only take him to Chucky."

"Let's put holes in the RV instead. Chucky said nothing about making holes."

This seems a good idea. The men take their Glocks from where they're safely tucked into their belts in the small declivity behind their backs. They like Glocks; cops use Glocks, and if Jimbo and Joesy weren't thugs, they might be something coplike. Each slides a bullet into the chamber and begins shooting at the Winnebago, starting with the tires, then windows, then walls. They take gunfighter positions; they spin around with their backs to the RV and shoot over their shoulders; they bend down and shoot between their legs. They reload and laugh and start shooting again.

"Fuck, I like holes," says Joesy.

"I could do this all night," says Jimbo.

Vaughn stands back by the lawn chair and says nothing.

"I like it when you can hear the slug smashing something inside," says Joesy.

"Yeah, like glass breaking. Neat!" says Jimbo.

But at last all great pleasures come to an end. A sense of economy prevails. "We gotta save some bullets for a rainy day," says Joesy.

"Let's put the nutcase in the truck," says Jimbo.

They don't ask Vaughn if he'd like to accompany them; they simply grab his arms and drag him. "I'm having a nervous shakedown!" shouts Vaughn. The Denali has three rows of seats, and Vaughn is shoved into the far back. Then Jimbo sits in the middle row and Joey drives.

"I need medical resistance!" shouts Vaughn.

"Shut up!" says Jimbo, but his usual indifference to another's discomfort is somewhat unsettled, as someone's stomach can be unsettled from eating a dubious piece of fish. *Maybe I'm not getting a cold,* Jimbo thinks. *Maybe I'm getting the flu.*

The Denali bumps back down the access road to Route 1. Joesy decides the sooner they get rid of the nutcase, the better. Let Chucky deal with him.

"You ever hear of anything called Murderers Anonymous?" asks Jimbo as he imagines a twelve-step program to fit his needs.

"Yeah, man, Murder Incorporated. Great! I saw the movie. Like that, right?"

"Not exactly." Jimbo decides to keep his doubts to himself.

We should take a moment to recall Jimbo's apple green sport coat. What would possess a thug to wear a garment that would make him stick out in a police lineup like a third tit on a debutante? Dr. Hubert Goodenough, our in-house shrink, might say the apple-green sport coat suggests Jimbo's conflicted nature about being a bad guy. Yes, he's been a bad guy since grade school, but maybe the years have taken their toll. Maybe it's time to quit and join Murderers Anonymous.

It's not easy to be a thug: no heath insurance, retirement, or promotions. They don't get their pick of the most beautiful women; they must make do with molls or worse; they exist on scraps tossed down by the boss. They break their hands on other men's faces and get broken noses in return. They drink too much, smoke too much, eat too much red meat, and in the wee hours of the night they worry about the future.

We're not saying that Jimbo is having a change of heart. After all, he *has* no heart, or at best he has a small one. But he's squeamish about handing Vaughn over to Chucky. It'd be like handing a child over to Chucky.

"I'm having a nervous shakedown!" repeats Vaughn. "I'm suffering from cardinal arrest. Damp weather's hard on my sciences!"

"Shut that guy up!" shouts Joesy, turning south onto Route 1.

"What do you think about gerbil warming?" asks Vaughn. "Will it be a cat's after me? The world's synapsing!"

"Smack him!" says Joesy.

"What're you incinerating?" says Vaughn. "Inflammable language scares me!"

Jimbo can't stand it anymore. He reaches a decision. "Dump him!"

Joesy's surprised. "Shoot him here?"

Vaughn is even more upset. "Deader than a hangnail? Where's close bondage among friends?"

"No, just throw him outta the car!"

"Pheasant rebellion!"

"What about Chucky?"

"We don't need to tell Chucky."

"Silence makes the heart grow fonder!"

Joesy hits the brakes. "Heave him!" Locked tires screech along the pavement as the back end fishtails.

Jimbo jumps out, grabs Vaughn by the collar, gives him a push to the side of the road, and jumps back into the Denali, which roars away.

"Emaciated at last!" shouts Vaughn. He takes a quick glance at the departing license plate: all that's needed to fix it in his memory forever.

It's past midnight, and Connor sees the flashing blue lights of police cars as he turns onto the access road to the RV campground. He brakes and puts the Mini-Cooper into reverse; then he thinks about Vaughn. Where is he? Connor has called Didi but gotten no answer. If Vaughn wasn't with Didi, he might have stayed in the Winnebago, which is now surrounded by police. Connor wavers a moment, thinking how little he wants to get mixed up with what lies ahead, but leaving Vaughn with a bunch of cops is inconceivable. He puts the car in gear and moves forward.

When Connor fled the casino two hours earlier, he'd gone to Linda's place in New London: a large house on Cedar Grove that had been broken up into six units with an outdoor covered staircase that led to Linda's second-floor apartment.

Answering the door, she'd asked, "So you're stopping by for coffee after all?"

Connor had forgotten the invitation for coffee. "Maybe decaf."

"It'll have to be instant."

He sat down in an armchair next to a bookcase full of travel books as Linda boiled water in the microwave. "Why'd you change your mind about the coffee?"

Connor didn't answer, and when she repeated the question, as she brought the decaf, he still didn't answer. She wore a thick red robe that reached her ankles, and her blond hair stood up at a variety of angles. Connor guessed she'd been in bed and was struck by how lovely she was. Sitting down on a sofa, Linda put on her wire-rimmed glasses and studied him. "Okay, I give up. Why're you here?"

Connor glanced away, but as she left his sight, he again recalled how two men had dragged him to the edge of the roof of a parking garage. If Vasco hadn't saved him, he'd be dead.

Linda pretended to clear her throat. "Connor, you have to say something. You can't just sit there. What's wrong with you?"

He still hesitated. Linda was earnest and concerned. He didn't want to get her mixed up in his troubles, but maybe it was too late for that. Nor did he want to remain silent. "You remember Jasper Lincoln?"

"Apple green sport coat."

"He and another guy tried to kill me a while ago. My brother saved me."

Linda studied his face as if it were a page in a book of uncertain seriousness and then put a hand to her mouth. "Tell me," she said.

So Connor told, told right from the start when Marco Santuzza was killed; told about Bounty, Inc. with Didi, Eartha, and Vaughn; told about Fat Bob and Jack Sprat; told about Sal and Fidget; told how he'd attacked Céline's nightgown with cuticle scissors; told about Chucky, while the cup of decaf grew cold. But he liked telling her, though he knew that "like" was the wrong word. Rather, he felt he was unburdening himself to someone he hoped could understand.

When he finished, Linda leaned forward with her elbows on her knees. She stared at Connor with a worried look. "You've been busy."

Connor started to speak and then shrugged.

"What do you plan to do now?"

Again he shrugged. "I haven't thought of anything except coming over here, though I tried to call Didi. He didn't pick up."

"Why come here instead of going to the police?"

"Because I like you and because I'd like to avoid the police."

Linda nodded as if it made perfect sense. "Do you think Jasper Lincoln and the other man are looking for you?"

"I expect so. No, that's not right. I'm sure they are."

"Then go to the police."

"I can't."

"So what will you do?"

"I'm trying to decide. Anyway, I'd better tell you more about Vaughn."

"What about him?"

"Well, first of all, he's an orphan from outer space."

This was the start of the conversation that sent Connor back to Brewster and the Winnebago. Once Linda heard about Vaughn, she especially wanted him to go, worrying that Vaughn would have no one to take care of him. Of course, Connor doesn't really think that Vaughn is an orphan from outer space, but if he received absolute proof that it was true, he wouldn't be one hundred percent surprised. And talking to Linda, he felt closer to her, or at least that he was *getting* closer to her. It wasn't like talking to Eartha or Céline. In those instances he was talking to their exteriors, their bodies. With Linda he felt as if he were talking to the whole creature, inside and out.

At some point during this time, Jimbo and Joesy were bundling Vaughn into the rear seat of the Denali, and we already know how that turned out. And where were the others during this uncertain period? Well, Vasco was driving south, taking a loop around New York City and crossing the Tappan Zee Bridge as he tried to decide whether to head for Atlanta or Phoenix. He had bank accounts in both places, but which would be safer from Chucky? His cell phone kept ringing, and he ignored it. The sixth time it rang, he opened his window and threw it out.

As for Didi, he and Eartha have a room at a Rodeway Inn in Waterford a few miles west of New London. The next morning Didi will visit his box at the New London post office, but at the moment he and Eartha sit on their queen-size bed playing strip Monopoly. Eartha has just bought Reading Railroad for two shoes and two socks, having bought Pennsylvania Railroad for a pair of sweatpants on a previous roll of the dice. Both players feel optimistic, but Eartha is sure that Didi is cheating.

Fat Bob nurses a Bud Light at the bar of the Bank Street Cafe, a serious biker bar near the corner of Montauk Avenue. It would be wrong to say he's in disguise, but in his black Harley T-shirt, black Harley motorcycle vest, Harley do-rag, jeans and boots; he's dressed like fifty other guys drinking and cavorting around him, because anytime's the right time to party. Outside the door a crowd of smokers gathers around thirty Harleys parked in a row, one of which is Fat Bob's Fat Bob. So Fat Bob is like a water buffalo hiding out in a herd of water buffalo. But he's not happy. He knows that Jack Sprat's out there just riding around, and sooner or later he'll make a stop at the Bank Street Cafe and Fat Bob will have to run for the back door.

In a Pequot Tower suite at the casino, Chucky sits in his La-Z-Boy Tranquility rocker and seethes. Crack an egg on his skull and it will cook in no time. We recall his large, hairless hands—the backs are shaved— and we recall their dampness and softness. Now they're spotted with dollops of sweat as he waits for the phone to ring. He wants to know what's happened at the Winnebago, and he wants to know if Jimbo and Joesy have picked up Connor. Of course he might call and ask, but Chucky never calls his minions; rather, his minions are supposed to call *him*. So he seethes. We hate to suggest he's a prime candidate for spontaneous human combustion, but were spontaneous combustion possible, then Chucky *would* be a prime candidate. It won't happen here, however. Tonight he'll only seethe as he tallies up the punishments he'll inflict on those who frustrate his wishes.

As for Manny and Vikström, both are asleep, though Manny, collapsed on his back, snores loudly, and Yvonne in the next room plans to give him a smack to make him shut up. Vikström and Maud, on the other hand, sleep quietly. Soon the phone will ring, but we'll deal with that later. Vikström dreams he sits in the back row of a huge lecture hall while in the foggy distance a Swedish professor shouts out to five hundred students, *"Arbeta hårdare och snabbare!"* But despite being a Swedish detective, Vikström knows no Swedish, and so he only frets and scratches his nose.

———

Connor parks the Mini-Cooper behind a police cruiser, climbs out, and walks toward the Winnebago. He tries to walk like Vasco, confident and self-assured, but his knees feel weak and his stomach flip-flops.

A uniformed state cop approaches and jabs a thumb toward the Winnebago. "This your rig?"

"No, no, I'm just visiting." Connor looks for Vaughn but doesn't see him.

"You got some ID?"

Connor hands over his license. The state cop calls over another cop, gives him Connor's license, and asks him to check it, as well as check the plate number of the Mini-Cooper.

Actually, we know this cop, who's a state police detective named Woody Potter. We met him when Manny and Vikström came out to Brewster and found the dead Leon Pappalardo. Later the three police officers went to the Brewster Brew, where Vikström made himself sick eating an oversize banana split.

"The rig's registered in San Diego, your license lists an address in San Diego, and the Mini-Cooper has a California license plate. Is that where you're visiting from?"

Connor has no idea who the Mini-Cooper belongs to. Maybe Didi, maybe someone else. He's trying to come up with a plausible answer, when there's a shout. Vaughn's galloping toward him, dropping pages from yellow pads in his wake. A cop begins to draw his weapon, but Woody waves him back. In that moment Vaughn leaps on Connor, giving him a fearsome hug and sending both to the ground.

Connor returns the hug while trying not to be smothered. He rubs the top of Vaughn's head. Vaughn's motorcycle cap has fallen off, and Woody picks it up and looks inside. "Marco Santuzza," he says. "A friend of yours?"

Vaughn yells, "Squat team, squat team!"

It's hard for Connor to conjure up a credible lie with Vaughn squeezing him. "I picked it up at the accident," says Connor. He gets to his feet with Vaughn hanging on to his arm. "I didn't see it was Santuzza's till later. Now it belongs to Vaughn."

Woody Potter regards Vaughn thoughtfully. He doesn't care about the cap one way or the other. It's a Connecticut cap, not a Rhode Island cap. He gives it to Vaughn, who puts it quickly on his head, pulling it down to his eyebrows.

"So what's with this kid?" asks Woody. "What's his problem? He gave me a license plate number. He'd memorized it. You have any ideas about that?"

"He's incinerating something," says Vaughn. "What's he incinerating?"

Connor puts his arm around Vaughn's shoulder. "I don't think anything's wrong with him. He's different, that's all. Maybe he's got Asperger's. He's terrific with numbers, so if he gave you a plate number, it's probably important."

"He says he's an orphan from outer space."

"Yeah, he does that. He lives in San Diego. I brought him with me."

"So who shot up the Winnebago?"

"I don't know. You'll have to ask him." He nods at Vaughn.

"They held me hostile! They wanted to shoot me behind my back!"

Connor thinks that whoever shot up the Winnebago was told to do so by Chucky, meaning it was probably Jimbo and Joesy. But Connor has no wish to say anything that would get Chucky arrested. He doesn't want to make Chucky madder at him than he already is. And he doesn't want to meet Jimbo and Joesy again. His plan, vague though it is, is to take Vaughn and drive back to San Diego. But whenever he thinks about this, he also finds himself thinking about Linda.

The cop returns with Connor's driver's license. "This guy's clean, and the car belongs to him."

"Me?" says Connor.

"It's a surprise to you?" *Who* are *these people?* Woody thinks.

"No, no, I guess I'd forgotten." Connor knows this is another of

Didi's tricks and that somewhere Didi has an IOU or a bill of sale show-ing that the car really belongs to Didi, but he won't claim the car until he's sure it won't get him into trouble—that is, it hasn't been used in a crime or in some other dark enterprise.

"Forgotten?" says Woody.

"I've got a lot of cars at home, and this one's new. It keeps slipping my mind."

Woody sees that Connor is lying, but he doesn't have a clear reason to arrest him. As for Vaughn, Woody doesn't want to take charge of him. He can't let him stay in the Winnebago; he can't put him in a hospital; he can't stick him in a booby hatch or jail. Although not a child, Vaughn is clearly harmless and childlike. Woody's worry is that he'll have to take him home until something else can be arranged, like a suitable halfway house. He figures his wife and stepson will put up with it, but Vaughn himself might protest. The whole business is a potential can of worms.

"You can't stay here. The rig's technically a crime scene. Do you have someplace else to go? You'll have to take your friend."

"We've got to evaporate," says Vaughn cheerfully.

"I've got someone in New London I can stay with," says Connor. *Sur-prise, surprise,* he'll tell Linda. *I've brought the orphan from outer space.*

"You'll be safe?"

"Safe? Why not?"

"Some guys put fifty bullets into your rig. It's not exactly a sign of friendship."

"I'll be fine." *Will I be fine?* thought Connor. He didn't know.

"Okay, I'll need your friend's name and address, also some other stuff."

As these details are sorted out, Vaughn goes to collect his yellow pads.

"Can I go inside and get some stuff?" asks Connor. "Like clothes?"

"I'm afraid not. You'd be tampering with a crime scene."

"What's the crime?"

"Shooting the blazes out of the place."

———

Around two in the morning, Vikström is awakened from troubled sleep by the ringing of the phone. Actually, Maud shakes him awake, calling, "Benny, Benny!"

It's a sergeant from police headquarters. "We got the license plate of that Denali you were looking for. It was spotted over in Rhode Island. You said you wanted to know if it turned up. And a Rhode Island state cop wants you to call him."

TWENTY-EIGHT

As a bowling ball gathers speed down a waterslide, so we accelerate as our friends join together at the finish. Some, however, can be left to their own devices. Angelina, thrilled by the way Milo Lisowski shot up Fat Bob's Fat Bob on Monday evening, has accepted his overtures, and they've begun to date, meaning they're screwing each other silly. Also, in Sunday's New London *Day* will appear Angelina's classified ad seeking members for the first chapter of Prom Queens Anonymous. The only nuisance is that Fat Bob keeps calling with threats and demanding his bikes back.

Nor will we see more of Orville Percival and Henry Lascombe. Their work in New London is done, and they're returned to the FBI field office in Detroit. We'll miss their upbeat appreciation of their own importance. Nor will we see Brewster police chief Brendan Gazzola, Rhode Island State Police detective Woody Potter, Caroline Santuzza, Céline, Fat Bob's friend Otto, Mr. Burns of Burns Insurance, Dr. Hubert Goodenough, and others—we wish them the best in new undertakings.

Others we'll see shortly. Fat Bob, for instance, spends the night cruising New London streets like a fly refusing to settle. Whenever he pauses, as at a red light, he hears the high whine of Jack Sprat's scooter getting closer. How Jack Sprat can so quickly figure out his location is a mystery to Fat Bob, even though his aftermarket exhaust pipes idle at one hundred decibels. But Jack is secretary of a local scooter club called the Vicious White-Faced Hornets. So a dozen of his scooter pals also cruise the streets, and after midnight Fat Bob's noisy pipes are child's play to locate.

In this instance the biker slogan "Loud pipes save lives" may lead to a contrary outcome.

Is Fat Bob to blame for Marco's death? We've discussed this before, and we're unsure. Sal wanted Fat Bob to meet him at his office at a specific time that Monday morning. The very specificity worried Fat Bob, so he offered Marco a test drive on a Fat Bob, since Marco was already headed for his own office in the same building as Sal's office. We know the result. Fat Bob swears he meant no harm, but Dr. Goodenough, if we had access to his services, might suggest that Fat Bob had an unconscious desire, et cetera. This isn't enough to send Fat Bob to prison, but surely it's enough to rile up Marco's murderous brother-in-law.

Also, Fat Bob knew that Sal was Dante Barbarella, and perhaps he made a modest attempt at blackmail, since he's always in need of money. Once Sal was dead, Fat Bob felt certain that Chucky was to blame. *Ho, ho,* Fat Bob might think, *if I can't get money from Sal, I'll get it from Chucky,* meaning that Chucky would pay to shut him up. Does this show Fat Bob's ambition, desperation, or incredible stupidity? Dr. Goodenough might suggest the last. In any case, Fat Bob knew that Chucky was looking for him, just as Jack Sprat was looking for him. But he wants to meet them on his terms rather than theirs, so he keeps moving.

Isn't it often true in life that someone fucks up and nothing happens; then he fucks up again and nothing happens; a third time ditto; a fourth, fifth, sixth, and seventh times ditto. Then, on the eighth time, the whole world falls on his head. That's what happened to Fat Bob. No wonder he calls life unfair. And every couple of hours, his ex-wife calls him with a message: "You fuckin' scumbag, I just sold your last bike to a scam artist for pennies and Milo's dick's a foot longer than yours. How d'you like them apples?" And of course Fat Bob calls back with threats of his own.

Early Saturday morning Manny and Vikström sit at their desks and consider the world's defects. One defect for Vikström is the defect that led a desk sergeant to call him at two a.m. to give him the Denali's

330

Stephen Dobyns

plate number: information that came by way of the trooper, Woody Potter. Then, an hour later, Woody called to say that the two thugs in the Denali had kidnapped Vaughn and shot up a Winnebago, destroying it. He also said he'd talked to Connor Raposo, who was, Woody expected, a person of interest for Vikström. Then Woody gave Vikström Linda's New London address: an apartment on Cedar Grove. Woody's call constituted the second defect.

Vikström tried to go back to sleep but could only think of the fucking Denali. So around six he went to his office, where he found Manny, humming. But the humming was the least of it. What made it a defect was the amount, because in a one-hour period Manny hummed or whistled "Riders in the Sky" maybe a hundred times. Vikström was certain that Manny was waiting for him to shout, "Shut the fuck up!" and so Vikström remained silent and suffered.

As for Manny, he wasn't disturbed by nighttime phone calls, because each night he made sure the phones in his house were turned off. But that doesn't mean he isn't brooding about defects. The main defect is whatever defect caused Yvonne to give a thousand smackers to Free Beagles from Nicotine Addiction, Inc. It didn't matter that it was her money; it's the principle of the thing, whatever that principle might be. So main defect number two was the defect that kept him from being able to locate the scumbag responsible for defect number one.

This is the trouble with defects: They never come singly. So defects one and two led to defect number three, which was more of a defective *situation* than a distinct defect. This had arisen from Manny's insistence that Yvonne knew more than she really knew, meaning she must be acquainted with the scumbag referred to in defect number two. This led to troubles, which formed further defects. Specifically, for the last two nights Yvonne had refused to make dinner and had slept in the guest room with their beagle, Schultzie. Tiptoeing up to the guest-room door late at night, Manny could hear his wife's giggles and the low, moaning howls that Schultzie made to express pleasure in having his belly scratched.

A further feature of this defective situation was that for two nights

Yvonne had refused to visit the karaoke box, forcing Manny to run the show himself. But Manny lacked Yvonne's charm as master of ceremonies. He tended to tell his guests when to sing and when not to sing. After all, he was a cop. Ordering was easier than asking. As a result, some guests left early and some didn't come back the next night. Also, without Yvonne, Manny's singing voice lacked its natural authority. He needed her praise. It didn't matter if others liked him or not. Sharps and flats were all the same to him. But last night one of the guests had actually booed.

Manny's catalog of defects has reached this low spot when Vikström asks, "You ever do any newer songs in your singing box?"

Vikström's words enter Manny's ears the way a dentist's drill might initiate a root canal with insufficient Novocain. Manny doesn't shout, but his syllables emerge from between his teeth. "No post-1960 songs. That's the rule. I've said that before."

"What about 'Hey Jude'?"

It should be said that Vikström's questions emerge from a mixed agenda. He wants to stop Manny from humming "Riders in the Sky," and he wants to show Manny his attitude change toward karaoke boxes as a way of improving office morale.

"'Hey Jude' is post-1960."

"You sure?"

"Fuckin' right I'm sure. It was released in 1968."

"So they might have sung an earlier version of 'Hey Jude' in 1960, like an earlier draft."

"It never happened. The Beatles weren't even formed as a band till 1960."

"But they might have had it on the back burner in 1960, like unconsciously."

"What the fuck's wrong with you!?" Manny shouts.

Part of Vikström's apparent attitude change to karaoke is his decision to try a little singing even though he's tone-deaf. But he doesn't want to do those old songs. He wants the Beatles.

"What about 'All You Need Is Love'?"

"What did I fuckin' say?" These are words that Manny shouts.

Vikström has begun folding an origami crane, which is something his wife, Maud, has been teaching him. But all his cranes look like paper airplanes. His paper-folding skills display a clumsiness that is equivalent to tone deafness.

"What if I introduced you to a new singing star as long as you kept it quiet?"

"Like who?"

"Me. I bet I could do it, as long as I could sing the Beatles."

Vikström's offer is for Manny the ultimate insult. It couldn't be any worse if Vikström had walked onto the little karaoke stage and taken a dump on the tiles. The affront would be as great. Manny jumps to his feet and goes to pick up a computer monitor. Perhaps he means to throw it at Vikström. Luckily for Vikström, their boss, Detective Sergeant Masters, appears at this moment.

"There's trouble in an apartment on Cedar Grove," she says. "Three people were dragged away. One was shouting about 'violet goatnapping.' Crazy stuff."

Connor and Vaughn reach Linda's apartment around 2:30 a.m. Luckily, Connor had called to warn her. Vaughn doesn't make eye contact with her and instead focuses on the ceiling as he holds his motorcycle cap to his chest with both hands. He has a red bruise on his chin from where Joesy struck him. Vaughn is smaller than Linda expected; his short, peroxided hair stands up at angles vaguely like her own. A head shaped like a loaf of bread with a pink bump of a nose, a blue left eye, a green right eye, a wide mouth, his uncertain age—Linda knows perfectly well that Vaughn isn't an orphan from outer space, but she sees how people might think so. But it's his voice that strikes her most, a rippling baritone like eddying chamois cloth. Maybe she's heard of Vaughn Monroe, she can't recall; maybe her parents listened to him. But Vaughn sounds just the way she thinks a famous singer should sound.

"Does he sing?" she asks Connor, as if Vaughn weren't in the room.

"I've never heard him sing." Connor turns to Vaughn. "Do you sing?"

Vaughn's smile shows even rows of little teeth. "Mission impassable. I'm a suppository of wicked notes."

"Is this how he always talks?"

"It's more pronounced when he's nervous."

Vaughn gives another beatific smile. "I suffer from inflammable language due to a deformation of character."

Linda feels the light-headedness often experienced by Vaughn's interlocutors. She retreats to the kitchen, leaving offers of hot chocolate in her wake.

Connor describes to Linda what he learned from Woody Potter and what he thought he learned from Vaughn about his interaction with Jimbo and Joesy. He again worries that he's getting Linda mixed up with troubles not her own.

After the hot chocolate, Linda works out the sleeping arrangements. She'd like to invite Connor to her bed but feels it's the wrong time. And Connor would like to sleep in her bed, but he isn't sure how to broach the subject. So he sleeps on the couch, and Vaughn sleeps on the floor on several yoga mats. Only Vaughn feels satisfied with the arrangement.

During the rest of the night, we hear tossing, turning, and a little snoring that we ignore as irrelevant. What's relevant is the pounding on Linda's door shortly after six. Linda hurries to the door in her pajamas. Maybe she thinks it's a neighbor with a sick cat. Before Connor can say, "I think that's a bad idea," she opens the door an inch and has it roughly shoved open the rest of the way by Joesy and Jimbo.

"Shark attack!" shouts Vaughn.

"Shut him up or we toss him out the window," says Joesy.

Linda approaches him angrily. "How dare you say something so mean?"

Joesy steps back. He hadn't thought of it as mean. It's just business. So he says harshly, "Business is business."

Linda looks for her cell phone. "I'm calling the police. Get out of here now!"

During this exchange Connor slowly gets to his feet and Vaughn sits on the yoga mats with a blanket over his head. Connor's impressed by Linda's behavior, but he's also worried by it. After a moment Linda finds her cell phone in the pocket of her winter coat. Before she can use it, Jimbo limps toward her, grabs the phone, and slides it across the floor to Joesy, who stamps on it. From under the blanket, Vaughn shouts, "Include me out!"

Linda gives Jimbo a push. "Didn't your mother teach you any manners?"

Connor, now standing, says, "They work for Chucky."

As Jimbo regains his balance, Linda gives him another push. We recall that Jimbo has had the third toe on his left foot eradicated by Vasco, so he's shaky on his pins.

"I don't care if they work for Donald Trump!" shouts Linda. "They need to leave! I should have the police on speed dial. Get out of here!"

Joesy has drawn his pistol and aims it at Vaughn. "Shut up or I'll pop the retard. I won't kill him, but I'll put a hole in him."

"You're basically a sissy," says Linda, stepping back.

Jimbo and Joesy look unhappy, which makes them look more thuggish. In their dealings with Connor, Vaughn, and Linda, nothing's gone as it's supposed to. The thugs have failed to inspire terror. In the casino parking lot, Connor had struck back at Jimbo, hitting him in the nose. Then Vasco had shot Jimbo in the foot. Next Vaughn had tried to hit them in order to save his yellow pads. Worse, he'd spoken an unintelligible language that gave them headaches. Lastly, this pajama-clad woman with spiky hair treats them with disrespect. Jimbo asks himself, as he's asked before, *Are we getting old?* And Joesy thinks, *Are we losing our edge?* Both imagine walking away, perhaps getting breakfast—pancakes or French toast—and then returning to the casino hotel to take naps. Regrettably, waiting downstairs in the Denali and expecting the imminent arrival—loutishly achieved—of Connor, Vaughn, and Linda, is Chucky. And Chucky, as the thugs know, hates to be kept waiting.

So Jimbo and Joesy catch their second wind, as it were, on the strength of threatening Vaughn. Joesy grabs Connor. Jimbo pulls Vaughn from underneath his blanket. And the thugs give Linda little pushes toward the door—that is, they give little pushes and jump back before she can kick them, which she tries to do.

"I bet you dumbos have tiny penises," she says.

Jimbo and Joesy hate this sort of talk. They shove her out the door and begin to push all three down the outside staircase.

Linda shouts, "Call the police! We're being kidnapped!"

Joesy claps a hand over her mouth, picks her up, and carries her to the Denali, where Jimbo has Connor and Vaughn. Chucky opens the door, and the three prisoners are thrown inside. Joesy jumps in the driver's seat, and they roar off.

They don't, however, go unnoticed. At least six busybodies stick their heads out of their windows and register each detail. These are the folks who, in a few seconds, will call police headquarters.

So how did Jimbo and Joesy get Linda's address? Very simple. Jimbo heard Linda give it to Vikström outside the back door of the Capitol Theatre. Thugs are good at finding addresses. They got Fat Bob's old address from the casino's personnel office, and they got his new address when Jimbo asked for it from Angelina. "That son of a bitch," she'd said. "Sure I'll give you his address! And tell him to quit calling or else!" The one address they don't have is Fidget's, and that troubles them, because Chucky demands it. Chucky is forever thinking of Sal's gold, which in his fancy has grown larger than the hoard of gold protected by the Rhine maidens in *Der Ring des Nibelungen.*

Fidget spends half of each day, sometimes more, lying in his tub. His skin has lost its pinkness and resembles the gray of wet blotting paper.

He still has food—beef jerky, Slim Jims, beer nuts, and five packs of Lance peanut butter crackers with "goodness baked in"—and he has enough vodka left for a day or two. What he'll do when it runs out, he has no idea. "One minute at a time" is his motto. But he is happy, that's the main thing. And perhaps because his memory has as many holes as the shot-up Winnebago, he can never recall being so happy.

This particular morning he got up at six, filled his tub, ate some beer nuts, and slid his long, thin body into the water. No soap—he doesn't use soap. Then he begins to get dressed, as he calls it, meaning he distributes Sal's gold across his body. With great delicacy he takes the yellow-gold curb-link bracelet from its place on the chair beside the tub and puts it on his wrist. Next, with the same care he might exercise to carry a Ming vase down a flight of stairs, he puts on his five necklaces: two yellow-gold hollow-wheat-chain necklaces; a yellow-gold solid Franco necklace; a white-gold chain with a hundred carats of diamonds, and a gold rope-chain necklace with a gold crucifix pendant. Fidget pauses to catch his breath and then puts on the rings: two yellow-gold nugget rings and a third nugget ring with a diamond cluster. The gold pinkie ring with a large ruby he puts aside for the time being. Then, as he might tiptoe a full tumbler of vodka across a packed dance floor, he slides onto his left wrist the Rolex Oyster Perpetual GMT-Master II with an eighteen-karat yellow-gold case and an eighteen-karat yellow-gold bracelet, plus a sprin-kling of diamonds, sapphires, and rubies.

All that's left is the Montegrappa St. Moritz Limited Edition Woods eighteen-karat-gold rollerball pen, which at first constituted a problem. Where could he put it? Then Fidget recalled Jack Lemmon playing the reporter Hildy Johnson in the movie *The Front Page*, and he'd carefully set his Montegrappa pen behind his left ear.

Lastly Fidget takes the gold pinkie ring with its large ruby and puts it in his belly button. Because Fidget is skinny, he has a shallow navel, and to get the pinkie ring firmly situated takes some pushing. But finally it's done.

Here, then, is the gold that drives Chucky mad, just as it drove Sal mad, just as it drives Fidget mad. "Mad," of course, is an overstatement, yet surely their mental well-being is, and was, at risk. But that's gold's job in the world: to upset cerebral equilibrium and encourage cranial entropy. It fucks you up.

So if we imagine Fidget lying naked in his tub and make the ruby in his navel the very center of a gold fixation, then Chucky, the police, and Fat Bob spiral toward the center of that fixation. The ruby works like a magnet works: stuff creeps closer.

Chucky knows that Fidget made his recent liquor purchases at a liquor store on Montauk in New London. And he knows that Fat Bob has a boarded-up house on Montauk. It's like striking a stone against a flint to produce a flame. Chucky strikes and strikes, and eventually a tiny idea begins to flare up. He decides the house on Montauk is worth a look. Afterward he'll decide what to do with Connor, Linda, and Vaughn. Nothing nice, of course.

Fat Bob isn't fixated on the gold, because he doesn't know about it. This is just as well, because if he knew the gold was lying in his crummy bathtub, his brain would pop. But he wants to avoid Jack Sprat, and he wants to visit his house on Montauk to make sure his last Fat Bob is gone, having been, as Angelina said, "sold to a scam artist," meaning Didi Lobato. And so Fat Bob zigzags closer to the ruby in Fidget's navel, as somewhere behind him Jack Sprat moves along as well. But he doesn't struggle to keep up, because this morning a new circumstance changed the rules of the game. We'll have to imagine it, because we don't know exactly how it happened. Be that as it may, Milo Lisowski, owner of the Hog Hurrah, has lent Jack Sprat one of Fat Bob's Fat Bobs: the red one. In fact, Lisowski's lending Jack Sprat a bike for a nefarious purpose is like Fat Bob lending Marco Santuzza a bike for a nefarious purpose. Lisowski was friends with Marco, more or less. Marco bought stuff at the Hog Hurrah and rented time in the garage to work on his bike, meaning that Lisowski would prefer Marco alive.

But it was Angelina, tired of listening to Fat Bob demand his bikes back, who initiated the new circumstance. Despite the restraining order she has against Fat Bob, he keeps calling and sending text messages. He even makes threats. We recollect the quarrels that Henry II of England had with Thomas à Becket, the archbishop of Canterbury, about "criminous clerks," et cetera, until in a fit of pique the king cried out, "Will no one rid me of this turbulent priest?" Accordingly, four knights took their swords and murdered Thomas à Becket at Canterbury Cathedral, on December 29, 1170.

In such a way did Angelina cry out, "Will no one rid me of this turbulent ex-husband?" Lisowski listened and initiated the chain of events that put Jack Sprat into the saddle of a Fat Bob. But Jack Sprat is a scooter guy and barely fits on the Harley. His feet hardly reach the ground. Worse, when he rides, he wobbles. But what he lacks in skill, he makes up for in determination. So Fat Bob must take care.

Then there's Manny Streeter and Benny Vikström. Manny's still furious, and Vikström's somewhat contrite, or at least apologetic. "Okay!" he has shouted. "So I won't sing 'Hey Jude'! Fuck the Beatles!"

"You're not singing shit!" shouts Manny. "You come near my house, I'll have you locked up!"

As for the house on Montauk, it would be nice to think Manny and Vikström had a sudden eureka moment about it, but that's not the case, even though they also know that Fidget made his purchases at the Montauk liquor store. Luckily, patrol cars keep calling in the Denali's license plate number. Vikström warns that Chucky and his friends are dangerous and patrol cars shouldn't get too close. Then, when a patrol car reports that the Denali is on Montauk and has just passed the liquor store, little synapses of understanding light up in the detectives' brains.

But that lighting up of synapses should have occurred earlier. This has been the trouble with Manny and Vikström. They quarrel on the job. Instead of focusing on Chucky, they wrangle about "Hey Jude" and the Beatles. Nevertheless, at this moment the small white house on Montauk is only a few blocks away.

TWENTY-NINE

C hucky gets there first. Perhaps he's seen a few patrol cars on his way over, but Chucky, being Chucky, thinks he's too big to catch. He was one of those ill-fated youngsters who saw *King Kong* on TV as a kid and bonded. Pushing open the door of the Denali, he steps out and sniffs the air. We might think he smells the gold, but it's all submerged in Fidget's tub, except for the Montegrappa pen. It's a sunny Saturday morning in mid-March, with hints of spring. Mourning doves coo and robins peck the ground, but Chucky and his thugs have no interest in birds apart from fried chicken.

Connor, Vaughn, and Linda remain in the third-row seat of the Denali. It's a bench designed for two persons, so they're cramped. They shift and try to stretch their legs, but it's no use. Linda feels increasingly irritated. Vaughn, staring at the boarded-up house, says, "It's closed for altercations."

Standing by the Denali, Chucky and his thugs look thoughtfully—relatively speaking—at the heavy sheets of plywood covering the windows and doors. The second-story windows are free of plywood but seem far away.

Jimbo wears his apple green sport coat and uses a cane because of his wounded foot. Joesy has on a blue New England Patriots hoodie. He may be a thug, but he's also a fan. Chucky wears a black turtleneck sweater, which makes his oversize head resemble an ugly golf ball with teeth. Oh, yes, Joesy has on black leather-soled loafers. This will be important.

"Open it up," says Chucky, jabbing his thumb at the small house.

Easier said than done, think the thugs. They can't reach the boarded-up windows unless one sits on another's shoulders, and even that would be a stretch. They circle the house in the opposite directions and return shaking their heads.

"Looks pretty tight," says Jimbo.

"What the fuck did I say?" barks Chucky. "Open it up!" Chucky is at least six inches taller than his assistants and outweighs each by nearly one hundred pounds. Authority to him is what burgers are for McDonald's.

Jimbo and Joesy separate again to check the front and back doors. The sheets of plywood are fixed in place with heavy screws. They pull at the edges but achieve nothing except broken fingernails. Maybe there's something they can use in the garage. Joesy peers through the glass of the garage's side door but sees nothing. The thugs look nearby for rocks. When Jimbo finds one of ample size, he returns to the window and smashes it. Then he reaches through the broken window and opens the door.

Back in the Denali, Linda says, "I'm sick of this. I'm not staying in here."

Connor's impressed and says, "I admire your guts."

Possibly joking, Vaughn asks with concern, "Are they showing?"

The thugs find no tools in the garage, but they find a fourteen-foot aluminum ladder. They carry it out to Chucky and set it against the wall next to the Denali. The ladder stops about four feet beneath the gable window above them. This is the window of the small bathroom where Fidget lies snoozing in the tub. We recall that his snoozing was earlier disturbed by noisy motorcycles circling the house, and now Fidget's ears are stuffed with cotton. Perhaps he dreams.

"I can't climb the ladder," says Jimbo. "My foot got shot up."

Joesy gives his partner a venomous look.

"Get moving," says Chucky. Of course there's no question of Chucky climbing the ladder. His status as boss frees him from the nuts and bolts of being bad.

Joesy sets a black loafer on the first rung. It's at this point we recall that he wears leather-soled shoes. His black loafer slips on the aluminum. He grips the rails until his fingers creak.

The door of the Denali opens, and Linda steps out. "I'm not staying in there any longer. It's stuffy. I'm walking home." She turns toward the street.

Chucky and his thugs are again deeply insulted that their victim refuses to accept her victimizing. They feel she's seen none of the right movies.

"Cut the shit!" shouts Chucky. "Get back in the truck!"

Jimbo grabs the collar of Linda's coat, stopping her.

"I promise I'll start screaming if you don't let go," says Linda coolly. Connor and Vaughn also get out of the Denali, but lacking Linda's moxie, they remain by the door. Connor thinks he should make similar protests but doesn't.

"It's only for a short time," whispers Jimbo. "I'll let you sit in the front seat."

Linda grudgingly agrees. All three get back into the Denali with Linda in front. Their little labor union has scored a blow against the bosses.

Now on the eighth rung, Joesy keeps slipping and is unhappy. The sunny, springlike morning means nothing to him. Jimbo and Chucky stare up at him. Jimbo could never imagine being grateful for his wounded foot, but he's grateful now: he's not on the ladder.

It's clear when Joesy nears the top that he'll have to stand on the topmost rung and brace himself against the wall to see through the window. He's reached a metaphysical moment. Should he risk falling and get his bones broken, or should he defy Chucky and get his bones broken? He keeps climbing.

Joesy moves at the pace of mold on a piece of angel food cake, but at last he's slipping and sliding on the top rung as he peers through the window.

"Fidget's in the tub!" shouts Joesy. "And he's got the gold!"

My gold, thinks Chucky. "Tell him to get down here or else!"

"He's got cotton stuffed in his ears!"

"Then break the fucking glass!"

"With what!"

"Use your fucking head!"

Now events speed up. The Denali is in the driveway to the left of the house, while the ladder is between the Denali and the wall. A car is speeding up Montauk. It's Manny's Subaru Forester.

Manny and Vikström are still arguing.

"What about Bill Haley and the Comets?" says Vikström. "I could sing 'Rock Around the Clock.' That's pre-1960, isn't it?"

"I already fucking told you!" shouts Manny. "You ain't singing fuckin' squat!"

"I bet Yvonne would let me. I've always been friendly with Yvonne."

Driving faster than he should, Manny spins the wheel of the Subaru and turns in to Fat Bob's driveway. He's about to shout, *No way, José!* but slams on the brake instead. Directly ahead squats the fat rear end of the Denali. The brakes squeal, but he hits the Denali with a metallic crunch.

Inside the Denali, Connor, Linda, and Vaughn are thrown forward. Outside, Joesy trembles at the top of his ladder and clutches at the bathroom window. Chucky, his mouth open, pauses in mid-rage. Jimbo puts a hand over his eyes. Connor, Linda, and Vaughn scramble out of the Denali as Manny and Vikström try to scramble out of the Subaru, but they're not young anymore. Stiff joints slow them. Manny hurries to inspect the damage to the front of his car. He grows indignant. He's never seen Chucky before, nor has Chucky seen Manny and Vikström, meaning he doesn't know they're cops. This is a problem with Manny driving the Subaru instead of a cop car. Chucky thinks they're trespassers after his gold.

But there's more. A loud motorcycle is approaching, and half a block behind wobbles another motorcycle. Fat Bob wants to make certain his last Fat Bob, the black one, has indeed been stolen from his garage, but as he turns up Montauk, Jack Sprat on Fat Bob's very own red Fat Bob turns after him. This is Fat Bob's first awareness that Jack Sprat has swapped his red scooter for a red Harley. *Angelina did this!* he thinks. He cranks up the gas.

Fat Bob doesn't spot the Subaru till he turns in to his driveway. He also sees a crowd of people and a man on a ladder. He yanks the handlebars to the right, bumps across the grass, roars along the right side of the house, turns left at his garage, notes the broken window, and turns left again toward the two vehicles and crowd of people, who are as they were when he last saw them: astonished. Jack Sprat on his red Fat Bob wobbles along behind. No telling what he thinks of the two vehicles and crowd of people. It's difficult enough for him to keep his bike going straight and not fall off without having to think as well. But he has determination.

Fat Bob takes another swing around the house. He asks himself, was that really Chucky, two thugs, two cops, the guy he had lunch with at the Exchange, and two strangers, one of them cute? What was going on?

But the scene has changed since he last roared by. Connor, Linda, and Vaughn run across the yard to escape from Chucky. Joesy trembles more actively on his ladder. Chucky pulls something fat and dark from his belt, probably a weapon. Jimbo limps toward him, yelling, "Don't do it!" Manny shouts angrily at Chucky that he's caused the accident by parking stupidly in the driveway. And Vikström, with a surer sense of events, runs toward Manny. Police cars approach, their sirens blaring.

Jack Sprat, though he keeps up with Fat Bob, isn't gaining. He decides to take a shortcut. So, rounding the back of the house, he cuts between the truck and the wall, meaning between the ladder and the wall, but maybe Jack Sprat hasn't seen the ladder, so intent is he on not falling off the Fat Bob.

Events speed toward their climax. Focusing at last on the ladder, Jack Sprat imagines he can pass between the ladder and wall. Perhaps he thinks he rides something small like his scooter. It's a brave attempt, and he nearly succeeds. But as he rushes after Fat Bob, he clips the edge of the ladder.

A scream comes from above. No longer on the ladder, Joesy flails in midair. He makes flying gestures, but they're ineffective. He drops like a falcon on a dove.

Chucky, still certain the intruders are after his gold, has drawn his pistol. Jimbo shouts, "They're cops! They're cops!" Vikström, moving quickly, has nearly reached his partner.

Gravity prevails. Joesy hits the top of the Denali, making a drumlike explosion. Chucky, startled by the noise, pulls the trigger. There's a shot. But consider this: A second before the shot goes off, Vikström has knocked Manny aside.

Vikström groans and falls. He's been struck by Chucky's bullet.

Patrol cars pull in to the driveway and onto the grass. Chucky is stunned when he sees the police. This wasn't supposed to happen. Some god of darkness has let him down. But he's not dumb. Hunched over, nervous New London cops creep toward him with weapons drawn. Chucky drops his pistol and raises his hands. Jimbo's hands are already up. Joesy is collapsed on the roof of the Denali, but he whimpers, surely a sign of life.

Connor, Linda, and Vaughn have stopped at the edge of the yard to watch. Everyone pauses to take a deep breath as all of their imagined futures swerve in new directions: better for some, worse for others. Fat Bob on his Fat Bob with Jack Sprat on his tail disappears up the street.

Vikström sits on the ground, holding his shoulder and rocking back and forth.

Manny approaches angrily. He'd like to kick his partner. "You son of a bitch, what did you do that for, you prick? You think you can start telling me what to do? You fuckin' think I'll start bringing you fuckin' coffee in the morning? I don't owe you squat!"

It's a pity that Didi has missed this display of the tradiculous, but after a leisurely breakfast at the Waterford motel he and Eartha ride Fat Bob's black Fat Bob back to New London to check the mailbox. This is possibly the last time he'll visit it. He's withdrawing from Bounty, Inc. for a while. He'll pick up a few things from the shot-up Winnebago, but basically the Winnebago is toast. Still, he's made several essential purchases. For instance, the Harley is pulling a black Cycle Mate XL-HD trailer with twenty-four cubic feet of cargo space, while attached to the back of the bike are a pair of black locking rigid saddlebags, because Didi can't go anywhere without his comforts. The Ford Focus rental has been left in the hospital parking lot, the same place where Didi picked up the Fat Bob. Didi likes Teflon transitions.

Eartha is eager for new worlds to conquer. She's changing her name back to Beatriz. In a fit of misplaced enthusiasm, she suggests to Didi that they get married, but Didi says they can't get married because they're related. Closely related? she asks. Close enough to have babies with two heads, he answers.

As for Connor, Linda, and Vaughn, a patrolman gives them a ride back to Linda's apartment on Cedar Grove. Later they'll return to police headquarters to give statements about what happened. All three remain shaken by events, though Linda's response is mostly anger. She says, "How dare they!" and things like that. Vaughn remains upset and shouts, "I'm having another nervous shakedown! They behaved abdominally!" Connor is angry he didn't do something courageous. "What a chickenshit!" he repeats. The patrolman is glad to get them out of the car.

Connor understands that Didi, too, will want to visit the post office, so once he has the Mini-Cooper, he drives there with Linda and Vaughn. He hopes to get there before Didi, but parked in front is a black Fat Bob with trailer and saddlebags. Eartha—now Beatriz—leans against the backseat rest doing her nails with a scarlet polish called Bright Lights, Big Color. Seeing them, she jumps off the bike and runs to them. "You're safe!" she cries, and embraces each with her wrists so as not to smear her polish. Of course, she doesn't know Linda, but Eartha likes giving embraces and doles them out energetically. She wears a black leather Harley jacket.

Now Didi runs down the steps toward them. He, too, wears a black leather Harley jacket. "I was scared shitless!" he shouts. "I thought you might be dead!"

With Didi's concern, Connor also sees in Didi a touch of regret that Connor has found him. "Where'd you get the bike?" asks Connor.

"Angelina gave it to me. It's a long story."

"Tell me."

Didi pushes his hands through his hair to express frustration and dismay. "We're done here, Connor. Everything's blown. Bounty, Inc. is shut down for the duration. Vasco ruined everything. I'll let you take the car back to San Diego, but you have to give it to me when I get there. Beatriz and I are going to see America!"

"But the car's in my name." Actually, Connor isn't surprised.

"That's just a formality. It means nothing."

Connor, however, isn't sure he's going back to San Diego, so he remains silent.

Linda steps around Connor. "So why'd Angelina give you the motorcycle?"

Didi's never seen her before. He looks indignant. "Do I know you?"

"Tell us about the bike," says Connor.

"Angelina gave it to me to piss off her ex-husband. It's a charitable gift, so she can take seventeen grand off her taxes. It's almost like real money."

There's an awkward pause, and then Linda says, "There must be more."

Didi gives her another indignant look. But these are bogus indignant looks. Who can guess what he really thinks? "Well, if you must know, I'm working for her."

Connor asks what kind of work, and Didi hesitates, says it doesn't matter, says they're in a hurry, says he'll tell him in San Diego. Then he shrugs. "I'm setting up meetings of Prom Queens Anonymous, setting up the whole organization. It'll be a job like any other." Seeing Connor's doubt, he adds, "Angelina says she'll have me arrested if I don't help her. It'll only take a week or so, and then we're heading for Florida. I told her I could help her set up a nonprofit organization, file papers with the state. All the legal stuff. Make everything on the up-and-up."

"That'll be a first," says Connor. "What about paying me?"

Didi rests a hand on Connor's shoulder. "I'll send you a check in San Diego."

He says this with such assurance that Connor knows he's lying. Connor's used to this: The more truthful Didi seems, the more the truth's in doubt.

"I want the money now."

They go back and forth, with Didi saying that he can't and Connor saying that he can. At last Didi takes a roll of bills from his coat. "Well, it'll have to be less than the check." He peels off ten one-hundred-dollar bills and slaps Connor on the back.

"You can send me a check for the remainder," says Connor.

They all laugh at such an absurd idea. Didi climbs onto the bike.

"What about paying Vaughn as well?" says Linda.

Didi's bogus indignation returns. "What's he need money for? He only buys yellow pads and clear nail polish."

"He needs it to eat." Linda takes out her cell phone. "I'm calling the police."

Didi's eyes widen, a sincere response to a disagreeable situation. He peels off another ten hundred-dollar bills. "You deserve a girlfriend like this, Connor. She'll cut your balls off."

Taking the money, Linda smiles sweetly. "I'd never do that to my friends."

Didi starts up the Harley. The noise wipes out future sentences and voices Didi's displeasure. That'll be the end of the talk. Eartha gives a little wave and mouths something; it could be "I'll miss you" or "I love you" or "Take care of yourselves." They can't tell. The Harley Fat Bob rumbles up the street.

Manny is late. He'd wanted to get to the hospital earlier. He'd wanted to give Vikström a piece of his mind, but he had to drop by police headquarters and oversee the booking of Chucky. Jimbo and Joesy are in

Lawrence + Memorial Hospital. Jimbo's foot is infected, starting at the spot where his toe was blown off. Joesy has a broken hip. They'll be spared jail food for a while. Chucky keeps demanding to see his lawyer, but it won't do much good. Chucky shot a cop, and no way will anyone get bail. It'll be a long time before Chucky sees the outside of prison, if at all.

Manny gets to Lawrence + Memorial Hospital in the early afternoon. It's also on Montauk, about six blocks from Fat Bob's house. Manny's been seething ever since Vikström was shot. He, too, has been wounded, but it's psychological. Even so, Manny is sure his wound is the worse of the two.

Vikström, being a cop, gets a room of his own. It's one of the job's little perks. Manny lopes through the hospital, holding his ID in front of him so no one slows him down. "Get outta my way!" he shouts. Maybe he's still seeing red when he bursts into Vikström's room; maybe he's not seeing at all.

"You son of a bitch!" he shouts. "You did it on purpose, you got shot on purpose! You're trying to obligate me in some way, fuckin' make me beholden. Fat chance, scumbag. I know your tricks! It's not going to work!"

But Vikström's not alone in the room; he has visitors. First there's Detective Sergeant Masters, supervisor of the Detective Bureau; then we have Detectives Herta Spiegel and Moss Jackson; then there's Vikström's wife, Maud. Together they form a quartet of matching facial expressions: surprise and disappointment fading to anger and indignation.

Vikström regards his partner with no expression at all, unless it's a small smile he can't conceal. He sits up in bed. He's been shot in the upper arm, and his arm and shoulder are wrapped in bandages. He'll be out by evening.

Vikström clears his throat and assumes a look of forbearing resignation. Somewhere deep inside he's laughing his butt off.

"I risked my life to save yours," he tells his partner. "I almost died so you could live." This is surely overdramatic, but his four guests all nod in agreement.

Discovery comes to Manny much as the New World came to Columbus. He knows he's been defeated. He knows that in the future, whenever he criticizes, mocks, or makes fun of his partner, Vikström can look at him sadly and say, "I risked my life," et cetera. Vikström has won. What an awful turn of events.

A snapshot of the awfulness is given to Manny the next day when Vikström picks him up to go over to Fat Bob's house on Montauk. Vikström heard from Joesy that morning that he'd seen Fidget lying in the bathtub draped with gold. The awfulness first appears in the phrase "I'll drive, Manny," then in "Stop humming, Manny," then in "Run into Dunkin' Donuts and get me a coffee and a raspberry jelly doughnut, Manny," then, at the house, "Don't walk in front of me, Manny."

The back door has been opened, and the detectives enter the kitchen. Both worry that Fidget might be dead. Vikström calls his name and hears no answer.

But no, Fidget is alive. They find him upstairs asleep in the tub, glittering with Sal's gold, his ears stuffed with cotton.

"Take some pictures, Manny, or nobody will believe it."

So Manny takes pictures with his smartphone. *How pretty he looks,* thinks Vikström. *How ugly he is,* thinks Manny. Then Vikström gently shakes Fidget's shoulder. "Silly noodle," he says.

Fidget opens his eyes and removes the cotton. Vikström thinks his smile is beatific. To Manny it's cunning.

There follows a pensive moment as the detectives stare down at Fidget and he looks back. Manny and Vikström consider the money that Fidget has taken from Marco Santuzza's flung wallet and from the pockets of dead Sal, but each thinks the other has forgotten it. To mention the money would mean arresting Fidget for whatever might be missing, though neither detective knows how much the two dead fellows had in the first place. And then there would be all the paperwork. Besides, what would be gained by putting Fidget in jail?

Let Fidget have it, thinks Vikström. *Let's forget about it,* thinks Manny. And Fidget thinks, *They don't remember the money!* Then he grasps his mistake. *They're letting me keep it!*

We guess it's about two hundred dollars. Perhaps Fidget will spend it wisely, but we don't expect that will be the case.

Fidget pushes himself into a sitting position. "I'm glad you guys showed up. I was nearly out of vodka." Then he sighs. "It's been a great holiday."

Vikström reaches down and helps Fidget from the tub. Then Fidget removes his bracelet and the Rolex and the gold chains and the rings and the rollerball pen. He gives them to Manny. Who knows what will happen to them afterward?

That afternoon Connor, Linda, and Vaughn sit in the Mini-Cooper in front of the train station waiting for Fat Bob to ride by. A spring breeze stirs up the sand pushed to the curb, the same sand dumped on the snow by city workers on Tuesday. Earlier they'd visited the Winnebago to see what they could salvage. It was high tide, and large waves beat against the Hannaquit Breachway. Linda said it would be nice to stay there for a while; Vaughn said that was an unreasonable preposition. They ignored the yellow police tape.

Little is left to salvage. The refrigerator has been tipped over; everything formerly on shelves now litters the floor. Food is spread all over, broken glass ditto. Half of Connor's clothes are riddled with bullet holes; the rest are scattered. Vaughn's clothes and the last yellow pads are also full of holes. They take what they can, but it's a dreary task. They fill two suitcases and put the suitcases in the back of the Mini-Cooper.

When they're parked at the train station, Linda says cheerfully, "So if you stay in New London, what kind of work can you do?"

This is the first Connor hears of staying in New London. He considers it and decides he likes it. "I can do substitute teaching until some-